Marianne E. Meyer

Family Code

Doris Day's Neckar Relatives

Death Is Not The End

The information introduced in this book was carefully researched and imparted in all conscience. However, author and publisher don't take any liability for damages of any nature that could emerge directly or indirectly from the usage or application of the data in this book.

drmarianneemeyer@gmail.com
www.marianne-e-meyer.com

© 2017 by Marianne E. Meyer, Tavira, Portugal
All rights are with the author

Cover photo: I. Kring Ucci, L. Holschuh
My Heart (Doris Day album)
Cover painting: M. Meyer
I. Kring Ucci 5, C.-P. Meyer 21, 117, 133, 139, 186, M. Vasek, L. Nahler 49, G. Groh, 61, A. Umbreit 79, 114, C. Troßmann 113, M. Rohde 134, 135, E. F. Braun 165,167,185, T. Shirvanian 170

Some other books by M. E. Meyer:

How Water Connects our Worlds
Spirulina, Survival Food for a New Era
Migrant Birds on Wheels
Cranberry Power Frucht
Psyllium - So bekommen Sie Ihr Fett weg
Spirulina - das blaugrüne Wunder

Production & Publishing:
BoD – Books on Demand, Norderstedt
ISBN 978-3-741-28233-1

Marianne E. Meyer
Apartado 320, P-8801 Tavira

Marianne E. Meyer has already passed through many stages of life with the focus on self-help and learned: We are our own best teachers, healers, and spiritual leaders. Formerly a doctor's assistant, she later studied with a focus on family therapy and gerontology in Frankfurt. She then studied food science in the USA. The dissertation case study on immune defense and Spirulina she published in her bestseller *Spirulina, das blaugrüne Wunder*. The author lived 10 years in the US, intervening in Southern Hesse, Portugal, and Morocco. Until recently, she worked temporarily with maladjusted adolescents in Portugal. She is inspired by a pioneering spirit and a passionate dedication on the well-being of the people.

TABLE OF CONTENTS

Visiting California after 15 years of absence	4
Exchange rate effect: Car dealers ticket to CA	8
Metaphysical phenomenon multiplication	10
Spirits in Hermosa Beach	16
Family repetition, a code from the past	23
Elective relatives in *Haus Tania*	27
San Francisco's nudists and paupers	28
Remote relatives on Doris Day's track	32
From *Haus Tania* to India	36
Christmas trees and phosphor bombs	44
Philanthropic Parsis	48
Cutting off the tresses	50
Goa at long last	62
Dealing, healing, gambling, dreaming	64
Odenwald family living in the 50s	72
Are we the creators of disasters?	81
Lost in flights and Lisa's departure	83
Lydia's leaving & Marianne's arriving	90
Developing psychic powers	95
Perfect Psychic: Hilde bumps into John Hudson	102
Sermons and Neckar rides	105
Jocelyn Brando's writers block workshops	112
The *Trail of Tears* and continued chronicle	114
Acting class appearance	116
Party George and property search	117
Dr. Fett and our new friends	120
Reiki in Venice and metaphysics in Mexico	122
Wien in Beverly Hills & Hay in Hollywood	125
Dan Barton commanding the bridal	129
Sizzling spring after warfare winter 1991	133
Fire walking with Michael Big Bear	138
New carriers on the horizon	141
Easy Eye and Malibu Inferno	145
George's UFO, Anza's ET and another prophecy	148
Attaché without a clue for taking the train	150
Hilde's karma uncovering	152
Buddhism & Reiki: Connecting past and present	154
Hasya and Hollywood's Poona Community	157
Water Code cracked?	159
Coming home to Berlin at last	164
What's on the wish list?	166
A little farm after all	177
Acknowledgments	181

California after 15 years of absence

Slipping back into the familiarity of a language free from the troubles of being socially befitting or sexually accurate was easy. But the ride from LAX to Pasadena in Ines' brand new BMW had not made me feel at home yet. We'd lived in the quiet Odenwald for so long. Growing older may be another factor for not using the fast lanes anymore. In the ten years of living with Peter in L.A., we had everything our ersatz-kids now own: a house with pool, fancy cars, and a good business. With the 2000charge company Ines and Wolf how he is called here made it a lot bigger, but Wolfgang told me about the constant creeping dread in his neck, that somehow it would fail.

Especially, in the US one has to be careful not to be sued. Even if you take care, the cheaters are always around the corner. Much too often, not the one who's right wins, but the one with the better lawyer. Since anything good or bad is leaping across the big pond, I just had to experience this in Germany too. A former friend whom Peter gave money for trading cars had abused my eBay account to sell a car. At the time of the deal, we were in Portugal and thus had never made any contract with any buyer nor cashed in any money. Still, I had to take back a car that I'd never touched. The first judge had ruled in my favor, but the tricky prosecuting party made it at the higher court. I now realize why my friend's daughter refused to be a lawyer and became a district attorney: The plaintiff's attorney purposely cheated me. He knew I was innocent. My solace if things go wrong is the existence of the highest court: the cosmic law. Since we can't get around this eye for an eye thing, I may have been the wrongdoer in a past life and thus have to deal with the cheaters this time.

The ride from Pasadena to Carmel was a nice change, also for the smoothly humming sports car. No way, I envy Ines for driving the route from Pasadena to LAX in her sleep. How often had I picked up guests from the airport? It's amazing, how many people had known us while living in L.A. One day after we'd a full house and no clean bed linen left, I enjoyed my solitude while restoring the house. A couple I'd met only once popped by and asked if they could stay over on their last day in California!

I'm very thankful for this, Ines.

With a twinkle in her eyes, she said:

It's my pleasure. Yeah, let's have fun. For you, it'll be a nice change, too. I truly admire your energy. Taking care of a big house with no help, two girls, a company where you are the what? Instructor. I train the employees. Oh here, let's have the best Hamburgers.

I thought TGIF had the best. Must be new. Typical white with red: stands for clean and fast. Three hours later, the M3 rushed through one of the most prolific areas of America. Steinbeck's home. Yum! Onion odor!

In the early eve, we arrived at the white Mediterranean dog-friendly bed & breakfast hotel Doris Day had purchased jointly with Denny LeVett. She may have had a similar motive as my mother who initiated building a guesthouse to have a livelihood for her son.

Ines had booked two beautiful rooms with king size beds in the Cypress Inn; mine had a view over a snug secluded patio.

I grabbed an apple from the fruit basket and opened a nut bag, abstaining from the other treat in the exquisite crystal bottle: a complimentary sherry as I'd later read in the guest book. But walking around the corner in the Carmel June breeze that felt like a gentle German January wind, I said, I should have taken a sip to warm up. Though, the red wine at the nearby crowded restaurant also helped. We had plenty of time to read all the honors the Italian chef had earned and actually, my salmon tasted excellent.

Next morn, I walked down, communed with a friendly Golden Retriever and helped myself at the breakfast buffet. The big screen above showed a scene from *Please, Don't Eat the Daisies*: Doris sitting across David Niven on a kitchen table. I was blown away by Doris's mimicry and moves reminding me of my mother's. My eyes filled with tears. Like a cry of remembrance flashed my mother's eyes through me. Slowly, the tears trickled down my cheeks. In the last half year of grieving, I had not cried truer. I missed my mother's loving eyes, the touch of her hand, her bell light voice she'd kept even in her 80th years.

I placed myself by the window under a photo, where Doris posed as the rambunctious, pistol-packing prairie girl Calamity Jane.

I'd read in her biography that this was one of her favorite movies, but it caused her nervous breakdown apparently from the physical "high jinks of jumping on horses, bars, wagons, and belligerent men or doing pratfalls in muddy streams...". Her following trouble breathing with terrible heart palpitations and fear of serious illness caused her deep depression. Because she'd not appeared at the Academy Awards singing the award-winning song *Secret Love* got her the annual Sour Apple Award from the Hollywood Woman's Press Club.

Ines joined me, cheering me up. After taking some pics of the interior, I flipped through the Cypress Inn's service book and found a dog sitter list. If I would live in the area, I'd love to do the job too.

Later we found a shop where I got large printouts of photos from Doris's Neckar relatives. We'd posed for her on the ferry in Neckarhäuserhof near Heidelberg.

Sitting opposite the bar at Edgar's staring at the big screen and the Quail Lodge golf course I enjoyed my delicious Caesar's salad. However, the food was not my central concern. I said to Rudy, I know Doris uses to lunch here every day. I'm a relative and would like to meet her. I'm sorry, said the bartender, since about a year, Doris doesn't come anymore. Oh, bad news. However, we enjoyed Rudy Gazudy's positive energy for another while. The name addition he got from Doris. He said she'd come because I took care of her privacy. I bet it was your warm smile and the way to make people feel comfortable. I guess, we can't do more than trying to find her house.

You can see it from the restaurant terrace. Ten minutes later we thought to have found the famous dog lover's place. The light fittings had cut out bones and other dog ornaments on the wall of the large premises. Leaving a note to be back in two days we left for Palo Alto where my other ersatz-daughter awaited us.

In the eve we were pampered at the Matta house. Next morn after we'd carried all the goodies from the kitchen to the garden table I said:

Wow, just like in the ad. Piles of vitamins.

More than you use to serve? Mandira asked with a funny facial expression. I shrugged off.

Where is Madhu? Still making coffee.

I know it tastes better in those fancy coffee makers but isn't the old-fashioned way less stress and less moldy? Right.

You're lucky. Madhu is such a darling. Yesterday he really worked his ass off. Wasn't it an outstanding dinner?

Yeah, he's great in the kitchen.

With a big smile on his face, Madhu came out to us in the sun carrying two mugs of steaming brown. I indulged in papaya pieces, sliced salmon on a roll and scrambled eggs. Half through the breakfast, I began to crochet again. It's hard for me to sit still and I had promised to finish Shiv's cap.

Madhu asked, so what are we doing today?

Lose our hearts in San Francisco? I suggested. Common consensus from all corners.

How far is it from here? Some 30 miles. Just behind the door. I made the last stitchery on the cap. Waving to the 12-year-old lad in the Hollywood-swing I said: Ta-ta, done!

Madhu said: You are amazing.

Whatever that means. I walked to the lad and put the cap on his head. With braces smiling he left it on. I need a photo for my potential cap business. I got such a lovely letter from Doris thanking me for her darling cap she was wearing all winter. Since the students from Baden are doing well with their Hatnut online store born on Baden's river of Neckar I may too.

Speaking of business, Ines went to the guest room to check on her E-mails. While the kids carried the dishes back to the kitchen, Madhu said, turning down his mellow voice:

Marianne, I don't know how close you are with Ines and... do you get along with her daughters? With the Indian way of waving my head, I said, I'm okay, thanks. I just want to let you know to feel free to come to us; the flights are cheap. That's very kind of you. If I don't meet Doris on our way back, I might do that. Mandira asked:

What do you want to accomplish by meeting her? Just see her. I want to find my father's relatives. How? Good question. I thought I'd already found one in the Hollywood Hills when Ingrid had sent me to the ex-wife of Al Ruddy. He is the producer of *The Godfather*.

Huh? Hasya's size, physique, hair color, eyes reminded me of my grandmother's. And during the group action, she'd often pinned me with a piercing glance. It was strange when she gave me the longest farewell hug of my life. If I wouldn't have left California shortly after ... anyway, I didn't contact Hasya again. Maybe Doris knows a lot of people in the area. She lives in Carmel since the early eighties. Her friend was even mayor there.

Clint Eastwood. Uh-huh. What I experienced in Hermosa Beach ... it's too important to bury. The oddity of both my parents' relatives living in Carmel could be the trim for the tale. Huh?

I don't believe the spirits visiting were droll ghosts making fun of me. What they told me, may be of interest for all of us. In what way? The overall message was mankind can't survive if we go on exploiting our planet and treating ourselves, each other and all creatures the way we do. That's nothing new. You know

---

DORIS DAY

April 2, 2011

Ms. Mariane Mayer
Apo, 320
P-8801 Taviva
Germany

Dear Mariane,

Forgive me for being so late in thanking you for my darling cap. I've been overwhelmed with mail, and I decided to take it as it comes and today's the day! The cap fits beautifully—I've been wearing it all winter.

Thank you again for thinking of me. Hope you are well and happy...and making more caps!

With love,

Doris and my babies

the joke? Two planets meet. The first one asks: How are you? Not so well, the second answered, I've got the Homo Sapiens. Don't worry, the other replied, I had the same, that will soon pass!

Yes, our ancient old suffering is based on failed experiments of mankind with nature. Most people think after me the flood.

True. But what can you do? We all need to know that the soul is immortal and if we lead bad lives we have to come back to our created mess. If we cheat we'll be cheated; an eye for an eye ... yeah but people don't care. Right, but finding my fathers' folks would prove my spirit experience. It would make people aware that the death of consciousness doesn't exist. Um! Don't you think if people realize they're surrounded by spirits they would lead better lives? Maybe.

I don't believe in chances. Maybe our living in California had been orchestrated by the spirit world. I don't know. My experiments with Ernst Braun and his water crystal photos made me crystal clear that souls communicate with us via water.

I don't understand. The spiritual world tries always to support us and to interact with us if we pay attention. We ... on my mother's side ... we perceive more than most people.

Madhu said: I know, second sight, but what's the use? Oh, it can be very useful. How so?

Once, my brother was with his handball pals in Paris. They left their hotel, drove around, stopped at several places and got lost. Well?

Suddenly my brother had a 3-dimensional map of Paris in front of his 3rd eye. He directed the perplexed driver to the hotel on a different route. And via my metaphysical experience, I got information on the field of water knowledge. What water knowledge?

You'd need the background information from my new water book to help accept the concept of soul energy and subtle vibrations of thoughts or feelings crystallized in water. It only recently crossed my mind that my early love was the artistic designer of my water crystal photos. Huh? I was engaged with Edmond Dembinski for 18 months. He was a waiter, but I believed in his artistic talent and got him to the art. He had vernissages in all large European cities. So, he may have created many of my soul stars.

Huh? He passed on in 2002. Strangely enough, his art is full of signs symbolizing beauty. They are also warning signals to take care of the environment! My great-grandfather's message was all about that too.

But how do you want to find your folks?

In 1902, my father's grandfather emigrated from the Hanau area. I could look through photo albums of Victor families with German roots. I still see him clear before my inner eye. But what do you want from them? I looked puzzled. Giggling, I answered, certainly, no alimony paid in arrears for my grandmother. It's just ... when you undergo something like that ... if my ancestors had only come to greet me in our first apartment in California would they've given me the lecture of my life? Changing the subject, Mandira said: I don't

remember, why did you come to California in the first place? Business reasons, but I'm not sure anymore! My thoughts drifted a quarter century back.

Exchange rate effect: Car dealers ticket to California

Most people emigrate out of economical reasons. We were no exception. You know we'd lived in the house in Frankfurt-Bergen.

Yeah, I remember the park like premises. Yep, we sold new luxury cars to Americans.

When the Dollar dropped, we were out of business. So we thought about another way to make ends meet. We'd seen a lot of rust free scrap metal on wheels in the three months we'd spend in California in the early 80s. Peter flew to L. A. and looked for suitable cars. Eventually, he was weary of the constant flying. So in 1986/87 we emigrated to L. A. and changed the country and also from import to export.

Just like that? No, before we decided to stay for good, we had a trial period. I'd have saved the rent for the house in Bergen. As a Sagittarius, I'm flexible and adapt to changes fast. But for my parents, it was easier to get used to losing us. My mother drove to Frankfurt twice a month to check on the house. Sometimes my father accompanied her, and they had little vacations. In these months, they slowly got used to the thought of having to let us go.

Where'd you go live? In motels and about five weeks at Jerry's house. What Jerry?

The Veteran who lost his leg in Germany.

Oh, I know, the guy with those blue eyes.

Yes. He hadn't even taken anything from us only the gifts from the German pharmacies. Huh? The geriatric pills from the famous Romanian Dr. Aslan worked wonders.

How'd you met Jerry? I'd kind of adopted him in the early eighties when he showed strong interest in our Mercedes convertible I'd offered on the car market in Frankfurt. We had given up our car lots, but we still bought fancy cars and sold them to dealers, through papers and magazines or at car swap markets. Jerry's fellow traveler, car dealer Jim Keller had talked him into shipping German cars to California. He tempted him with the reward of doubling his money. Aha!

At this moment I sensed the chance to scout the US since Peter wouldn't simply fly to a foreign country and explore it just for fun. No? Why not? We would never have visited India if you had not lived there. That's why I lured the Californians to our home. The words, I've got two other nice cars at home I'll make you a package deal opened Pandora's box. The men followed me to Haus Tania.

Peter sold them a green sedan and took them to our favorite Italian restaurant for dinner. Next day I cooked salmon, sauerkraut and home fries for Jerry since he didn't get fish with Kraut at the Altänchen. Why not? Good question. They were selling herring next to their fatty pork food. So he ordered fish and sauerkraut, the grease on the side, please. The waitress didn't get the joke and was offended by Jerry's order. He said: She truly seemed pissed off. How can they sell their stuff if they treat their guests like shit? I told him that Germans are used to being treated rudely. The reason you'll find in history books.

He said you have to come to the US! There you'll be treated like a king. I'd love to. Sure, come over, you can stay with us. So my cooking earned me a ticket to the Wild West but finally it was quite costly.

That I know.

I thought about our pleasant days. At the flea market on the river of Main, Jim bought some antique clocks, and I detected Jerry's love for swap meets. During this week Jim put a bee in the bonnet by telling Peter with exporting fancy cars you can double or triple your money.

Not much later, we crossed the big pond. Peter wanted to make quick money by exporting European quality autos to the US. I suggested to test the procedure of converting to American regulations with only two cars. Sending me a ridiculing look, he said: It'd be not profitable and not worth the effort to start with in the first place. So my daring fortune hunter invested our money in mostly convertibles and shipped them across the ocean.

We followed later to keep a strict eye on the conversion specialist. Without any doubt, we had a great time with his family. We also had the opportunity to stay in the condo owned by Leonard Bernstein's brother in Escondido for a weekend. I asked Jonathan, who took care of business to get Mr. Bernstein to trade his condo with our green Panther J 72. Regrettably the deal fell through. Peter wasn't interested in taking in any real estate. He said anything immovable makes us immobile. A few months later, EPA and DOT were still not satisfied with the technical modifications and exhaust standards. Thus we returned to Europe empty handed.

Before we left the USA, Peter appointed Max Högele to sell our cars. He had a tiny house with a fenced lot in Venice between Lincoln and Strand. Our fellow countryman was rather into smoking pot. His eyes popped out of his head after choking attacks. Max only sold a champagne metallic Mercedes convertible to a film director at Twentieth Century Fox. For Max, selling this car seemed to have been too much work. So he chose an easier way, taking off with another SL and was never seen again. The rest of the cars we had to ship back to Europe.

Yes, I remember.

Then we started on the roller coaster ride all over again. When the Dollar was at its peak, we had enough money back to buy a new Mercedes and got bank credits for some more. They sold like hot cakes. When the dollar dropped again, we imported vintage cars. Then we figured it would be more fun to emigrate to L.A. and change from import to export. What did you do with your furnishings?

Some of our furniture we were able to sell. The rest landed in my mother's huge bedroom and the adjacent attic. Both our tomcats had to stay in Michelstadt until we bought a house. Back in California, we found an apartment in walking distance to the beach. With plenty of cash, we were like most Germans not used to plastic. So we had no credit line and the manager said, you need somebody to vouch for you. Peter wanted to pay for months in advance. Sandi said that won't work. Finally, Jerry guaranteed for us.

Peter's partner Bernd Bonello was the founder of the *Markt*, a German magazine for classic autos. He lived in a rented trailer in an exquisite trailer park in the harbor area in Newport Beach. Peter didn't want to squeeze his 6.3 feet in such cramped conditions. We think differently today since life is taking place mostly outside. Back then we preferred our apartment in Hermosa Beach. We were happy there. I'd go for it even today. Since everything's in walking distance, supermarket, post office, library, bookstore and tennis courts. Apropos, I saw Steffi a 5 min ride from us in Manhattan Beach beating Martina and ranking #1 for the first time. I also snapped the baffled Martina in her typical cleaning specs stance. The only disadvantage of living in the bay area is the May gray and the June gloom, due to the marine layer. Too often, the sun loses her battle against the murk, while victorious just a mile inland.

Facing the pool from our sized living room, it was quite entertaining and Peter's belly, grown during the weeks without sports, melted. Except for the bed, we had the used furniture from our friend Hans-Jürgen's liquidated law office in Beverly Hills. He borrowed us a fancy leather couch, an antique flap table, 2 lamps and two stylish seats. Some household goods, I took from Jerry's garage. To repay him for having us, I systematized it so at least his silver Mercedes did fit in. The relentless California sun can be especially harsh on this metallic color. I worked all day, stapling the bargains our friend had hunted for by strolling through the swap meet. Jerry made me take anything of use for us. What a great feeling of freedom after 35 days of using our friend's space. Though, it had been mostly only nights due to the long ride from and to work. I loved my first walk-in closet. We even had a German speaking Torrance policeman as a second manager. The nicest cop, I'd ever met. Walter's mother lived in Bavaria. Our first manager was a petite lady in her late fifties. She always carried a slight vodka breeze like a streaming banner behind her. If I wanted the key to the gym, I'd to go to Sandi but didn't want her to feel caught in the very act of boozing.

In these days, I learned a lot about the American way of life. We used to consider the Yanks as being wasteful, but it is just the system and the way things are handled leading to wasting energy. At first, we were astonished about the 850 dollars rent for a 1 bedroom apartment. Our flat in Frankfurt was larger and less expensive, but we had to pay extra for electricity, heating and water. Of course, if everything is included we use more. I wasn't much different from the US citizens. I indulged in a bubble bath almost every winter day, possibly the reason I had prophetic and past life dreams more than ever. At least Goethe used spa therapy because he realized that the heavenly messages had flown better.

In the morning, we used to walk to the beach and had breakfast at *Good Stuff*. Peter drove with his red Mustang Convertible to the office right after. I did some housework and shopping first. One morning at the checkout at Von's, stacks of the same book caught my attention. I recognized the famous actress on the front page and was stunned: Shirley McLaine writes, too! Impulsively, I bought *Out on a Limb* and took the printing to the office. My spontaneous actions had accelerated after my connection to the Reiki energy, a millenarian old cosmic healing system, rediscovered by Mikao Usui.

Following the initiation, I sensed a strong feeling of being as if a different spirit accompanied me. From stop light to stop light, I forced my streamlined convertible forward.

A feat feeling centered in my body like in my childhood when I'd fallen in love with my cousin's toy cab. Passing through the tunnel of LAX airport, my heart extended to higher spheres. I'd arrived at home again. There was no doubt in my mind we had done the right thing coming to California. I only missed seeing my mother but our letters crossed the Atlantic three times a week, and she'd planned to visit us for one or two months every year.

Metaphysical phenomenon multiplications

At the office, I flipped through the pages. Wow! The woman has guts, writing about her experiences with spirits and extraterrestrials. That could take away her career. What would I have to lose by informing my fellow students about my unlikely? In California, almost everybody can tell stories about own metaphysical experiences. Riding on the crest of the health wave, I had quit drinking coffee and alcohol as well as eating meat. In the library's computer, I found more than one hundred studies on coffee. Alas, I had not searched for one that makes one get off the black poison without withdrawal symptoms.

My main foods were salads and vegetables. I got pimples, which I never had in my youth.

Later, I accepted them as detox symptoms. Back then, I blamed the L.A. smog. I had more prophetic visions than ever. Most true dream contents became a reality in the following days. Also, so-called coincidences began rushing through my life with metaphysical speed. I thought about someone and right away he or she called. One morn I woke up with the remnants of a dream and asked Peter: Do you know an Oliver? Nope.

I dreamed about a young man named Oliver.

Well, I guess I better watch out ... no joke, he showed me a one page commercial for a stereo sound system in the *Stern* magazine. It was himself, dressed as a bird seller. A few days later in the office Bernd said, I've to pick up Oliver from LAX. He wants to work for us. An hour later, a tall blond man arrived showing us the very photo I saw in my dream.

On Friday, May 13, 1988, we flew back to dissolve our house In this night, I conceived. I knew it at once. In the following dream, strangely enough, it was on Mother's Day, I took our blond boy to my former prof who also headed the Family Counseling at the Jewish Community. Günther glanced at him: Is this your boy? Yeah, he caused me no pain at all. Three months after the dream, we visited friends at a pond site near Limburg. I held my belly and said, I'm expecting a son, but Peter said, he only wants a girl, a boy he'll throw into the garbage. I knew he didn't mean it. Peter often says strange things. He must have been reminded of his wild sons he had to take care of when he was still a kid himself. Talking rubbish may be an Aquarius thing, too. Modern Talking Dieter Bohlen, also born in early February proves it every week on TV.

Whenever I said to my mother, I'm not sure if I can stand this forever, she soothed me, come on let him talk, other than that he's a good sort.

Our rich friend Karl-Dieter said don't worry, if Peter doesn't want the boy, I'll take care of him. An hour later, the problem was solved by itself. Or by me? Could I have avoided the miscarriage? Had I forced it subconsciously? I was standing on one side of a wooden board. Kids jumped onto the other side forcing me to hop up abruptly. I felt a pull in my lower abdomen and our son I had named Jan Jasper went back home waiting for our return.

I'd asked myself if I'd only imagined this. But whenever a person had tried to read from my hand, he or she said you've two children, the incise on the root of your little finger shows it. I remember another time missing my menses for 3 months. When I did my apprenticeship at the emergency doctor I had to do a lot of x-rays without radiation measuring devices.

On Friday eve I put on my just finished sweater in a red, gray and white material mix. It was pitch dark and time to leave for the reader circle when Carlo with a drumming staccato of his paws demanded the kitchen glass door to be opened. I left the lighted living room. Energy conscious I didn't switch on the light when entering the kitchen saying: Why don't you go upstairs you lazy son of a gun?

Our two tomcats had the freedom to leave the house through a gap from the bedroom door. Of course, it was easier to order me to the kitchen than to get up the steps and down on the tree attaching the garage terrace. I opened the glass door a bit, waited a few secs and closed it again. Passing the kitchen table, I felt something warm on my chest. Touching the area, I noticed the wet and detected the attacker on the table, peeing at me. Pissed off Carlo had developed this attitude when our landlady Margot Weber next door made a shrimp salad for a party. Carlo had smelled the seafood and meowed his heart out. She had opened him and filled a bowl with milk. Carlo took this as an affront and approached her brand new couch. With his lifted tail he discharged a strong jet onto the floral print. Instead of ranting and raving, Mrs. Weber got quite excited by realizing the reason. She laughed her heart out and rewarded him for his nasty behavior with a few shrimp!

Of course, this reaction made Carlo adapt the pissing manner in order to get what he wanted. I hurried up and changed. I could not show my new sweater but had a funny story to tell. With the German edition of *Out on a Limb*, I'd purchased for my mother, I headed for my last literature group meeting and was curious about my former fellow students and our hosts' reactions.

Günther and Gisela sort of represented our progenitors. Sometimes, parents have problems granting their kids the freedom to stand on their own feet. Members of other groups may have disengaging difficulties, too. Günther Feldmann, one of the faculty members of the Goethe University in Frankfurt may have established the reading circle so he could see the most familiar of his students twice a month. During a colloquium, he invited me to the Friday eve's literature event he had set up with his life companion Gisela. Had I also joined out of detaching problems? When the joy regarding the tops diploma grades had faded, the connection to the Uni seemed lost. As long as I was still able to look in the known faces, I kept a part of the university activities, the solidarity spirit, the stimulating discussions, and the feeling of being young and free.

Sitting around the table, amply set with plates of cakes and cookies the initial small talk started. Günther ended it with the query: who has anything to read? I said, I'd like to read a few pages of Shirley MacLaine's book *Zwischenleben (Out on a Limb)*. Gisela said, why, I didn't know she writes, too. I like her acting. So she may be a good writer too. Yes, and you'll be one of the first Germans to learn something different about her. The paperback in German just came out. As an awakening sensitive, she steadily reflects upon her life. Shirley came across spiritual helpers and friends who guided her to greater consciousness. I started reading the part where the medium Kevin Ryerson went into a trance, and two different ethereal entities came through. In distinct speaking demeanor expressions, they answered Shirley's questions and wonderfully explained the meaning of existence.

Perplexed silence followed the reading. Some of the attendees intently studied their cake plates others kept their eyes closed in brooding mode. A minute passed. We could have heard a pin falling. While reading, there was also no single sound of impatience: no chair shifting or clearing of throats. So at least the subconscious was engaged. Nobody seemed to have been bored. Yet the unspoken question hovered in the air and was readable in the consternating faces. Why did she confront us with this? What has it to do with our reality? Was it a mistake to release this other world on them? Had I expected them to share my enthusiasm about the power of the universe and men? Not even Professor Nietzsche from Basel was understood when with Zarathustra he released his second sight onto his startled equals.

My friends were partly atheists or agnostics, skeptic individualists. If they'd ever been worshipers caught up in concepts and liturgies, they'd outgrown it. I'm not against any religion if it helps people to radiate love and goodness, but the senses of most mortals seem extinguished. As if they have lost trust in their inner wisdom and listening to their inner voice. The only jurist of the group digested the amazement first. Why'd you choose this reading?

It's my reality right now. I thought since we are going to live in California and I may never see you again, I wanted to show you a side of me, you had not known. The spiritual is part of life, not only the things you can see and touch. Or how do you explain that: I dream about an occurrence and a few days, weeks or months later it happens just like envisioned. Why! That happens by chance, said Wolfgang.

What chance is it, when my mother at age 12 dreamed about the death of an old neighbor and the next day she had died and everything was like in her dream.

Okay. But what's the use?

Oh, it can be very useful if we listen to our inner voice. It just happened the last time when we flew back to Germany. Peter walked with the suitcase towards the car and was about to open the trunk. I shouted, put it in the backseat. Why? Dunno. Peter didn't listen and broke the key. That's a coincidence! I still think it's a belief. Belief! If you wouldn't know anything about the metamorphosis of a red caterpillar into a fluttering moth, would you believe, if I tell you by showing you a larva that it'll turn into a beautiful butterfly?

This reasoning yielded admitting sounds and shining eyes. So why should we not be able to incarnate in different bodies, too?

What difference does it make if I know or not? The difference is, if you know you've to come back, you'd stop living like after me the flood. If cheaters or murderers would know they'd to come back and live through the same misery they've caused their fellow humans ...

Superstition, there is no proof. Would the world not be a better place if we knew good and bad comes back to us? Would the tormenter not think twice if he knew, he'd be the victim next time around? That's the meaning of an eye for an eye. As a legal expert, you should know earthly justice often errs. That's different.

Isn't it a relief that there's a properly working universal law? Whatever we do is gathered in a kind of library. Nonsense. I bet, in a few years, you'll change your mind.

I don't think so. I thought like you before. You may have just gotten rid of your internalized Christian or Semitic principles, and now I come with such! But don't we all recognize the works of Fowler, Piaget, and Erikson? So?

They show that only the ones reach the highest stage of the conscious life, who actively go on to search for the truth. In California, you can talk to everyone about the metaphysical who can mostly offer their own occult experiences. I met a young woman who's uncle appeared to his widow as spirit and told her about the whereabouts of important documents she then found. I also met a woman who had an operation by an ESP surgeon. Nobody said anything. I felt rejected. At least I had expected some regard and to have gained respect all these years as an earnest person. Daniela cleared her throat and said:

Em, I didn't want to talk about this outside the family anymore. Huh? I've also prophetic dreams: mostly accidents and other negatives, but I'd never prevented anything by telling my friends what I saw in my nightly visions. So I don't speak about it anymore only to Herbert. With his nodding, the former reverend cleared his Swiss-born psychologist wife. Of course, he had witnessed Daniela's metaphysical experiences as Peter gets to know mine all the time.

Daniela said, there's something else: Whenever anyone in my family dies, a crystal glass in my vitrine breaks apart without touching it.

Eagerly I said, a similar experience had Renée, my friend's daughter. She was 12, when a box of bird feed flew in a high bow from the shelf, rattling down to the ground. Renée screamed, Uschi hurried to her room. What's up? Something terrible must have happened. I think a spirit has thrown the box. An hour later the phone rang, and Uschi learned about her stepbrother's passing. By the way, when Uschi was her daughter's age or even younger, she felt earthquakes thousand miles away.

Once, when I stayed overnight, I saw her grabbing the rail of her bed, looking odd and asking, didn't you feel that? Some hours later, in the news, another temblor was announced. All these experiences seemed to have no effect on our friends. They had not generated our knowledge by experience, so they were confused. Maybe, they'd not recovered from the archetypical fear of the witches terrors.

But it cannot be denied that globally psychiatrists and parapsychologists demonstrate that prophecies lived up to and mediumistic transmissions from the ether help to master certain situations and ills. E. g., Ian Stevenson did studies with kids who spontaneously talked about their past lives and showed connected psychological and physical characteristics.

Of course, our group of 10 persons may not be representative. But if two out of ten have mediumistic abilities a good guess might be millions of Germans avoid being laughed at. Why do US citizens have more self-confidence than Germans? This is certainly due to the different socialization. Poverty and hunger were less known among the many self-sufficient US farmers. Looking at the Kraut's history controlled by gangster governments, their state of mind must not be questioned. The German serfdom towards authorities and institutions is based on historical injustice: outrageous deliveries of small farmers to feudal men. Even now few people can afford to own land. But German counts can still count on millions of taxpayers euros if they cannot afford to restore their castles. Biographies from "good old times" state how intelligent and professional people in degrading ways had to fawn to get a badly paid job. Germans used to discipline and order learned to obey and act according to orders; for corrupt seducers an invitation for manipulation.

The two lost world wars and twice the loss of savings by currency reforms were not conducive to generate confidence either. The date of the last reparation payment from World War I was on October 1, 2010, to the day exactly 12 years after my father had left his body. What have the Americans so far paid to Vietnam for reparation? What have they paid to the thousands by the defoliation agent orange physically and mentally crippled Vietnamese? NADA! They constantly repeat the shame of the Holocaust in films and reports without ever coping with the genocide of Northamerican natives, still treated as second-class people. US students learn about their "superiority" in school. A friend was brought up in the US. For her, it was hell to visit Dachau with her school class.

Germans reappraise their dark history instead of suppressing it. An anniversary day of shame would do US citizens also good. To compensate the half a million Vietnamese, who like the man in the photo suffering from the consequences of Agent Orange, would be long overdue. Since the poison is still in the food cycle, it is estimated that even two to four million people are affected by the sequelae. There is no point to sue the almighty US or corporations. The Europeans, should they be as stupid as to agree to the Free Trade Agreement with the USA (TTIP) without ifs and buts will learn it too. To sue for damages is a US domain. How it goes knows every child. Those of the young Americans who do not yet know what they want to study take law. On the other hand, complaints are hardly in the interest of the traditionally subservient South Vietnamese and their economic dependence on the USA. Justice should be called

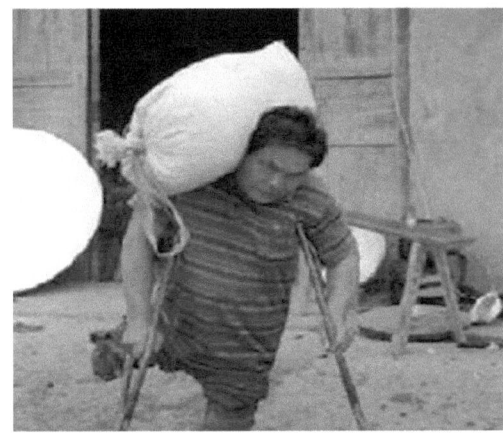

for by a global community. But the US itself did not pay the 2.4 billion US dollars for military and paramilitary actions in and against Nicaragua despite being sentenced to pay by the International Court of Justice in The Hague. The US themselves sent judges to the Court. Doesn't mean superiority integrity?

And why are Germans different?

The indoctrination of hundreds of years had stirred up anxiety and benumbed the inner voice. But we better pace angst-free, healthy and happy through life. Instead of listening to priests, politicians, physicians, scientists and other authorities we better trust our feelings. Searching people are in the catch-22 situation because the church conceals a lot and scientists are avoiding to prove the soul. The above psychiatrist Stevenson, as well as Elisabeth Kübler-Ross and Raymond A. Moody and few other scientists count to the laudable exceptions. It will be beneficial for humankind if science finally includes the spiritual in all research fields. Let's hope we don't need another Sodom and Gomorrah to wake up and build a heaven on earth.

At the university, we had acknowledged the reputable Swiss scientist's work. So, at the end of the eighties, when her research results had been published in the LA Times, I'd been certain that the world would recognize there's no dying. Dr. Kübler-Ross proved that we only change the life form. She sat on beds of dying persons, usually kids who like their family members were involved in disasters, mostly car accidents.

On the verge of making their transition, she asked them about their experiences. For instance, the kids said: Mama and Peter are waiting for me. The dying only named family members who were already on the other side and never the ones who survived the accidents. Many of the studies on deathbeds had been witnessed by hundreds of students in the auditorium. The scientist had also sat at the deathbed of a dying woman who was blind for many of her last years. When her time had come, she was able to see again and answered questions about the color of the scientist's blouse and the amount of buttons it had. Dr. Kübler-Ross had proved beyond a reasonable doubt that though our frail bodies someday will turn to dust, our spirit never dies. Her research results may not be common, but many of us have personal experiences about this natural event. My mother told me, that as a toddler I talked about strange things, though she had not remembered anything. I recall at least one happening, I certainly tried to tell her. I'd gotten a glossy colorful ball on my 2nd birthday and hopped out of the house with it. Passing the steep street off ours, I saw a girl down on the corner of Hieronymus St. making a sign to throw the ball. I thought she wanted to play with me, so I dropped it. The girl lifted her apron, caught my lovely present and vanished northward. I was shocked, beside me. Abruptly hovering above, I emotionless looked down on the little girl and figured there's nothing left to do for her than to go home.

I don't recall ghost meets, but my grandnephews had contacts with spirit relatives: Tall Moritz with Oma Maria's half-brother Christian who lost his life in the Russian campaign. For two years Jonas (right) had gotten in touch with Simon, a brother lost as a fetus. Jonas made me happy when he was talking about his older brother Simon. Someday I also may see my kids whom I lost. Jan Jasper would be 28 now. In Jon Mc Gregor's novel "If Nobody Speaks of Remarkable Things" I read about a Buddhist temple south of Tokyo with hundreds of rows of similar looking little Buddha statues and all have names. Mother's go there when they'd an abortion or lost a fetus or a newborn. They bring tiny clothes, sweets and little gifts. Though the temple may be fiction, I visualize me going there for Kai and Jan.

In a Donahue Show, in the eighties, I learned about this process of babies developing further in the ether: A surgeon lost a little girl on the operating table. She came back saying: I've been in a beautiful park with my dog and my older brother. The doc who knew his patient was an only child asked the girl's

mother. Blankly, she said, I had lost my son as a baby, but I'd never told my daughter about it.

Spirits in Hermosa Beach

Back on the Pacific Coast, we enjoyed our new habitat. It was a mild Californian winter day when Peter left the apartment while I allowed myself a little time after the domestic work and drove to a secondhand bookstore. Studying the book's backs, I grabbed one on automatic writing from the shelf when the adjacent booklet by Lynne Palmer fell right into my hands. The title Your Lucky Days & Numbers awakened my curiosity. The astrologer writes, in a house with #11 or the total of the digits respectively, the chances to experience the occult are utmost. People who live there are used to be interested in utopia research. Not only our house number 1820 amounted to 11 we also lived in apartment 11. No wonder, I thought walking back to the Toyota. For the first time, I consciously checked on the number plate: 1 ESP 660! Wow! Why hadn't I realized this earlier? The three letters accustomed in California were: ESP! The shortcut for Extra Sensory Perception referred to me. And the total of the digits amounted to 4, Peter's birth number: adding day, month and year and cross count. So it seemed our first car had chosen us! Ever since our license plate numbers were fitting us.

Entering the apartment a Freesia smell swept over me! Walking through the rooms, I wondered about the floral scent. No flowers anyplace. Somewhere I'd read the floral smells announce a spiritual visitation. But nothing happened all evening. I woke to a knocking. Sleep drunken, fussy and panicky, I realized that the dawn had not even begun to cast its shadows. Did I hear wrongly? Who could want anything from us at this ungracious hour? All kinds of Kafka's obscure and threatening descriptions were rushing through my gray matter. Without any warning, a medium aged woman in white and a lean elder man appeared in the door frame of our bedroom. The female's mellow round face surrounded by medium blond curls stood in striking contrast to the man's oblong one with graying dark brown hair, bushy eyebrows and side whiskers. The woman pointed to the tall man in anthracite pants and light blue shirt and said: That's him. He adopted the name Dieter Victor and used to live in the Carmel area.

Instantly, I knew this was my great-grandfather! Ad lib, I began a lively conversation without saying a single word. Whenever a question started forming in my mind, the spirit visitors answered in a split second. Their vivid descriptions of the meaning of life, the ongoing projects on other heavenly bodies and the careless way we treat our nourishing planet touched me deeply.

Humankind straightens rivers and causes flooding. Mining is ruinous exploitation. Mortals must be conscious of the fact that the earth needs its coal and metal for the water to become fully developed and for the soil to mature. There is free energy available not harming the planet and its living being. But this natural power is suppressed by calculating, irresponsible and ignorant individuals. With the continuous use of fossil combustibles, chemical herbicides, and genetically modified foods humankind is withdrawing itself from the foundation of life and ruining the earth. This concerns the inhabitants of many other planets since with the destruction of a planet the universe loses its equilibrium.

Moved by the overwhelming abundance of data about the inexhaustible wisdom and simplicity of all things of creation, I thought about writing down everything I grasped. At this moment, the ethereal woman said, we must go now. Pale light shimmered through the break of the negligently drawn bedroom curtain. All of a sudden an icy cold wind inflated the fabric like a sail at high seas. Both spirits vanished as abruptly as they appeared.

Quite confused, I looked around and wondered about the sudden bright daylight when Peter's terrified voice reached me.

What's wrong with you? He'd bent over me.

Why? You looked dead. You didn't breathe.

Didn't you see those two? Peter looked at me doubtfully. I must have scared him. Just what had happened? I heard a knock and was upset by the disturbance. The beings in the door frame. Why had Peter not seen them?

Somewhere, I guess it was in the Steiner writings, I had read: Everything below on the material level also exists above. I apparently once again had left the physical plane in order to communicate on the immaterial one. I faintly remembered the long marches to the line keeper's lodge when I was a little girl. On one of those, my grandmother Maria had told me about her having a different father than her siblings. I could not remember any specifics from what she had said and picked up my red day book from the desk next to my bed. But, considering the mass of information, there was not much left in my mind from the lecture of my life. I even wasn't certain anymore if I remembered my ancestor's name correctly. However, it made me aware that there's no dying truly that we still go on living, just without the ballast of the body.

Shortly after, my mother called: If you want to have me, I could come to visit you beginning of February. Oh, good, I'm glad. Me too, but I've to be back for Andreas' confirmation. When is it? March 13. Hey, I still have an open ticket. I think I'll fly with you. Oh! Good. For how long? Two weeks at the most. Peter needs me. Better than nothing.

We purchased a custom made couch that turned into a very comfy double bed with an extra thick mattress. We were delighted about those sofa manufacturing stores. We took the model we liked best, choose the fabric and the best mattress and paid not more than an ordinary couch would have cost in Germany. But it wasn't my mother who initially slept there but a customer from Tokyo.

The young dentist had bought a Mercedes convertible from us the previous year and wanted to visit us in Frankfurt. Reaching the house on the hill, our former landlady told him, the Meyers moved to California. He said, no problem, I'll visit them there. I want to buy jet skis anyway. Another funny coincidence with Japs: Marita and Willie, another happy customer couple who became good friends after buying a Mercedes from us. We had purchased it from the Japanese embassy. Some 300thousand kilometers later two Japanese car engineers bought the car for more than it was worth just because it had a high mileage. They wanted to study the wear of the engine, axle shaft, gear etc. My numerology study results: Willie's birth number is a 6, the luckiest one.

Ma arrived two days before Peter's birthday. Long before the dawn, I heard her rumbling in the kitchen. I groped for my glasses, put them on and tiptoed tiredly to her. She held her forearms under the faucet and let cold water run over them. On the gas flame stood a pot with water. Is it the jet lag? I glanced at the clock: It's only five!

Jesus, that was close. My mother's dramatic voice alarmed me. What's with you? I forgot my heart pills in the morning and in the evening. Why? Flying westwards it was never dark. I've not thought about taking them she said with a forgiving smile. Jeez! couldn't feel my pulse. You know how I realized it was serious? You tell me. In a dream, I'd seen picture frames ... pretty broad oval ones with people laughing and dancing. They lured me to come. Ma made the typical sign with her index finger.

All of a sudden, I realized ... these people were dead relatives and acquaintances except for Elise. It was in her house in Schönbrunn. I said no, not here with Marianne. I pulled myself together ... oh, Jesus, that was close. I said: What a nice start in America. Indeed.

Do you need anything? No, it's okay now. I could massage your arms, I said while my heart was swamped with love. No, it's okay. I've taken a pill already, I'm fine. Go back to sleep. You too. Just a short round. Later, we'll go to the beach. I'll show you our town.

Two hours later, we had a hearty breakfast with soft boiled eggs, smoked salmon, cream cheese, yogurt, bagel, and coleslaw. What's that? It tastes good! It's shredded cabbage, carrots, onions, sour cream, mayo, and spices. You can have it everywhere. Yummy. We should be able to buy that at home, too. Works like a broom I guess. Yeah, perfect jet lag food. Water and walking help too. Let's get some air. Stepping down to the pool area, I said, here you see our freshly cleaned heated pool. When Peter sees people sitting in the whirlpool, he hotfoots in his swimsuit, grabs a towel and whoosh splashing falls in the circle.

On the bark-covered path, we walked towards the center of Hermosa Beach. A few neighbors walked their dogs. A young woman stretched her long legs on a bench. Another jogger passed by. Ma said, well huh. I like it here. I'm going to walk every morning. I wish we had such a dog's path. Yeah, it's nice, in the old days, it was a railway. I pointed to the tennis courts on Pier Avenue. Those are our community courts. Everybody can play for free.

Really? Yep. Each town provides for some playing fields to their citizen's disposal. Isn't that great? You pay less tax and get more for it. Yes, but how about social security and health insurance for everybody? I don't know. I don't have any at the moment either. Michelle, the 20-year-old daughter of our car converter got monthly $200 for her two kids living with her at her parents' house. I guess, she'd gotten more money if she'd lived on her own. That was funny, she went to her daughter's father and asked him for alimony. Without any money but with her second daughter Sarah in her belly she came back home.

Look there, our library: also cost-free. We only pay a few cents if we keep the book longer than agreed. Marveling the perfect serve of a player, I said look, only two courts are occupied. We never have to wait. Why don't we play a game in the afternoon?

You think I can handle it?

Sure! You play badminton. It's not much different. Minutes later, we reached the pier.

Now, I'm going to show you the memorial of one of the Challenger victims.

The teacher? No, not the woman, but I know Mrs. Jarvis, the astronaut's wife. I pointed to a round structure. That's it. We can sit there for a while. How did you get to know that woman? We have the same yoga teacher at the adult education center. Here we are, Gregory.

This man lived here in Hermosa Beach?

Yes, like a lot of interesting people. We could visit two right away. Herta from Wiesbaden. She's married to Wayne Haedrick. Nice couple. We can visit Herta in her little art studio. She makes copies from original paintings.

Is that allowed?

She does it for the artists, they pay for it. How's she doing it? If I got her right, she gets the effect by the light-dark contrast between the free basis of the sheet surface and the picture itself. How'd you got to know Herta?

Oh, well! Another coincidence for the album. When we were in Germany last October, we visited Mila, the taxi driver from Sigmund Freud St. Have you met him? He's that giant who came to Germany as a youngster in the Prague Spring. I don't think I know him.

Anyway, when we told him that we now live in Hermosa Beach, he looked puzzled and said: Christine's girlfriend lives there, too. By the way, on Saturday, we are invited to their party. I think Herta's sister-in-law from Germany is visiting; then you'll get to know them.

In the penultimate week of her stay, Peter said, you didn't show your mother much. Curling his lips, he added impeaching: Universal Studio and Disneyland. I said, how about the ride with Martin's Budweiser buggy through the desert in Yuma? And Griffith Park with the trains and the Western museum added my mother. We still plan on the picnic concert at the Hollywood Bowl. What about all the sightseeing while looking for cars? Peter made an adversary gesture:

That's business. Turning to his mother-in-law, he said encouraging: How about driving up PCH and showing you San Francisco?

That's not necessary, just for me. I mainly came to see my daughter. Ma gave me an affectionate look.

No, that's okay, we need a vacation, too.

Because we only had the two convertibles, we chose my reliable Toyota. I scrambled into the little backseat. On our first stop along the coast, Hearst Castle, the sweet smell of the hill slope embraced us. Peter and I had visited the site of the newspaper mogul already in the early eighties. Entering the grand building, Ma released a cubic yard of air.

What a pump! A bit too much for my taste.

People died for being a guest of Mr. Hearst. They got expensive presents: sports outfits, tennis rackets, golf equipment etc.

Look at the wooden ceiling! It's from a cloister. Ma marveled at the shiny crystals and exclusive china. That's quite a dining table!

How funny, the mustard and ketchup plastic bottles between all the elegance! By the way, Herta is the godmother of one of the Heinz' kids. That was to shock his guests, Peter tossed in. Their reaction told him a lot about them. This way Hearst preselected their ranking. Yes, Peter said, fascinating guests sat closer to him. Boring ones at the end. Hearst's broad hint the invitation had come to an end and the person should better leave, I added. Ma said, I don't know if I'd wanted to be invited, though the guest houses are a little cozier.

Back on Highway 1, we were almost alone driving up North. In Pismo Beach, Ma said, what a funny name. It reminds me I soon have to visit ... a powder room? No, in restaurants you ask for the restroom. In private homes, the powder room is what we call guest toilette. Isn't that beating the bush?

Around the bush. You picked up quite a bit.

Yes, compare to Ludi I learn languages very fast. When I was in Turkey for 5 weeks, I could get along with the village people pretty quickly. Of course, Mike helped me, but I never had to ask him more than twice.

After a short stop, we went on riding along the ocean. Miles up the beautiful granite coast, patched with pine, fir, and cedar, we made it to the Carmel area. Cruising through the 17 miles drive, we watched the cute squirrels and the wet brown seals. Look, he's waving! Yeah, they are talking to you. Near the beach, we got a nice parking spot. Ouch, I said, stretching my cramped extremities turning my head from side to side. Here, I feel familiar. We come every year to the classic car events, auctions, and races.

Ah! I stretched my legs and arched my back.

Ma said, poor thing, I told you, I'd get in the back, too. That's out of the question, you are my mother, 25 years older, and 2 inches taller. Not anymore, I shrunk at least one. You can do yoga to keep your size, flexing the spine.

The sun painted a gorgeous picture with the water and the clouds. Have you ever seen such coniferous trees? They look quite mystical. These free flowing branches. I wouldn't know how to cut them, though Ludi and I had taken a course in tree cutting.

They look like fox tales. The dark heaviness of the cypresses displayed a direct contrast to the flour soft white sand. Yin and Yang. I got my shoes off. The fine crystals flowed between the toes. Giving me a conspiratorial wink, Ma conformed to the barefoot ritual. I felt like we were in a movie. The solemn sunset atmosphere and the sheer overwhelming beauty of the panorama made me feel blessed. On our way back to the car we passed a blue-gray house with a broad gate out of high brown boards. I said:

That looks strange! Like a stable entrance.

Abruptly, my mother stopped and asked: Tell me, Marianne, has anyone of us ever told you that your great-grandfather emigrated to America, leaving behind Mine Oma with a two-month-old problem? Uh-huh! Oma once mentioned it. The connected experience two months earlier had slipped my mind. Too much diffusion. Living in the fast lane, I had so much to do, driving around, looking for cars, the many guests, business meetings, parties and other strange metaphysical experiences. My mother said it was kept a secret. Mina married right away and Marie was considered a 7-month child.

Do you know his name?

No, we only know that he lived near Hanau.

Could he have been related to Lina Eisele from Steinheim? I don't know, but Lina was related to the Meckes family. Incest!?! Well?

Hadn't she rolled her tongue and shouted like a cuckoo? No, that was Stanzi. Huh?

Remember, Stanzi and Franzi? Um!

My father has a cousin here somewhere, too.

In California? I don't remember. We got parcels from America. I only recall the clothes. I got a dark blue woolen skirt and a beautiful white-yellow dress, an exquisite thin fabric, floral, roses, I believe. On the only class trip to Karlsruhe, I was allowed to participate, I had it on but couldn't enjoy it for long.

Why not? In the bus, a girl threw up on me.

Boo! Why didn't you take part more often?

It was too expensive. We were three girls and not enough money. We'd to work for the farmers and in the house since Mamme had worked in the forest. I'm sorry. I was able to go in for everything and had taken it for granted. Class trips were about the only likable school events. With three grownups making money we could afford all of them. Oma had the easiest and most dependable job as a line keeper. As a bookworm, she had plenty of time to read in her lodge while waiting for the trains. She could also write her poems and letters to her friends. Not a bad way to make money: sitting most of the time and having a great pension. (Doris's great-grandfather had done this job, too: in Heidelberg, just an hour ride away. I also would've gone for it.)

Oh, look Stierlin. I bed there's no street named after him. Who? That's our Prof from Heidelberg. Helm is one of the pioneers of the multigeneration perspective. Huh? He thinks that families for generations own their own value system ... a code that expresses itself in rules, sayings, and communication styles. Its origin lies in the family's past.

We reached San Francisco in the dark. Next morn, we walked to Fisherman's Wharf, watching seals and having clam chowder in a bread crust and salad for lunch. Pointing to a strange artifact, I asked: Have you seen this metal thing here before? It's a submarine. Do you want to get in? Why not? We entered the narrow U-boat and climbed through the holes from one compartment to the next. I'd not dare to stay here for weeks. It looks bigger in the movie. Why don't we show Alwine Tiburon and the artist town?

Oh yeah and the house on Sugar Loaf, I wanted to buy. Only in your wildest dreams! It's such a cute little wooden house just hanging above the San Francisco Bay. And the nice view to St. Quentin, Peter added disparaging.

The Bay was covered with boats with wide wound up sails. In the lovely Belvedere artist quarter, we had coffee and apple pie on a house boat. I said, if it had gone my way, we now would own a house here uphill. I like it here much better than in L.A. Peter moaned.

With the weather and business-wise, we are better off in the South bay.

Yes, but instead of having lost all the money by shipping the cars to L.A., converting them and ship them back to Germany we now would have a fully paid house and no rent to pay. Get out, Peter snapped, to keep a house costs more than to rent an apartment.

Maybe, but I'd rather own a house and have fewer cars.

And what are we going to live on?

The Americans always say, do what you love to do, and the money will follow.

You and your American soap bubbles. I like to race cars. Do you think anybody would sponsor me?

Then why not be a test driver?

Yeah, Peter curled down his lips, they are all waiting for me. Just visualize you're doing it! Meanwhile, you can sell a few cars. A flash from a hostile eye struck me. Ma said laughing: It's good to listen to you, just the way I carry on with Ludi. Makes me feel better.

Your daughter hadn't been like that when I met her first. She was such a sweet girl. I think I'll give her back to you.

Why? If she has changed in your company, then you must have done something wrong.

Huh? Peter hesitated, then laughed aloud. You made a point. I haven't thought about that. Or, I thought, I've learned from scratch.

On our way back on the solitary coast stripe Big Sur the sun skipped over the ocean gilding the hills. While climbing the zigzag winding roads, the trees thickened. Here you're buried, Peter said. I'd not mind living here for a while. I used to live secluded like this with Günther on a little farm.

Hey, listen I married a used woman!

Haha! Ma marveled at the array of colorful mail drops. The mailboxes right on the street would make our lives much easier. I agreed, thinking of my family's unusual work. When they had given up the restaurant after 4 years of hard work they'd started in the newspaper business. My father was hired by the *Odenwälder Heimatzeitung* or the *Darmstädter Echo* respectively. He developed sales and employed and coordinated the deliverers. Heini had quit his mechanic job and until recently picked up newspaper packages from the printers in Mainz and Darmstadt and drove them to the deliverers till about 6:00 a. m. If one of them got sick he, Ma or Pa had to drive the papers to the readers. Heini's night work made it possible for him and Ma to build the bed & breakfast all by themselves within 4½ years, starting every workday after lunch.

Admiring another bank of mailboxes, Ma said: I'd love to have those at home. I added:

I like the postman's taking the mail when the pointer is up, saves us the ride to the post office, saves energy.

At the *Ventana,* we enjoyed the fantastic view at the Pacific. The grandeur of the redwoods and the silence made me inhale deeply. Isn't that a sole smell? Yeah, clean, moist and sweet. I've just read Henry Miller's book *Big Sur and the Oranges of Hieronymus Bosch*. About his life here. While reading, I often thought about Heini.

How so? He interacted with his kids just the way Heini does with Andreas. Also the lifestyle, his liking of seclusion, the radical individualism. At the end of the book I found out ... oh look, a buzzard or is it a hawk? The bird as if he'd heard me, stretched its wings and went up. Wow! An eagle!

So what d'you find out? Hem! Both have the same names Henry and Heinrich, and Miller was also born on the 26th of December! That proves astrology or numerology. Peter tossed in: That's true, Bolko and I were born in the same delivery room ½ hour apart and we both got married at age 19 and had two sons.

I added, both divorced and lived for 7 years in cohabitation before they married a second time.

My mother asked, what's numerology?

You count your day, month and year of birth and add all the numbers. The cross sum is your birth number which is 6-6-1924=1.

You look up 6, that's, by the way, the luckiest number. Pa is a 4, the least lucky number. Mine is 7, Peter's 4.

We both have less lucky hubbies. But 6 and 7 are lucky numbers. That's sharing trouble. Yeah, it seems, we not only look for contrast in looks and acting. With our partners, we choose what we don't have.

What's the use of knowing my number?

In numerology books, you find out what you came for to learn in this life, what talents you have and so forth. I'll show you a book when we're back. How long did Miller live here?

As long as the kids were little. The school in Big Sur only went to sixth grade. Like in Schönbrunn, we were all ages in the same classroom, Ma said.

We too, said Peter, in Manor Moorbek; coming from the big town, we had always trouble with the farmer kids. Ma said:

I hate to think about it. Kohler always picked on me. The others had problems with math, too. But it was always me. I was the well of this sadist's amusement. Only when he needed me to sing on festivities, I was good enough.

Why do you think he'd tortured you?
No idea! The plump gnome was just evil.
His wife took her life. Well!
His daughter, too.
And you had it all, pretty and tall.

Dunno. He was just sinister and corrupt. His censures hadn't depended on general criteria. With every tray of fresh eggs and every slice of bacon, the grades got better. Since we'd only dreamed of grease our grades weren't great. Must be hard such persistent humiliation. Uh-huh. When we got the young teacher, Willie Kern he was stunned by our bad grades.

Oh, look! Let's see the Henry Miller Museum. It's time to move on, said lowbrow Pete.

Okay, then next time. By the way, Miller's father was a tailor from Bavaria, and his mother grew up in Hesse.

What does Heinrich mean? According to the stem, house, domain, ruler.

Isn't Heini the master of a huge house?
Ma said, without me, he wouldn't have it.
Why, because you helped him build it?
Not only that, I wanted it more. Of course, it was for him so he'd have the bed & breakfast to make a living.

He doesn't seem to appreciate it, I said.
Well! Do you know what Alwine means?
I think a noble friend. Skeptical smiling, Ma said: How do you know all that? I read it somewhere.

Oh, well! Paper doesn't blush.

Maria means idealistic, wise, thoughtful, loved, wasn't Oma that? Am I? Ha! Ha!

Family repetition, a code from the past

After another half hour of chatting, I said:

Could we get going now?

Madhu put on a broad smile: Absolutely!

Mandira recommended wearing something from her: We better prepare for the San Francisco wind. I followed her to the private rooms. Shiv called:

Marianne can wear my red windbreaker.

Hey! It's been a long time when a handsome young man offered me his parka. I was 15, sitting on a bus on our school class trip to France. The thinkable life with my handsome schoolmate in all likelihood flashed through my mind. Did I even realize back then that Jürgen mostly walked a roundabout way home to be with me a bit longer? He's short. Reflecting my childhood undergo I fancied tall men.

Though I am as tall as Angela Merkel, in my class, only one girl was shorter. We usually search for what we don't have. I agree with some of Freud's theories, but I had no Oedipus complex. At age 4, I asked my mother, why did you marry such a short man? Now, in the fall of my life, I learned that I married a father brother mixture. A blend of habits, like my brother's occasional boozing, antics, and his leaving tools behind wherever he works and my father's switching TV channels without asking, his yawning and sleeping through the westerns and Colombo series.

Mandira, grubbing for clothes, soft, worried:

So how's Peter? He's ... I lowered my voice ... I don't know.

Things have changed for you, haven't they?

For Peter more. But there are also good things about his losing the money. Huh?

He'd quit smoking five years ago.

Good for him!

For me, it's almost the same. I don't need millions to be happy. Peter loves racing and fancy cars. Yes, those hobbies are costly.

I'm on Spinoza's track. What do you mean? Status and consume has no importance anymore. Had it ever? Not really. I don't need status symbols. I only collect knowledge. And by the way, I'm a Google multi-millionaire, ha ha!

Huh? When you write Marianne E. Meyer in the Google space bar, you usually find between 7 and 23 million entries. Anyway, I'd be happy with a little farm, pets, literature, and music. Entering the beautiful bathroom in violet tones, I glanced at the flat TV on the wall over the tub: Of course, I wouldn't mind having one like that. But Peter doesn't like spending money on beautiful things in the house. By the way, the husband of Doris was the same. She even gave back a landscape of $400 for domestic peace. Just as Doris described the winter landscape, Ma once gave me one for DM400 for Christmas. Where did your money go? Phony investments. Of Jobs from Apple Peter is particularly annoyed because he dropped the company in which he invested $30,000. How so? It has developed a program for Lotus, which Jobs then did not take. He wanted the company to pay 10 million then Apple would have taken it. Since then, Peter has been demonizing all Apple products. But he is to blame himself because he always wants only more money instead of enjoying himself for the sour earned and enjoying beautiful things. He sent a king's ransom from Michelstadt to the sons of our neighbor. The tall blonde? No Anda, the little redhead. I do not know if I've introduced her to you. She looks like Kevin Costner's partner in Dancing with Wolfs, just older. I do not think I've met her. Have you not dealt with classic cars? Yes, there we'd made money, but all start-up companies, except for *Wonderware*, were wrong investments. Poor Peter, sighed Mandira. I told him, if you do not enjoy your fortune, the spiritual world will lose interest in helping you, but he never listens to me. Well, I still have the confidence that we get part of our dough back. Doris had gotten hers too, and I think that this is a family repetition.

How do you mean? Doris's hubby had lost all their money in phony investments which the attorney Rosenthal had reason them into it. Terry then filed a lawsuit. The judge awarded Doris over $ 23 million.

Who is this? Terry, her son. He was a musician and a producer. He has written songs for the Beach Boys and the Byrds. Remember the Manson Family who'd murdered Sharon Tate? Polanski's pregnant wife, yes. Charles Manson wanted to kill Terry because he did not want to record the music of the Manson Family. How so? They were not good enough. But why did he kill Sharon? He and Candice Bergen had lived in the house on Cielo Drive six months earlier. Ah! Terry had to hire a bodyguard for two years. And Doris's house was also guarded around the clock.

How come? Manson has instigated his followers from prison to kill him. Sick! Yes.

And who is this Rosen ...? Rosenthal was the attorney who invested everything Doris, her hubby, and Terry earned in his very own favor. When I read their company's name ARWIN, I thought, heck how fresh. I bet, Rosenthal coined that name. Why?

Attorney **R**osenthal **win**s. He ruined a lot of celebrities, some of them chose suicide.

How do you think you'll get your money back? I don't have Doris's cash for costly lawsuits. I'd invest in a motor home trip. We could try to get hold of George Boyd & Co. and convince them before they meet their maker to be gracious enough to give their angel investor's money back. Who's George? Brix was our 2nd company we invested in, a ¼ century back. At the time when my father had sold my Ibiza apartment, Brix was already making money. They sold the software Ralph's is using. Then, George needed extra money. He planned to shrink all his software to sell it to many customers. He sounded trustworthy when after Dennis Morin's success with Wonderware he said to Peter and Jerry, I'm glad to be able to give my angel investors also at least ten times their invested funds. He probably never wanted to go public.

What can you do? Nobody thought he'd be lying. How'd he lie?

Maybe not exactly lying, but his behavior is bad karma practice. Huh? Morally wrong.

Why? Peter later told me he signed something that the money will be lost if the company doesn't go public or is taken over. I would never have signed that. It was my money. I should have seen George myself. I know people by sight. Well? Yeah, even by voice. Once, a guy called, he wanted a car. I said Peter don't sell him the car. I don't trust him. Peter didn't listen to me as usual. The guy cheated him and vanished. Only years later, a cop called from Paris that Peter could get his car. Oh, my!

Anyway, the shrink wrap was off. What only shrunk was our funds. And good old George built himself a multimillion$ villa in the Santa Ana Mountains. Jerry said in South France, too. Peter said he'd also gotten ten million in liquidated damages from Ralph's. Jeez! Some people are not able to get enough.

Jerry says he can't reach him, but of course, for him, it doesn't matter, he has enough dough. Jerry who? The bright blue eyes. He introduced us to the companies, a former broker, studied law. It's a family repetition again. Though our Jerry's not the cheater but still, same name same profession and so on. So I hope we get some of the money back, too. Because, with my expected €255 pension for some 30 years of working, I may survive in Portugal. But I'd love to live in California again. It's so silly to increase rents by the same percentage. Huh? What does a senior with a €10.000 pension do with 5% or €500 more? Give it to the bank. Exactly! For Peter with his €270, 10% would make a difference! Twice a month eating out or a visit to a concert once in a while. We'd take less money from our small savings. I'd scale the pension perhaps with up to €500 10%, up to €1000 7.5%, up to €2000 5% and so on. That'd strengthen domestic sales and be much better for the economy. Why will you get only 250? Because crooked politicians spend money from workers for crony capitalism projects and bankrupt banks. I think, for 33½ years of work and study I should get at least 500! Sure.

Why is the export world master not able to give their old people a pension similar to the Austrians or a basic annuity like the Netherlands? Huh? When I was there on a 5-day excursion with my professor in the 1980s, the seniors already received a basic pension for 5 years of working. Back then, I said, we better look for a job there. A fellow student replied, don't worry when we retire we'll have a basic too. Shit, we have. If seniors with small pensions apply for social benefits, the government tries to get the money back from their kids. Most of the elderly rather go hungry.

So how do you want to get your money back? I'll write a book and warn my fellow humans only to invest in Joint Venture companies when there's tons of leftover money.

That won't bring your dough back.

I believe in the cosmic law of cause and effect. If you give freely you'll get it back one way or another. Mandira's questioning look made me go on: Keeping a diary, you'll recognize it. I had once given 2 lectures on Spirulina for free. Soon after, I got a 4-day freebie trip to Berlin that was at least three times the cost. Mandira said, then good luck. When I put my jeans on she came close. Looking at me in the big bathroom mirror, she said:

Where are your wrinkles? Huh? Still there. You better get an eye check. You look definitely 10 years younger than last time I saw you. Em. Maybe this one week without Peter? Ha ha. Last time you looked frail. I sighed, I'd tons of problems two years ago: a depressed mother, an invalid husband, a flooded flat. How do you feel about your mom's passing?

I still don't realize it. I feel close to her. Last week, on what would've been her 87th birthday she'd reminded me of something.

How's that? On June 5, I said to my brother's wife, tomorrow after my root canal care, by the way, I'd done without an injection. Why?

Dentists use too much novocaine. I use to bite my lips and didn't want to fly with a big lip. I said to Edith, on my way back from the dentist I'll visit Ännchen, she's my mother's friend. Next morn I woke up hearing Mom's light melodious voice: That we don't forget this! I sensed her around my shoulder, on my cheek ... like a nip in my soul. Um, well ...

I was glad. Ännchen was also pleased to hear about her friend's still being around.

How was her mental state?

Not as usual, insecure, embattled, vulnerable. I was stuck in between her and Peter. Who needed me more? Rushing to my mother to see if she's up, helping her get dressed. Then cooking her lunch and walking with her, in the eve cooking for Peter and me. Um!

Mentally, I turned over my internal album.

I saw me sitting in the car, trying to blink my blurred vision away, fighting my shortness of breath and the fear these stress related symptoms could get as severe as when my first lover stalked me. Our misfortune in that period of time tore down all the effortless and the trusted. Mandira's question made me close the inner record album:

What was with your flat?

Oh, terrible! Every time it rained, you know how often it rains in Germany, our bathroom was full of water. I always had to wash the floor coverings, often to renew the grout on the tiles and to paint the walls. We'd better deducted the rent. We were stupid! Because when we moved out we'd not even gotten our security deposit back.

Why not? Never trust a lawyer. Our landlady is not the first one who'd cheated us. How so?

Patricia promised to deduct our heating costs and send me the rest. Last week when I arrived at her house she said the radiators were stolen so they couldn't read our usage. Well?

The winter before we were in Portugal until the end of April, so we had not much oil used and estimated a cashback of €500. Anyway, I was glad to leave. In our 8 yards long house on wheels, we have less stress.

When we arrived in Portugal Peter with the truck and the trailer in front and I following in the Hymer ... if the Atlantic wouldn't have stopped us I could have easily driven to the States. Of course, the promised house was not ready, maybe Joáo lied again because the house doesn't have the view Mila had envisioned in his dream. Huh? Didn't I tell you?

No. Mila called a few years ago. He had visited me in a dream where I'd lived in a big white house. He described the very place on the golf course Joáo had shown us before the project was planned. In his dream, the Guardiana bridge that connects Spain with Portugal was under construction. Mila saw two towns though at the time there was only Ayamonte. Now, there are lots of buildings across the river. Since a proven psychic had not seen the loss of our investment I'm still trusting. And if not, I quote my mother: *We'll pass the little time we still have.*

Where's your furniture now? We left our moving equipage at the first farmer right after the bridge entering Portugal. He's one of the many Joáo relatives. We now stay right on the river of Guardiana. Isn't that a little close for comfort? Sometimes, Peter is noisy indeed. Either he talks or watches TV. If he offends my ears, I press my index fingers on them. Same when he's ever listening to Bob Marley or the bald guy he used to get drunk with in Malibu ... em, what's the band's name? Huh?

Great sound. They performed at Clinton's farewell party ... anyway, I'd never guessed I would stand it in the Camper that long but not having to take care of a place has advantages, too. I'm often in the library, writing books and blogging on my website. What website?

Marianne-e-meyer.com

But don't you like a house? Sure, I'd take yours right away. But at the moment, I enjoy the serenity of the water and the freedom. Are you still taking Spirulina? Of course, without

I'd be night blind. Does it help? Yes, it's beta-carotene. Okay?

Some years ago, when Peter raced on *The Ring* his young co-drivers weren't as fast at night so Peter did five night hours. Good for him. Good, I didn't know only later. Yup! That was when Hans-Joachim Stuck said, it was his hardest 24-hour race.

Well? And what was with your mom?

She was in the home of the Workers' Wefare Association where she belonged to the board of directors. I wanted to take her with me. But the chief had gone nuts ... a wholly choleric guy! He's in the wrong business, I guess.

Uh-huh! When my mother and the other seniors had their lunch, he came to the table and said, your mother can't go back to Michelstadt. I said, have you forgotten that she begged you crying because of being homesick? If you don't want her in the AWO home, I can look for another place in Michelstadt. My mother can choose, she's not in jail. That triggered an outburst that made me think he's totally unfit for the job. His eyeballs almost popped out of their sockets. He spun around like the Grimm brother's Rumpelstiltskin and yelled, not with me, I'll call the court. Really?

Really! Of course, my mother's and the other senior's appetite was lost. So what happened?

I told the judge they just pump my mother full with drugs. If I'd take her with me to Portugal, she'd be better off. Two weeks before, she'd walked as limber as a deer. But after she'd been drugged up to the brim with Haldol she walked as rigid as a Parkinson's patient. The judge and a shrink said I couldn't take her to Portugal right now, but I could get a second opinion. So I called at the Frankfurt University. I'd read that Prof. Pantel treats depression with a minimum of drugs. They keep the patients active. My mom was real active: a council member, a juror for 20 years, involved with adult education, seniors counseling and other voluntary work, two dance groups, gymnastics, the choir. A few years ago, she'd even sung solo to dedicate a temple. Well! Anyhow, I made an appointment with Dr. Israel. But on the day my brother and I'd planned to get my mother to the hospital without informing me he went alone and according to him, Ma wanted to stay. I believe with the correct treatment she would be still alive.

Mandira said: It's so sad what they're doing with the elderly. You know what's odd? Huh? When my brother informed me about my ma's transition on Jan 1, 2011, *The Love Boat* had just started on TV. They were on Tahiti. I said look, Ma here we were very happy. Strange! What? One of the guests suffered from sarcoidosis, the rare disease my mom had.

That is strange. I clapped the hand on my forehead, Mac ... Fleetwood Mac! Huh? The music Peter plays a lot. Yeah, good sound. Still quizzical, Mandira said so you really don't feel cramped living like that? No, I'm okay, our life is mostly outside anyway. We move our bodies more than ever. We ride our bikes almost every day to the beach or library.

Sounds like fun. Uh-huh! Except sometimes we have an enervating neighbor. Lucien is a French guy but looks and talks like a woman. He gets on our nerves often. He'd worked on an atomic submarine. Huh! The fallout may have affected not only the gonads. Jeez. But we use to keep close contact with all kinds of neighbors I said with a twinkle in my eyes.

Yes, I can confirm this, Mandira said thinking of the seventies when at age 8 she had adopted us as ersatz parents.

Elective relatives in Haus Tania

The roaring sound of the white beauty made everybody in House Tania aware of our return. Peter turned sharp left and parked the Porsche Carrera without any staggering but with the last baritone bellow. Walking from our private car park to the impressive entrance of the light gray marble building was rather uplifting, like going on vacation. Walking under the red protective cover was like entering a fancy hotel.

When we reached the white marble stairs, a little girl with long black braids greeted us with a big smile. Hopping up and down a stair, the cute dark skinned kid said without any shyness: Hi, how are you?

Hanging in there, Peter replied.

You look like interesting people. Why don't you come to our next party? We party almost every weekend. We live in the Penthouse.

We live right here on the third floor, I said pointing to the third balcony over the canopy. What's your name, cutie? Mandira, but my friends call me Situ. And how old are you?

Almost nine. And you? Her refreshing frankness made me laugh out loud. I'm the almost 26-year-old Marianne, and Peter is 33.

Good, my parents are just a few years older. Outgoing as we were, we agreed to come. We like to explore different cultures. As a child, I'd wanted a black baby sister. I'd put a Winky doll with a lump of sugar for the bird on the windowsill. I don't have to mention that my mom didn't perform the, therefore, necessary task. But a substitute little girl had been coming along.

We had seen Situ's handsome father and his beautiful wife in the entrance hall or elevator wearing classy Western world clothes.

But when we rang the bell and the door opened, our host appeared in a caftan elegantly holding a cigarette with a silver tip. Gaily he said: You must be Marianne and Peter from the third floor. I am Satish and this is Maya, he said raising his hand in his wife's direction. It was arriving in a different world when a gracious woman in a red sari with golden embroidery greeted us. The large home had modern western style furniture though the smell was quite different. I was not used to Indian spices and scents. Maya, what a pretty name.

Matching the pretty woman, Peter added,

She said I'm just an illusion hard to realize.

I glanced at her blankly. She explained:

That's the meaning of the word Maya. Smiling, I said, I hope, we are not intruding. Peter added, your little communicative daughter asked us to visit you. Yes, Satish said, giggling as if ashamed and proud at once, she loves to make friends. We all do, mentioned Maya gaily, with a big smile. I walked to the panoramic window and marveled at the great view.

Maya chuckled when I explained her daughter's advances in detail. She said, let's sit down. We all dropped onto the sea green landscape interior. Is whiskey okay?

Sure, I said thinking, the plus of not asking for my poison of choice: I'd only have one. Bunny may have triggered it.

Bunny? I asked with a funny face.

That's my son Vivek's nickname.

He's curious about your variety of cars.

We all wondered about you, flashy folks.

What do you mean by flashy? I asked.

Great looks, fancy cars, Maya replied with a teasing sub tone. Satish asked:

What are you doing for a living? I worked as an IT consultant at the Metallgesellschaft. But because I had some income from rent and lease, my tax adviser told me it would be better to start my own business. My only interest is cars and racing. So I decided on dealing cars. Aha! And where's your business?

I've two car lots in Frankfurt, one in Sachsenhausen and one just a few blocks from here. No wonder, you drive all those luxury cars. Are you managing both yourselves?

No, the one in Sachsenhausen is run by Harald, a very promising young man.

Yes, I said, he's quite busy. Next to selling cars, Harald manages a disco and arranges concerts for bands like The Searchers and Dave Dee, Dozy, Beaky, Mick & Tich.

Maya said: Isn't *Love Potion No. 9* from The Searchers? Yes said, Peter. And *Needles and Pins*, I tossed in. We got to know both bands after their concert in Frankfurt. Satish asked:

How is the car business these days?

We are very busy. I had no chance to wash my hair for a week I whined. There are only

12 cars fitting on the little car lot on Friedberger Land St, and we turned them three times this month. I don't know whether I'm coming or going.

That is good responded Maya. It's paying the bills. Peter said why don't you come by tomorrow, look at the cars and have a drink. Marianne is known for her coffee. That's so strong the spoon almost stands up on its own in it. He added reflectively, his shining roe deer eyes scanning nirvana: Soon we'll have another salesman to have competition between the two branches. Yes, that's good thinking. I'm going to ask my pal, Volker. He'll quit his job anyway. Then we'll have time to travel.

San Francisco's nudies and paupers

In my Italian-German elective kinswoman's BMW, we followed the Mattas' Mercedes from Palo Alto to San Francisco. Though I agree with Goethe's concept of elective relatives, I did not think about the subject when I kind of adopted Ines almost a generation after Situ. Just in time for the Northridge earthquake, she and Wolfgang had arrived in California. They still looked like kids, their faces barely blemished by the wounds of growing up. I wouldn't have guessed that the pale blond boy I sold a red VW Porsche a few months earlier would walk his talk. He'd told me to come back with his girlfriend to stay for good. They came with $1,500 in their pockets and rented an apartment a ½ mile from our house. It was destroyed by the same temblor that rumbled through our bedroom like an express train and made me jump under the desk like Bernie Shaw in Baghdad.

Our Desert Storm did send the TV, paintings, and dishware to the floor. Its epicenter was 10 miles deep but only 4 miles away. The motion was not restricted to the ground. I got enlightened by the meaning of the expression: It scared the shit out of me. The adrenalin rush forced my 25 feet gut to two shock evacuations of freshly cooked applesauce lookalike.

The night after the kids had slept outside with me next to our pool I was searching for the half-year-old kittens who'd disappeared. At night, they'd shown up on our outside bedding just for a few secs and vanished again. Two days later, when the worst rubble was cleaned up, Lisa and Mickey returned.

We felt the need to take Ines and Wolfgang under our wings. But with their creative power, their will to win and fortune they'd done it easily without us. Lucky Ines won the green-card lottery in Italy. She had sent several quests thru her grandma's in Italy and from Germany. Wolfgang did not show strong desire to work as an auto mechanic, same with Ines. She informed me about the hairdresser business in the US. The same sweat we now have in Germany, adding up to a salary that's not enough to lead a decent life. Ever since, Thanksgiving and Christmas eves, we celebrated with our ersatz kids.

Situ had studied in Stanford and visited us a few times on other occasions with Madhu.

On my first visit to California after 15 years, I learned why Peter prefers L. A. It was July, and we were wearing sweaters and anoraks.

But after the first 100 steps along sunny SF harbor, a crowd of bare bikers showed up! I raised the camera. Omigod, Peter won't believe this. Times have changed. We've never seen naked men in the US in the 11 years we'd been there. When we went to Malibu beach, Peter always watched out while changing clothes. He'd say, if an older Lady sees a single pubic hair, she may call the police. I don't feel offended by naked people, but personally, I don't feel comfortable showing everything. As a toddler, I even was ashamed of peeing in front of a cow. However, in the seventieth, I felt ashamed wearing a bikini top. At St. Tropez beach, everyone was bare bosom, even a girl with a breast looking like someone had sewn a button in. Finally, peer pressure made me take my top off. It also made me think about the 3rd Reich. Would I have mounted the barricades to be shot? I'd have left the country. It would not have helped the Jews either. To make up one's mind about someone else one has to be on the very spot.

We passed several homeless people sitting or lying close to their belongings piled up in shopping carts. I aimed a silent curse at the Congress fools who waste billions instead of helping the homeless with lodging, detox programs, and job training to get back on track.

Isn't it a shame for highly developed societies not to have shelter for everybody?

They may want to live like that.

Perhaps a few. It's no fun being kicked around by cops. Most of them may have lost their jobs because of disease, bad luck or mistakes.

Don't they get welfare? That's what most people think. But I know from a street lawyer that the homeless get tons of problems from the bureaucrats, like no address, no form to send, not calls to be returned. Then they drink away or use crack. To get the drug, they sell it. If they get caught they go to prison. This cheap and highly addictive drug costs society much more than all the needed programs. Just think of all the crack babies, who will always have to live at society's costs.

There's lots of charity going on.

I know, some super rich avoid paying taxes by spending money for all kinds of bull, genetically modified food causing cancer, harmful medicine or other ruinous stuff and nonsense. But who gives a rat's ass about the things that could make our planet a better place? What do you mean?

Freedom! Security! Dignity! A basic income for the most urgent needs. No other social benefits would be needed and no control agencies. That's costly! Well! Many people are struggling because of big concerns not paying taxes but giving their top managers fat salaries. Don't they pay taxes too?

Does it justify the immense difference in wages? Families got poorer in the last 10 years. The average income didn't change, but energy costs have doubled, making it difficult to make ends meet. Most top managers and celebs made 10 times more than ten years ago. It's difficult to understand the enormous increase of management's and celebs' earnings. Yeah, but that's our achieving society.

Alas, but people who love their work, like bosses, actors, soccer players, and race car drivers shouldn't use tax havens. Without others' ideas, efforts, works or watching and worshiping they couldn't collect their dough.

Um! That reminds me of a Doris song *Life is just a bowl of cherries:* "You work, you save, you worry so, but you can't take your dough when you go …". By the way, in Germany, people can avoid paying death taxes by investing everything in their companies. This adds to the increasing gap between rich and poor. With more fellow feeling a fair distribution and paid taxes would be common.

Isn't that idealistic? Maybe. Sure is. But I'd love to live in a society that provides all people with their basic needs, allowing them to stay pure and spotless from the world's mess.

Let's stop with politics. Okay, I just hate to think about some persons' greed hindering our heaven on earth. What do you mean by that?

J. P. Morgan is such an example. We wouldn't have to live in fear of nuclear catastrophes if the banker would not have been so selfish. How so? Morgan had invested in all of Nicola Tesla's inventions except for his free energy generator he'd installed in his Pierce Arrow. The speed of the car was 90 miles per hour. There was still enough energy to illuminate his house. Huh? I've seen it on the internet, also the patent number. Guess why Morgan feared mass production?

Conflict of interest? Exactly. He had previously purchased two copper mines. Electrical wires are made of copper.

What has this to do with the homeless?

With free energy, we'd be a lot further in providing every individual with a basic income to pay for food, clothes, and shelter. Who should pay for it? The taxpayer like always. Many companies produce, come hell or high water, and when they create financial problems they ask the taxpayer for help. So, wouldn't it be fair that they pay taxes for every running machine, for any assembly robot? Big companies used to pay no taxes at all and often even not for energy. This is unfair. And if politicians wouldn't spend taxpayers money on corrupt bankers and senseless projects and subsidies there would be a lot for everybody.

But wouldn't people stop working? Some of course. Would you stop working with 800 or 1000 bucks a month more in your pocket? Nope. Me neither. Most people enjoy working in their field of interest. It's good for their confidence and their commitment. In principle, we all wish to do something for society to be accepted, to be loved. Few people work according to their likes and talents because they couldn't make ends meet if they'd do. True.

Oh, look there, what's Gandhi doing at the market? Promoting vegetarian foods? It reminds me of the venturing in food that makes people starve. With $800 or $1000 a month all man could do the jobs they love and still make house payments and have babies. This kind of security would help the economy better than any halfhearted trade booster. How?

An unconditional basic income would be spent on goods meaning more jobs and more productivity. More money would be spent for better education helping the economy. With better training, people make more money, pay more taxes and have more retirement money to spend. Sounds good, I'd also know what to do with 1000 bucks more in my pocket.

Hey, you're the first wealthy man I met who looks at it this way. I ignored Madhu's verso gesture. The rich who are against the citizen money better think about their own benefits, less work time and more security, to name just two. Well! Why security?

Because, without despair there's no need for stealing or dwelling on destructive thoughts.

Politicians may not want it, they fear about their security, their pension. No need to. Like I said, more money, better education, more things made, more taxes obtained. Politicians are paid by taxpayers and should be interested in high salaries and a basic income.

You could have made it in politics. Yes, they'd asked me. But I remain rather a one woman party and free to say what I want. And I hate to talk to large crowds.

Dropping the camera after a more distant pic of the metallic granitic Great Soul I missed out on an enormous physical object passing by, a 6.5 bare muscleman on roller blades.

Omigod, did you see that?

What, the homeless? No, the nude dude. When I was a kid, I used to dream me walking naked through town ... my worst nightmare. And this guy does it freely without shame. Is Eden nearing? Where do you think he hides his keys or his money?

Probably in his boots.

Back in Palo Alto, Ines rushed to her room to make some phone calls. What a change from the early nineties when she and Wolfgang came to California empty-handed. In the mid-nineties, they were already living with their dogs and cats in a rented house in a cheap Pasadena area. Now the busy business woman leads a 16 soul company with her husband spending more than double the sum they jointly owned arriving in the US just on school money per month for their 2 girls.

I marveled at the Mattas new kitchen. Average families build houses for the amount of the remodeling. I'm proud of my well off ersatz kids. Having just read Irving's Water-Method Man, I compared Fred Trumper with Mandira Matta: both academics and from academic families. Fred's father, urologist, not supportive. Young father Fred's main worry except for his erectile organ: avoiding the bill collector. Situ's grandfather, once surgeon general of India and her parents immensely supportive. She only had to lose hair in her first year after her study. Luckily, the habit of harassing young physicians has eased. Or was the harassing reason Situ's skin color? Now, the prospering pediatrician is chief of a clinic earning social prestige. I wonder what she'll be in her next life. Though Christian born, I find myself more understood and my metaphysical experiences better interpreted in Buddhism and Hinduism. Was it luck or destiny? With their lesser educated backgrounds, Ines and Wolfgang seem to be financially better off than the Mattas? At least, the Kring's fleet of vehicles expresses it: the newest AMG Mercedes, Porsche Cayenne, BMW, Mini cooper, and Harley. This couple made the American dream reality. Did they deserve their wealth in this incarnation by having led a former life of sacrifice and goodness? The last ones will be first! And the first ones last if they hoard their bucks like Dagobert Duck instead of helping their fellow humans. Money isn't the meaning of life but love and cherishing all living things.

Shiv and Rija freed me from my thought process by asking to come with them to the park to play some soccer games. Are you serious? Why, yes. Okay, if you don't mind playing with a granny, I'll certainly enjoy playing kid for a while. On our way, Shiv and Rija took turns on the skateboard and the ball. I said, it's a bit chilly. The 10-year old who had her jacket around her hips got it off and reached it to me. To the kids' astonishment, the gray garment with anthracite animals fit beautifully. Our former landlady's singsong voice popped into my mind: Mrs. Meyer can wear everything. She'd even look right in a potato sack. I wondered about how both had grown since I saw them 2 years ago. Shiv's voice had become a bassoon. When we showed the children our old area in Frankfurt, Rija was quite funny. I'd talked to Situ about my and my mother's fear of talking in public rooting in early disgrace, same with Doris Day. As a little girl, she had wet her pants on stage. And both Doris and my mom leaving their sect is another similarity. Cute black braided Rija had stemmed the back of her hands against her waist and briskly called: Who the heck is Doris Day? The kid looked so funny that we had burst into laughter.

Arriving at the arena, Shiv handed me the skateboard and ran with the ball to the wall. I'd never tried to cope with that plank on wheels and lay down on my stomach. Shiv shouted: Be careful! Huh? That's dangerous. Is Shiv playing the father role? Later, Rija told me, Shiv had an accident in this very position.

After 15 minutes of kicking the ball against the wall, I was happily short of breath. It's strange sticking in an old body. Since the soul never changes feeling at 30 isn't different to feeling at 60. Without mirrors or reflecting peers we may never feel old as long as bones don't stiffen or bladders weaken.

A little later, Rija dropped onto the piano stool and made me listen to beautiful strains.

Wow! I admire your effort in whatever you're doing. You swim daily to become a world class swimmer. And your playing needs many hours of weekly work. Shiv plays, too.

Yes, I've heard him, but … not as skilled I thought: Your mom must be very proud. At age 11, I also had lessons but the 12 marks my grandma paid per hour was a waste of money. Why? I developed a cataract in both eyes and couldn't read the notes. Whenever my teacher played something and told me to repeat it, I played out of memory.

Too bad. I wasn't ambitious anyway. Well …

So Rija, tomorrow you've your room back. It was nice to let me sleep in your comfy bed. As soon as we'll be in the house, I'd like to buy one just like that. Situ asked: When do you get the house? Dunno. João promised us last year. Right now there's not much building business going on in Portugal. I wonder what our furniture will look like when we empty the truck. It's been sitting there for 1½ years.

My memories went back two years when things began to change for us. We had to think about moving again. It was the aftermath of another Peter escapade which our landlady commented with: Now I understand why you don't have kids. You have enough on your big one. Don't throw bricks when you live in a glass house I thought. A line on my astrological chart appeared before my inner eye: The need for change is very important. Our last change in life was also after Peter's strange proceeding: material for another story.

I always wished to write novels but doubting my fantasy for good plots. Is Peter helping me collect stuff for future writings?

Remote relatives on Doris Day's track

How do we handle our moving? Peter called from the kitchen. Huh? How do we get our furniture to Portugal? We could buy a 7,5t truck and do everything ourselves. The cost would be about the same and we'd be more flexible time-wise. Later, we could sell the truck. Hem! What hem?

Shit. This coffeemaker makes me mad.

We also could convert it into a motor home.

Yeah, right! That's much too expensive. We'll end up paying more than buying an original one. Though I didn't believe it I gave in:

Okay, anything you want.

In the worst case, you can make a junkyard

selling the truck in parts. And you don't know how long we have to wait for the house, you know Joáo. When did he say it's finished?

He promised so much. I know.

We may not get it at all.

I still have hope. The psychic had not erred with everything else. Marilyn said, I don't see the money lost but it'll take a very long time. Remember Mila's dream of visiting us in a big house overlooking a golf course and a bridge. You and your dreams. Damn, Peter gave the filter a whacking blow, there's something wrong with the drop stop mechanism.

I filled the Google space bar, searching for a photo of the plant that filled my mind lately. Why the heck do they call psyllium flea-seed? I may have chosen the healing plant as my writing project much earlier.

Peter uttered, half the coffee's gone.

Not at all interested in my work, never read any page of my books, only interested in news, car races, and stock analysis. As a determined optimist, I see the positives in his lacking involvement: I can write about anything for he would never force me to blacken a line.

I opened the internet portal of my favorite uni and filled the empty research space bar with Plantago ovata. The phone rang. Usually, I ask Peter to answer it. Since I heard him still rattling in the kitchen, I grabbed the receiver. Aunt Anneliese's light voice bubbled over in my ear: What are you doing?

Working on a book about the best substance to lose weight and to detox.

Well, you can talk to me about that later. I've to tell you something important. Okay?

On Sunday, I went with Lisbeth and Hilde Wiswesser to a ferry feast in our birth community. In Neckarhäuserhof. Yes, they will celebrate every year now around June 20 to get some money for the ferry ... to keep the ferryman in business. Well!

Next time, you should come too.

Sure. How was it?

They had set up tables and benches in front of the Grüner Baum, in Neckarhäuserhof. A musician was there too. It was quite lovely.

Um! You've to come next year, too. Settled.

We had delicious home smoked trout and guess what I found out. Huh? We are related to Doris Day! What? That's strange. What?

Lately, I saw a picture of her in the tabloids and had a familiar feeling, reading that her grandmother stemmed from Mückenloch. So?

I'd only torn out the page. Well!

Isn't it a pity that we hadn't known about it when you'd visited me in California? Uh-huh!

Whenever I saw Doris in a film with her jerky hip movement or her grumpy guttural sound I thought, just like Mama. Oma said it, too. But who does not know people who remind them of someone?

How is Alwine? Still reclusive but crystal-clear. I bring her lunch. She just doesn't want to go out to the others feeling inferior to anyone else. Why? She's one of the best-looking and best-dressed women there. Her closets are bursting, but she complains to have nothing to wear and no money. She saved plenty. Yes, I know, but when I remind her she says I can't sing anymore or I can't write anymore, all signs of severe depression. You think, she has

Alzheimer? No way, her short time memory is better than mine.

How so? Recently, in the pharmacy, part of her medicine had to be ordered. I asked to have it delivered to her apartment. Later, we had an unplanned engagement near the pharmacy. Ma said, then we can pick up the drugs ourselves. She thought about it. I didn't. Um!

So why had she been given Alzheimer pills instead of antidepressants? The psychiatrist asked her about the date and the President's name. She answered correctly. They want to keep the looney bins and old age homes busy. Is it otherwise less socially agreeable? They'd live too long and break the pension fund!

Aunt Anneliese pulled me down from my pulse rushing excitement and impatiently stopped my evermore raging monolog:

I just wanted to tell you how I got the news.

Why, yes, I forgot. Go ahead! The rising of her phone bill seems to be ever on her mind.

Well, you know how I am, I approach all people. I talk to everybody. Like me. Um, yes.

Mrs. Wiswesser sat on the balcony in her wheelchair. She's 90 years old, an ex-docent. I turned to her and said hello, I'm a daughter of Lydia Augspurger. She was appreciatively surprised. She said, oh, from Lydia, I always liked her. Just come up to me. She spoiled us with cheesecake and coffee. Now, I stopped my aunt's flow of words.

So how are we related to Doris Day?

Hilde Wiswesser said, through our grandma, What's her name? Eleonore Nollert. How does Hilde know it? She said it's official. You could get proof from the town council. Like most times, she finished the phone call in her abrupt manner: That I only wanted to tell you.

Okay, thanks for calling.

I was exhilarated, moved, proud, amused ... a mixture of feelings. Who would not be flattered by a relative most people had heard singing *Que sera, sera* or seen in many motion picture movies. Do you want a coffee, too? It's past two, too late for me though I may not be able to sleep a lot anyway. Filling the Google space bar with the singer-actresses' name I said:

Have you overheard my conversation with Anneliese? Sort of. So you are married to a distant cousin of ... wow, she is still the most successful actress of all times! Quigley's 'All Time Number One Stars' list puts Tom Cruise at No 1 and Doris Day at No 6, just behind her friend Clint. Don't get overexcited. Heeding his mockingly twisted lips, I snapped, how would you act if you'd find out to be related to John Wayne?

Your relationship with this woman does not get us a single nickel in our pockets.

Money! Money!

We better concentrate on our business.

Ah! There's the ancestry. Indeed her grandmother Anna Christina or it's her great-grandmother ... a born Nollert like my great-grandmother. They are 9 years apart. Likely been sisters. Endorphins rushed through my veins.

Peter enervated, so what?

I excited: Ma may be her second cousin.

Does that get us anywhere?

Neckarhäuserhof has only about a dozen houses. It must be that. There may be more Nollerts, Wiswessers and Augspurgers related to Doris, enough for a family fan club, haha.

Don't you have serious things to do?

Ma is only two months younger than Doris. From all the distant cousins she is her the most alike, the looks, the singing voice. And Anneliese is a real standup comedian.

You make me sick. If you don't stop, I'm leaving. We have the stress with that Ubbe bastard, and you waste your time with nonsense. Hey, wait a minute I shot back, you are the one who's always giving the cheaters money. The stress we have is your sloppiness. Who told you from the beginning not to give Ubbe any money? Peter pushed his blockhead cheekbone forward looking like a kid.

I even advised you not to take him as a testdriver. You still may have your job at AMG if ... Yeah, in the end, you always know. No, not in the end, you'd also known that he'd lied twice. Once when you tested the brakes in Italy when he got the mirror torn off the right-hand car and when he had the accident. You also heard Bolko saying that he squandered Rosi's pharmacy. So you were warned not only from me. That's all history. Well? Now, I've to think about how to get some of my money back.

Why has the history always to repeat itself?

Huh? Your problem is that you never learn from history: Britta, Strott, Zimmerlein, Joáo, George Boyd, Clemens Martin, the Rosen Brothers, Rost, Neidhardt, now Tyarks, did I forget anybody?

Who's Britta? I forgot her last name. You'd lent her and her husband 6.000 marks for that cleaning business, before we met.

Jeez, the Schnitzlers! Peter shouted, puffing with annoyance, that's eons ago! Just think about what Hans use to say, the cows get fat only under the eyes of their owners.

Yeah, yeah, I know, but I don't like working without partners. My father had partners, too.

From his eyes, brown hate rays with golden dots took aim at me.

Reconciling, I said, oh my, why do you always make me reproach you with the catalog of my disappointments? Peter laid his hand on my shoulder. I stroke it with my cheek. Softly, I said, look I'd always helped you, but I had no help with my writings and sold thousands of more copies of my first three books in the first 6½ years than Dan Brown. Um!

And he has a supporting spouse! Why don't I get a chance in my field? I don't ask you for help, but I don't like anybody telling me what to do or not to do. I wonder why I haven't left you long ago. Because I still make you laugh?

Sweetly smiling, Peter cocked his head to one side and tickled me under the arms.

We better invest in good film camera equipment following Ubbe's advice: a sitcom by just letting the camera capture our daily interactions. He thinks we'd be funnier than what's on TV. Well! While Peter got himself another coffee, I thought about Betty from Glendale, the real reason for sticking with Peter. The aged artist painter, my friend Ingrid worked for urged me to think closely about leaving him. She had kicked her hubby out because of their constant quarrels. He had another woman right away, and in the long years living alone, Betty even missed her hubby's spats. Ingrid always said: Whatever happens happens for a reason. Actually, my astral chart indicates losses. Since from early on I was used to saving money there were always people coming into my life who helped me to experience losses. Edi crashed my Cabrio. I got a poodle from Günther. Tony was run over by a truck in our 9-house village (another Family repetition: Tiny, Doris's same-aged dog got run over by a car too). Günther also convinced me to vouch for Edi's sister. 1½ year long, half of my paycheck was seized. Ma wondered why I was always short on cash since we kept strong emotions from her. Though Peter helped me get the money back from Claudia he provided me with loss experiences big time. The judge's comment was, you can do various things with your money, you can treat yourself. You can save it or you can throw it away which is the same as giving guarantees.

Searching on Amazon, I didn't find any biography in German and ordered the one Doris had written with A. E. Hotchner.

The phone sprang into life again.

Peter answered. It's Maya.

Say hello, giggling, I added, tell her the news. I found the website of the Doris Day Animal Foundation (DDAF). Wow! She's also blogging! A celeb did a no-no with his dog. She writes he should please cease doing so.

Peter, sad-voiced, I can't come, I may never see India or the States again. I grumbled:

You make me sick with your mantra! You are perpetuating everything by repeating. Why don't you repeat positive affirmations? Oh great! We are looking forward. No, I guess they can all sleep at Csöpi's. You've seen her large house. She'd like to have them. She admires Vivek. Say hi to Satish. Ciao.

As if called, our neighbor friend appeared at the terrace glass door. As a typical Saggy, Csöpi is a clear cable for the other side, too. She still questions her clairvoyance though she'd dreamed about Peter's scooter accident.

Mandira and Madhu are coming with the kids in August. Is that Vivek's sister? Yes, she's the pediatrician near Palo Alto, who's specialized in treating obese kids. You'll like Madhu. He's cuddly like a teddy bear, a pleasant guy. How exciting!

I asked the thin air: How old may Situ be now? Um ..., Shiv is 10, her medicine-study was quite long, she must be almost 40. Wow, time travels fast. Remember, when she always came to us? We were her second family. My thoughts drifted back to the mid-seventies.

From *Haus Tania* to India

My lovely ersatz-daughter came to me for a little chat or a private coaching in math. Mandira said when you explain it I understand it right away. My teacher complicates everything. When Situ showed up for the first time, I had asked her: What do you want to become professionally as a grown up? Quick as a flash, she answered, a pediatrician. On her next visit, she carried her friendship book along. I wrote her an assuring poem in it and painted a doctor-patient scene next to it. We also went to places together.

One winter morning, when I entered the Zoo with Situ, a tall gentleman in a dark blue coat walked in our direction. When he was some 20 yards in front of us, I held my breath, then whispered, do you know who that is? No, answered the kid with a counter-question: Who?

In an erect naturally authoritative manner, the gentleman walked towards us. Good morning, I greeted. He kindly greeted back with a nod. I felt elevated but only for a split sec. Looking down on me heat struck my face. Extremely embarrassed I said, here I am in the middle of all these animals wearing a leather trench coat and leather boots. Mandira turned to me with her left leg lifted, mine are also leather. Her red turtleneck shining out of her duffel coat still increased my scruple.

Grimacing, Situ said, you didn't kill the animals. Yeah, but it's the way we are, thoughtlessly buying the things that are in fashion.

A spur of impatience in her voice Situ said: So who was that man?

Professor Grzimek. He's on television all the time. With his son Michael, he'd filmed the wildlife in the Serengeti. Their film even earned an Oscar. Michael was killed there in an airplane crash. Situ asked:

What kind of professor is he? A vet, I guess. Have you never seen the Bernhard Grzimek show on TV? Nope. Now, I was a bit agitated. I can't believe it. He always sits there on a desk talking about the Serengeti or showing some films. He usually has little lions or monkey babies hopping around.

Situ's face cleared up. Yeah, yeah the excited little girl exclaimed, I've seen it a few times.

Often, we went shopping wholesale groceries and drinks for the parties, or we'd driven clothes-shopping to Obernburg, the town known for apparel wholesale. Once, on our way back, Bunny and Situ got hungry in the middle of nowhere, only corn fields in sight.

I said: If you like corn and only take two that's considered theft of comestibles. It still felt like stealing, but at least it stopped the hunger of the two poor little Indians. One time, when we were already quite familiar, Situ rang at the door. Peter opened.

She asked: Is Marianne there?

Yes, he said, but she's taking a bath.

Let her in I called from the bathroom. I had left the door ajar since Carlo used to use our toilet, too. Peter asked: In the living room?

No, let her come to me. I just got in the bathtub and didn't want to be rushed. With a big smile, Situ asked so what are you doing?

How does it look like, I said laughingly, splashing the water with my forearms: Indulging in a bubble bath.

No, the kid said, I mean after that.

I said, chat with Situ? So, what's up?

Nil I just want to see you. What's up here?

Not much but I had an odd dream last night.

Huh? I lost a pretty worthy ruby ring. Can you imagine, I showed my stretched out fingers, I don't wear any jewelry. Guess where I lost it? Huh? I think in the Grand Canyon. In fact, it was only the little oval gem from the setting. I realized it in a casino. By the way, do you know how the Grand Canyon was carved?

Not exactly.

A Scot lost a nickel and searched for it. Ha ha! Carlo's paw pushed the door open. The tom jumped onto the toilet seat. Unhesitating he peed in his usual rocket-like position: four paws in front, the bum in the bowl. With a sudden outburst of laughter Situ said:

Did you see that?

Yeah, he does it all the time. Carlo absently stared into the promised land. Short he got up and scratched the seat of the pot thoroughly.

Situ said: That's awesome! Yep!

You should snap him. I did.

I mean you should make the pictures public.

I've sent two photos to the *Stern* magazine. They've this page where they show cute animal pictures. One shows Carlo sitting with the high bent back: On that you even see the dropping copper bolt. Another one was just like you have seen: Carlo staring into nirvana.

They didn't want them. Carlo pushed down the curtain ring on a string. Wow! Carlo, great! Situ shouted joyfully: Unbelievable.

The tomcat left with his tail erect. He doesn't flush all

the time since I did not train him from the very beginning. I once talked about Carlo with a fellow student. She'd said, my cat can flush.

Situ again yelled gleefully.

So where have we been? I asked.

In the casino. Wow, I'm known for my good memory, yours certainly can compete.

Okay, the dream, the ring, while I was washing my hands, I felt the sharp edges of the setting. Strange dream! I don't own a ruby ring, but it could be something in the future. I had a prophetic dream a few weeks ago. Do you remember the day when the little boy was run down by his mother's white Beetle?

Uh-huh! Situ grimaced, terrible! She reached out to grab the soap and played with it. I said, it happened, when I talked to my mother. I saw the boy flying through the air. The poor woman screamed like crazy. She had no chance. The youngster must have jumped right in front of the car. Yeah, Situ tossed in, he had recognized his mother's car. She'd lent it to her girlfriend. Exactly. I'd knelt on the kitchen table, watching the street and talking on the phone. My mother had called with the *news*. I made an apostrophe sign with both my index and middle fingers in the air. She said, your classmate Inge's father's dead. He hung himself. I said, I know. That was two or three months ago. No, my mother replied resolutely, it was the day before yesterday.

Huh? But I know ... I must have dreamed about it. It had something to do with his son. He had an accident with his bike. My mother said, do you now start with prophecies, too?

So, did you? Situ said.

Yeah, this may have to do with Tikale's lymph cleansing and alignments. I'm more receptive than before. Is he the guy you always come back with your hair smelling? Yup, as if I had fasted for 5 days. Um!

Please, reach me the bath towel. Uh-Huh!

My mother had foreseen things through dreams all her life. Have you ever dreamed anything that later came true? Not that I remember. Have you ever been in a place you felt as if you'd been there before? Situ's absent-minded face seemed to fish for something. I was once in a part of Bavaria I believe. I suddenly felt strangely familiar with the area ... I knew before what would happen next. Yes, I had that too. My mother had her first prophetic dream at your age. One morning she told her mom a dream in which an old neighbor woman had died. She'd described all the details of the room where the lady laid in a bed behind a door. When she'd come home from school, her mother said you were right the woman died. Both had gone to the house they'd never entered before. Everything was as seen in her dream, even the bandage around the dead body's cheek bones.

At around this time, I had a red Porsche 356 as a daily driver. I soon changed it for a little green Italian car. I often was anxious about getting a dent in the mint car. With the Autobianchi, my parking problems at the university had vanished. The handling was much easier. It felt like driving a go cart as if united with the street. Even my Professors enjoyed the rides in it. Only Günther Feldmann was a little scared sitting in this speedy little automobile with not much sheet metal around him. After Satish had a test drive with it, he asked Peter to find an Autobianchi for Maya, too. She'd just received her driver's license when Peter found a neat yellow one. It seemed to have had a weak battery or an ignition problem, since the following winter, several times in the early morning the doorbell rang. Satish asking Peter for help, sleepy Pete grabbing keys and jump start cables, driving his car from our car park to the Caroli's, putting the black cable to minus, the red to plus, and after the motor purred, returning and slipping back into the feather bed. This went on until they drove the car to a garage for an adjustment. Our tours together to German tourist regions were the most enjoyable gather, but nothing topped relaxing with Maya and the kids on the big divan in the family room. We laughed a lot and watched TV or Videos: Grease, Tina Turner shows, Queens concerts or other musical events. There, pleasing my fanny on a pillow, I learned to drink English tea. Kesin, the family's skinny servant served it in a silver teapot on a silver plate. Maya poured sugar and hot milk the way we all liked in our tea cups. Before I never had tea with sugar and milk. But the way the tea is cooked by the East Indians not just brewed it is more agreeable that way and extremely delicious. When the family was traveling, Satish gave Peter the key and asked him to check out if everything is in order. One time, Peter entered the spacious living room where Kesin was resting in Satish's high chair, feet up, having a whiskey and smoking a cigar playing big boss. Just like Carlo. Whenever Peter or I opened the door, he'd jumped down from somewhere since I don't like cats on tables or kitchen counters.

Peter said: Should I mention Kesin's behavior? Why? Do you think Satish will check the booze suspecting you of abuse? Peter still told him, perhaps because of what I'd said. Satish chuckled saying, that's okay. He grew up with me. He's like a brother. But believe it or not, though Kesin seems to like to sit comfortably he never slept in a bed. He has his own apartment in the house, but he always sleeps on the rug in front of the bed. Like many of his countrymen, he's not used to sleeping in beds.

When Situ was 12, the family left Frankfurt to live in Delhi again. A very emotional farewell. Their closest friends came from Hanover and Saarlouis. We all laughed off when Peter arrived at the airport with Chico on a leash. The middle-aged Pekinese I retrieved from people who for some reasons wouldn't want to take care of any longer, one was bad breath. I knew the lively little bundle would be best off in India with our caring friends. We still had contact through the phone and Maya once came to visit us. Peter drove her in Alois' blue Rolls Royce with golden

Emily through Germany. When Peter informed them of our planned visit, Satish said, I hope you've been in Morocco before. Nope! Why? It would be good to go there first, so you already have an idea what to expect.

Does he think we cannot handle the people there? They cannot be more enervating than the Gypsies that come to us trying to negotiate prices for hours and to trade in their rugs. Peter said I don't mind their wheeling and dealing. Most of them are quite nice. That's what I mean. We don't need the Morocco test.

On Dec 31, we entered an Indian Airline Jumbo with a suitcase full of animal product gifts: salami, bacon, ham in tins, salmon in jars and various kinds of cheese for the family. In those days, there were no sausages to buy in India and only two kinds of dull cheese. The whiskey for Satish we had planned to get duty free on board. Over Nuremberg, the stewardess served our bottle of champagne she had put in the refrigerator, an hour earlier.

Looking down on the yellow, red, and green lights, we celebrated the New Year. Since we had married on 4th of November 1980, on Ronald Reagan's inauguration, this was virtually our honeymoon.

Almost eight hours later, we were in the middle of a world of mystery. A Sikh with a blue turban drove us in an archaic Ambassador with crunching joints to an affluent Delhi suburb. The man went up and down performing strange contortions caused by a knocked out steering. When we arrived at our friends' house, a party was in full swing. After the guests had left, we emptied the suitcase with the goodies.

Satish's face grew longer and longer, where's the whiskey? I said, we wanted to buy it on board. But the crew didn't show up with the duty-free stuff, so we forgot all about it. Satish wailed: Do you know what a bottle of Scotch costs on the black market? 270 marks! Peter said I'm sorry since the crew didn't come we should have asked. I tossed in: They may run a business with the booze in Delhi. Peter later bought the Scotch for Satish in a 2-hour ceremony in a palace. We enjoyed Mayas vegetarian cuisine. Kesin helped her cutting the veggies but the cooking and flavoring she did.

Next morn, we ate the Indian fresh cheese with bread, healthy but bland. We didn't want to eat the foods we brought for gifts. Used to salmon and eggs, we walked a bit hungry through the first two days until we got used to the vegetarian fare. In the eve, we accompanied our friends to a party, where typical spicy Indian dishes, kebabs, and chicken were served. Outside on both sides of the street leading to the house, old men were sitting on the ground holding their plates of food in their laps. With their white garments and turbans, they lightened the street like a welcoming committee.

Next morn after breakfast, Peter drove with Satish to the office. The typical sounds from the street merchants reminded me of my childhood. There were also people coming, who offered to sharpen knives and scissors, collected old metal, paper, and fabric or sold fruits and veggies. Situ came into my room and said, it's so nice to have holidays. You cannot imagine how different school is in India. Frankfurt was peanuts. How long is your school day?

Expelling a cubic yard of air, she said:

Till 4:00 p. m. But it doesn't stop then. We have a lot of homework to do. Poor thing! Fetching a sigh, rolling her eyeballs, she said:

Mostly things we'll never need. I said:

That may be the reason why more Germans get Nobel prices than Indians. We do not fill our heads as much, leaves room for creativity.

Situ said, come with me in the living room. My music teacher is coming. You've got to see him. He looks funny. Are you playing an instrument? No, but he brings one you've never seen, I get voice training. A man with a big box came in. He placed the wooden instrument on the floor. It reminded me of a zither-harmonica-mix. The middle-aged man with strong gray curls sat down on the floor. His caftan under a red vest covered his bent knees. Situ placed herself next to him.

The tones you have to get used to; sounded a bit like stepping on a cat's tail. Same with Situ's singing. Listening to her false tones, I thought, wasted money. Mandira may have sensed my feelings and made a funny face.

Later on, I went with her and Bunny to the nearby village. Passing a football field, Situ said: You cannot imagine, how excited Mummy was when you said, you'd come. It took three days cleaning everything in and around the house. Poor Kesin, getting the Ambassador touched up took him five hours. After passing a huge palace ruin, we were in the middle of medieval times: hens, piglets, sheep, women in brightly colored saris, some with loads on their heads, smiling.

Hey! I like it here! Me, too!

Some women stood in line before a store.

Situ said, with their stamps, they get sugar and flour. Some ten men of all ages sat down on the dirt in a circle playing cards. I said:

They are poor, but I don't see anybody looking unhappy. And it is like everywhere, poor women work, poor men play games dreaming of better times. The scenery had something surrealistic to it. Strangely enough, I didn't feel strange at all. I felt more at home than at the party, the other night. But considering all the news about brutal raping, I may have been a little idealistic.

When Satish and Peter returned, we invited the family to the most impressive hotel I've ever seen. The broad white marble staircase we stepped onto affected me immensely.

In the restaurant, Satish said: Peter, you can order beer, wine, and whiskey but for Maya and me I order tea. Heck, what happened to you? Are you sick? The waiter came and took orders. After he'd served the tea, the soft drinks for the kids and the wine and beer and for Peter and me, Satish waited for the waiter to leave. Conspiratorially and cautiously he looked ahead and behind. Then he filled his mug with beer and Maya's with wine. We can't drink alcohol in public, Satish explained but drank more than ever approving the well known: Forbidden things taste twice as good.

Tipsily, we walked to the family's yellow Mercedes. Because of the high import tax, this car was considered a house on wheels. Satish fiddled in his pocket for the car key. Finally, he got it out and turned it over to Peter. With eyelids dropping to half-mast, he uttered, I'm totally drunk! You've got to drive. Peter said I had as much beer as you. Satish replied in what I suspected a phony slurred voice, I'd two scotches more.

Giving in, Peter said, and you think I can handle the traffic. Sure, dude! You're used to driving. But I've never driven amongst cows and goats on the wrong side of the road.

With an eager gesture, Satish said, you'll handle it. And be careful, you now bear great responsibility. Giggling ... crucial cargo.

I'm not jumping at the chance, Peter replied. Looking at me quizzically Situ asked, are you sure?

Since I had my share of wine, less alert and afraid I said, don't worry! Peter was a racer. If he can't handle it, nobody can. Besides, he'd eaten a lot and it's been three hours. The three beers and two whiskeys will not matter much. Peter said:

Well, Satish! But you've to tell me where to go. Certainly, dude! The dandy Hindu touched Peter's arm and slipped onto the passenger seat. Maya, Bunny and I sat in the back, Situ on my lap. Peter started the diesel. Leaving the building, I noticed a few rain drops on the windshield. I said, Monsoon is in summer, isn't it? Laughing and choking we reached the main street. Satish shouted amused: No, Peter, the other side! We are not in Germany. Bypassing a bull with an extremely calm impression, a feeling of great relief floated through me. A great serenity came over me. I impulsively started to sing: I'm singing in the rain...

Situ and Maya attuned right into an audible pitch and more or less even the men joined in. After Gene Kelley had left the mental screen swinging his umbrella, the medley consisted of Perry Como's Raindrops, Doris Day's Sentimental Journey, Tom Jones' Delilah, the Beetles Yesterday, Blue Bayou, Hello Dolly, Mr. Sandman, Strangers in the Night and New York, New York. Uplifted, I said, if I could sing all the time, that would make me very happy. So why don't you do it, asked Maya?

You mean, professionally?

Why not, she reasoned, haven't you finished university? Oh, yeah, I answered, I'm stuck with Peter, dealing cars, having no ties to the music business. Besides, I just started a doctorate in gerontology. You could check it out anyway. Yeah! What else? Cooking, cleaning, car sales, university! By the way, I just had a strange experience with my professor, incidentally, she's from Finland and loves the rain. Anitra Karsten, I pronounced the "R's" in her harsh manner, is going to initiate the university for seniors. We had a meeting at the uni tower. Together with some other professors, tutors, and selected students, we prepared a petition for the foundation. The most baffling part was that against my usual habit I took a highly active part in the discussion. So?

I was surprised were all those brilliant ideas came from. I submitted the most constructive contributions, all accepted for the petition. Maya said: So you'd one of your better days.

No, I'd never experienced anything like it. Most bizarre was, at the end, my fellow student Margit Fath asked me, what I'd meant by that and that. I had no clue. The words had passed off my lips and I heard my voice as if it came from outside. Situ said, sounds spooky.

Yup and the meeting had ended with my offer to take a copy of the concept outline home. You know Wolfgang Mischnick's son lives on the first floor; the politician from the Free Democratic Party. I'd offered to ask him to give the petition to his father so he could submit it also from sides of the FDP to the secretary of education Armin Klaus. Satish tossed in, didn't he always come in a yellow BMW with seven bodyguards? No, said Peter, Mischnick sat in the Mercedes with three bodyguards, the other four were in the 500 Beamer. We used to make jokes about the crowded flat or when we saw them walking with the family. It must be very inconvenient to have people around every minute. Satish yelled:

Slow down, now the next right. Thank God! We made it. I said: We better hit the bed fast. Why do we always go out late when we have to get up early?

Four hours later, the dusk had begun to ink out the stars, when Satish dropped us in front of the bus to Agra. New Delhi was already in full swing. In front of the little huts on the sides of the streets, the people were cooking their tea on heaped up stones. The one-room huts without windows looked like big cardboard boxes. Most curtains in front were tilted over the tin roof so we were able to look inside. There was nothing else to see but a few bamboo or plank beds. Where do these poor people go to pee? Just around the corner or behind a tree like dogs. But there's no privacy! I'd poo in a plastic bag inside the hut and drop it in a trash can.

In the rising sun, we marveled at the marble Muslim mausoleum, the famous Taj Mahal.

Situ's lecture about Shah Jahan crossed my mind. The emperor had loved his 3rd wife who bore him 14 children and served as an advisor and confidante to him, so much that he'd build this beautiful building for her burial. Getting closer, I gently touched the red, green and yellow half gem inlays in the white marble. Inside, I walked to the sarcophagi. Their marble was finer and the inlays more delicately shaped. I tried to visualize the emperor and his wife lying in there and made a mental note to ask Situ about their embalming.

However, looking at the body as an instrument bearing the soul, I think burning it would be better for the environment. Had the Muslim sovereign anticipated the crowd of people visiting the Taj Mahal? Today, tourists can't get as close as we'd been. But they can touch the ivory inlays on wood carved dishes or flower pot stands in the nearby tourist traps.

Next morn, Maya took us in her black Ambassador, called The king of Indian roads, to the vital and colorful heart of Delhi. The car of British origin based on the Morris Oxford III model is manufactured in India since 1958. On our way downtown, we talked about the few people of the then 700 million soul society that can afford to study in the US. Today, about 35 years later, India has 80% more people, and the middle class increased to an extent that now more rich Indian cousins come to visit America than the other way around.

How many people live in poverty, I asked?

We have an upper class of 5%, a middle class of 15% and a lower class of 80%. And what could be done to strengthen the middle class? Our cast system is the main hindrance, Vivek replied. How can we get a stronger middle class when most Indians believe they are not to leave their cast? If you are a servant and you believe you should not strive for anything else you and your kids and their kids will remain where or what they are. That's as easy as that.

I bought a white cotton fabric with silky embroidery as a gift for Ma and a light blue printed fabric for me. We went to a tailor, and for a few rupees, I ordered slacks, a caftan, and a scarf. On the market, Peter said, unbelievable the price of chickens! You should do a business a la Wiener Wald.

Yes, that would feed us all. We should run a chicken farm together. Looking in my hubbies face, I could read: Cobbler sticks to your last.

We have to think about it.

Sightseeing with Maya and Situ was a funny venture, joking around and laughing at most stone sculptures. On the grounds of a magnificent mansion surrounded by a 2-miles-long red stone wall, Peter pointed to something of sexual content. Maya, said jestingly: That's nothing, wait until tomorrow in Khajuraho. You may even learn something new there.

At the dinner table, Satish wasn't fond of our business proposal. Much better than chickens are cinemas. That's true, said Situ. Have you seen the long lines? Bunny agreed:

We certainly need cinemas. Satish suggested: We could start with one cinema and from the profit we could build another one.

All these business opportunities may have been better than shipping cars to the US. But we would have lost the money, anyway. If we have to experience losses, it may not matter what we do. The best is not to attach to things and to find bliss by working in the loved field.

Sitting on a green meadow in front of Khajuraho's famous temples a youngster in Jeans and square shirt came near us asking: Could you take me with you as a servant?

We only have a two room apartment.

Tis no matter, ma'am, said the likable lad. I can sleep under the table or in the garage.

I'm sorry, we only have a ground garage and a cellar, and I don't believe our landlord would agree with you sleeping there.

Our next stop was Jaipur. We were the first time alone in the middle of the mishmash, trying to pass without bumping into people, vendor trays, and merchandise on the floor. The human potpourri of puggree men in diaper-like dhotis or kurtas (caftan), women in saris or salwar kameez (long blouse, pants, and shawl) and all the noises, colors, and odors somehow got to me. I'm usually not shy with all kinds of people and creatures and don't mind big crowds as long as I don't have to give lectures. But in the middle of those strange smells and the hullabaloo, an eerie feeling rushed up my throat. A skinny man in a dhoti pushing a rotten wheelbarrow passed by touching me. The 6-by-3-feet frame with raw planks had only two big wheels in the middle. All of a sudden I realized what the unusual freight under the dirty white shroud was! An older man in front had one hand on the cart, probably to pay attention to the dead body not to slide down. The covered corpse gave me the rest. My system revolted. Hyperventilating, I was close to throwing up. I made Peter a sign to follow me away from the masses of human flesh. I rushed in the direction of *The Palace of the 7 Winds* since it was not as crowded there. Passing the front of what I thought was a building, I stopped stunned staring up what looks like the frontage of the motion picture industry. Just a pink facade, a wall with stairs in the back. I got upstairs as far as I was able. The motion was good for my emotion. Relieved, I looked down on the scene and laughed the rest of my inner turmoil away.

During the next few weeks, we visited the Jagmandir Island Palace in Udaipur and other beautiful places. Peter bought me a ruby ring in Bangalore as a late wedding present. We resided in former guest houses and hunting lodges of Maharajas. We were woken by tooting elephants and rode on them.

In Mysore, Peter was on a drunken spree with some natives. He came back at 2:00 a. m. and talked about the guys he'd met: We were five men in a scooter; that was quite funny. Up the hill, we had to hop out and push. I pictured the boozed crowd behind the black and yellow tin can on wheels.

You can tell me tomorrow. We have an appointment with our driver at 8:00 a. m. Driving tourists had been the teacher's sideline job. With four girls in a row and still trying for a boy, he was always in search of side jobs. He said: Only a boy will later take care of the family. You never know, I replied. One of your girls could make it in the movies, earning millions.

In the morning, I had a hard time to awaken Peter. Though we were on our honeymoon, I had no other means than shaking him up. Since we had lived together in cohabitation for seven years, the refined ways to wake a man up didn't work anymore. In the seventies, living together without the blessing of a higher authority was not as common as today. But even my mother with her strict, severe and ascetic upbringing said, you did right. All couples should live together for a while. How else could they get to know each other? By the way, Doris said the same in her biography.

Hubby finally opened a frenzied eye: Whom did you let in? I yelled: Get up, now! Peter's jolted voice cut knife-like through the air:

Turn around and look whom you invited in. Moving my head, I shrieked. Lined up, a cute sandy monkey family stalled there, holding hands: monkey dad still on the balcony door, the smallest monkey kid near the bed. My screaming made eight eyeballs popping out. I felt a bit sorry when they slowly walked sidewards step by step back out of the glass-door, fixing their optic organs on me. Peter grouchy, that's because you always leave everything open. Glancing at the bedside table, he said: Fortunately, my Rolex is still there.

We made friends with fellow travelers, a nice Parsi couple from Bombay. By the time we got to know them, we already knew a little about their religion. Most Parsis are living in Bombay since 1995 called Mumbai. There in the Hanging Gardens, we had already visited the Tower of Silence. On its top, the Parsis lay the corpses of their loved ones out as fodder for ravens. This may sound soggy to some people. But I think of it as a clean and practical thing to do. Whether you are picked off by birds or nibbled by worms, what's the difference? We went into the tower with a guide. He said, pointing to some jewelry in a glass vitrine on the wall:

Made from human bones. Peter asked:

Are you taking us for a ride? No, it's true. Oh my, how would I feel if I'd wear Granny's bones around my neck! Peter replied jokingly:

I would say, Grandma looks nice on you.

In reflection staring, I said, Oma Maria was my darling grandmother. It would be the most personal memorial piece from her, actually, the only one. I haven't gotten even her wedding ring she'd said would be the only thing I could inherit from her. Though she had her pension, there was nothing material left. She'd spent all her money on us, her family. She'd also helped friends with money and clothes. I'd often searched for certain pieces, Ma had made for me. But they already had new owners in Glückstadt: Annegret and Silke. This was another way of getting used to losses. Only much later, I figured that letting go is my lesson in life. Oma's pension first faded away in the household; later for purchasing the brown house in Schönnen, for cars, and other things. However, she had left me lots of treasuring memories worth a million.

Christmas-trees & phosphor bombs

In her mid-fifties, my father's mother had left the line keeper's lodge to live with us in Michelstadt. Of course, she had a lot more to do, since she still worked as a watching woman for the German Federal Railway. She usually walked the four miles to the Post 19 in Schönnen. I often accompanied her. After her husband's brutal death in the aftermath of an accident at the railway station, she was living with two foster boys. When I was a toddler, my parents dropped me at the two-story stone house on top of the meadow hillside. During the week, they drove around with their split window Beetle. As sales reps for a Black Forest firm in Freudenstadt they sold quality fabric merchandise all over the Odenwald: table clothes, bedding and linen goods.

Next to cranking the railway gate up and down, Granny spoiled me rotten. She brushed my hair until it was as supple as thread algae and shined like oiled. She used to say, as a princess you get your hair brushed with hundred lustrous brush strokes. Oma cooked me whatever my taste buds asked for: cherry souffle, potato pancakes, and filled cabbage were some of my favorites.

She also knitted me a wide skirt from multi-colored wool rests. I loved its wavy effect while doing my pirouettes. Oma also made cute clothing for my dolls and moved me around in a wicker chair. My brother and my foster uncles Hänsi and Karl-Heinz also took turns. One time, the chair abruptly stopped, and I fell onto the floor. While they all comforted me, I sensed their guilt feelings. We often went to the forest and picked blueberries. The boys filled my cans, and I proudly pronounced my diligence. Once, they even had prepared the extremities of my doll with twine to entertain me. When I woke up, my doll was walking towards my bed. I was enthusiastic, but only for a split sec. My family's laughter turned me off leaving me humiliated for believing the doll became alive.

When Heini came home from school, we were roaming forests and fields. One time, GI's drove by in a jeep. They had called us from their open windows and jokingly offered us gifts. Of course, we were running for our lives. Since, in the German language, a gift means poison we were scared of being killed. The soldiers seemingly had a lot of fun and tried to allure us to stop. We still ran, trying not to fall into the ditch. One GI laughed hysterically. When taking off, they threw something out of the window. Our curiosity survived the fear. We cautiously walked towards the gift. There was a flat silver can that looked like a contact mine. Since a boy from a neighboring community had lost an eye by playing with one, Heini stretched his arm sidewards to stop us from going there. He carefully bent down to the object: It's wrongly written, but I think it's chocolate. But be cautious! Everyone take something! Heini chose the contact mine handing me a high size can. We took our poisons to Grandma. Six queasy eyes observed the excruciating turning of the threaded cock at the flat silver can.

I asked, is it shoe cream? I don't think so.

Oma removed the cap and the white crackling paper: a disc of pitch dark chocolate appeared. Not a good one, though. Only Oma liked it. My can contained beans in a spicy tomato sauce. Yummy! Nobody shared my excitement about the beans. I ate almost all at once. I had never eaten better beans.

When the foster boys' mother picked up her sons to live with her, Oma moved in the other top floor flat next to ours. But we missed the forest and the free life in the red sandstone house, where Heini was born a day after Christmas 1945.

Grandma stirred sugar and cocoa in a bowl of oatmeal, added a handful raisins and poured in milk from a pitcher. The door bell rang. Seppel shrieked from his birdcage on top of the sewing machine. Oma put the bowl in front of me onto the large kitchen table and walked to the door. A gasping pedlar rummaged about his merchandise and said, gosh, these stairs are draining. How can you handle this every single day? Maria made a gesture trifling. Whether it was his trick to raise guilt-feelings or her constant being used to going up and down the stairs wasn't clear to me.

She said, why you are younger than I am. But, good man, she added quickly leaving no time for compliments, I don't have much time now. What do you have to offer? I have earthenware ... best quality. He got three pieces out of his knapsack and put them on the floor. Well, just get me that little milk pot. There were always sellers coming to the door. Oma only bought practical things or foodstuff. Had a hawker nothing useful to trade, she usually offered him a bowl of soup. In the old days, we ate soups before all meals and had mostly leftovers. Whereas I enjoyed my sugary breakfast, Granny made us scrambled egg sandwiches to go: with butter and chives. The melted fat smelled tempting. I could have easily eaten those as well. But here even my beloved grandma was able to say no.

While she wrapped the bread in grease-proof paper and afterward in a dish towel, she said:

We have to hurry up since we walk today.

Oh, Oma, why don't we take the train?

Because I have to stop by aunt Liesel. I want to ask her if she needs to be picked up by your papa next Sunday for the divine service. Why? She has problems walking. We still may have time to drop by uncle Otto and aunt Anna.

Oh yeah! Grandma's trump card. She knew, I liked her half brother and his wife who radiated calm and security. Compare to them her husband's folks were quite boring. Uncle Otto had a model railway installation as big as a king size bed. He also was a bird breeder. On Christmas, I got Seppel from him. Since then, the green parakeet mostly fluttered freely around in our flat. He liked to sit on our shoulders or heads and nibble on our lips or on Heini's exercise book. In the evening, we had a hard time to catch the bird. His high pitch yelling and complaining was one thing. Seppel also could be so quiet that we walked out with him on the shoulder. One winter morn, Ma went downtown when a woman stopped her saying, you've a bird on your shoulder.

Turning around on the spot without touching Seppel, Ma walked home quick as a flash.

The long marches with Oma Maria, I didn't mind. First of all, I'm an outdoorsy girl. Secondly, I liked the fascinating and sometimes gripping stories I made her tell. Half way to aunt Liesel's two careworn women and a little girl walked towards us. I whispered they look odd! Why do they wear those weird scarfs? They are fugitives. Huh? They had to leave their homeland. Why? Because, we lost the war. Is this, why we sing *Maikäfer flieg, der Vater ist im Krieg; die Mutter ist in Pommerland, Pommerland ist abgebrannt, Maikäfer flieg*. Yes, but this was another war. There have been too many. Perhaps my father did the right thing taking off to America. Huh? I guess you don't know that. My real father went away to America.

Why didn't he take you along? I wasn't born, yet. I was in Mine Oma's belly, only this tall. She stretched her pointing finger and bent it.

Why didn't Mine Oma go with him?

I don't know. Maybe she didn't want to leave her family. Had your papa not want you?

He may not have known about me. Um.

My interest in the war outweighed the family business. Tell me about the burning Christmas trees and the shrunken bodies!

Oma sighed: Again! Why do you want to know all these terrible things? I couldn't tell her. I was most fascinated by brother Grimm's horror stories, but those were bed-literature. Her war stories were a thrilling pastime.

Oma pleeease tells me again about the bread loafs and the Christmas trees. Can people not cover or step aside when they fall?

No, they were not the problem, they were just markers for the bomber pilots. Only the phosphor bombs set fire to everything. They shrank people, animals, and trees.

Kids, too? Yes, they were not bigger than a loaf of bread. Have you seen them? No.

Then how do you know? When I visited aunt Hedi in Glückstadt, I met a woman from Hamburg. She had seen it herself, she lived through the Operation Gomorrah.

Huh? Like Sodom and Gomorrah? Yes, the bombs made everything stiffen. The quarter where the woman lived lay in ruins and ashes. She saw shrunken families sitting in a circle. On the street stood a horse, froze in an erect position. Omigod! Poor thing!

People were walking in the streets, and all of a sudden their bodies were sat alight.

Couldn't they blow out the fire?

No, they just tried to escape. Thousands had thrown themselves into the river of Elbe, or they dug in the soil. They had to remain there because whenever they raised an arm, it started to burn right away like a torch. Why?

Phosphor only burns in contact with oxygen. If burning phosphor is poured on you, your skin looks like leprosy. Huh? Like when you burnt scrambled eggs. Their relatives came day and night and brought food.

Were there kids too? Yes, many. They were the bravest; didn't scream nor cry. They even felt sorry for their relatives. Why? They were desperate. Huh? Couldn't help them. Who threw the bombs? The allies, Oma replied promptly. Huh?

The Englishmen and the Americans. Why?

Maybe because of The Final Solution. Huh?

The Nazis killed the Jews. What Jews?

Remember, you'd seen those pictures, those poor skeletons and piles of dead bodies in the pit with bony faces... uh-huh, the bones sticking out from their stomachs. Yes, horrible! Ugh! Oma muttered, they should've ended the killing by gasoline embargo and bombing the railways to the camps. Why kill innocent people? Huh? All those horrible killings are senseless. This will still give us a hard time thanks to Adolf Hitler and everybody who helped him. Hopefully, you never have to go through something like that. It was a horrible thing they did with the Jews and also with the youths. Huh? Using them as puppets ... you won't get that yet.

What did the people in Hamburg do wrong? Maria sight. Not only in Hamburg, many other cities were also burnt down. Michelstadt, too?

No, only large towns, but in the darkness, we'd seen the flash bombs going down in Darmstadt like burning Christmas trees. 80% of downtown Darmstadt was destroyed.

Why? Why what? Why they burnt the people? Do you remember the photos of the skeletons and piles of dead bodies in the pit with bony faces? Uh-huh, the bones sticking out from their stomachs. Yes, horrible! Ugh!

Oma muttered they should have ended the killing by gasoline embargo and bombing the railways to the camps. Why kill innocent people? Huh? All those horrible killings were senseless. This will give us a hard time thanks to Adolf Hitler and everybody who helped him. Hopefully, you never have to go through something like this.

Why? Why what? Why they burnt the people? What did they do wrong? Um! Most of them had been entrapped, deceived and later they had no choice. Huh? We had a fascist regime, the Nazis seized power and persecuted everyone who'd a different opinion. Huh?

It was not like today. We couldn't say what we wanted. We never knew, what our neighbor thought. We even had to be careful in front of the kids since the teachers were urged to spy on them. They advised the children to spy on their parents and to report anything they said against Hitler or if they listen to foreign senders.

I wouldn't have sold you out. I believe you, certainly not on purpose. It was such an evil time, full of fear and horror. What happened to the kids in the water? That was so sad! The officials tried to find a solution. After a week, soldiers shot the poor condemned in their heads. Up in arms, I shouted: But why? They hadn't done anything wrong! It was for the best since they had intense pain. The poor! Oma repeated her mantra: terrible things happen when countries are at war. Hopefully, you never have to go through one. I'd to go through two wars. My beloved brother Christian had died in Russia.

Why did he go there? He had no choice.

Why not? Men who had refused to recruit were shot according to martial law.

He could have run away. Some did, but it was deadly dangerous. They couldn't hide forever. And whoever helped a soldier, was also shot if caught. That happened often since they pressured children at school. The kids didn't want to betray their parents, but they said something making the Nazis suspicious. Huh! In the 3rd Reich, we had tribe detention. Huh? If your papa's papa had robbed someone, all members of the family were also imprisoned or had to work in a labor camp. The kids, too? They usually came to distant relatives or in an institution.

Aunt Liesel's house came in sight. Oma said: I hope she doesn't offer her Blümcheskaffee again. I knew, she meant thin coffee.

Why is it called flower coffee? That's an old expression. In the old days, all coffee cups had flower patterns. When the coffee is too thin, you see the flowers shining through. We left the old house faster than assumed.

The couple was about to take off to visit my favorite Hörr family. Passing the beautiful old building of the district magistrate, I asked:

Are Hänsi's and Karl-Heinz' parents in jail? No, why? Because they said some wrong. No! I'd taken the boys because their father was killed in action and their mother had to work.

Maybe your dad wanted to go to America because of all that. Why, no! In 1902 were no wars only a miserable time and no chances for a better future. He may have wished to see the world. Me too Oma, me too! I believe you will. Why? There's a saying that people with gaps between their teeth travel the world. Can we go to America and visit your dad? Maria sighed. I don't know where he is. I only know that he lived in the Hanau area. Is that where aunt Lina lives? Yes, she lives in Steinheim, but I don't know if my father's from there too.

Maria used to write lots of letters to her friends and sometimes Lina Eisele wrote back that she would come to visit.

So your dad never saw you. No, he may have been already on the ship to New York in early 1902. I was born in October. Luckily, my stepfather married Mine Oma right away. Nobody knew I was no purebred Hörr. Huh?

With a mysterious smile, she said: I now told you a family secret. What? Why? At that time, it would have been an enormous shame if my mother had gotten me out of wedlock. Huh?

Having babies without being married was dishonoring at the time. Even today, it's not just. Therefore, you better keep yourself till your wedding. Huh? That's when a man puts a ring on your finger. Look here. Stretching out her hand, she showed me her wedding ring.

The philanthropic Parsis

This would be quite a personal memorial piece, Peter said with a funny-faced glance at the human bone necklace. I pictured my grandmother lying in the open coffin in front of the old chapel the wedding ring on her finger. Ma wasn't able to take it from her. I didn't mind back then. Now, I'd like to have it, if only to keep it for potential seances. At least I've got some of her poems and embroiderings. Her late life she'd dedicated to her grandchildren. I was the sunshine of her life. Shortly after my fiancee had taken me to Frankfurt, she found nothing to fill her emptiness.

Even when I was still at home, she once had locked me in to keep me from going out. Not long after I'd left for Frankfurt, she'd taken refuge from reality and for many hours walked about the grassland bordering the house or sat in the car looking down at the town.

Not being able to let go and to adjust to changes may be the main reason for old age senility. Maria was washed and swaddled by her son. Ma couldn't do it. When I studied in Frankfurt, my parents once engaged me as a Granny sitter over the weekend. During this time, Oma's senility had disappeared. Like years back when I returned tired from work as an emergency doctor's assistant, I asked her to make me a sandwich. Quick as a flash she rushed to the kitchen and instantly slipped back into her old role. We'd read and talked and behaved like in the old days. What would have happened if I'd taken her with me to Frankfurt? Would life be easier, if we all had a school subject, where we'd learn something about constructive relations?

Would we avoid problems if we'd be prepared for all stages in life? Or have we chosen to undergo our experiences? My parents returned with bright eyes, wagging with a booklet. The cover showed a photo of my Afro head surrounded by a halo. We found that in a Swiss pilgrimage church. Yeah, a photographer friend, Lothar Nahler, had taken photos of me and sold them. Wow! The title story "Who am I?" Stark! My very topic!

Our guide hoped for a high tip by asking: Would you like to see the top where the dead bodies are laid out for the ravens? Without waiting for an answer, he stepped up the winding stairway opening the door and saying: I'm sorry, this is as far as you can get. I looked at a musty wall. To see any corpses I'd had to jump up to double my size. Later, the *Stern* published a photo made from a helicopter. It showed the circled rows: the bigger outer ones were for men, the middle ones for women, and the small inner circles for kids.

Parsis are known for their generosity, not only towards birds. Lodging at the Bombay Oberoi Tower, we called the Parsi couple we'd met during an earlier tour. They picked us up in a cab and invited us to their home for dinner. Because both were lawyers we expected them to live in a fancy apartment. Arriving at a barrack yard with several rows of small houses, Lidia said, my father-in-law was a military man. He has Parkinson's. We live with him. We were stunned how close they lived.

The old man looked like Gandhi, so he was in my good books at once. I started a conversation with the funny talker whose hands were trembling slightly. The dinner consisted of rice pilaf, mushrooms, green peas, carrots and other fatty looking vegetables piled up on oval plates. Then the couple proudly showed us around the house since we only had seen the dining room. Entering the bedroom, I was quite puzzled by two double beds, only 2 yards apart. In my frank Saggy manner, I asked:

Are you all four sleeping here? Yes, Lidia said. Why don't you use the dining room as a second bedroom and put the table and chairs in the living room? It's big enough. They both just smiled at my practical suggestion. I wonder why they didn't do it in the first place. Perhaps that was their kind of birth control.

Next evening, we had dinner on top of the Taj Mahal. I felt uncomfortable with all the waiters around our table. One came with water, one with napkins and two dishes with lemon pieces in water, one with wine, another with the menu, the fifth droned out the specialties. There were two other waiters in their bright red uniforms with yellow-green collars standing nearby on the lookout.

I bet, the next one asks me if I want to have my feet cleaned. I don't like them to hover about. It disturbs my privacy.

Why! It's their job. But it bothers me. Peter's bully amusement with his quirky laughter made me steam. You want privacy in the bedroom. I want it when I eat too.

Next morn after breakfast, we left the hotel area and its private beach through a door in the fence. We walked for almost two hours. In the far distance, the bom Bahia turned into a long stretched bend. Peter said: Now whenever we see Bombay on a map, we can say we walked the beach there. As we got close to the bending, I looked down on my feet. Watch out! What's that? Peter sidestepped and said, looks like a shore worm, a very big one, though. The closer we came to the curve, more brown worms lay in the mud.

That rather looks like dog shit, I said, meandering through them. 100 yards from us, just about as close to the Indian Ocean not to get wet, sat two men in white caftans, a yard apart. What are they doing? Peter said: They talk to each other. Suddenly, I realized, what the shore worms were: human excrement.

Pooh! I'm used to dogshit, but this is disgusting! I feel sorry for people who have no toilets, but I can't ... ugh, I feel nauseated. We turned on the spot, and two hours later gladly reached our beach resort's safe haven.

All afternoon we remained in our clean Oberoi room. It was the first time on the trip we ordered our meal through room service. Down on the path to the beach sat a beggar with his hat on the floor. I watched him for about an hour while Peter studied a map. Once in a while, I said yep, a bill again. When the man left the scene, I said, if we ever get poor, we know where to go. Peter asked:

Where? You're never paying attention! Huh?

I can do three things at once, you not even one and a half.

Annie get your gun! Blah! You wouldn't believe how many people dropped their dough into the beggar's hat. Not only coins.

It seems to be a good business, indeed. How about we follow him tomorrow? Maybe his Mercedes parks around the corner.

From Bombay, we flew south to Goa. Of all the India we saw, we were most affected by this former Portuguese enclave. I tried to talk Peter into buying a hut by the beach. The price was only 20.000 rupees. Nowadays, you won't get anything under a million. But like always when I come up with a great deal, he said: Immovable make us immobile. Don't own anything, only use everything. The best is to have all belongings in a suitcase and live in a hotel. I screamed: Jesus Christ! Reconciling, with a twinkle in my eye, I said, He had not even a suitcase. Goa was different from the rest of India, not only because of the Portuguese buildings. The way of fishing, I'd never seen anywhere else: 30-40 feet high stands of rods and bamboo of a triangle or trapezoidal shape, holding a net inside. The fishermen loosened the fixed ropes on each side and slowly lowered the structure into the water. After a while, they lifted it up again and inspected the catch.

Some people from the furthest western state of Europe remained in this region after the Portuguese colonial dominion ended in 1961.

I said: I could live here for a few years, I only have to get out of my Jeans. Let's get some light domestic clothes. I approached a vendors booth. We selected slacks, caftans, and blouses made of a thin diaper like cotton. Then, I detected something Peter could wear in the evening.

Look, that's like a magician's outfit. Peter rubbed on the blue and red velvet vest and touched gently with a phony whistle over the golden embroidery. He said flippantly:

Heck, what a load of ornaments, and to me in a lowered voice in German, I shouldn't show appreciation that only increases the price. I'd not wear it at home. I'll give it to Ecki. He can wear it when he does his nonsense at the Quodlibet. Yeah, Ecki will like it.

I mentally moved back, when I met Peter's friend and roommate Eckard Drexler seven years ago. I wondered, how he'd gotten along during the past years. Still celebrating life in the pubs or visiting his pop in heaven. He was 32 when the doctor told him he'd suffer from Hodgkin's disease, and if he'd quit boozing and smoking he'd live another half year. I'll always remember the day in January 1974 when my Wilhelmshaven born lover HP had sent me to my Wilhelmshaven born future husband CP and his friend Ecki.

Cutting off the tresses

On Friday, I took the metro from my college in Nordweststadt to visit HP, only three stations further. He hadn't seen me since I cut my long silky brunet mane and created a huge henna colored curly Afro.

Why did you do that? Don't you like it?

No! Yes, it's great! How much did the Figaro charge you for this piece of art? I smiled proudly! Touching my hair, I announced:

Homemade. You're kidding.

It's true. How did you do it?

I pattered: I washed my hair, took a strand, cut it and rolled it up on a curler. I took the next strand and so on until I had all the hair cut and wound up. Then, I put the stinking perm stuff on, then the fixing, after that the Henna and here I am. HP's skeptic expression had eased during my explanation.

Next morn, we were greeted by a sunny winter day. Sitting at the kitchen table, we indulged in a zesty breakfast. Looking at my Afro magnificence, HP said:

So why you changed your look? The way, he said that I suspected jealousy. Could that be? He spoke openly about his other girlfriends! With one he had visited Günther and me twice in our rented Odenwald farmhouse: once, when my groom to be organized a class reunion and his teacher and classmates came from Frankfurt, the other time for a grass course race in Michelstadt. I said: A while ago I was with Günther in the musical Hair in the city hall in Offenbach. Marsha Hunt struck me big time.

Okay, okay, HP said, I believe you. Tidily he wrapped the salami in grease proof paper and put a rubber band around it.

Didn't you want to buy a car again, since you have a cheap habitation now?

That's what I told HP when I'd met him by chance on my first student's protest demo. My thoughts drifted a few months back. My clueless way of pleading for more BAföG money had likely cost my career as a pedagogue. I'd just quit my job at Deutsche Bank. Oddly feeling I walked through Frankfurt in an unusual outfit: Afghan sheepskin jacket, bell bottom hipster slacks, John Lennon hat. This was not the habitual walk of a sensuous blue-eyed brunette strolling through the zoo or park.

Suddenly I felt a strong urge to look back. Behind a red banner marched HP, my ex-fiancee's classmate. With his curly hairs and bright blue eyes, he looked like a giant angel. I gave him a blank look joining the group. Puzzled gazing, he asked:

What are you doing here? Aren't you a doctor's assistant in the Odenwald? Proudly, I replied, we moved a year ago and separated a month ago.

Abruptly, HP lifted me and dropped me on the sidewalk. Haven't you seen the SS? Huh? The state security takes photos from communists. Nonpolitical as I was it hadn't crossed my mind that a few communists could harm democracy. When the students grow up and make money, they usually fall for consumption anyway.

Speaking of family repetition: More than ½ century ago, my father was also wrongly taken for a communist. He'd driven his GVP party pals Helene Wessel and two future German presidents to election meetings. Gustav Heinemann advised him and his other passengers to join the SPD. It was foreseeable that the GVP wouldn't surpass the 5% hurdle.

When 41 years later, during an election campaign Johannes Rau congratulated my father to his 40 year SPD membership, he asked:

How come you missed a year? We were all honored last year. With a growing grin, my father looked up to his famous friend. Sitting in listening range at the bodyguard's table, I heard my old man saying: The pals didn't want me. They thought I was a communist because I furnished evidence for one. Alas! That's bad luck. Yep! I was the only witness, so it was my duty, to tell the truth.

On this sunny fall day, HP asked for my phone number, handing me a pen and his palm. Writing on the soft flesh, a feeling of cheer came over me as if I was a teenager again. Was Amorous shooting? Another 6.6 man, poor Dad! Or was HP just the mediator to lead me to CP?

So, how is it living in a big city? Great! I feel free! Nobody knows me. Don't you miss anything? Only a car. I always had a car. I can't afford one because of my expensive flat.

Since I now had a cheap room the grinning giant handed me the Frankfurter Rundschau: You can look in the advertisement section for a car. Sliding his key in my direction he said: You can take my Beetle.

I laid out the paper on the floor of the flat's free room. It was the nicest, furnished with a gray-blue bed with matching bookcase cabinet. I'd have taken it right away, so would have Karl's girlfriend but they wanted the perfect third man. For many weeks HP and his roommate had looked out for a fitting male to complete the three-bedroom living community. But the expectant were either too radical or too fundamentalist. To me, they didn't seem to be bomb throwing anarchists or archaic thinkers. The hearings were quite entertaining though I didn't understand much. I found three Beetles and called the cheapest and even newest: a 3-year-old Beetle for only 3,300 marks. A sonorous voice said hello. I'm calling about your Beetle. Yes? Is it still there? It's still there, but there are people on the way.

What color is it?

Light blue. Though this was not my favorite color for a car, I asked: Where can I see it?

Sigmund Freud St 76. There's a sign outside that says, Haus Tania. It's off Eschersheimer and Hügel ... I know the area. My ex-fiancee's family lives on Hügel St. What's your name?

Meyer. I'll come by right away.

Happily, I ran into the kitchen and said hurriedly, I found one, I've got to run, there are other people on the way. The 6.6 bear embraced my 5.6 105 pound body and said, take your time, today I don't need the car anymore.

12 minutes later, I parked HP's ivory Beetle ten yards away from a little group of people standing on the blue one: a modest young woman, a middle-aged man, whose stout beer belly expanded over his three quarter pants and a tall slim dude in elegant green trousers, surrounded by a performer's aura. The salt and pepper coiffured hair with a quarter size bald spot on the back of his head made him look older than his wrinkle-free face showed. None of the individuals matched my Afro look, not to mention my Afghan jacket and jeans with colorful embroidered seams.

I was seemingly too late and pitied myself. Nevertheless, coming closer, I inquired with a sturdy voice after Mr. Meyer, approaching the man with the Bavarian waistline.

I'm Mr. Meyer. The warm baritone hugged me shaking hands with the two who left the scene. Walking towards me the dandy also squeezed my hand. How about a test drive?

Why not? Mr. Meyer took off his brown woolen blazer and put it on the backseat. A breeze of his beguiles Eau de Cologne emitted from his yellow sweater. Not bad! Whom will he attract? Of course, I didn't care about my Afghan getting wrinkled. I pushed the pedal to the metal, saying: It seems slower than my friend's Beetle.

Yes, this is the cost-cutting version with less horsepower. Okay? It was not important to me. The car should only take me to and fro.

Convincingly, Mr. Meyer said, it needs less gas and turning the wireless on, the radio works perfectly. There seemed to be nothing wrong with the car. When I parked it, Mr. Meyer said nonchalantly, do you want to see the title? Okay?

It's up there, in the apartment. 3rd floor.

Hey! Why don't you have it with you?

It's unsafe to take the title along in the car.

How so? Because, if somebody takes it, hops in the car and drives away I've no proof of ownership anymore.

Walking under a red canopy, we reached the glass entrance. The opening took eons. Is Mr. Meyer living here or just visiting? Light emanated from sparkling crystal balls in the entrance hall. What an extravagance! It's daylight! Well!

In the elevator, Mr. Meyer mouthed some words. I had not grasped a bit of his American slang. After the third que-ry, I got what was important to him: the *know how*. His tanned face made me ask:

Have you just come from Mallorca? Gosh, no! It's not in to fly there. It's considered the scrub woman's island. I hadn't flown anywhere and wouldn't have minded to mingling with the cleaning club. Okay?

My suntan is still from the summer.

The elevator doors opened. The elegance of the hall's white marble walls and glass dropped to a green wall to wall carpet and orange walls, reminding me of my old apartment near the Zoo. I'd preferred a blue carpet with a light gray wall. The spacious size made room for imaginary seating accommodations for my psychic counseling office if I'd ever be able to rent an apartment here. We turned left. This time Mr. Meyer had the mahogany door open in no time. He took the Afghan from my shoulder and hung it on a clothes rack next to his brown blazer. For my taste one color too much. I'd only two colors: gray and brown, except for the seams on the jeans and the tunic.

My expectation of a fancy flat with modern furniture and all the things a Parvenu's heart desires was spoiled though I liked the parquet and the open kitchen & living room area with the glass front reaching from the kitchen all over to the end of the living room. The white woolen Berber sofa and chairs reminded me of my similar pieces of bourgeois furniture.

I'd sold mine with some minor cat artwork to a lady in my neighborhood and changed to a lower level sitting since all my fellow students lived on mattresses. Mr. Meyer said why don't you take a seat and handed me the registration certificate, here, the pedigree. I sat down on a blue painted chair facing the kitchen. Its rear legs on the parquet I was also able to overlook the parlor. Glancing at the gray document, it looked to me more like a penal record.

Why three owners in 3 years? Is anything wrong with the car? My eyes dipped into the attractive owner's fawn ones feeling an eerie familiarity as if our souls were scanning each other. Nope! Three owners! That makes me a bit wary. I don't really know what to do.

Um! Those velvet eyes!

The phone rang. Hello. I don't know for sure. I'm in negotiations right now. Could you call again in an hour? Yes, thanks, I appreciate it.

He's got refined manners, I thought and said:

I wonder why your name is not on the certificate if it's your car. Mr. Meyer said:

Look at the picture on the wall! This is my Ford Escort, I used to race. See there, the wheel in the air! The Beetle, I bought because I sold the Escort, but the buyer only put 200 marks down. He never came up with the rest. Now I have two cars and both advertised. You can buy the Escort as well. But all owners had the car for only a year! What could be wrong?

The velvet eyes looked baffled. I'd rather drive my old car than this since it's faster. This Beetle is not at all quick as you have noticed.

That doesn't sway my worries. People usually sell their cars when they expect major repairs. Mr. Meyer said: Then, the last owners may have already fixed the car. So it could be your advantage. I glanced at the plump secretary alongside the wall on my left. On it's top sat a chessboard with an ongoing game. I got up and followed the fight that was in full motion. The white dame was in danger. The melted caramel candy voice addressed me: Are you playing chess, too?

Yes, since I was 5 or 6. My father liked to play a lot and lured me into playing for prize money. He even gave me his dame. So do you want to play a game? Not knowing what to do, I studied the books in the bookcase cabinet on the cross wall. Since I was not sure whether to buy the car I thought at least about buying time and said: Why not? Great!

But this game is not finished, yet.

That's okay. My friend Ecki may start a new game with me later. He took the chessboard and placed it onto the blue kitchen table.

Do you want something to drink? I make myself tea, do you like some, too? Yes, good idea. I use to freeze when I'm excited. Those eyes! I still didn't know whether to buy the car.

You don't mind, if I get my sweater off?

Not at all, you are at home. He hung his cashmere garment with the tiny gray dots neatly over the back of his chair. Setting the pieces, I watched him work with the kettle and the tea egg. He would look better wearing his gray shirt outside. Tucked into the pants made his high hip line more prominent. I felt in good hands in this man's company, no need to play games. What's to do now? Should I go for it or not? For what? Withal, it was the first time I looked for a car all by myself. I said:

When I bought my former three cars, I'd always taken men specialists along making air quotes with my index fingers. Their inherited technical know-how had never helped. Why? The cars turned out to be real failures. How come? I bought a green Beetle from the VW dealership in Michelstadt. We couldn't even test drive it on our own. Why not? Aping the sales rep: That's our policy.

There was certainly something wrong.

Yeah, the steering wheel behaved oddly. Ah! I'd a severe accident. I was nine days in the hospital with a concussion. On the first day, the cops came. I still had no recollection. I got a fine of 340 marks for reckless driving. Next day I remembered a truck cut a curve. I'd the option: either the trailer or the slope.

So you got screwed from all sides. Yep!

Too bad. It's risky buying at a dealership.

Why? Selling new cars the dealer has to take all kinds of junk cars in and somehow has to get rid of them. Course, after this see, I'd never again buy a car without driving it myself. You better watch out your dame is in danger.

Oops, you are right. I would rather exchange my knight with your bishop. I can certainly go down a bit on the price. Everybody wants to negotiate. But this Italian yesterday ... he was quite insulting. He only wanted to give 2,800. I said no way, that would be too much of a loss. Oh, that's nice, giving me that hint. I haven't even thought about negotiating the price and said could I have the car for 3,000?

Mr. Meyer's 'hem' didn't allow any rushing. For a few seconds, his fawn eyes deeply immersed in the blue of mine.

I think I can live with that. Deal? Okay!?

So, he asked, what do you study?

At the moment social pedagogy at the FHS and next year psychology at the university.

What have you done before?

I did an apprenticeship as doctor's assistant at an accident insurance consultant, my hardest job ever. Then I worked in a hospital and finally stranded in the education department of the Deutsche Bank and by chance ended up on the school bench again.

What do you mean by chance?

Yo! Great listener! I met my classmate Ingrid. She sat right next to me, a very helpful girl. She's the cousin of our lottery fairy Karin Ludwig-Tietze, blond too.

In what way helpful? What a great observer! I was developing cataracts and had a hard time at school. I'd to read and write through a thread counter with less than a square inch of visual perception. Ingrid had helped me to find cities on the map. Or in handcraft, she got the thread into my needle. You had a rough ride. Yep. Ingrid told me she'd love to follow her brother studying social work. I thought: a perfect profession for her. I read some of the bank's psychology and pedagogy books and developed an interest as well. That's how I got to study social pedagogue. My boss, Dr. Beine was not pleased. He said, finally I got a secretary with brains, and now I've to let her go. Uh-oh!

Now, let's talk about you, what do you do for a living? I'm an economist without ambition. What is that supposed to mean?

That's a long story. Wanna you hear the entire prehistory? Why not?

I studied because my father wanted me to. Why? He wanted me to work in his company.

Chess. Huh? My dame is in danger again.

What company? Wine, liquor, tobacco. Um!

At first, I resisted and started an apprenticeship at an Opel dealership. Of course, he didn't like the idea of his son to have his arms in oil up to here. My opposite pointed to his upper arm. With 19, I was forced to marry. How so? My ex-wife Erika was pregnant at age 17. Gosh! My 2nd name is Erika, too. Really? Nodding, I said, boy, that was early! A heavy load. Yeah, a heavy boy, too. 10 pounds. Man! Then, I changed to Mercedes and sold trucks. I'd to deal with the farmers. They were used to celebrate the deals with hard liquor. This and the stress of having a young family at age 20 I got stomach ulcers. I finally agreed to my father's offer to finance my study and support my family until I could work in his company. But shortly after I'd finished my father died. I'm sorry. Thanks. Wasn't easy. My younger brother Joachim had worked there for a while. He wasn't happy.

My father's companion Mr. Klett didn't want me in the company.

Why not? I guess, he wanted to remain with people he could handle to his advantage. So I worked as a director's assistant at Karstadt in Wilhelmshaven, then in Münster. But, because most races were in the Rhine-Main area, I moved with my family to Sulzbach and worked as an EDV organizer at the Metallgesellschaft. With a conspiratorial smile he said, at times, I sneaked out and worked on my race car.

While the game of the kings was in full swing, an untidy downcast male shuffled on in a gray bathrobe and greeted grumpily:

Moin! I placed a questioning look at my chess partner. His wide nose and tanned skin reminded me of a mulatto GI kid. The liberators had left many brown war babies. Only in my little hometown, I know two of them personally. May I introduce you to my roommate Ecki Drexler, and this is the new owner of my car, Miss...? Holschuh.

Hey! Why don't we call each other "du"?

It's okay with me. We also address our profs and lecturers informally with "du". My name is Marianne. I'm Claus-Peter, also called CP or Peter, rarely Claus. Ecki bent his 5.8 physiques towards the beer case on the bottom of a respectable homemade birch floor-to-sealing shelf that awakened my artisan aptitude. He took a bottle, opened the crown sealing with his teeth, emptied the bottle at once and repeated the procedure with another bottle.

Don't you worry about your teeth?

Haha, his father was a dentist. Ecki sat down with squinting eyes annoyed by the dazzling sunlight. I looked at the smear on the window's glass surface that caused the ray's diffraction into a brilliant pattern of colors falling across the stubbly chin and the puffy eyes of a drinker. Eckard is a specialist in pickling herring. Try one? No, thanks, I've just eaten. I was so excited that my throat would have been too cramped anyway.

The doorbell rang. I placed the white knight next to my bishop and said: Checkmate! Crossly, Ecki shuffled along to the hall and pushed the door opener. CP sighed:

You surely beat me! You know how to play chess. His approval seemed honest. But this was no guaranty for being any different from Günther after a while. In the beginning, my ex-fiancee didn't throw the pieces across the room either. We had chess fights almost every night. As an insurance agent at the time, he could sleep away the mornings, but I had to go to work early. I was stupid enough to win and triggered his need for revenge. I don't like to lose either.

While waiting for what I expected another customer, my doubts about the car slowly subsided. If so many people are interested, it must be a bargain. I glanced at the big modern tinted glass balls hanging over the living room glass table. The old Persian rug beneath looked worthy. A smart common face dominating a body neither small nor tall, neither thick nor thin moved forward in the manner of the homeowner. He introduced himself, Liebe like Amore. I replied:

Holschuh like, get a shoe.

Is this a living community? No, said CP, we just know a lot of people in our area. Ecki lives with me since my girlfriend left me under cover of the night half a year ago. She emptied the flat. Boy, was that a shock, she even took the light bulbs. I sat there in the dark. Mr. Liebe said: Well, do you still have the scrap metal?

I didn't understand the question.

Peter said, walking to the desk, this young woman came for the VW. While he got a contact form out of a drawer, Cupid shot his arrow. I ignored the vague look. CP put the form in front of me and said, I can also register it for you. Do you have your passport or ID card with you? No. Then why don't you come on Monday with the money and your ID and you can wait here for the registration is completed. Okay, I said, still doubting the deal a bit. While CP finished the contract with his signature, Mr. Liebe left the apartment. Handing me the pen, Peter said, how much can you give me as a down payment?

Oops! I didn't expect to buy a car today.

I groped for the purse in my pouch and counted the bills. I've some 80 marks. The bell rang again, followed by a knock on the door.

Ah, that's Bebóo, our Dalmatian. He lives on the same floor. Ecki opened. The knocking dog turned out to be a Croatian student of engine building. Looking about my age he reached almost Peter's 6.3 but with a shorter waterfall. Hi, folks! Well, what's up today? What shall we do with the broken afternoon? Bebóo's hollering voice and his a bit rough approach reminded me of a doggy's after all. I began to like this bubbly house changing my view towards skyscrapers. Who'd expect an 8-story building to be something like a huge living community? CP said: Meet Marianne, the new owner of the car ... actually not before Monday. Will you come around nine? Sounds like an arrangement. Bebóo said, don't bother, just go on with your paperwork. He sat down on the Berber chair next to the bearish stubble-bearded beer lover, who meanwhile had traded his bathrobe for jeans, shirt, and sweater. The Dalmatian's white woolen pullover mingled with the nap pattern of the Berber fabric. He stretched his jeans legs under the glass table as if they didn't belong to him staring at the spherical shaped white boob tube that looked out of a science fiction film though it was not turned on.

Still holding my moneybag, Peter said, just give me 50 marks. You may need some cash over the weekend. The rest I'll unhook from you on Monday, he said easily with a sly twinkle. This talking didn't match his refined manners. I glanced through the floor to ceiling glass front towards the Taunus mountains. The setting sun cast a purple shadow, transforming the firmament into an incredibly beautiful effusion of blood red. When I arrived at HP's flat, the umpteenth hearing was still going on with lots of intellectual talks. I sensed, the guy in question was close to expectation. Good vibrations all around, lots of laughter.

My boyfriend asked, so did you buy a car?

Yes, the cheapest Beetle in the paper and I even bargained it down to 300 less.

Wow, and how's the car? The way he said it, he seemed surprised, as if it went too fast or he'd expected me to call him first for advice.

You'll see it on Monday, I said. HP laughed and was right back to his mellow mood.

During the weekend, I often caught myself thinking about the easy going bunch. How old may CP be? Over 30 surely. Never trust anybody over 30! But I considered this man trustworthy as if I knew him.

On Monday, I took the street car. Getting off Eschersheimer Land St/Hügel St, I walked all the way from Hügel St. to Sigmund Freud St.

Passing my car, I had no warm feeling as I still disliked the slip blue color. When I reached the apartment door, Peter said, have you seen? Eh? Somebody broke the antenna.

No, how come? That happens often. I'll buy a new one. If you come on Wednesday, I'll build it in for you. Heck, could it be that he screwed me by having it unscrewed himself, so I'd have to come again? I was amused at this idea.

Entering the living room, the dark escritoire on the light wood floor troubled me again. It would be the first thing I'd throw out. Ecki's coarse pitch knocked me out of my interior decorator's dream. You've any barbiturates?

No, what for? CP said, Ecki has Hodgkin disease, that's cancer of the lymph nodes.

Yes, I know. Are you in pain? His grumbling was not conclusive. CP continued, the surgeon said, if he'd take his spleen out and Ecki'd quit boozing, he'd have a half year to live. Ecki laughed sarcastically. With a sly smile and a glance at the beer bottle in his hand, I said: Of course, this advice you'd followed right away. Peter handed me the car title and the registration certificate saying see both in your names. I gave him the money. Now you are mobile again. Yeah, thanks, but now I've got to rush. I'll be late for a seminar. After its ending, I drove to HP and showed him my Beetle. He half-bent went about it and drove around the block. Coming back, he said it's a slowpoke, but I can't find anything wrong. I'd go to a VW dealership and get it checked through. They'll find out if something's wrong with the car.

On Tuesday, I left the Beetle at the dealer. When I picked it up the next afternoon, I got a list of faults amounting to 270 marks. Mr. Sigrist offered to fix everything right away.

I've no time today I'll call you, I said. Straight off, I drove to Haus Tania and presented Peter the fault list. While he studied it, his grim grin turned into a broad smile. That's nothing. They are just stinky that you haven't bought a car from them. Wearisome, I said I didn't see they had any used Beetles to sell. CP, leaning on his desk and shrugging his shoulders: They just want to make money.

Hanging on, not knowing what to say I must have looked deranged. Warm eyes entered the mine and a sustained 'hem' made me feel silly.

Peter turned around, opened his briefcase, got a bundle of 100 bills out and counted to three. Reaching me the bills, he said:

Are you happy now? At a loss, I locked eyes with him. Why? Yes? Well! I saw the tenderness in his look. Was he interested in me? So what are you going to do now?

Why? What d'you mean? We had planned to go downtown to play pool and later pick up Bebóo's girlfriend Anni at the bar and perhaps go to the disco. D'you wanna accompany us?

Heck, three men and a gal, as a title of an old time movie. I felt like in the old days when I'd roamed the streets with my older brother and his friends. I hadn't planned anything for that day, and there was no educational activity the following morning. Well, why not?

I had to admit being interested in the likable man with the familiar doe eyes. Lots of laughter in the car, after Bebóo said in his Dalmatian German: Just make yourself comfortable! No easy task since the stiff roll-bar of the rally car was in the way. My experience in handball, throwing darts and shooting roses on the fairground didn't help much at the pool table. I had a rum and coke. At about 10:00 p. m. we were on route to the red light quarter. I'd never been in a bar before. But I couldn't get more than a glimpse of the silky milieu. We went in and out within a half minute and rushed away as if the house was on fire.

In the car, I asked: What do you do there?

Nothing much, I just talk to men, make them drink a lot and make them pay me drinks.

Can you drink as much? Nope! We order cognac, and Gil gives us tea from a cognac bottle. Don't the men want more? Some want to go to bed with me. Anni pursed her lips. I say, I've to work two more hours and leave it open. When Bebóo picks me up, I hurry out the back door. Isn't that dangerous? Shrugging off, the 19-year-old girl said, it just happened. Aren't bar girls working till the early morn?

Not the ones under age, Bebóo tossed in, turning his head. Anni yelled:

Look ahead, don't crash the car. Turning she said coolly, I have the early shift from 2 to 10.

We parked close to the Opera. Entering the disco nearby, we mingled with the boisterously dancing crowd. The Cuba Libre made me tipsy. As soon as the first slow dance started, I melted in Peter's arms.

At the end he took both sides of my face in his hands, his gaze reaching right inside me. Gently he put his lips on mine. Just once then he withdrew. He looked passionate with queasy hope in his eyes in a lovely face. I came after him, my tongue trembling on his.

After the 2nd rum and coke, I'd quit thinking of driving home in my new car. My room near the uni wouldn't see me tonight. Back at Haus Tania, I had no chance to take the couch. When I returned from the bathroom, Ecki had already settled in the living room.

I entered a white painted room with one black wall behind a tasteful white floor to ceiling wardrobe opposite a French bed. Next to it, the white square low table had a huge yellowish stain on the side of the following mattress. Staring at the spot, I said: What happened there? Um ..., yeah, living with Ecki is quite dangerous. He uses to wake up in the middle of the night starts to smoke a cigarette falling asleep again with the burning butt. I always keep a bucket of water next to me.

Had he always drunk that much, or just since he knows his diagnose? He already boozed at school. Nevertheless, he was an excellent student, best grades in math, even in Latin.

And after school? He studied economics. The secretary of economics Schiller was his professor. But Ecki doesn't do anything with it, just wasting his brains boozing. So let's stop talking about Ecki. What about you? What did you do as a doctor's assistant? X-rays and assisting in fixing injuries of labor accidents. In summers, we had a Turkish vacation replacement. He'd let us do a lot of things like getting legs in plaster and removing fatty tumors. I once even got my mother's ear fixed. She'd gotten caught with her earring and tore up her self-made earlobe-piercing. I took everything I needed: a sterile scalpel, a bent needle, twine Novocain ...

So you're good at handicraft. Well? And then? Dr. Fischer became a surgeon at the new hospital in Erbach. I got a job there, writing operation reports and discharge letters. It would have been boring, but I had interesting colleagues. With the first one, I started to work before the clinic was fully furbished. Once, we stepped out of the elevator and thinking we were in the kitchen. We opened one of the huge fridges. But instead of food, a dead skinny woman's body rolled towards us. Oops! Yucky! Yeah, that was something! We also once watched two operations in green sterile outfits and masks. The first one was an appendectomy. Ugh, I had a ruptured appendix when I was at boarding school on the island of Wangerooge.

That's dangerous! Yup. I was carried to the hospital on the back of a bicycle. Wow!

So how was the operation? It only took a ¼ hour. The next one even less. When they'd opened the abdomen, I knew the man ... he was a neighbor. His blood gushed in all directions like a fountain. His intestines were covered with cancer looking like dozens of tiny cauliflowers. They closed the abdomen, and the man died three months later.

Um ..., could we change the subject, please?

Would you rather hear anything about your lungs? What do you mean? My next colleague Mrs. Michel-Diez had worked in the pathology in Heilbronn. She said she'd seen a lung from a heavy smoking 18 years young Italian. It was pitch black. So? Ours may be looking not much better. Ouch! Don't worry! If we quit smoking, in 7 years, our lungs should be like new. Why? They regenerate.

What else did you do?

When we got bored of writing, we did some EKG's. I'd my office next to the only ophthalmologist in the region. I owe him this little comment in my driver's license. I got the gray paper out of my pocket and handed it to CP.

Why you look different on that photo.

Yes, *17 Jahr, blondes Haar*, I vocalized the refrain of the Udo Jürgens song. Turning the document, Peter said: So you wear contact lenses. I'd have to wear glasses as thick as telescopes. But what had this eye doctor to do with it? Dr. Libal is a rude little man. Once, he got loud with a patient. He yelled so unrestrainedly that I opened my office door and looked at the poor old woman with a granny knot standing there in tears. I steamed. Looking straight into the doc's eyes, I quietly said, this is not the way to treat a patient. We need a competitive ophthalmologist here then you'd have to act humanely. Of course, it wasn't diplomatic to express me right off. Dr. Libal hadn't said anything.

But he took revenge, said Claus-Peter.

Yes, I got an official mail. I should have returned my driver's license. According to a law from 1956, people with glasses 8 diopters and more are not allowed to drive a car. Of course, when this law was written, contact lenses were not invented. So I had to go to an eye doctor in Frankfurt. She wrote me a letter denoting with the contacts I have the full angle vision. So that's how this command came into your driver's license, Peter said.

Yes but this wasn't my main problem these days; I got chased by my ex-boyfriend. How come? He was a hairdresser, working near Heidelberg. We dated only on Sundays. Once, Alfred caught a cold, and I had to visit him three evenings in a row. I got extremely bored and felt imprisoned in his company.

Why? He was interested in subjects as what restaurants have the biggest meat portions or fill up the beer glasses best. I told him my feelings, but he still came to the hospital every Monday. I'd asked my colleagues to say, she'd already left. On Sundays, sometimes, Alfred was lucky when he tried to pick me up at home. He said if you don't have another boyfriend, why can't you just come along with me? I had a hard time breathing and was scared of having TB or lung cancer. I went to different doctors. The x-rays didn't show anything. Naturally! Not a single physician asked me about personal problems. Even the doctors, I worked with, passed me in a hurry like a breeze. They'd never asked me about my breathing, though, I had often grasped at air.

Carnival 1969, Alfred finally gave up. He saw me falling in love with a waiter in a restaurant, an Austrian baron just coming from the school of hotel management in Salzburg. I had no more trouble breezing.

Poor Alfred, Peter said. When I'm stressed, it always affects my stomach. At the hospital, I had a great doctor. He told me, Mr. Meyer, I can't tell you what to eat or drink, you have to find out yourself. We're all different. Most people agree with oatmeal soup, some swear of rice, others of bananas.

Yeah, good doc! I agree with puffed rice.

And I even found out that coke helps me.

So, what did they do there? Nothing much. They thought, I just needed to rest.

Good thinking! It didn't help much. After 3 days, following a hunch I left the clinic, went home and caught my wife with another man.

There my grandma's proverb *youngish wed never regret* goes down the drain. A soft feeling for this man touched my heart. Of course, you always have to hear both sides.

So what about your Lord? Baron. Edmond Jean-Pierre François von Dembinski. Okay, did you get your nobleman? I was in love with him for one and a half years. Then with Günther, I lived in cohabitation for three years. Maybe next time I'll be engaged for 6 years then for 12 if it goes on like ... do you know the chess story?

You mean when the king granted the winner a wish and he asked for a grain on the first field and 2 grains on the second and 4, 8, 16 and so on and the king ended up poor?

I nodded. You still didn't tell me about your waiter baron. He treated me with care, but also cheated on me. A true lady killer. Since most members of his family were painters, I asked him to try some artwork, too. I went with him to the art academy. The professor, by the way, looked like Sigmund Freud. He liked his work and shortly after, Edi began his study. That was also the end of our relationship.

Que sera. Yep! He betrayed me with a girl I knew. They had an accident. He drove under the influence, and she broke her arm. He claimed, she'd blackmailed him, not to say anything to the police if he married her. So?

Just a week after he had left me for Corina, a local gastronome called. One of his guests was in need of a model for his new newspaper, the *Odenwälder Nachrichten*. Günther was another giant, even an inch taller and very handsome. Too bad! Yeah, having a short father kind of darkened my childhood but my mother's 5.7½ had helped. So how tall are you? Almost 5.6?

So, what else? Günther made photos of me What happened to Günther? His paper failed, he went back to Frankfurt and took me along.

Why'd you separate? I've no idea. Huh? It just happened. Maybe he wasn't fond of my study ideas. He suggested getting separate apartments. We lived only a 5 min walk apart in front of our castle, sitting on a bar stool surrounded by boots and shoes. So, next to a new man, I had a second job, as a reporter and an advertising agent. In not even two weeks, I went from an abandoned crying girl to a self-confident young woman in love again.

What happened to Günther? His paper failed, he went back to Frankfurt and took me along.

Why'd you separate? I've no idea. Huh?

It just happened. Maybe he wasn't fond of my study ideas. He suggested getting separate apartments. We lived only a 5 min walk apart and used each other until we made it on our own. Why the bank? Huh? Why didn't you work as a doctor's assistant anymore?

I didn't like the dark workplace they'd offered me at the hospital. There was another add in the paper. Director Dr. Hoog from the education department of the Deutsche Bank looked for a secretary. The teacher in me responded. The boss seemed to like my appearance. I had a ready tongue and a cute hat matching my coat.

And a cute face, Peter added, earning a big smile. Though I'd never been a secretary, I had no doubt in my mind not to be able to do the job. But I guess Dr. Hoog had his doubts. He chose 32-year-old Mrs. Zia, and I got a job in the library. I started typing, cataloging, drawing and enjoying the 180° view from the 18th floor of the skyscraper overlooking the Hauptwache and Rosemarie Nitribitt's apartment. A few months later, another director's secretary came down with a disease and ever since I worked for Dr. Beine. He came late in the morning from a Taunus town. I wasn't working to capacity. So? In the evening and on weekends, I took a second job. Why that?

I bought furniture on credit, and I can't stand having debts. So I worked as a typist for 10 marks per hour at the Schutzgemeinschaft der Kraftfahrer (Association for the protection of motorists). I think I've heard of them.

What exactly are they doing?

The founder Julius Székely had created an express expert report for his engaged appraisers to quick asserting of unjust repairs from auto shops to get money back if repairs weren't correctly done.

Sounds good. I've heard of them. They also blacklisted unreliable repair shops.

Yep! It was a good thing and good money. I wrote the letters for the appraisers. But unfortunately, the nice *The Good Soldier Schweik* resembling Hungarian defected to South America still owing me 75 marks.

How come? I should have foreseen it and asked for my money. How so? I came into his office and like in the movies he looked at me as if caught in the act. With both arms, he raked in a whole bunch of foreign bills, in his desk drawer. I think I made him hurry up. He'd gotten cold feet. Days later, I saw his photo in the paper. Peter said: It's a pity, I should go on with this association. And why did you leave the bank? I had time to read psychology and pedagogy books. Then my classmate Ingrid came along. Peter nodded in recognition. The blonde. I had blondes all the time, didn't bring me any luck. I stopped dying my hair blond three years ago. But I think, we should stop talking about me, how about you?

No, go ahead! What's with your classmate?

Ingrid told me about her plans to study social work. I followed her to college. How do you support yourself?

I'd worked more than five years after my apprenticeship, so I get full BaFöG. Parents don't have to support two educations.

Isn't that the professional training furtherance law? Exactly. Of course, 613 marks wasn't enough to afford my 360 marks flat. So I got a large light room, facing a park, but it's oven-heating. I hadn't thought about the winter. I pretended a shivering of cold. I could have also rented a dark heated room for also 100 marks, but frost was not on my mind. Peter said I didn't tell you yet. I'm going to fly to the Canaries with my friends from Wilhelmshaven. If you want, you could stay here from next Wednesday on. Um! Think about it. You can pick up the key on Monday. Yo! I laughed diffidently, feeling like a princess who'd been offered a palace. Until now, the sun was shining every day, warming up my room, so I had not used the oven at all. I'd covered my back with a blanket and sat in front of the desk in my antique chair, the single worthy thing I owned. I'd given notice to the landlady not needing the room anymore. Owning a car, I wanted to drive forth and back to Michelstadt. But I liked the idea of my tan angel spreading out his wings around me even better.

On the weekends, Edi mostly drove home. Since he had a VW van, I asked him to take some of my stuff to my parent's home. We stuffed the van, I followed in my Beetle and spent the night in his room at his dormitory. I still felt comfortable lying next to him in his bed, but there was no Amorous darting along anymore. Fawn eyes had been interfering.

I arrived at House Tania on Monday. Peter greeted me with a soft smile and said:

I wasn't sure you'd come. Fawn eyes were deeply dipping into mine. Peter whispered gently, I'm glad you did. Where is Ecki?

He already left. I thought he'll fly to the Canaries with you. No, he wants to stay with his friends in Wilhelmshaven. He may not come back because he wants to get the operation. So if you wish, we'll have the apartment all to ourselves. By the way, do you like fish?

I like almost anything edible. Why?

Bebóo cooks for us tonight. It's Anni's day off. He's a pretty good cook. I only can make lard with onions and apples or eggs sunny side up. Sounds delicious.

But don't worry if they start one of their fights. Bebóo's from Croatia, Anni from Serbia. Some of their dishes had previously burst into pieces.

The studio smelled fishy. Bebóo had cooked potatoes, carrots, red and green peppers and the fish in a huge pot, sprinkled parsley over it and poured half the content of the pot in a big soup tureen. He held it under my nose and said: How does it smell? Yummy! Peter said:

Hopefully no fish-bones. You won't suffocate, Bebóo said, Marianne must be a master of the Heimlich maneuver, aren't you?

With one of my cats, it worked fine. We made it through the evening with lots of laughter and no flying knives. When we were about to leave, I said, next time, I cook you a Turkish dinner. My mother brought a mixture from her trip to Turkey that makes everything taste like Turkish food. Bebóo asked: A spice? It looks like grits. There's one certain herb making it taste distinctive. Peter said:

You could make it on Thursday for all of us.

Why I thought you leave on Wednesday.

No, I have checked the tickets again. I was

mistaken. We'll fly on Friday morning. Um! Why don't you get some of your things? From here it's close to your college. Okay!?!

I listened gladly, anticipating another steady relationship after nine months on my own. To remain HP's 3rd girlfriend wasn't one of my favorite dreams. Of course, I never demanded a change. It was not en vogue in the early 70th to call for monogamy. But that was what I wanted. I never felt satisfied with no commitment or once a week relationships. I saw Edi every day, either in our homes or on vacations.

With Günther, I lived in concubinage, in three different places. Only in longtime relationships do I feel at home, accepted and loved. Still, in my two marriage-like relationships it took me months to feel unrestrained enough for consummation.

I needed less than five inches of space in Peter's wardrobe to hang up my clothes. When the friends from Wilhelmshaven arrived, the Turkish meatballs and the mixed veggies were ready to eat. It took them a little longer than planned since they had picked up an actress from Hamburg. The blond girl sat at the kitchen table in her light blue sheep leather jacket. Probably a brand new gift from Bolko. George, a bistro owner, said:

Yummy, you've got to give me that recipe.

Well, that will be a problem.

Why? I'd like to add this to my menu.

Certainly, but I never pay attention what spices I use, it changes every time I cook. And I'm not sure if you can buy this breadcrumb like stuff anywhere. My mother got it from a small village near Izmir.

After just two drinks, the troupe was dead-droopy: the result of eight hours on the road. We took care of their bedding and left the apartment to sleep in Bebóo's studio. We had a couple more drinks while Peter filled us in on his favorite guests:

Bolko I know from the delivery room. He was born 20 minutes earlier. Anni asked:

Have you heard anything from Ecki?

Yes, he is scheduled for an operation in two weeks getting cut out his spleen. Anni asked:

What for? I said: For cutting off the white blood cell production. Bebóo said:

How about sleeping a few hours? Okay.

We dropped down onto the broad sofabed. I slept like dead but woke up early and listened to our host's soft snoring.

Deep down ventral, I sensed an increasing flame. Bad timing, but my last chance. The charter jalopy of the never come back airline could fall with my new lover into the ocean.

A burning sensation in my lower abdomen kicked off a hormone bonanza turning off my thinking machine. Dazed, I slid atop Peter's body. Kissing his tender lips, I felt an electric current of love and his desire in the trembling urgency of his tongue. Hugged by a hot musk breeze and greeted by an ad lib responding phallic I was amazed about my immodesty. Unrestrained, climax leading to a climax I covered my cries of release. It was as in Doris's song *Move over, Darling*: "has me waving my conscience bye-bye?" There was a built-in intimacy as if we had a steady relationship for eons!

In the following night, I had a dream where I watched CP racing. I waited with his friends, Helmut and Marianne whom I'd just met. When in one round, Peter was missing I felt my heart sink. Waking up, I had an empty feeling of having lost my life. Luckily no true dream, but a heck of a hint: This is the one!

Goa at long last

Yeah, Ecki will like it. Do you realize that he lives seven years longer than his doctor's death sentence? If he'd quit on the booze he may be already dead. The new long white cotton blouse and slacks hugged my body. A light feeling made me wish to live in this former Portuguese enclave. During breakfast, Peter asked: How about roaming the half-island?

A little later, we got in a beat-up bus, not knowing in what part of Goa it would take us.

A guy said, they all stop at the local market. Some shrill dressed women escorted by hens and birds were already sitting. The fowls fluttered anxiously in their cages as if they knew their fate. After five minutes, the boarding still went on. My escort became edgy and got out of the bus. I observed the animals and guessed the women's talking. Peter came back in a better mood, though, nothing had changed: I haven't seen any sign. It may start soon.

After another five minutes, the bus had filled up to capacity. Shortly after the bus driver arrived. I said, now we know why there's no signboard: there's no timetable; the bus departs when it's full. Two rows in front of us to the right, two blond men were the latest to enter the bus. They seemed to enjoy themselves a lot in the middle of the locals. On the next stop, several vendors with oranges and a beggar approached them on the open space where windows supposed to be. They just smiled, shook their heads and said, no thank you. Strangely enough, they were not bothered any longer. With us, the locals were more persistent. On the next stop, I walked forward and asked: Hi, where are you guys from?

A duo answered: From beautiful San Francisco. Ah! I'd like to go there. Yeah, you'd like it. Have you been in countries like India before? We've been in Malaysia and Morocco.

Aha! The vendors look for timidity since with nonchalant persons is no rupee to earn. On each stop, the Californians handled the annoying crowd smoothly. I said: If all Californians are like the two, I'd like to live there for good. We got off the bus at the market. I liked the place a lot and pictured myself in the role of a marketer. The people were pleasantly content. Peter bought a bunch of bananas and a pack of chips. He said in admiration: Did you see, how easy these guys handled the enervating salesmen and beggars? I said:

Yeah, they've got the practice. Guess so. At least, there are not as many beggars in Goa than in the rest of India. I should not have said that. Peter peeled a banana. After the first bite, he threw it away. Out of the blue, an ugly leper touched him with his corroded fingers, begging with the other stretched-out open hand.

Peter screeched, don't! Afraid of contagion, he stepped back. Peter tore off three bananas and walked forward. The man who shook his head. I yelled they're green! Afraid the leper would approach him again, Peter handed out the chips. He kept them, but it didn't stop him from stretching out his leprous hand. Offended hubby stepped on the poor man's sandal.

Peeeter! I shouted. It wasn't stout. I didn't hurt him. Look, he's gone, he's learned. He's not hungry. Just another example of the beggar industry. You can't say that he's ill. This cast consists of large organizations. I've read they steal kids, bring them to far away cities and amputate a hand or a foot. This way they can panhandle for money in a more heart appealing manner. Back in Delhi, we talked about our experience. Maya said, a week ago, a boy from a wealthy family, was kidnapped and mutilated. A most horrific way to break the rules of the cast system.

Our Goa beach hotel was not more than a plain building where we had our meals and little 1-bedroom houses spread out on the land. Every day we walked along the beach to the only high-rise hotel on the other side. There were no buildings but a few huts in between and at daylight almost no tourists in sight.

I only remember a young Italian who once ran naked around screaming like crazy. Somebody told he had a thorn-apple drink. An Indian with a turban and no clean clothes had a bunch of long Q-tips in his hand asking: Let me clean your ears. No thanks!

You, western people, are not hygienic at all.

Every evening, we walked to a bar booth with a bamboo roof got a sundowner and went back to the beach. That was the only time of the day the people gathered, devotedly looking as our energy spending fix star sunk dark red behind the broken up heavenly clouds.

Orange and peach-colored gleaming rays flared like fire over the blue-green Indian Ocean. I took Peter's hand and said: Here I'd like to grow old with you. Squeezing my hand, he gave me the look of a kid under the Christmas tree. Standing next to my handsome husband holding the glass in my hand and watching the spectacle in the sky I reflected on a life in the little beach house. I'd paint some pictures, write some poems, cook some healthy dishes from my self-grown veggies.

Let's go, said Peter calmly, still impressed by nature's serene play. When I didn't react at once, he gently touched my arm, his look of love penetrating my soul. On our walk back, the fire enchantment was fading away. The firmament had changed into a delicate lavender violet.

We had already survived about 20 starts and landings. I had enough of all the Turboprop flights. There had been no problems, but I always expected them since I'd developed a distinct fear of flying due to two earlier flights. When we had visited Bebbós parents in Croatia in the late seventies, the Tupolev-Tu154 was tossing about in a severe thunderstorm. Also, on our last flight back from the Canaries, the plane suddenly did a nosedive. The Cologne dome came closer and closer.

I wouldn't have mind stopping the tour skipping southern India. I had a feeling as if I'd reached a point: deal done, lesson learned. Deep inside I knew what I want from life. Had the Frisco men implanted my enthusiasm for the US? They left a definite impression on me and evolved my desire to visit California.

Dealing, healing, gambling, dreaming

After the failed Californian car trade trials, Peter flew to the USA with his friend Uli Degenhardt who had relatives in Fairfield, CA. The junk-yard owner who lived like a health nut because of fearing to get cancer didn't buy any cars. But he bought my red wooden house in Tiburon. Not long after the purchase he had died of bowel cancer at age 48. I think one of the reasons was his sucking gasoline from his junk cars with a hose. Though he didn't swallow it, having it in the mouth for a sec, the poison penetrates through the mucous membrane right away. Little by little, it adds up. Uli's fear may have further triggered the cells to degenerate. He urged Peter not to smoke and to drink less coffee. Do we foresee our future or do we draw the events by our fearful thoughts? Anyhow, I had a prophetic dream about it and asked Uli to see a doctor. He said, I just had a check through at the Mayo-Clinic ½ year ago. A strange similarity:

When I walked with Uli's wife to the hospital's cafeteria, she told me about her premonitions and personal cancer experience. Birgit had a check-up at her gynecologist with no result, but half a year later she had cancer. After her uterus cervix removal, the doctors wanted to add cobalt radiation. Birgit refused because she had to take care of two toddlers. Ever since she had no problems. At the time, I didn't know Dr. Hamer's cancer theory of a previous shock experience. But since reading about the disputed physician, I'm asking persons with malignancies about drastic experiences. Until today I have not met anyone who had not suffered a severe injury or a psychic trauma before developing cancer. Oma Maria proved the theory also a friend's brother, H. J. Kneupper who fall from a 3-story building. But not everyone suffering severe accidents or other shock situation will develop cancer.

In the 5 weeks, Peter was away I remodeled our apartment and enjoyed being on my own. But one evening, the TV news terrified me. A downed and drowned plane in the US!

Since Peter and Uli flew all over America, I was afraid they were on it. When watching on TV the rescue of a man in a light blue shirt looking like Peter, I was a little relieved. But this disaster made me think of my situation. What would be, if he would not come back? Could I keep the apartment? I had to check it out. I called the Frankfurter Rundschau and placed an add: Buying Mercedes spot cash.

The rate of the one-liner including my phone number was only 11 marks. Not a risky invest.

On Saturday morning, I was painting the bedroom wall when the phone rang. A nice man offered a red 280S for DM 8,500.

Oh, too bad. The SE is the desired car. The S is a gas-guzzler. But if you give me your address I'll have a look at it. If it's mint, I may take it anyway. I'm living an hour from Frankfurt, the man said. On Monday, I'll be in the office downtown. You can see it there. When I came to see the red car with the white interior, I was impressed. It looked like new. After the test drive, I said okay, there seems to be nothing wrong. But still, could you just give me a break for the S? The 280S is not very desirable. I got a bundle of bills out. I've got 8,000 cash here, we could finish the deal, and you could take the train home. The man agreed. I showed the car to a dealer on the Mainzer Land St whose daughter also studied social pedagogue. I sold the car to Maurice and was pretty sure I could make it without Peter.

On the following Friday, I headed to Michelstadt and drove with my parents to the Geo-Hydro-Institute in Igelsbach. Johann Tikale, aunt Anneliese's neighbor had invented a system to regenerate the spinal column by cleansing the lymph in the presence of certain frequencies and a series of stretching and chiropractic like alignments. We belonged to the society and worked for the research of this health system. In addition, Anneliese voluntarily did Mr. Tikale's paperwork and acted as his advocate. Thanks to her advice, Ma was completely healed from a stiff back due to an accident while building the bed & breakfast complex with Heini. I had gotten rid of hay fever.

In the car, Ma said: Last week, Heinz had another x-ray. So? His worn and slipped disc has disappeared. Wow! What did the doc say?

He couldn't believe it and asked to see the x-ray. When his assistant handed it, he said: Not that one, the one of Mr. Walz! When the woman said, yes, that is Mr. Walz's x-ray, the doc was surprised. It was cowardly of Heinz not to say this was the work of the Igelsbach charlatan. In and around Eberbach and Heidelberg, Johann Tikale was known as a deceiver. But he was accredited by foreigners. The selfless brave man had never asked for money. Members of the society had only paid 48 marks as a yearly due per family. Tikale was solely interested in his research and in helping his fellow humans. Many doctors were in fear of losing their business when their patients told them about their recoveries from chronic diseases. Due to conflict of interest, many filed lawsuits against Tikale and the IRS was on his tail. Anneliese, who's adept at handling people got him out of trouble and even saved him from a night in jail. Though he was never charged with anything the sensitive man who had done so much good for so many people had suffered greatly from all those legal proceedings. Anneliese's former physician Dr. Hartmann from Eberbach regrets the government's lack of providing this genius with research money.

I acknowledged Johann Tikale's work in my book *Wunderwesen Wasser*. The former holistic dentist Willie Melischko from Haßmersheim whose work I introduced in my book *Wasser-Code geknackt?* has also worked with Tikale's equipment but in a different way.

On my way back to Frankfurt, at a traffic light, an African male offered the newest issue of the *Frankfurter Rundschau*. It was the only time I bought the paper when Peter was gone.

Back home, I searched through the DB section and found a 220 at a reasonable price. I called the owner, who was at his work close to the river of Main. After the general questions, I asked: Can I see the car now?

No way, you can have a look at it on Monday. Do you have it with you?

Yes, but I want to show the car to all the customers next week. I didn't feel like taking part in an auction and said, I have to drive to the Main anyway. Because of the storm, I've to check on our boat. This plea had popped into my mind since we had a boat there. The man finally gave in. But it took me more than an hour to write the contract. Back home I called Helmut, Peter's friend, and colleague. What would you give for a yellow 220? I know the car is in the Rundschau but forget it. He wants all owners to show up on Monday. Yes, but I bought it. Silence at the other end of the line and after a moment: Yes, then, congratulations. How did you do this? At the end of my story, Helmut said:

Yes, beginners have the better bite.

In these weeks, I'd snatched some cherries from under the other dealer's nose, though I rarely left the apartment. In the third week, I was working on the table of the wooden kitchenette. I'd bought it because I didn't like the colored table and chairs combined with the light-wood storage. The top of the new light-wood table already showed knife's cuttings on the top. I rented a machine tool from the nearby do-it-yourself store. While grinding off the top layer, the phone rang.

It was Klaus Zimmerlein, another car dealer:

I have heard you are looking for cars. So? I've got a nice 280 SE from a private woman. If you are interested, I'll pick you up in 20 minutes. I cleaned up, jumped into my boots, threw my coat over and drove with Klaus to the car. We sat a while quietly in the living room until we could see the car making me suspicious. From the backseat, I glanced at the indicator for the oil and said: The oil doesn't build up correctly. No, that's okay. Huh? It should have jumped to 3 right away, but it only climbed to 1.7. That's good enough, said Klaus hastily. At that time, I'd not experienced colleagues cheating among them. I thought at least to get the price down a little. Of course, that would have minimized his commission.

Nevertheless, I took the car. Later I learned it only ran after a jump start. But it was a desirable model for export. I spent hours cleaning the engine, the interior, and exterior. When I drove it to the car meet on Sunday, a dealer said, shoot, what a beauty, gleams like a pocket watch. It was so terribly cold that I left the engine on until two dark skinned men came and bought the car for a thousand more than I paid. Calming my conscience I told myself, they still must have made money since nobody came or called complaining. The only regrettable thing was that when Peter came back, I gave him all the money I earned by selling four cars. I worked my ass off refurbishing the apartment and dealing cars while he was on vacation. Why did I give him my earnings? Stupid me.

He already had my savings for the business.

I still have the contract of my lending 20.000 marks to Peter at a 10% interest rate. But he wasn't interested in handing out the interest, only in reinvesting. He said you get the money when Joáo pays back. I'm now managing my money myself.

When the Dollar drifted to heady heights, we sold a lot of cars to the US with the help of a blood young American dude who stemmed from Lebanon. We had a lot of fun with our ersatz son and his girlfriends. We also became gray marketeers. US citizens bought their fancy automobiles, preferably the cars with the stars, directly in Germany. Therefore, we asked friends and acquaintance with businesses to conclude agreements for new cars at the dealerships and paid them commissions.

Because of the high dollar, we sold the cars beyond the original price to the US citizens and finally, my dream came true. We were able to rent a big house in Bergen-Enkheim. Wasn't that what I always wanted? The house with the garden was surrounded by a wall protecting our privacy when plunging into the pool. It had a view over Enkheim and Eastern Frankfurt. The floor to ceiling windows and doors to the terrace extended bent shaped from the fireplace to the dining area. We didn't care about the heating bill. The rent of 1,760 marks was reasonable because in the little flat belonging to the house used to live the landlady. Many people would consider this too close for comfort, but we reasoned it an opportunity.

When traveling, we had Mrs. Weber to take care of our cats. Our relationship with the elegant half-Jewish widow consisted of paying calls via the round cellar stairway. Once, she said there's a little something on the step. 6-month-old Foxi tail-brushed Mrs. Weber's leg. Spotting the dropping, I said Foxi have you done that? The tomcat looked at me as if I was kooky, jumped in his covered litter box placed on the deepest step and peeked out looking overtly into my eyes. Mrs. Weber translated his thoughts:

Look, Mom, that's where I do my muck.

During the Hitler war, Margot and her brother almost had been sent to a death camp. Their father thought to avoid his fate by stating he had two children with his Aryan wife. That was when Mrs. Weber's mother's ordeal to save her kids began. She had to travel to Berlin three times until her appealing finally had saved her children. There are still people denying the holocaust while the rest still brood about its incomprehensible nature!

When my mother came to help me sewing the curtains we'd no stove yet. We drove to the shopping mall having lunch at the Chinese restaurant. There was no empty table available. Unlike in the US, where guests used to wait to be seated, we looked for free seats. We asked an elegantly dressed woman in her late thirties and took seats opposite of her. We talked about our newest prophetic dreams while the dark-haired lady tightened up a bit.

I said, you may think we're mad. She loosened somewhat and said:

Not at all. I never wanted to talk about this again. I had an exceptional experience, too. It's not easy for me to tell you this since my aunt didn't take me seriously. I was in a hospital and was considered clinically dead. My aunt was there. Later, I told her what she said, but she only smiled at me as if I'd been crazy. She treated me like a kid. I had the most wonderful feeling of lightness. I came back unhappy because I felt rejected and misunderstood.

Yes, my mother said, I also had that feeling of lightness. I was in the hospital with toxemia. I had levitated a few feet over my bed. My mother had called me. I know some people have a hard time to accept things they have not experienced themselves. The woman said, about this time, I also had a vision of living 200 years from now. So? Not desirable at all.

What did you see? The people live underground. They wear tight suits like in the science fiction films. I said, some of the movie makers may be prophets too.

On our drive back, glancing at the spider-web-like snow covered hill made me feel blessed. Locating our home, I was proud, we finally lived in a house, though it was not our own. I enjoyed the week before we got the oven. Americans may move so often, just to have more of those interesting intermediate gets and less of the everyday life. Speaking of Americans: Greg Farhat, our Situ substitute, came to the house every day. Our best customer from Boston had ordered several cars. Peter said: I've to take a train to pick up a car in Hanover. There's also a BMW in Bavaria Paul wants. Got to go. Take Greg along and buy this car. There's only one problem. It costs 13,000 marks, but I only have 11.000. I'm sure you'll find something to negotiate.

From your lips to God's ears.

200 miles further south, the owners of the green sedan opened the garage. Father and son ran a textile company. There was not a single scratch on the shiny lacquer of the limousine. Immaculate from the inside. I got cold feet.

Hey, it's chilly today, I should have worn socks. Hating to waste time, I felt wrung.

Can you please open the hood? Luckily, there was something I could not evaluate.

It seems it had an accident. Look at this line. Had the car many owners?

I'm the third owner. Aha! Can I test-drive it?

Sure. We all got in the car. I said, it drives okay; they must have fixed it well. But I don't know what to do since this is a car for export. The Americans pay more for it, but they don't want any accident cars. It's chilly, I expected it warmer in the south. We can go inside, the older man said, I could get you some socks. Oh, would you, that might help, thank you. The white cotton socks didn't match my outfit, but it was a relief.

Thanks, much better now. Do you want a jersey, too? No, thanks, this will be fine. Of course, I couldn't tell the men my cold feet were stress related because the content of my pocket was 2,000 marks short. I said, so let's talk prices. How much could you go down? 12,500 the car should bring. I sighed. If it had no accident, I could go for it. But if my American customer doesn't take it, I may be left with it forever. A nerve-racking ½ hour later, we were at 12.000. Regretting to have turned the knitted garment down I was about to give up when suddenly a wicked spirit got me on another track. Automatically I said: I don't want to waste our time any longer, here's my final proposal. I'll give you 11,000 cash, and you can write the bill as low as you wish. I sensed the relief in the seller's faces. They lastly got rid of us. Outside, Greg whispered:

That was awesome. Proud, but with mixed feelings, I drove to the next gas station.

We informed all our friends about the house. Most of them came to visit. Maya called from Delhi: We'll not be able to come, Satish had a severe accident. A truck ran over him. He has more than 50 broken bones. I don't even know if he's going to make it. Shortly after, I woke up with a vivid dream.

Wow, Peter, I dreamed Satish visited us. He came on crutches, had kind of a homespun tennis shoe on one foot. He walked very slowly. Something was strange. Huh? With his cigarette, he made an ugly hole in the seat of our Mercedes. But the velvet wasn't brown like in our car. It was light gray and boy, it did show!

Several months later, Satish on crutches, Maya and 17 years old Situ came to visit us for a week. At the dinner table, Maya said:

So what happened to you since we saw you in Delhi? Why did you give up your car marts? On Friedberger, you can buy Big Macs now. The Sachsenhausen site was also sold; they'd built a house there, and I'd lost my driver's license. Oh, my! Yeah, shit and because of the RAF terrorists, there were lots of controls. One time, on my way home, they stopped me in the Ferrari. Luckily, it had no consequences, they were only searching for terrorists. Since then I felt shaky and didn't want to risk getting into trouble. In the car business, I need to drive.

Maya said you could've hired a chauffeur.

He had a chauffeur, I said, quite an expensive experience, Peter tossed in, yeah, fat Rötschke stole my 30,000 marks. A Waldorf student! Is that what they learn there?

I said Rolf or the pub owner found Peter's wallet in the john and shared his money. By the way, a chauffeur doesn't keep you from trouble. One full moon night, Rolf drove us home from Oberursel. I sat next to him. Peter slept on the backbench. We had a police car on our tail. We stopped at our car mart. They got out and asked us for our ID's. Rolf showed him his and I searched for mine.

The skinhead cop pointing to Peter snapped:

What about him? I said, his ID is in the glove compartment. While I opened it, the troublesome officer got the backdoor open and shouted at Peter. Attuning to a higher pitch, I said: Why don't you let him sleep? I have his ID here! The man touched Peter's shoulder. Getting out of the car, Peter muttered I'm going to sleep in my trailer. He was about to open the door to the car mart when the cop grabbed him. Don't touch me, Peter mumbled, I want to sleep in my trailer. I yelled, why don't you leave him alone? I have his ID here! What did he do wrong? Is sleeping forbidden? To make a long story short, Peter called the bull Nazi pig, and the whole thing escalated. Peter ended up in jail. He has a uniform dislike ever since Polish soldiers had put the toddler and his family up against the wall.

Oh, my! What happened next? The good cop said: We've always a lot to do on full-moon nights. Well, I said, you could have avoided this easily. Your colleague must have missed psychological training. Satish asked:

So how long have you been in jail?

I left beaten up in the morning. I said:

At court, the tough cop was immensely angry because of the verdict. The judge asked Peter to apologize for what he did. The cop almost freaked out when Peters fine was 1,000 marks to send to a police dependent charity. Maya said:

How was the business without the car lots?

Okay. I had help from Hugo Schubert. He also once had a shop on Friedberger Land St. He could talk like a priest. With his blond hair, blue eyes and the big belly, he looked pretty trustworthy, but he was a big gambler and lost everything he made on the roulette table. He was even jailed, because he'd sold his cars twice. I said: Yes, another not so good friend, but he could be very nice, too. The way he surprised us on November 4, 1980, I'll never forget. When we left the city hall registrar's office, he was standing there in front of the Römer with his wife handing me a big bouquet of pink roses. Very nice indeed. A split personality. Peter said, when he was in jail he tried to make a deal with a man who was about to be released. He told him to get a cheap car, run into my Ferrari and ask for 30.000. 10 grants for himself.

I said: He was a good guy, he warned Peter.

Yes, I was lucky, Peter tossed in. Since blackmail is a felony and driving without a license a misdemeanor, I showed up at the criminal investigation department and told the offi-

cer about this as if it had happened to a friend. The criminologist said, I'll also ask the district attorney, but I'm sure if you, um, your friend... if he files a complaint against the man, you, um, he won't be fined for the misdemeanor.

Oh my, said Maya teasing, you're leading a pretty exciting life. So do you, I said, looking at Satish's foot. Yes, said the invalid, driving in India is becoming ever more dangerous. I had no chance. I didn't do anything wrong. This huge truck just smashed me, broke half my bones. I was lucky to have survived. I'm sorry, Maya, I should have called you right after my dream about you visiting us. I could have calmed your worries, but I'm never dead sure about my dreams. I always tell Peter, especially when they refer to cars like the one I had just the day before you arrived. I wrote it down in my little red notebook, though I doubt, it's a true dream. Why? We were each driving a red Jaguar E-Type Roadster when all of a sudden, I had an accident. These cars are such rare items. And both in red, the best color for a Jag. Highly unlikely.

Next morn, I woke up with another vision. Oh Peter hopefully, no prophetic dream again. Why? I had to stop directly on the railway of the streetcar that comes from Eckenheimer and goes to Homburger Land St. When the traffic moved again, I couldn't get the car to move an inch. In the back of me a bus, in front a streetcar. It was embarrassing. Later, sitting at the breakfast table, I told our friends about the dream. I said if it is a prophetic dream we are going to buy a red SL soon.

When later, I made a photo of Situ in her lilac pants, she seemed truly happy to see me. You're a little lady now. Think three years back in Delhi, you in your gray and dark red school uniform! You lamented about the long school days. Yeah, it's even harder now, too much to learn. How about your music teacher? Has he given up on you like mine in trying to make me a pianist? Didn't you quit because you couldn't see notes? Yes, my cataract. Excellent memory! But I wasn't hot about it anyway. I had no fun playing by notes. Can you read notes? Not very well. Same here. Not primal to me. But when I hear a song, I mostly can sing it right away. You could think, I'm a page singer. Situ started to sing a sweet song I didn't know. Well done!

Yep. my teacher did a great job.

At the dinner table, Maya said:

We forgot about that yesterday, what happened to your friend who blackmailed you?

Hugo was in the open house already. He got back into closed prison again.

No, I mean after he lost everything? When he met his wife, she made him get barred from casinos so he couldn't play anymore.

They then opened up a flower store. Apropos flowers, one time, Hugo won big time at a casino in France. Since there was no flight to Germany at the time, he hired an Air France plane just for himself. The chief asked:

Monsieur Schubert, can we bring any flowers along? Hugo said: When I pay exclusively, I fly exclusively.

There's a much better story about Hugo. His gambler friend Heiner told us recently when Hugo had lost everything, he spotted an older lady on the roulette table. She had several chip towers sitting in front of her. Hugo said:

Permit me, Professor Dr. Orloff.

With a bow, he took place next to her and started to lay out her chips. As he worked the towers down, the lady got ever agitated. The groupers had problems to restrain laughter. When all the chips were raked in, she said:

Monsieur, how do you want to solve this little problem? The tall, stout man stood up bowing again and saying jovially with a hand kiss: Madam, upon my honor, Professor Dr. Orloff, my knowledge, your money, today, unfortunately, it didn't work out. Hugo jerked around hiding his amusement and left the casino. Of course, the lady gasped for air.

Peter said: The groupers had a hard time suppressing their grins. Don't you think, the bank should have refunded her? Maya asked.

Perhaps they did. But the better part is still to come. When Heiner drove home with Hugo in the 6.3, the gasoline level dropped to zero. Both had no money. At the next resting place on the Autobahn, Hugo said, turn right. Further, from the restaurant, they got sight of a beat-up Opel. Hugo said, hand me a screwdriver. He took off his Homburg, bent down and stabbed the tool into the gas tank. After filling his hat, Hugo transferred the gas to the tank of the Mercedes repeating this procedure several time. When Heiner drove off, Hugo said, hold on, roll back. This piece of junk isn't worth a continental. No use to get a new tank in. Hand me a match. When the car burnt in full blaze, the huge limousine moved slowly from the resting place. Hugo said it's the best solution for the poor owner. At least, he'll get some money from the insurance company.

Hugo reminds me of a Balzac figure.

Satish said: I've never been in a casino.

That we can change right off, Peter stated.

I said, let's go tomorrow evening. We'd some wine already. Peter said: You've the choice of Wiesbaden or Bad Homburg. I said I like Bad Homburg better. By the way, my first time in a casino was due to Heiner. Do you remember Willie Caspari, the hunter from the first floor? Of course, said Situ, Gabi, his partner for life's daughter was in my class. Maya asked: She was in the flower business, right?

Yes, but Elfi's philosophy was the same as Willie's. They both lived the financial equivalent to the bible quote look the lilies on the field. The bailiff was there every month. Peter said, the whole area around House Tania had belonged to Willie. He inherited a fortune from his grandfather. But he knew Willie's preference for gambling, fancy cars, and pretty ladies and enacted that he shouldn't get it before his 35th birthday. But it took Willie only three or four years to get rid of everything. I tossed in: Willie once made us lamb liver with lots of garlic when the official came. They invited him to eat, but he only drank a cup of coffee. It was quite funny and entertaining. After Willie declared not to have anything the bailiff said, next, please! Yeah, Peter threw in: One time he showed me a fancy extra on his Carrera: the bailiff seal right next to the tailpipe.

So, Marianne, how was your first time at the casino? Maya asked. Well, Willie, Heiner Thoma and Gerd Grünewald, the gas station owner on the Homburger Land St had been in Bad Homburg. Willie called at 9:30 p. m.: We've such a good run, come asap and bring as much money as possible. Peter asked me if I'd like to go. I usually like to stay home evenings. But I go for anything new. When we arrived, Willie had almost a hanging tongue and reminded me of a dog when he asked, how much money you have?

Peter said: I can give you each 500 marks and need it back tomorrow eve. I have to pay for two cars. They immediately approached different gambling tables. I followed Heiner, and when he laid out the chips, I said aloud: 27. Nobody put anything on 27. The ball rolled, rien ne va plus. And what came? 27. Next time, I said: 11.

Heiner placed lots of chips on the 11 and some other gamblers followed him. The ball rolled, rien ne va plus. And what came? 11.

Yep! Heiner got about 2000 marks.

10 minutes later, all our three gamblers ended up empty handed. Laying out chips by hand that is shoved back by a slider, what's to expect? Willie, still full of whims said, I'm hungry, let's go to the restaurant. That's why I like to come here. Their food is so much better than in Wiesbaden. Peter said, but you took my last money, too! We don't have anything left. Sitting down, he said, that's no problem. Just take a look at the menu and start from the end with the expensive stuff. We deserve it. I had delicious salmon. When the waitress came with the bill, Willie said, why, you already have our money. And that was it. The woman seemed to have known Willie. She shrugged, turning away. Satish said let's go tomorrow.

Maya said: We better go shopping and let the fortune hunters gamble. With one voice they said: No, we'll only enjoy the ambiance!

Two days later, Peter detected the hole in the passengers' seat. Satish denied having something to do with it, but this time even hubby remembered my prophetic dream. Meantime, we'd exchanged our brown DB500SE for a blue one with gray velvet. Peter also had bought a red SL from Trier which I drove, because Peter was working and the Carolis were on the road in my Golf GTI. On my way home I was about to turn from Eckenheimer Land St into Marbachweg that leads to Homburger Land St when the traffic came to a halt the four wheels on the streetcar rail. All went on as in my dream. I was cool, not the least ashamed.

Peter drove me to the SL. He started the car and backed up. Nothing wrong, he said, it's an automatic car. You should've switched to neutral or parking. Why didn't you say so when I told you the dream? Next time I'll be more persistent in evaluating things thoroughly. I could've avoided this. Who's sending all those messages? Wondering if our loved ones on the other side will get impatient because of our ignorance, I thought about Grandma Maria and our long marches to Schönnen. If she'd be the spirit in charge, I can count on her patience.

She was the best pal one can think of. Listening to Doris's heart moving song *Make someone happy* I think about Maria. She'd the desire to making me happy. She knew:

*L O V E is the answer,
someone to love is the answer.*

Odenwald family living in the fifties

Oma, when did you marry Opa? Oh, Dear, more than 30 years ago. You and your father were not even there. Where's Opa now?

Didn't I tell you?

Yes, in heaven, but was he not in that big bathtub with a cover? Sure, sweetheart.

Did he get out of it?

No, his body is still in the coffin, but his soul, his real but invisible being is in heaven.

What's he doing there? He's watching out for you. You can tell him anything you want. Um!

He's your guardian angel. Passing the school in Erbach, Oma asked:

How about taking a piece of cake along?

Oh, yeah! Nearing the confections bakery opposite the hospital, I jumped for joy.

Coming close to the glass cabinet, I pointed to the chocolate covered conically shaped product and spelled: S h e l l – s p l i n t e r.

Oma, why is it called shell-splinter?

Probably a leftover from the war. Can I have one? Why, of course, how could I turn you down on that? We'd better not tell your mama.

I felt a rush of complicity. A minute later, the tasty top was gone. Mmm! Yummy! What's it made of? I'm not sure, you want to hear this. Huh? They make it with all the leftovers they couldn't sell, mix everything together add rum and cover it with chocolate.

I couldn't care less. After 1¼ hour walk, we reached our destiny. From down the street, the line keeper's lodge seemed spirited away. All summer it's covered by a symphony of bushes and trees. Oma unlocked the corrugated sheet booth next to the brown house and opened the window. The familiar smell of motor oil hung in the air. Grandma got ready for her line-keeping job. I left the bottom part of my fatty piece for her and licked the sticky chocolate from my fingers. I was satisfied and wishless happy. Was it the alcohol or the chocolate? Great combination! In these days few people did know that such culinary pleasures lead to inflammations. Not many doctors knew about healthy nutrition. Some do not even now. Therefore, important organs of the immune system such as tonsils and appendixes were cut out wholesale in large quantities like useless crap that has nothing to do in the body. Men often think creation is erring but it was human errors that caused my lung infection, pleurisy, ear infections, mumps, tonsillitis, and my old-age cataract, I got fixed at age 13 by resistance fighter Prof. Wolfgang Jäger at the University Clinic in Heidelberg.

I listened to Grandma's warmhearted voice. I loved her reading to me, though, I was able to read myself already. When Heini was doing his homework, I was watching. But I learned to read from Oma. When she read the newspaper, I pointed to the first letter of a word and asked her to speak it out. One by one, I connected them. Oma then provided me with children books from the library. A parrot man was my jolly friend. Globi did things in different, sometimes strange ways. His nib was almost as big as his head under his Bask cap. I roared with laughter about Globi's antics. Oma looked at her watch. I must go outside. The 9th will come shortly. She grabbed the handle of the winch turning down the railway gate. It still took a while until the clack of wheels against the rails got louder, and the red embroidered black engine came noisily puffing between green bushes under heavens gray in sight. The trail of white steam followed the train wagons like a bridal veil. I wished myself inside to feel the train's rhythm, the rocking and swaying. As the wagons rumbled by I said a bit disappointed, it's almost empty. Yes, dear, most people who work in Eberbach or Heidelberg have taken an earlier train. Well, look who's coming! Only when Mr. Walter came close, I recognized the rail-keeper, tall, skinny wearing a heavy black cotton suit. He walked head down towards us taking one split tie beam after the other. He took his cap off, sat down on the table and opened the leather loop of his worn case.

I stared at the creepy man's black mustache. He'd taken out a thermos can, a wooden board, and an oval metal box. From this, Mr. Walter took out a boiled egg, an egg holder, and a folded buttered sandwich. He fished a jackknife out of his pocket. With great consideration he cut the bread in small stripes, the size of the little sherbet powder rods, I loved so much until ending up with a sore tongue.

The eating celebration went on dragging. I almost faded of tension. When Mr. Walter dipped the bread stripe into the liquid egg's yellow, I felt the yolk running in warm swallows over the gums into my throat. Three times he soaked each piece of bread in the egg yolk and with his long yellowish teeth he snapped a piece off. My mouth was watering. Last time I was also fascinated by his ritual eating habit. He had picked up gingerly a smoked mackerel from the skeleton and slowly ate the tiny flakes. No sound had mingled with the fish bones. It had lasted so long that I'd have died of hunger. In our family fish meals were accompanied by spitting sounds. With Mr. Walter as a father, I might never have had indigestion because good chewed is half digested. There would have been no reason for me to write health books. Providence had it differently, and everything happens for a reason. We used to eat pesto. Emperor! I called when I had finished first. The gulp fare then had rotted for hours or days in the bowel. If I'd learned to chew well earlier, I could have spared myself a lot of pain due to constipation. The latter was also a result of my taking antibiotics without gut flora structure.

The time was rushing away in a flash. When we were about to leave it got murky. I said:

Hopefully, our show will not fall through.

Yes. Let's pray for good weather tomorrow. Oma looked out of the window. Fortunately, I brought an umbrella. It's real dark, hurry up.

From the meadow arose the aroma of fresh hay. The path to the federal road was usually only used by farmers, hunters or people collecting wood in the forest. The melting gold of the evening sun dissolved hazy behind the bushes. A few mosquitoes were dancing in the last reflection. We turned right on B45. When passing the paper factory, Oma said, your father worked here as an electrician in his youth. Was this before the war? Uh-huh. Tell me again, how Papa had jumped on the tank and how you burnt his uniform. I didn't burn it. I was thinking about it, but your mama wanted to sew something from it. I only did hide it. Your papa was on wedding holiday to keep him from being sent to the front. So he was not in the war? No, he didn't serve. After his basic training in the fall of 1944, he suffered diphtheria. The throat? I touched mine. Yes. Very dangerous. Ludi could have died. Then he'd to repeat the basic training in Thüringen. There, he had contact with an apostolic family who listened to foreign broadcasts and heard that the war would be ending soon. In February 1945, he'd to go to driving school in Hanau. Your mama had visited him there. Ludi had suggested getting married since this was the only way to get a holiday. They'd hoped the war would be over until the end of their honeymoon. It did, didn't it? Yes, dear on March 24th, was the wedding, a few days later

the GIs came. Jumping up on my feet, I said: Tell me about it! Um, we first thought it was an earthquake. It was still dark. We were wakened by a grinding, vibrating noise. A tank of the US Army had broken through the barrier. The wood had splintered away. The house was shaking. Why had Papa jumped up the tank? Well, he was glad that the war was over. He shook hands with the GIs and chattered cheerfully. I said impatiently: Hadn't Papa put on an idiot, so they wouldn't think he'd be a soldier? Didn't you burn the uniform while Papa jumped up the tank? Why, no! God almighty, when this metal colossus came clattering ... well, we were full of fear. Why? There'd been soldiers hiding in the deposited gravel down at the creek. Ludi went down and made the Americans signs. The men were sent hands over heads in detainment.

Why did Papa sell them out? He was scared for himself and for them, too. There were still lots of deserters shot in an instant. It was for the best. There was also a hiding soldier in civilian clothes, in our hen house, but he'd disappeared. Nobody knew how hiding a soldier could be taken by the allies. Just before, hiding a Jew was for sure deadly dangerous for the entire family. Fighter pilots had dropped their bombs and shot at anything moving. Your mama and her sisters almost got killed. Eh? We were rattled and shaken. We didn't know what to expect. When they'd burned the books in 33, we thought those idiots can't last long. Most people learned to cower in fear of the Nazis believing it'll pass. 6 ½ long years. I'm 5! Yeah, dear. Nobody thought it'd last that long.

A gray cloud layer darkened the sky like an unwashed curtain. Arriving at the alley with its beautiful oak trees, Oma opened the umbrella though it only drizzled. The march made me tired. Between Lauerbach and Erbach a car stopped next to us. A man asked through the rolled down window, Frau Holschuh, can I get you a ride? Oh, this is just too kind of you, thank you so much. You come like called. You're welcome! One can still find men making the life of an old woman easier. Ten min later, at the corner of Bogenstraße, we got out of the car. Thanks again! Now, we have only a few yards left. Sure! God rewards goodness. Oh, we wanted to go to Uncle Otto! Yes, but they don't run away, we'll visit them some other day. I didn't mind. Though that nice guy gave us a lift, I was dead tired.

My parents were about to get dressed for the choir practice. They both belonged to the big choir of around 130 singers. Mama fiercely brushed through her curls training the whirl on the back of her head. She was the conductor's most awaited singer. On events, Herr von Hamm didn't start before she was there. Usually, they went by the Beetle, the only car on our street. Mama complained about a headache and said, the fresh air will do me good. She may have thought, Papa never moves his body, and it would do him even better. Though tired I followed an irresistible urge to climb the 4 feet high bookcase under the living room windows and watch them. Papa made his distinct twitching nod of the neck as if ordering his hat in place. He turned his long arms so I could see his palms, almost as if he paddled. In his poplin coat, he walked on the pavement and Mama down on the street. This way they were of the same length. I felt shame and at the same time guilt for being embarrassed. We went to bed right after we'd eaten and brushed my hair with 100 strokes. I felt like a princess from the Grimm Brother's stories. Oma was the best Lady's maid and a great reader of fairy tales. Her marriage bed only used up a fourth of the right angled spacious room that I shared with her. I slept in Opa Ludwig's bed but wasn't aware of it.

Now, older than Maria back then, I understand how hard it must have been for the warm and caring woman to lose a husband this way. She'd always kept her home open for people to come with their problems. Ludwig senior was a trainman and principal of the Apostolic community, full throaty in his sermons and singing. End of the 30th during shunting he was pulled off by a train and dragged with it several hundred yards. He lost his forefoot and had seizures ever since. Afterward, transferred to Schönnen both spouses worked in alternating shifts as line keepers. The otherwise gentle man could be dangerously wayward through his attacks. Once, he got an ax from the shed and said, I'm going in and smash up the furniture. After the initial shock, his brave wife while laughing the fear from her eyes clapped her hands and called: Oh yes Ludwig, great idea, just do it! This unexpected response forced a smile lightening his face and an embarrassment whistle eased the condition. Of course, this was no sound environment for a young family with a small child. Plus, there was still Maria's awkward mother Mina in the household. After Alwine's long months of inquiring in the town hall with dozens of eggs and other bribe items, the officials finally fetched a little flat for the family in Michelstadt in the Walther family's Zeppelin house. When the seizures got worse, Ludwig had been taken in Goddelau's psychiatric care. There he had hung himself after an electroshock therapy.

Listening to Oma's mellow voice, I nestled to her warm body. Ma didn't like my sleeping with Oma but never suggested any alternative. My mind wandered to the adjacent room where my brother lived in Karl May's imaginary world. Originally, this was the Pahler family's kitchen. On the spot of their sink, Heini had a pale peppermint green painted chest of drawers. From there, we loved to jump in his bed. Our parent's bedroom was the most fun. There, we leaped from the wardrobe into Ma's bed. Later, she'd ordered a manufactured built-in wardrobe from light alder tree to match the other furniture. This made it difficult to jump. As if Oma sensed my being absentminded, she put the book on the bedside table and said: It's time to sleep now, Jannche, have a sweet dream. Her lovely smile of pure goodness and the luster of love in her eyes warmed me. Good night, Oma. I turned to the window, from where Heini used to do his stunts, mimicking his idol Armin Dahl who's motto was, rather 10 minutes of fear than one month of work. Though Kirk Douglas did a lot of stunts himself, at times, Armin helped out. Heini used to climb from our window to his and from there to our bathroom window. That was built in the gable roof like our parents' flat bathroom window. He even would have wound up a rope to walk with a balance pole to the Poländer family who lived in the neighbor houses' similar flat slightly above ours. Though he wanted to secure himself with another robe, Ma fiercely forbade him this dangerous task.

I had installed a cord to the Fischer family on the first and the Gippert family on the 2nd floor. We kids used it to get things from one flat to the other and also fill the cans with gravel to wake us up for early excavations or treasure and thief hunts. For the next special day, we had planned to use it for waking us up. We wanted to be early birds in preparing our big event.

After munching the usual vegetable soup right across Mama's garden with apple fritters, Heini said: Hey, let's go down again. Maybe we can help. I didn't take his demanding requests as orders since I mostly liked his suggestions. I was proud to be accepted by him.

We walked to the kicker's meadow, on which Heini usually played soccer. Now, it was the perfect place for the open air stage. The rehearsal was in full swing. A heap of clothes laid on the floor. The doctor persuaded his assumed patient to get his undershirt off. A neighbor boy emerged with two Chinese lanterns. Rubbish, I forgot the matches. I said: I can get some! Oh good, go ahead. Glad to have a job right away, I turned around on my heels and ran back home. My strange affinity to fire, I couldn't explain. Around Christmas, I used to pile up fir twigs in a big ashtray and lit the heap. After absorbing the cold emanation of the stone steps on my feet, I hopped up the six creaky wood stairways.

Hi, Oma, we need matches!

For what? For the lanterns. Just be careful and don't set about anything. In an hour you come back, today you'll take your bath sooner.

Ay, ay, we are right back. Ma called:

Wait, come here for a sec. You've to try on your dress. I want to have it ready for tomorrow. Just try this on. I took the light blue tiny checkered tube with both hands. Ow! Careful, the pins! Ma took the thin fabric project back and slowly put it on me. Except for the unavoidable stitches of the needles, I loved the fitting: her hands on me, the naphthalene smell of the chalk, when she marked the seam, the reaching of the pins. She took them in her mouth if I'd been too fast. I only need to sew on the pocket.

But it's too long! No, it'll be much shorter after I elasticize the waistline. Huh? Look, this wide, Ma showed a 2-inch gap between her thumb and forefinger, I'll sew a few rows of rubber thread, so the dress will be tight in the middle like a belt. Come on, get out. One pin did hurt as usually, but in a flash, I was down the staircases and back on the street. After delivering the matches, I asked:

Heini, can we do our acrobatics?

He reacted with one of his distant looks.

The one when you hold me up in the air on my ponytail? Sphinx-like, my brother refused to provide his opinion. Or the one when you put me in a box? Huh?... Huh? Distant and aloof, Heini left me speechless. After an hour, Oma called: Heini, Marianne, come in now! Her voice wasn't as demanding as Ma's, so we just overheard it. We put chairs and benches on the sunburned grass glancing at the stage of the rehearsals taking place. A hypnotized boy jumped like a lion through a ring of fire. At 7:00 p. m., the show was scheduled.

Axel Bär, an older boy in our street used to organize events to entertain us smaller kids. Once he'd arranged a soapbox racing, where I won silver. Anni Fohr was the winner. But my prize was more appealing than her box of candies: A big tablet with a laurel bunch fixed on it! Had Axel also taken a look into the future? Or had he gotten a hint from the spirit world?

We'd quit on Ma's biting-toned call: Heini, Marianne come in now, I won't call again! We did not want to jeopardize the climate of confidence. Thus, we got our asses in gear right away. Oma had already carried through with the procedure of the bath preparations. She'd taken firewood from the drawer under the baker's oven to the bathroom and split logs of wood with a sharp knife. She'd arranged the latter crosswise in the little oven under the man high boiler over some rumpled old newspaper pages and set the heap on fire. The thick woods were already burning for a ½ hour. When we arrived in the bathroom, it crackled cozily. Heini's body looked like a modern painting. How'd you get those purplish marks? Um! Does it hurt? Nah! In a certain distance from the little cast iron oven door where I once got a massive brown blister on the back of my leg, I watched the water flowing in.

Sitting next to each other Oma clocked our alternating dipping into the depth of the sitz bath. Mama still treadled the pedal of her beautiful black Singer sewing machine with colored and golden embroidery. Seppel grumbled at his mirror image because the dame of the house had occupied his innate stand.

One minute 10 seconds said Oma, as I arose.

When Heini plunged, she handed me the stopwatch and said: You can check now. She walked the small hall to the kitchen door and said, Alwine, you have to see that. See what?

Heini's body is full of bruises. Pronto, Mama followed her mother-in-law who she sometimes would have liked to launch into outer space to be alone with her family for a while. Her gray-green eyes rushed over blue-green bruises and wandered over her son's poker face as if they'd wanted to land on it. Seemingly calm, she asked: What happened there? No reply. From a throbbing forehead, attentive eyes stared at the left side of Heini's athletic little body. On thigh, pelvis, buttocks, hip and ribs boasted bruises in all colors.

Does it hurt? Nah! Have you fallen? Silence. Heini's eyes stared like a face from an Egyptian sarcophagus. Mom's look reflected failure and resignation. She left Heini's silence unpunished hanging in the air. A penalty would not have helped anyway. Her Capricorn could be very stubborn. She'd let him taken refuge to his room. When I came in, he puttered on an invention. What is it? A gambling machine. A real one? Sure, how else could I get hold of other people's money? But Opa Wilhelm got banned from using gambling machines because he was known for emptying them.

The doorbell rang stormily. Honey! Are you going to open? Her husband stood there in leisure mood loaded with bags. He put them down on the floor and lifted his beautiful wife. Her shouting of joy came out half annoyed and half ashamed. Releasing an irritated sigh, she got down on the floor again. Ludi kissed Alwine ruffling her dark curls. A bag fell, two oranges tumbled down. Making a grunting sound, Alwine twisted her hips on the down bend and grabbed the orange that was on its way down the staircase. The Saturday was Pa's best work day since most people were at home. He was in high spirits. His order book needed not to be ashamed. Papa had sold two fridges and a vacuum cleaner. In the kitchen, addressing the thin air, he demanded a knife and the large dish for making a fruit salad. For all works, he called for assistance whether at packing or electrical work. Pa always wanted to be attended by getting things done. On Saturdays, when he made his famous salad, there had been only empty plates and no salty rain. My tears only drop-ped on Wednesday's sugar beet mash hash or on Friday's spinach masses that used to cover up potatoes and eggs or fish like lava, making the meal, I now enjoy, inedible for me.

Alwine said, Heini's body's full of bruises, but he doesn't say how he got them. On her way back to the sewing machine, she turned her inquiring look towards her wet haired little girl on the chaise lounge: Do you know anything? Nah! Maybe he got them when he throws himself playing soccer. He's the goalkeeper. Um! But they are also on the back of his thighs. Changing the subject, I asked: Can Uschi have any fruit salad? Sure, it's plenty there. My best friend next door also liked Pa's Saturday dinner. She was a year my junior but as tall as I was. Of course, her father was taller than mine but less likable. He left his wife and four kids.

Pa certainly took his time chopping the oranges, thereby clamping his lower lip between his teeth. The tongue tip at times protruded from his left mouth corner. Like a kid working on something strenuous, he wheezed occasionally. The bananas he'd cut faster, finally the apples. He stirred them under to avoid brown spots from exposure to oxygen.

Usually, Ma made amusing remarks about his acting. But now she had other things on her mind. Pa enriched the colorful fruit salad with nuts, raisins, and condensed milk. Much later, I learned that sweet fruits or sugar with milk (ice-cream!) forms fusel alcohol and is the main reason for abnormal liver function.

While Oma and Mama buttered the bread, I ran to the neighboring house and, taking two steps at a time, Uschi and I hastened back. I plunged next to Heini on the chaise lounge, Uschi next to me. Pa sat on my right on the heads end, the women of the house opposite from us. Grandma's false teeth made their usual clicking sound. Oma said with a sigh, my denture still doesn't sit right. I was at the dentist, but he couldn't fix it properly.

After the early dinner, Oma gave us pennies for change. We hurried outside heading south. The scent of roses and pinks mixed with the smell of home fries escaping from the 3-story blocks of flats followed us. Where Georg Glenz St meets Hieronymus St, we walked westward towards the stage hut. The seats were neatly placed in a half circle. All of us helpers, amateur artists, and players, collected the entrance fees: 4 pfennigs for kids, 6 for grown-ups. Gradually the open air theater filled better than we thought. Of course, in the fifties there was not as much entertaining as today: Carnival and the two county fairs Bienenmarkt and Wiesenmarkt. There were only a few balls and musical events in Schmerkers Garten, across from our school. On their stage, Ma sometimes appeared as a solo singer within the scope of the zither club. For some folks, it was the highlight of the week when she let her bell-like soprano clang. Today, since most activities are confined to TV or PC the large-scale event's destination made space for several charming single family houses.

Next to occasional cinema visits a few times during the year we had another celluloid extra-curricular activity. Two boys in the neighboring clerk's apartment block had 8-track simultaneous recordings. Whenever they had gotten new films for a few pfennigs entrance fee, they'd let us watch them. It took eons until the film roll rattled in the projector and the boys' father switched to forerun. But the enervating procedure only increased the excitement. Agog with the expectation we eyed at the flickers of geometrical figures slipping by, ripped perforations, white flashes, black jags, dirty yellow lumps, and finally the picture appearing on the coarse-grained canvas. We watched Laurel and Hardy, Buster Keaton and other film comedians. If someone had told me about my future opportunity to meet a Buster kid in America at Herta & Wayne Haedrick's Party or one of the Three Stooges in the Motion Picture Hospital, out of my rash tongue would have slipped: Sure thing! I'll also meet the emperor of China. Though Oma had told me with my wide-set teeth I'd travel the continents, Ma's mocking made me doubt her saws.

Before a sizable audience, on the knocked together platform a man tried to ask the doctor something. The medico interrupted by asking his suggested patient to take off his clothes.

Several times, Ma's eyes wandered around the seated crowd. During the pause, I saw her standing with Heini's classmate. One could

throw a ball through Rolf's bowlegs. The rickety boy had not only suffered from a lack of vitamins but also lost his mother. Though, she'd died young, she'd already looked like

Oma: a dark dress with an apron and a granny knot. A man had hauled her dead body in an open hand cart to the burial ground, likely her husband. But I had eyes only for the poor woman. I was struck by the cold-blooded affair, the disgraceful way Mrs. Arzt was brought to the graveyard. Why did I feel so humiliated for the careworn woman in this cart? Had I felt the agony that had caused her early death or recollected a similar past life? I suppose, people often die to get out of unsatisfying relationships. They usually lack the guts to run away or depend too much on their partner. Disappointing circumstances and missing money may be the main reason. Therefore, I plead for a citizen's money, at least for the ones who commit to several hours of freely chosen work for the community. This would help the economy increasing domestic trade. It would lessen illicit work, lead to better education and more satisfying jobs, more tax yield, less crime, less depression, and other diseases. Often, people work in unpleasing jobs in disagreement with their skills and hobbies, since only with a high paid job they can make ends meet. A basic income would lead to happier people. Some of the crap, politicians spend taxpayer's money on, often only pleases their own, their friend's or their allies' purpose! Spending citizen money on the citizens would be useful for everybody not only for a few state-subsidized firms or groups. With a basic income, a neglected or beaten woman could get out of an unhappy relationship. Since women still earn 20% less than their male colleagues in the same jobs, a basic income for all would also ease this unfairness.

Ma came back to us. Harsh voiced she said:
Of all kinds! I'll tell her what I think of her! She'll not get away with this! Pa said:
Yo, darling! Why are you so angry?
This Pfeiffer beast had done it. What? She kicked Heini. But why? I called outraged.
She'd been peeved by him. Huh?
She'd dragged him outside kicking him. Heini had fallen down the staircase. The hallway with the shining oak banister rails flashed before my eye. I'd loved to slide them down or ran my hands down their sleek shaft. I also knew Heini's classroom. We met there every Sunday with our church community, a split group of the New Apostolic Church. As in American religious communities, the preachers to which Pa belonged, spoke about times subjects on metaphysics, philosophy, and social politics. Mahatma Gandhi and Albert Schweitzer ranked highest on the Sunday's program scale of the Christen unserer Zeit. On weekdays, it went on less Christlike.

On Tuesday after the open air theater, Mama braided my sun strained hair as usually. How about going to school today? Oh yeah, I called jumping for joy. At this time, I was still fascinated by school, full of expectation. When Ma asked me to wear dark blue pants with a white blouse and a hand knitted brown based jacket with colored rectangles, I protested by raising my voice to a higher pitch: This doesn't fit at all! Enervated, Ma helped me in my blue darling cardigan that looked less handmade. We had a last glance at our pleasant appearances in the head high bedroom mirror. I was proud of my mother's look. Her self tailored shift dress accentuated her waist and her neat bottom. A head of full dark curls framed her beautiful face. Her gray green eyes were matching the sea green gown perfectly. After the ½ hour walk in the morning damp, we got up the wide old stairs towards the massive dark oak door. Ma's sturdy knock got an immediate response from inside. The teacher may have expected the principal. Entering, we could have heard a pin falling. A second later, the silence changed to a rising whispering and chuckling. Without any doubt, the whole class knew why we'd come. I sensed a conspiracy and supposed all students were on our side. Mama sounded sore saying:
Can I talk to you in person, Mrs. Pfeiffer?
The teacher approached us. A shaky smile

broke across her visage, changing into a poker face. Her eyes locked with Ma's. Some 50 souls sensing the anxiety. The air sizzled from tension. Yes, certainly. Let's go outside.

Mama said, now with soft timbre, Marianne, it's best you stay here. Proudly, I stood in front of the third graders, who to me looked pretty much grown. Standing in front of them, I felt fantastic celebrating the birth of my educational work. Later at home, I installed a register. Heini provided me with the names of his classmates, their skills, and qualities. Two boys in front I recognized: grimacing Rainer who lived in our house on the 1st floor and one of Mrs. Ensinger's four boys. I once had heard Ma say: I could never argue with this woman. Raising four boys without a man on her side is quite a task.

Mrs. Pfeiffer came back inside. Ma waited for me in the doorway. Come Marianne, let's go. Her relaxed voice made me feel comfy. But I would have liked to stay longer. When we left the schoolyard, the sun was about to break through the clouds. I scanned my silent mother's face. What did she say?

Ma absorbed my tension and said smiling:

I said, why'd you kick my son? Guess what?

Huh? She denied it! What'd you say? I said you can't deny it. I know it from your pupils. You don't have to say anything. I only tell you this: If I hear anything again, whether it happens to my son or to any other child, I won't come to you anymore. I'll go straight to the rector. And what did she say?

Nothing. You know, Heini can be real stubborn, and you can't get anything out of him. He never says what he thinks or feels the way you do. But to kick him like that, he could be dead! In Schönbrunn, there was this rigorous teacher Ries. He'd killed a 12-year-old neighbor boy. He'd lived next to the oil mill. How? Why? The creep had kicked him in the kidneys. The boy's funeral was on the very day of aunt Hilde's chaff cutter accident.

Jeez! Ma's often described scene of her 14 year old sister's being ripped off her scalp made me shiver. But Hilde married her tall handsome Heinz while her tall pretty sisters had fallen for two insignificant looking little men.

Heini and I were quite different kids. Maybe we came together, so my blunt Sagittarius temper would be a balance to the stubborn Capricorn. We may all come together to learn from each other. I, to keep my tongue in check, so it will not always hurry miles in front of the brain. And Heini to be able to learn, that it doesn't harm to open up, because then, you learn more from others. Could Mrs. Pfeiffer have learned something from Heini, too? That we have to accept people ticking differently, and divergences are chances to learn and grow. Maybe she stopped taking the indifference and independence of a child personally and avoided unlawful actions. At least we haven't heard about another tortured child. But she pestered the staff of the nursing home and was described as a beast. Well tempered and proud of her performance at school, my mother said, boy, have I changed. When I think about my teacher, if you may call him that. Kohler was a sadistic monster. Why? I had problems in math. But instead of helping me or leaving me alone he enjoyed to call me to the blackboard and tease me. We got bad grades because we were not rich like the farmers. They bribed him with ham and butter. Um! Only, when he wanted me to sing on festivities, he could be kind to me, too.

In the Braun Street, Ma stopped at Läppe-Lui. Stepping up the stone stairs to the textiles and haberdashery store, she said: We always got our clothes at the Jews, even when it was very dangerous. Why? It wasn't allowed to buy in their stores. Why? The Nazis wanted them out of the country. They thought if nobody buys from Jews they'd leave. But why? Why what? Why'd they wanted to kick them out? They said they were profiteers. Huh?

They would only think about their gaining. Why did you buy from them? They were cheaper than other stores. We were too poor to buy elsewhere. We always sneaked in from the backdoor. If they'd caught us we'd been put away. I knew what that meant: the concentration camp. Mama and Oma almost had to endure this experience. Tell me about the wooden shoes again. How old were you then?

19. I refused to work because my shoes were kaput. I was forcibly conscripted by the BBC. What's that? That's a dangerous bomb attracting place, an ammunition factory! I had a supply ticket for new shoes, but there were none to buy. I said, without shoes, I can't come to work. After three days of absence, my colleague Mr. Dewald came urging me to go to work. He said, girl, come tomorrow! They're planning something. So I got papa's wooden shoes from the stall and walked to work.

What'd they say? They'd burst out jeering when they saw me. Entering the store, the door-bell rang. Tell me again, why had Oma almost gone to the KZ? Marie had 14 friends and relatives from bombed out cities in the brownstone house in Schönnen. The Nazis had allowed slaughtering only twice a year. Since she had to feed her folks, she butchered a swine illegally. A neighbor of the Nazi, who'd gotten wind of it, convinced him not to report her. Would they've killed her?

I don't think so. But the KZ was a dangerous place with hard labor and diseases. Jeez!

Go, open the door again.

After the second ringing, a slightly bent man with few strands of white-yellow hair came from the backside, asking for our wishes.

This young lady needs new pants matching a brown jersey. At the time, the price for these pants wasn't much more than it is today. What had changed was the producer's exploiting: outsourcing the fabrication to Third World countries. Meanwhile, miniature trains from Märklin & Co. had been sold in the Braun Street. Though the producers from Göppingen still make high-quality model locomotives many of lesser quality trains are rolling from China to North America. Business sucks.

Some 30 years later, other toys, preferably classic cars, were sold in L. A. like hotcakes. We were busy searching for these rare items.

Are we the creators of disasters?

On the last day of my mother's stay, she came back from her walk to the beach quite excited. You won't believe this, outside stands an antique chest of drawers next to the garbage cans. Have a look, if you want it, I'll help you bring it in. I ran outside and took two drawers right away. Returning, I said: It's got lockable drawers. Usually, only genuine antique pieces of furniture got them. The newer ones are mostly not lockable. But the keys are missing.

Speaking of missing, I'll miss California. The five weeks staying went by like five days.

When we have a house, I hope you'll stay longer. If it wouldn't be for Andreas' confirmation, I'd stay longer. If I'd be 10 years younger, I'd even come for good. I said, I have to reconfirm my flight. In a finality tone, Ma said, my luggage is packed.

I'll pack tonight. You've got some nerve.

Okay, now I want to thank you for the grand trip to San Francisco. I'd like to invite you for dinner. Peter said: Great, we could go to the Red Onion in Redondo Beach. I said: We all like fish. Couldn't we go to the seafood restaurant where you get the bibs?

Only when you eat crabs.

No, I think, we all got them.

But half the pier is gone after the storm. You are exaggerating. Let's go and see. We've got to call first. Okay, go ahead.

You always have to have the last word.

Why? Your friend Bolko says, who's got the idea, should do it. See what I mean?

The damage was visible, but the boardwalk seemed okay. Peter was cranky because he'd have to do without his teammate for two weeks. Most changes use to make his mood barometer plummet. He grumbled: We should have picked up the Jag.

Why didn't you tell me yesterday?

Why must you fly in the first place?

We'd talked about this at length.

But we have so much to do at the moment. Soothing, I said, it's only for two weeks. After dinner, there was peace again.

Apparently, Peter's blood sugar had dropped dramatically. In addition, comes the tension before any flight no matter who's flying. But fear of flying he rejects outright. However, he's extremely distracted shortly before departure. At times, you have to watch him like a first-grader. He leaves his briefcase someplace at the airport or he forgets his passport. Once, he was permitted to fly to Germany with his sports boat license since he was known as a frequent flyer. Of course, I had to send his passport to Germany. Peter would not have been allowed to enter the States without it. Arriving at home, I started to pack. Peter accepted his fate. He reconciling joked around and worked on the mail, he wanted me to take to Germany.

In the middle of the night, I woke up bathed in sweat. I still had the last picture in my mind's eye: A jet submerged in white smoke! I toddled to the bathroom. Peter yawned.

What happened? Our airplane will have an accident. Come now! You had an angst dream. Washing off the cold sweat, I said, I hope you're right. The bird, fluttering in my chest, still wanted to get out, but its wings were becoming lame, and I soon rested in Orpheus's arms again. In the morning, I woke up aware of a follow-up dream, in which I begged Peter to cancel my flight. He did it right away.

When I told Ma about the dreams, she didn't believe me and masked her letdown behind her sharp tongue. I can't believe that you let Peter persuade you. No, it's true, I saw the smoking plane. I wish you wouldn't fly either.

No way! I'll fly! I won't miss my only grandchild's confirmation. I've to be there. Grabbing her windbreaker she was out the door, just like in the old days when she had quarrels with her mother-in-law or my father. As a kid, I didn't know that she only needed the physical exertion to calm down. I was always anxious my big beautiful sister wouldn't come back. Had this anything to do with my self-sufficiency or my early independence? I wonder if my sisterly feeling come from a former life.

When Ma came back from the beach, she had her cool back. I repeated my concern about her flying. Resolutely she replied:

That's out of the question. I'm flying. I hadn't dreamed anything dreadful. There was no use to say another word. I wished that my clairvoyant mother's warning system was still working. It was the first time we stayed at the airport waiting for the Boeing 747 to vanish on the horizon. Palpitating pressed in the passenger seat I lingered about the following hour. Peter said:

Now she may be passing over Las Vegas. Split by inner restlessness I said: Who knows where she is. Our afternoon program kept me from brooding. Our last appointment was with a male couple in El Segundo, who offered a 280SL. Peter asked: Why do you sell the car?

We're going to move to the Bacha. Why? Don't you like it here? I asked. Yes, but it's too expensive. We couldn't afford a beach house. There, we almost finished one. Every time we drive down, we take some lumber with us in our pick-up truck. We only need the utility car.

Peter said, I'm sorry, but for the price, I expected a nicer car. For this one, I'd pay 9,000 ... 9,500 at the most. If you change your mind, just give me a call. Peter handed him his business card. We went right around the corner and enjoyed Orville & Wilbur's Happy Hour and the sunset with hot live music.

I loved all the goodies you get for free if you order a drink: raw vegetables with dip, filled eggs, and tuna pizza. Peter added 2 jumbo shrimps for 60 cents and 2 oysters for $1 each saving me cooking dinner. Back in the flat, I brewed herbal tea. Of a sudden, the phone sprang into life. ALWINE! Peter shouted stupefied:

What? What is it? I yelled at Peter. He ignored me. Impossible! What's with my mother? Impatiently, I pulled on the sleeve of Peter's pullover. At times, I still believe in his ability to do two things at once.

We're coming. Hanging up he said:

It was exactly the way you have dreamed it. Get ready! We'll drive to Westchester. All passengers are staying at the Amfac Hotel near LAX.

15 minutes later I was greeted by my mother who with the other travelers sat in the hotel's crowded conference hall. You witch! You were right, Ma said merrily, and I didn't believe you. Sit here! I kept the seats free for you. Some passengers seemed informed of my newest second sight subject greeting me like a pop star. So what happened? Jeez, about 40 minutes after departure ... all of a sudden there was a jolt ... there were a lot of young folks around me, but nobody made any sound, unlike the movies. We listened to the stories of the air passengers next to us. The waitress asked: What can I bring you? Just water easy on the ice and Caesar's Salad, please. Back then, I didn't know that fruits and salads in the eve are acid-forming and hinder digestion. I used to wonder about my bloated belly. Now, I only eat papaya and avocado after 4:00 p. m., exceptional raw foods helping digestion.

The airplane couldn't be fixed. The next day, all travelers had flown with Air New Zealand.

What would have happened, if I had accompanied Ma as planned? After all, during my coffee withdrawal depression I had often thought, it would be best to crash together with my mother ... I had even mentioned this in letters to friends. After this experience, it was crystal clear to me:

If the soul is troubled or the body deprived of nutrients, it affects the whole.
We create our reality by thinking, talking, and writing. We cause the disasters in the world and, therefore, we take responsibility for all life around the globe.
Hence, it should be our prime desire to live in a society with happy people.
This shows clearly, how we are connected.
We are all in the same boat.

The richest, most powerful people depend on what even the poorest think and how they feel. The increasing catastrophes and burn-outs point to a lot of negative stimuli. Depression can cause destruction. Thus, we should be interested in making us and other people happy! Isn't that the real meaning of life? I'm now careful not to send unreflected statements out into the ether. They could become a reality. When the tongue is faster than the brain being cautious about words and wishes is a real tough task! Better is to be quiet. Since loose lips sink ships ... and crash airplanes.

Lost in flights and Lisa's departure

Though I missed my mother, I also loved the change to be alone again. Before Ma came, we had much distraction: customers, friends, looking for cars. Now I'd appreciate some time to read and write. Opening my neglected red record book my ghost experience hit me!

I re-read the lines. Wow! It had been in Carmel when Ma reminded me of my great-grandfather! In the very area, he supposedly had lived: Victor like victory! This name would also be on my shortlist if I would adopt another name. Swiftly, I wrote a script and a synopsis. In August, on our next trip to the Monterey vintage car auction, from the White Pages, I got the addresses of five Victors around Carmel. I did send the synopsis with a letter to them. No respond.

Peter said Ray found me a mint red 280SL in Phoenix. By the way, he advised me to get at least the Gullwing and the Ferrari to Yuma because of the expected Earthquake in L.A. Carole did, too. Who's Carole? His mom. She said Nostradamus predicted the big one. So?

They have garages for their racing cars, our two cars would fit in, too.

A week later Carole Madrid a German looking fair skinned freckled woman with medium blond curly hair arrived with her son to help us move the cars.

I said you look strangely familiar to me.

Carole answered with a canny broad smile as if she knew more than she wanted to tell. I got onto the passenger seat of her BMW. We followed the red sports cars to Yuma. Glancing at my hand, Carole said:

That's a nice ring you've got. Just give it to me. A bit reluctantly I handed it to her. Closing her hand around the ring Carole said: I see an elder graying lady with curly hair, blue eyes, about 5.7, 170 pounds, big Busen. That's German! I said as if I'd been more amazed by her talent for languages than by describing the very person who'd given me the ring. Yes, my grandmother's German. She taught me some words. Carole must be a great psychic. Or could she have seen a photo of my mother-in-law? Inattentively I said, originally it belonged to Peter's little Granny Köster I used to exchange letters with. Until age 84 she had managed her 3-bedroom flat until she passed on in her sleep. Carole said I see the woman who'd given you the ring.

Tcha, that's Lisa, Peter's mother. My thoughts drifted back to the beginning of the end of Lisa's life in the flesh making her presence felt and proving my new view of eternal life:

The bell rang. Had Peter forgotten anything?

Seconds later, I looked into Walter's friendly round face. Do you have a moment? Sure.

I bought an SL, but I've got a problem with the soft top. I don't know how to get it down.

Let me have a look. Happy to be of help, I stepped into the wash house vapor of the marine-layer. That wasn't what I'd in mind living close to the Pacific.

How are you this morning?

A little broody. I had a not so nice dream in which Peter's mother had died. Omigod! I hope it's not happening soon. Our 2nd manager seemed overly touched. It's hard for me to think about my mother's dying. It frightens me a lot. Do you think it was a prophetic dream?

You know about prophetic dreams?

Sure! Why not?

In Germany, you hardly find anybody talking about these things. Why? What do they say if you do? They may not say anything, but they give you funny looks.

Foreboding dreams are common. People in Germany may just lack confidence, so they suppress anything a bit out of the ordinary.

Have you ever had a dream where you were a different person?

Not that I remember, have you?

Just recently. In this apartment, I'd more metaphysical experiences than in the last ten years. I think I was a shepherd youngster in my last lifetime. What makes you think that?

In the last two weeks, I'd dreams where I was a shepherd, who got killed, a woman with a Quaker headdress like on the 2 cent stamp whose husband got killed in the civil war, a gladiator killer, a Jewish girl living in a ghetto, an English-speaking actor living in a hotel, a very pretty blond woman who got pushed on a ladder wagon having a difficult life, a fat dark man from Polynesia who got feathered and teared. Wow! I think in my last life I was the shepherd. Why? My last dream was the same as the first one where I was the shepherd boy. Jeez! Not really great lives. So you should have a better life this time around. It seems so. We reached Walters covered parking.

Here it is. Wow! What a beautiful pagoda! Walter opened the driver's door. Where are the handles for the soft top? Our 2nd manager looked puzzled. No wonder, I couldn't move it. I found the tools in the door pocket and gave Walter one of it. I placed it into the slotted opening on the passenger side and said, now do the same on your side and move it. The top clicked off. That's it. Ah! Thank you. In a lower voice he said, I hope, Peter has not to undergo his mother's death soon. I hope so too. We'll see her soon. Are you going back to Germany? Only for a short trip. Peter and his brother want to sell their property. Okay, then have a safe trip. Thanks, I wish I'd be back again already, I don't like to fly.

On my way back, I listened to a typewriter sound next to Walters apartment and envisioned me as a writer in a house surrounded by lush greens and old trees. Working on my books and loved by my readers like Joan Wilder in the movie Romancing the Stone.

I'd just watched this venturous film that starts with a scene of the author, played by Kathleen Turner who for years had written adventure books without ever having a daring life herself. With smashing a plate, she decided to help her sister by following her in the jungle. I identified with the author and would have loved to overtake her flat including the cat. Withal, I'd traveled enough and longed for the quiet to write. This movie effected me in many ways. I had even touched Michael's white linen suit at the secondhand shop *A Star Is Worn*, on Melrose Avenue. In a fit of mental derangement, I purchased a German top model's white 3 part evening outfit. A friend urged me to buy the dress. I'd never worn it. The corsage required a larger mass. I'm pretty sure the girl on the dress owners' photo was Heidi Klum. I remember a short name. I'd not known her. Heidi's popularity increased much later. I'd like to find somebody who'd fit in the glossy western style outfit. A few years later, in the Moroccan Himalaya studios we've seen the paper mache airplane used in the film. Back in Spain, my father's cousin showed us Michael Douglas' pink mansion a few hundred yards from his home.

Our flight was interrupted by a dinner with turbulence, two motion picture movies and a breakfast with more turbulence. A good friend of foods two feet away from Peter asked: Have you also been on holidays in California? The noise of the moving flaps poured out a portion of adrenalin and cramped my extremities. No, Peter answered puffed up with pride. We live here. And where if I may ask? In Hermosa Beach, not far from LAX. I deal with antique cars. Ah, I guess the sunny state is an Eldorado for rust free automobiles.

You're right, these tins on wheels just wait to be pushed or driven from the backyards.

Good for you! A bit regretful the man who filled out the opposite aisle seat continued: On Oct 12, I've to work again. Too bad.

More than 10 hours later, the double-chinned giant asked, how did you come up with the idea of dealing vintage cars? Economic reasons. We sold gray-market cars before mostly Mercedes. Peter said, addressing the puzzled face, that may sound half-silky, but it's all legal. Because of the high Dollar exchange rate many US-Americans purchased their high-quality cars directly in Germany. We asked friends with an own business to order a new car. They got a good commission, and we sold the autos over new price to US citizens. Where on a car lot? No, we had a house in Frankfurt-Bergen. Since we were almost flying over that house, our last landing popped up in my mind. Sitting stiff like a chair, my gray matter grasped on the memory of our last safe landing:

Peter had announced, now you can see the Hanauer Land St and our house. Pointing with his index finger, he'd said mockingly, look there, Mrs. Weber just waved. Ha, ha, I had counterfeited fun, breathless waiting for the roaring thunder. What are we going to do with the cats? We better leave them at my parents. For two months it doesn't make sense to fetch 'em. Think about all the distraction with the garage sale. You're right, as long as we don't have a house, they'll better stay with Alwine and Ludwig. I missed my pets wondering when we can take them with us.

My safe landing mental work had killed some time. Not the fear, though. The jet slowly went down, side slipping to the left, I balanced it by turning right. Meadows, fields, and forests came closer. Peter said: When the dollar dropped dramatically, we were out of business and had to think about how we further on can make ends meet. Yeah, the man tossed in philosophically: Nothing remains as it is. How did you get the idea of dealing with the classic cars in the first place?

When we traveled to California in the early 80th, we already got to know some oldtimer freaks. Later, I flew to L. A. and looked for decent cars. When we unloaded the first haul on the Mainzer Land St in Frankfurt, a young man fell immediately in love with an immaculate silver XKE 12-Cylinder-Jaguar. His rich girlfriend from one of the best families in Germany ... wealthiest ... I tossed in to be precise. Yeah, she bought the gem for him. For me, that was a good omen. I did this a few times. Eventually, I got tired of flying back and forth. Therefore, we emigrated to L. A. and changed our business from import to export.

Where do you store your cars? Peter's black curled aisle neighbor asked while a mysterious dissonance troubled me. My icy fingers clenched the armrests. Peter replied patronizing, in a large storehouse on Century Boulevard next to the Hilton in walking distance from LAX. So our customers don't have to drive around much. We've got a deal with a shipper there. He rented us some of his space, and of course he gets the freights of our customers on top.

That's quite convenient, said the giant, looking down on the greenery. Peter announced: The landing flaps already extended.

I've heard it, finally. Fixed on my seat, I fastened my seat belt still tighter waiting for the long hoped-for pulling power sound of the curbing jet. I love this auditory sensation! The jumbo landed smoothly. A united bunch of mortals radiant with joy some slightly tipsy but happy to be alive jumped off their seats.

We had expected a mild, red golden wooded autumn, but it refused to obey the clichés. Father Frost had already spread out his morbid mantle. Crisp freeze had eaten its way through all cracks. The muddy weekday in our cold homeland made our immigration seen as the right move. Helmut drove us to our 280 SL that still hadn't found a new owner. We picked it up from a befriended car rental company.

Peter took the opportunity on the Autobahn to put the pedal to the metal. I like the rolling traffic in L. A. better if it rolls 65 miles per hour 10 over the permitted 55.

When we entered my parent's living-room, we were greeted by the entire family. My father's aunt was visiting. They all just watched a TV news program, a political affair: Had Uwe Barschel the Christian Democrats governor from Schleswig-Holstein known too much about anything critical? I looked at the confused staring man on the screen. In his trench coat on the empty street surrounded by bare trees with some last leaves sailing in the wind, I said: Omigod, he doesn't live much longer.

Huh? What makes you think that? Pa asked perplex. Dunno just crossed my mind. He looks desperate. Was it telepathy? Had I read his mind? Had he at this very moment thoughts of suicide or angst of assassination?

Three days after my premonition, Uwe Barschel was found dead in the bathtub of a Swiss hotel filled up with a deadly mixture of drugs. Until today, there are speculations. The CDU was able to blame the social democrats for the Waterkantgate. There are other theories about the Stasi, the CIA or an Iranian arms dealer, set by the CDU, to avoid increasing damage to the party. Or Barschel had known too much about a submarine deal with South Africa. Recently, the expert witness Prof. Hans Brandenberger in the Uwe Barschel case states the fact that the chemical analysis data agreed in all details with a murderous sequence which the former Mossad agent Victor Ostrovsky describes in his book *By Way of Deception: The Making and Unmaking of a Mossad Officer.* According to Brandenburg, Ostrovsky claimed that "Barschel had been the victim of a Mossad killing command because he had opposed the execution of secret arms traffics between Israel and Iran in transit in Schleswig-Holstein in 1987 and threatened to go public with his knowledge of the matter." The investigating state attorney Heinrich Wille is also convinced that Barschel was killed.

Aunt Sophie left, and we exchanged some personal news. Ma went to bed early as usual. Pa retired to his bedroom an hour later searching in the boob tube for one of his beloved Western. Do you think we'll someday have separate bedrooms, too? Peter seemed far away. In a trance-like mental state, he said out of the blue: At age 16, I only once had a dream in which I was a different person. Huh?

I'd fought in the American civil war. All my signal lights turned on red.

What makes you think about this dream just now? Huh? Peter got out of the trance state. What movies have we watched on the plane?

Any of metaphysical content? Ishtar with Warren Beatty and Dustin Hoffman and the comedy with Bette Midler. My gray cells were working in extra shifts. Bits and pieces of my visions whizzed through my cerebrum. Had it to do with my past-life-dream in which I was a woman with a dress closed up to the throat and a white lace-cap? A simple life with kids, a boy, and a girl in a small house with only a bedroom and kitchen with tiny windows. We had a maid who slept on the kitchen bench. My man in uniform I saw only on one occasion watching him doing exercises on a high barn with others in a blue uniform. The dream ended with me staying with my kids and father-in-law on the village meadow when a man with a megaphone announced the casualties. I heard my husband's name read out from the list of the killed. Could we've had a life together some 150 years ago? It would explain Peter's familiar eyes and his trusting by letting me stay in his apartment all by myself after only a week; also our preference of large rooms, glass doors, and large windows. In our domiciles, high costs for heating or cooling never discouraged us. Thinking of the midget home in the dream, anybody who'd ever lived in such cramped premises would strive for different conditions in another lifetime. Also, if, after a life of frequent separations in which the Grim Reaper broke in much too early a longer relationship would be preferred another time around.

Would it also explain, why we had no children together? From age 27 on, I did not practice any birth control. I also was certain, when my mother asked me, don't you miss kids? Nope. Abstractedly, she'd replied: Um! I guess you can't miss what you don't know. Who knows? If we had a past life together, it would explain my unrestrained pudenda when we first made love. I didn't need any time to settle in. It was as if we continued where we'd left off 1½ century earlier trusting us on the soul level.

In Wilhelmshaven, we visited Peter's mother in her elegant apartment. Peter's brother and his life companion came with their little daughter Anna. Lisa talked a lot about her death. Strictly, she ordered us not to make any fuss about it. I don't want any ceremony, got that? The urn shall be interred, and that's it.

Peter appeared awkwardly uneasy. Because his 76-year-old mother had no ill to complain about, he said: Come on Mutti, don't think of dying, you'll survive us all. Peter appeased himself more than his mother who unwavering said, no wreath and no music. Peter gets the pantry and Joachim the car. I'd never experienced my mother-in-law as stout in her expression. Earlier, she also talked about her death. On Omi Köster's funeral, she'd said in a pathetic way that she would be next. This time, it sounded different. I thought it had to do with our staying in California. She must have felt lonely especially since Jochen was about to sail to the Caribbean with his family. The boat he'd built himself was almost ready for taking off.

In the second week of our stay in the cold homeland, I wanted to visit another lonely soul, a namesake of Joachim. Peter didn't know the cranky painter from Forstel whose teacher wife had passed on. He asked:

Do we have to go there? I've got a feeling I won't have another chance. I'm very grateful for what the old oddball did for me. I always felt at home there. Um! You'll like it. What did that man do for you? He watched me playing badminton when I was 15 wearing thick cataract glasses. Boy, had he questioned my father closely about it. Why? He knows best how it is to be different. The Hitler war had cost him a leg. For me to wear those ugly nose bikes, wasn't easy either. Jochen said the glasses are so thick that a dumdum would rebind in full strength. It's no good for the psychic developing to walk up to the world with cow eyes. Anyway, I didn't wear the glasses often just at school and home. I had my glasses usually in a pocket or under pullover or jacket sleeves and saw the world as surrealistic paintings. I didn't greet anybody and was probably considered arrogant.

Peter blew a cubic yard of air against the window. I hope it'll not take long.

Eh! I'm sure you'll like him. He is as funny as you after a few drinks. He's like a kid, bubbling out all thoughts without paying any attention to its propriety. Then he's more like you, said Peter slandering. I know. We have to work on things we recognize on others. What's the bible say? You see the sawdust in your brother's eye but your own plank you ignore or the like. Hubby replied, I only know HE is the boss. Yeah, sure, if you'll do what I say.

When we reached the snug house, Jochen came out and opened the electric gate. I said:

He had no barrier before. I guess old age makes anxious. The artist started immediately with the examination of the new. I think, he's quite okay. On the picture you'd send me, he looked like an ass with ears. I thought, what kind of an old primate she'd picked out.

Though Jochen ignored Peter completely, hubby seemed quite comfortable. I said:

Peter's uncle Adolf is also an artist painter. But his wife the sculptress Hanna Koschinski is better known. Jochen ignored the comment meaning I could go on talking. So Peter had experience with the Bohemia. His Rotary-Father was a sponsor of the Fine Arts. He'd wanted to be an actor, Peter tossed in jokingly. He'd often recited in front of the mirror. Jochen smiled mockingly. I said:

His father had known Heinrich George. Jochen snapped: Hadn't he kicked the bucket in the concentration camp Sachsenhausen?

Yes, I think he died there of pneumonia.

His eyes turned to Peter. What about him?

Peter's artistic side? Jochen's brusque nodding made me continue. He's not like Edi not even like Günther though his grandfather was a violinist in the Kiel Orchestra and his uncle Adolf a painter from Bavaria. Peter looked at one of my friend's graphically precise paintings. I followed his eyes to the bit morbid dreamlike piece of art. He could act, though. I'd say comedy. But let's talk about you. How are you doing all by yourself?

Nobody's showing up. It's as I'd already be pushing up the daisies. Oh well! Norma had been your cable to the outside world. Turning to Peter, she'd always visiting friends or colleagues from school. Apropos, have you ever seen her in a dream or so? Lurking, Jochen said: What d'you mean by or so? His cynicism couldn't hide his curiosity. A friend of mine had seen her husband several times, standing next to her bed. He also had talked to her. Jochen cleared his throat and said: One time I saw Nora, but I believe it was just wishful thinking, probably caused by the booze.

No, no, I gentled. I read about these things. That happens quite often. Jochen got up. My son's dissertation is about the occult. He handed me a light blue book. I read aloud: Johann Joachim Gestering: German Pessimism & Indian Philosophy. A hermeneutic reading. Sounds exciting. Jochen shrugged his shoulder. I've problems believing in it. For me, it is not believing. I know these things are for real. I'm always experiencing metaphysics. How?

Remember when our acquaintance from Steinbach hung himself because of grieving his son's death ... yeah, he died in a motorcycle accident. Exactly, but I had dreamed about it months before it happened. Maybe my father's father had telepathically informed me, since he had hung himself, too.

Jochen tossed in giggling: And then your folks live on the *Gallows Hill*. Sensing Jochen's thoughts about dying, I said: If we'd know how much better we live without the distress of a body, we'd be less scared to let go of our fleshly hull. How can you be sure? I had out-of-body experiences. At about age 20 in our old flat. I was on a different plane in a circle of intimates. We communicated through our hearts. I didn't perceive me as a person anymore, I just was. Um! Yeah. I felt a refreshing well of unity. I knew everything, pure consciousness, unconditional love all around, a thousand times more rejoicing than the love of my loved ones. I was incredibly sad and felt empty when I returned into my body. I asked myself, would I ever find this kind of love in the physical world? I paused in remembrance. Jochen asked: And the other times? Totally different. A neighbor girl had run off with my beautiful ball, a gift for my 2nd birthday. I was practically out of me. The other time, I had visited my parents and was lying in bed in my mother's bedroom when all of a sudden, I was hovering over the door and saw myself lying there. That was the least emotional experience. I just looked at me for a while and then returned into my body.

Jochen missed showing offensive activities against a subject, people in Germany don't like to discuss. I had the feeling that I'd cheered up the old kook. Peter missed out on his usual repellent remarks over my liked subject either. Evidently, he'd also sensed that our conversation had been beneficial for my friend. Jochen hadn't let Norma wait long.

Shortly before the flight back to California, Peter's brother called us at my parents' house. Lisa had been hospitalized: She'd fallen down the stairs and broken a thighbone. This was the second time she had a leg fracture. Since her condition was stable and she was feeling fine, we had not been overly concerned.

Two weeks later, Joachim called again. My mother-in-law was used to sleeping pills and affected by withdrawal symptoms. She had to be taken to intensive care. In the chilly room, she had developed a lung infection. Peter wanted to sue the hospital. I said:

You always say, one crow doesn't pick out another ones eye. You won't have a chance.

On Nov 11, at almost 11:00 a. m., I walked to the gym. I always looked first for somebody working out before I asked the manager for the gym keys. I was lucky. The 911girl was on the treadmill. Have you been on duty last night? Oh my, what a Wednesday! I'd no quiet time at all. It wasn't even my shift. I'd to overtake for a colleague.

Why don't you sleep now? I can't. I still have a day job at a restaurant in Redondo Beach. Speaking of work, I've got to rush. Could you return the key, please? Sure.

Moments later, I got edgy and wasn't in the mood for the machines anymore. I dropped the key in Sandi's mailbox and met Peter in front of our door. You go? I've to fix my Firebird. Inside, the wall clock showed 10 past 11 a. m. I got it from Jerry's garage. Together with a toaster, popcorn maker, pans, trays and dishes it had a more meaningful existence in our apartment. On my way to the bathroom, I passed by our brand new queen-size bed. Out of the blue, I dead stalled! I couldn't move my extremities and collapsed onto the bed. My body felt like filled up with liquid led. The faint fear of being seriously ill only lingered a second. Following a hunch, I asked into the thin air: Lisa is that you? The eerie episode ended on the spot. Arms and legs were lax again. Was it providence that I'd just read Ambrose Worrall's book? He was a clairvoyant working as a mechanical engineer. One of his co-workers was on his way home for lunch hit by a train without realizing his being dead. Coming to work again he was upset since his colleagues did not respond. Ambrose saw him grabbing through the tools and did send him back to the railway crossing. Through this I learned, when we some day irrevocably leave our material body, it can happen we do not consciously notice our being out-of-body. As in sudden death when involved in an accident, having a heart attack, or being intoxicated by alcohol or drugs. Such deceased persons are confused because they want to go on with their habits but are not noticed by their relatives, friends or colleagues. Thus leading to spook.

I felt odd talking to my mother-in-law's spirit: You've left your bedridden body. You can now travel as fast as you think. As the minutes passed, I wasn't as sure anymore. Was that for real? An hour later the phone rang. Jochen confirmed Lisa's passing. I said, it was about an hour ago. Jochen said I don't know. They just called from the hospital. It was exactly 11 minutes past 11 our time when I felt your mother's transition. I called my mother and told her about Lisa's haunting. Isn't it amazing she'd chosen this date? Uh-huh! She knew that Peter has a hard time memorizing dates. He surely won't forget the beginning of carnival. I was paralyzed but only for a sec.

Ma said: When Mamme passed on I had that too. I know. But I was 20 minutes immobile like glued on a chair. My colleagues in the textile factory did not know what to do. Maybe Oma occupied you because you are the most responding. I don't know. My mo-ther's furred voice seemed lost in infinity. Did I sense guilt feelings? I was always her buffer while I did the most work. At age 14, I had to work a year of compulsory labor at the rude farmer Reimuth. Hard labor from daybreak to darken, not enough food, and disgusting eating habits. I slept in a shabby garret.

Ugh! I'm sorry. That was not all. What else?

Once, while sleeping, a black rat bit in my ear. Jeez! Visibly! Yuck! I packed, walked seven miles home, and showed Mamme the bite. And? She had no mercy. I had to walk right back.

That's tough, how could she? They were the times. After hanging up, I remembered our most life threatening time some 30 years ago.

Lydia's leaving and Marianne's arrival

Ludi, the doorbell rang. Whoever could that be? It's Sunday evening!

I have no idea. It's after 8!

We all grew excited while Lydia Augspurger wheezing reached the last stairway. Her daughter asked almost as breathless:

Mamme, how did you get here?

By train. Her son-in-law asked:

Why? What's happened?

Nix, I just wanted to visit you. The entire escapades of her generate whizzed through Alwine's gray matter. Lydia was moonstruck all her life. After a hysterectomy, four years earlier psychic problems had developed. Thyroid troubles may have mixed up her hormones. She'd talked about inner voices ordering her to kill herself.

Composed again, Mama declared pragmatically: There's no train to Eberbach, now. You can sleep in Heini's bed, and tomorrow we'll look further. I'll take a day off tomorrow. We'll drive to Schönmehl. Mamme once had tried to get help from my homeopath in Goddelau herself for another health problem. After the somnolence had demanded its tribute, muted confidence ruled again. While our tall, sad grandma tried to find rest in her grandson's bed, Heini turned from one side to the other on the firm pink patterned chaise. In the middle of the night, he heard a noise and a tiptoeing. Somebody walked into the kitchen and fumbled about the oven. All of a sudden my 11-year-old brother was wide awake! He got up and ran to our parent's bedroom screaming:

Mama, Oma turned the gas on! Mama came out, turned off the gas, led Grandma back into Heini's room and locked the door.

I belly flopped back into the deeps of sleep.

Next day, our parents drove with Oma Lydia to the health practitioner. Mr. Schönmehl said:

I cannot take responsibility for this. My advice is to get your relative in psychiatric care. If you want to, I call the clinic in Heidelberg and get you admittance. Alwine said: If you think so, but I cannot decide this alone. I want to talk to my sisters first. After they'd got Lydia back home, the family gathering turned out to accept the homeopath's advice.

Next Tuesday morn, I sat with Pa on the kitchen table. He yawned so wide behind his Spiegel that his body shuddered. His reading task was in danger this week. On Thursdays, the *Stern*, Pa's other obligatory reading material is issued. To be always well up in is quite stressful. My mother had taken a day off and came out to us beautifully styled.

Ludi, you could have set the table for once! She got a new piece of butter from the refrigerator. The addressed said smiling:

The bread's already on the table. Yes, she replied walking to the kitchenette and getting out a little plate, because your mother had cut it when she fixed the kids' school sandwiches.

Mama? What? Sigh! She put the plate on the table, scraped the butter from the grease-proof paper, glanced at the ceramic wall clock and looked questioning to me again.

Isn't it time? What's cooking? I don't feel well at all. Did you catch a fever? Touching my forehead, she said: I don't think so. My throat hurts when I swallow. Today anything important at school? Nope! Then stay at home and we'll see how you'll feel tomorrow. Um! Or do you want to come with us? We'll pick up Oma and drive her to Heidelberg. Oh, yeah! My face lightened up.

That's all I wanted anyway. Who needs school? Happy, not having to go there, I heavily spread homemade plum marmalade, known as Latwerge onto the zesty rye bread. Oma called it Ladwaye. Papa got up and pranced like a lovesick goat around Mama who walked to the trashcan and then to the sink. He lifted her while she chuckling tried to get off. I was scared, Mama could fall onto the oven.

Let her down! I shouted.

Papa may have only tried to cheer her up. Embarrassed I thought, luckily none of my friends had seen it. It looked too funny. A tall jiggling woman raised over a short man. When she finally got down, Papa patted her butt and asked: Sweetheart, we have some sour milk left-over, haven't we?

Disgusted I called: Eh! Pooh! How can you eat that? Yucky! Papa said: Yummy! It's the best matter in the world. Mama reached him the milk pot. He poured the clabbered milk in a soup plate and broke bread into it. Grandma entered the kitchen. She had left the doors of both flats ajar and evidently overheard that her part of sour milk could have been in danger. She loved the crumbled dish at least as much. They surely had no other competitors in the family. There was enough left, and her son poured the rest in Maria's soup plate. This time the fascinating clicking sound of Oma's dental plate didn't disturb me. I was so happy about my school free day. Usually, I felt disturbed by all kinds of noises. Probably because of the many antibiotics therapy without following reconstruction of the intestines with beneficial bacilli. Thus, yeasts or other invasive parasites perpetually nibbled off my sugars. I tried to scratch them away from eyes, ears and bellybutton. All warm spots itched.

Oma said, on Heini's anorak the zipper's broken. I couldn't help with anything other than a safety pin. Her daughter-in-law grumbled. I had to use it only on the top. On the bottom, it still holds together. Alwine defamed: Typical Holschuh's Marie! Oma propped her look against Mama's. What should I've done? Heini was late already. Um! Of course, with your sewing machine, you would have stitched in a new zipper right away. Since you've to get up every morning before five, I didn't want to wake you up.

Placatory, Mama said: I can do it in the evening. Simply, Heini has other things to wear.

He didn't want anything else.

You always have to have the last word.

Papa didn't pay attention. He'd finished eating and was passionately sunken in his mag.

Two hours later in front of the hospital in Heidelberg, I waited with Papa in the Beetle. He has submerged again in this boring publication which had not even colored pictures. Many years later, when the Berlin wall went down, Pa had donated his 50-year collection of Mr. Augstein's mag to the citizens of Rudolstadt in Thüringen so they can leaf through the West German history.

I got out of the car, stepped into the building, hopped up the steps and opened a door at the end of a dull hallway, smelling of urine.

When I entered, Mama looked perplexed.

How did you find us? Shrugging, I said:

I just wanted to see Oma once again.

In her restless excitement, Lydia walked up and down the corridor seemingly losing her soul on this endless lonely way of despair. The string of her fluttering dressing gown loosened as if trying to draw attention.

Obviously, we both had premonitions. When I out of the blue had arrived in the hospital room, Mama had sensed a certainty in my performance as if I knew it was the last time to see Grandma Lydia. And when Mama saw the dangling string of her mother's dressing gown, she had the pressing urge to take it off.

I was still thinking about that phone call. Had I sensed guilt feelings or anger in my mother's voice? She was not at once for the looney bin and may have blamed herself to have followed the homeopath's advice. But at the time, the public didn't know much about the origin of illnesses or any alternatives. Only much later, we learned from Janet Frame that the stigma and the fear of shock therapy force many patients still further into insanity. The author of two autobiographic novels received more than 200 unrelieved shock treatments. According to the level of angst, each was suchlike an execution. Janet Frame described shock therapy as a "treatment that snatches everything from you and leaves you alone and blind in the nonentity. And like an animal one seeks touchingly the spot that gives solace. Then one wakes up, small, jittery and the tears flow indefinitely and in nameless grief."

Turning from Freeway 101 eastbound to interstate 8 Carole said: What happened to Lisa?

Huh? Where were you? Still roaming the past? I thought how everything started and got caught up in my childhood. I guess I dwell too much in the past. Right.

Yeah, okay, Lisa. She had a hip fracture, died in the hospital of pneumonia. Yeah, that happens often. You better stay out of clinics.

My mother knew that, too. I also had pneumonia at age six weeks. Probably the aftermath of my birth. She kept me at home and may have saved my life.

I couldn't help. Again, my thoughts drifted away to my birth. I was way too late. I was expected to arrive around November 6.

At the end of the month, Alwine still moved her big belly back and forth. She went to her parents' house for delivery in Eberbach. But her mother had no experience with a baby that keeps its relatives on tenterhooks. She sighed:

It is long overdue. We've to do something. What stops it from leaving your womb?

Alwine moaned. I doubt it'll come out on this filthy rainy day. To the day 3 years and 11 months ago Heini came just on time, but this pregnancy is totally different. He had not kicked that much. So I hope it's a girl this time. Alwine had wished for a girl before. Heini's long hair in the first five years proved it. When Maria without asking cut his curly mane, she was furious. She grew up as the oldest of three sisters, in the first years on a ship. Wilhelm Augspurger was an inland navigator until his 2nd daughter Hilde started to crawl. Later, they took care of two little half orphan foster kids. In the icy winter of 1940, at age 16, Alwine sewed a coat for Anneliese, a suit for 5-year-old Willie and a coat for the toddler Gretel. She'd liked the idea of making pretty clothes for her own little girl, too.

Lydia said, look it boxes again! What a fighter. Why doesn't it find the exit? Alwine groaned. What is it, labor pains? No, that noise makes me mad, I'm not used to that any longer. Since 1940 after a long period of having no work, Wilhelm was employed as an ostler. Ever since the family had not much quiet time. The shrill grinding sound of the sandstone in the stone-mason mill Gütschow was the family's nine years ear deafening reality.

Tomorrow, it'll be quiet, thank God it's Sunday. This morning, Wilhelm's workday started as always at 6:00 a. m., with the walk around the house to the attached stable.

Cleaning out the droppings took a little longer than usual. Had the horses digested Alwine's birthing problems? While filling the hay into the fodder crib, Wilhelm thought about the birth of his eldest. He was rather nervous on June 6, 1924, and a ½ year ago, when Hilde's first daughter arrived, he was quite anxious. It looked like the little something wouldn't make it. Heide hadn't even weight three pounds, and Hilde placed her in a shoebox with padding. When Wilhelm had seen the 8-months baby for the first time, he'd said: How'd you do it with such a tall man? She's just a tit-bit. Though he always wished for a son, for his beautiful firstborn's 2nd child, he hoped for a girl.

Gosh had he wished for a boy after Hilde. However, Anneliese has at least guts like a guy. In the reign of Nazi terror, she'd crossed borders under cover of the night to see her Max in Thüringen. Boy did he feel bad when a year after her, the lost fetus had announced a boy. On the other hand, we at least can be sure girls are not used as cannon fodder in some senseless war. Listening to the grinding and crushing sounds of the odd-toed ungulates, Wilhelm thought about his somber war experience at age 21.

Attacking Verdun with heavy artillery, general Falkenhayn had hoped to bleed France to death. Wilhelm's only hope was to be back home soon. Away from the abysmal world of trenches full of stinking mud, blood ripped bowels and genitals. He had thought of his mother. She was certainly not comforted by her sons' being heroic. The growing death toll had devalued the worth of any scarifies. The prospect to die and prepare for it daily and still the rare moments of hope to get away from the shells craters and to keep off the madness. As a soldier of the Fifth Army, under his namesake Crown Prince Wilhelm, he survived the *Hell of Verdun* month after month. As one of the few survivors of the lost battle, coming home in fall 1916 rattled and shaken, he'd never thought of ever having to fight again. Two weary wars were hard to swallow, even for the jolly fellow he was. Nonetheless, Hitler's henchman had shown no mercy when after a nervous breakdown, without more they castrated him. No need for generating unworthy life. He was not tall and blond with blue eyes either: just as plain as Hitler, Goebbels, and Himmler.

Wilhelm thought about the following 9 years as an independent skipper. Would it have been better for his family, if he had remained on the rivers, and seeing his wife and kids only every other weekend? He would have made a lot of money, but wouldn't have seen his kids grow.

In 1918, he had earned a great deal and modernized his parent's house having disposed of the oil lamps and installed electric light all over. However, he had nothing from his self-sacrifice. The oldest, *Crooked Heinrich*, inherited the house. In the early 30's he had forgotten about his brother's generosity when the dire time of unemployment made the Augspurger girls to eat plain bread. When they asked for something on top Lydia used to say put your fingers on top of the bread.

The grinding poor brother had to move with his family to Schönbrunn, in a house that belonged to the community. On the side, it harbored a fire truck, and in one room through a hole, one could look through to the cellar. The *Hole House* was considered a wrecking building. One time Lydia wrote to Hitler's sister Paula about the condition of the house. She obviously had an open ear for poor people and did send a commission to Schönbrunn. But the mean mayor showed them a better house in Ober-Schönbrunn. Instead of writing again, Lydia gave up.

Wilhelm thought about his chances if he had remained a skipper or followed his cousin to America with all his earnings. His relative had done the right thing. Straightening Max's black mane he pictured her far away from the wars with all the fear and horror. She never had to follow senseless orders and go through the strict discipline of a totalitarian system nor to feel declassifying and starvation.

Wilhelm pulled the bridle over Max's head, leather straps between the forelegs and straight across the forehead. As it was Caesar's turn, the common dance with the stubborn stallion started. When Wilhelm tried to get the bit in his mouth, roaring Caesar kicked and acted up as if driven to the slaughter bench. Finally, the bit was uptight in his mouth. Putting the harness on was the most life-threatening part. When it clang on his chestnut back, Caesar pranced and ruffled up. Everything living in his surrounding was in danger. Suddenly the devil broke loose, and run off before Wilhelm could fix him to the lorry.

Heck, always trouble with bloody Caesar, but a good stable-man knows his horses. This one dies for apples. Wilhelm went into the cellar, got an apple, jumped on Max's light brown back and followed the fleeing horse. It took him half an hour to get Caesar back and fasten both horses to the lorry. Lydia came out asking: What took you so long?

I had to capture Caesar. How did you do it?

Wilhelm smiled proudly, with a lasso of course! Huh? No, an apple worked perfectly.

Lydia said that's smart. Just give him more fodder. Same as with kids: always give the bad ones two slices of bread instead of one. It's good that Max has such a pleasant attitude. Yeah, nice and quiet just like Anneliese's Max.

Is Alwine awake? No, she had a bad night. We better let the midwife come tomorrow. When it's quiet, the baby will hopefully come. Now get going, they will wonder why you are not coming. Dragging the empty lorry uphill to the quarry was the horses daily routine. After the lorries had been filled with stone blocks, they'd rolled down the rails with a breaker on top.

Today, most of the 43 quarries around Eberbach had closed down. As a result of the competition with other structure matters of the 32 masons, only the Schmelzer company had lasted.

The forceps delivery took place on the dark-gray rainy Sunday of Nov 27 at 5.15 p. m.

The midwife had pulled me out with a metal thing. She'd called: A girl! But she is blue. What did they expect after my suboptimal prenatal experiences? First the funky birth control, then the frightening moves to make me move. And some 10 months later Patentex-Marianne should hop out as the perfect baby!

My mother was happy to have a little girl. But at about 8 p. m., grandma Lydia was so knocked out that she relaxed her heavy body on the nearest pillow. Luckily the motherly instinct worked perfectly. Before I ended my 3-hours life by suffocation, the beautiful girl saved me from the pillow.

At age 6 weeks I'd caught a lung infection. Sleeping I'd sounded like a purring cat only interrupted by occasional choking signals. The doctor had prescribed penicillin and suget them in Yuma.gested to hospitalize me. But my caring mother had said, no way! The nurses would not pay enough attention. She'd wanted to keep a close eye on me training her ears 24 hours. The slightest change in breathing had made her wake up. All the Nightingales in the world would have been impressed. I certainly was learning at this early age that disease snatches a lot of attention. On the downside, I'd rather passed on lying with feverish convulsions in her lap. I'd also rather cut out the increasing and decreasing sounds like the blowing of a ram horn and the agonizing visions of a rotating earth and rolling fire of apocalyptic measure. The torturous sound was surely no angel song. Was it caused by the drugs, with which in my early years I was filled up to the brim? Some thirty years after my postnatal experience I learned ways to heal that don't lead to illness.

Carole pulled me back to the present again:
Look, the Yuma sand dessert! They make lots of movies here. I glanced out of the side window into the sun's eye, wincing in pain.

That's where Martin rides his buggies. Huh? Remember the Budweiser commercial? Uh-huh! He's German, too. Nice guy. You should meet him. He grows his own veggies.

There was at least one good thing about the Nostradamus prediction: the L.A. traffic. Nomen est omen, Freeways were as free as in the 1950th. But back then, the cars were prettier. Two weeks later, we drove the cars back to L. A. Before we had fun with the Madrid family.

I liked the dogs, the kids, and the easy way of eating. Lots of Mexican food, my favorite baked beans, from the fridge to the counter top, so all family members and guests were helping themselves. Peter got a chiropractic adjustment from Dr. Ricky in his office.

I told Herta about our sour tour. Laughing, she said, I think I can top that story. When I worked as a stewardess, we had an earthquake prediction for L. A. I changed my flight schedule and flew to Tokyo. There, sitting in my hotel room way up in a skyscraper, I endured a pretty strong temblor. The building slid forth and back. That was a strange feeling! It almost made me seasick. No quake in L.A.

Of course, we promised ourselves no more to give anything about predictions we had not foreseen ourselves. Yet I still miss acting on my own ones. Only recently, I dreamed sitting in a fancy black limousine with Peter and two Bavarian friends who are more or less holding the same stocks. I crashed the side of the car on a wall a little. I told the men about my dream. No one sold a single share. When the stock market plunged, I said if I never move on leads, I might not get briefing anymore.

Developing psychic abilities

Nicole called. Could I come right away? I have to tell you something. Of course. In the 25 minutes of waiting for her arriving my curiosity about the thing, Hans-Jürgen's French wife had to tell me grew. She had never called me before though, we had similar likings such as books, writing, and spiritual ambition. We also celebrate our birthday on the same day, yet had never met without our husbands. I prepared tea and snacks.

When Nicole arrived, she said let's sit outside. I took everything on a tray to a table next to the pool. After exchanging the latest family news, Nicole asked: How was TM? Okay. So? You get a mantra and ... where was it? In Manhattan Beach. Would you recommend it?

Um. I don't know. If you wouldn't have Reiki yet, I'd say, get Reiki first.

Is it worth the money? Without the student's rebate, I wouldn't have done it.

Where did you get your initiations?

On Ventura Blvd. in Encino. Joyce Morris is leading the Reiki-Center together with her son in that cozy wooden shopping mall.

How was it for you? An eerie feeling as if an icy wind pulled some of my hairs. They seemed to stand straight up.

No, I mean, did your life change somehow?

I was in seventh heaven, lost 5 lb in a few days and felt in tune with the world. Did you feel lightness?

Yes, like walking on air, I felt an inner glowing and a deep connection with creation, especially with animals. I use to feed the seagulls at the pier. After the initiations, they greeted me with a cacophony while sailing around me. The birds picked the stale bread from my hand and moved along with me when I walked the beach. I felt almost blown away by an extraordinary wave of happiness.

Did Peter feel the difference? Um! I guess, but he's so much involved in his business. Making money is his prime goal, and everything else seems to bother him. But even strangers recognized my elation. Once while feeding the birds, a Japanese tourist approached me. Why you look so happy? I smiled shrugging. Pointing to his camera, he said: Do you mind if I try to catch the radiance of your beautiful blue eyes?

Nicole's voice got a nuance deeper:

Do you still have those psychic powers? Well, yes, but don't we all more or less? Yes, I know, but I haven't experienced anything you have. I found something interesting, a 3-month block seminar. What's it about? Developing psychic abilities. I'd like to go there. Yes, do it. It'll be great for you. No, I'd only do it if you'd come with me.

How much is it? €340 or 360.

Hey! That's quite a lot for finding out, what I already know. I know you have these prophetic dreams and all, but it would be good for you too. You will learn to perceive persons in their momentary environment and to say something about someone by touching a personal object. I tossed in: Psychometry. Well?

Okay, you got me. Good! Yeah, I'll do it. I'm curious to learn something new.

Next morn, after threshing the balls over the net, we walked to the beach and had our breakfast at Good Stuff. With all the endorphins from moving our bodies, we were quite happy and laughed a lot. Peter said:

My mother always said: Birds singing in the morning are eaten by the cat in the evening. That wasn't the first time I detected Peter's a little more common way of prophecy.

Our perfect world was indeed interrupted by a cat the following night. In a vivid dream, I saw our orange Armin Dahl of the cat world imprisoned in a cellar-like room, jumping up a gray roughly timbered door, desperately meowing.

All day long, I was agitated and couldn't concentrate at any work. Again and again, I thought of our little hotspur. I visualized him in the dark dungeon, only lightened by an old white fridge and a washer. In the early eve, I called Germany. My nephew was on the line. I asked: Is everything alright with the cats?

Andreas answered Foxi hadn't come to the feeding twice. My parents were once again traveling to Ibiza, and my brother's son was taking care of the cats. I described Andy the basement and begged him to ask the neighbors. Two days later, he called. Foxi's back. I had to refill the water bowl three times. He didn't eat anything. Animals are wise when it comes to healthy living. They intuitively know eating after fasting wouldn't do them any good. They live according to the rule of nature: only water, a bit grass and the next day solid food again.

Usually, I dream things that happen days, weeks, months or years later. This time it must have been a telepathy. Had Foxi transmitted his despair to his mama? Or was it my soul body drifting to our homeland and detecting the 2-year young tomcat's distress? Or else?

Taryn Krivé, who with sparkling eyes performed her weekly psychic readings on TV, greeted us in her large apartment. Her cute Persian cats played along with the 16 person group. The petite psychic who looked like a 12-year-old girl said, if someone wants one, Susie will have another litter in five weeks.

Before we start the psychic development class, I'd like you to advice not to eat any red meat and not to drink alcoholic beverages before the sessions. It would be best to omit these foods and drinks at all. Taryn got a glass bottle from the fridge and opened it.

This green algae powder called Spirulina is a multivitamin food. It contains 65% vegetable protein, three times more than meat. I take 1-2 teaspoons powder in apple juice or applesauce every day. It was the first time I heard of the supplement that years later, through my dissertation and the books, I had made public in German-speaking Europe and Russia.

Now let's start with psychometry. I'm going to do a meditation first. Then you work in three groups with each group getting a hat. You put in anything from you, a ring, a watch, a chain or whatever personal object you have with you. Then grab a piece, and try to get information about the person, verbalize whatever comes into your mind.

First, let me tell you some about this phenomenon. We live and evolve in energy fields. An object also has an energy field and transfers knowledge regarding its history. We also emit a certain energy transferring to frequently carried objects: crystallized matter.

Via scanning such an object we can learn about the character or the life experience of a person. It may involve past, present or future because spiritual dimensions seem to be a continual state. Any questions? Okay, now sit comfortably, take a deep breath and think you are a tree with your branches reaching out for the sun's rays. Your leaves take up moisture from the air. Your roots grow deep into the earth and take up the essential nutrients.

Instead of a tree, you can visualize yourself in a huge pipe that's fixed in the earth and goes way up into the sky. Feel a bright light coming from above, bathe in it. Any questions? No?

Then go ahead, grab anything from the hat. I got a ring. Instantly, I felt a heat, then cold, followed by heat again. Offhand I said, the owner of the ring may have a problem with the stomach. A dark haired short woman in her 40th identified ownership. I had the feeling of something serious. I said I recommend you to see a doctor soon. She said, I already have an appointment because of a stomach problem. The woman didn't come back to the seminar.

The next test to prove our psychic abilities, we did in groups of two. Taryn put me together with Tom, an American with multinational roots. She thought of us as her most mediumistic talented students. Think of a certain person you know very well. Just tell your partner his or her first name. Write everything down what your partner verbalizes. Then change places. Tom said, his name is Hal, short form for Harold. In front of my inner eye, I saw a pale blond man in a light blue checkered wind-breaker, looking like my father. I said: He looks German. Without any respond, Tom asked, how old is Hal? I said around 50ish. My partner made notes but didn't give me any feedback. I thought all my finds were wrong, but then I touched a spot on Tom's head and asked: What's that? My partner lost his cool: Um! I wasn't conscious about that anymore. Hal had an accident. On this spot, his hair doesn't grow anymore. You must have seen him from above. If you'd stand in front of him, you wouldn't have seen it. Okay?

How does Hal's house look like? I said: High. Either it has at least three stories or it stands on a hill. Tom said both is correct. That's strange! What? The Grimm brother's Frau Holle just popped into my mind. Tom grinned agreeing: Every morning, Hal's Frau shakes out her feather beds. Wow!

Can you see the color of the house? I see blue, but also green, maybe turquoise?

Blue is correct, on the walls grows ivory.

Wow! Quite an amazing result!

Taryn came close to overhear our conversation. Hal is indeed a 53-year-old German professor. Incredible. Now, you. I visualized my gray-haired mother and said, her name is Alwine. Tom said I see a pretty woman with dark curls, but her original hair is straight. She's wearing a self-tailored elegant suit. But strange! What? She's wearing old lady shoes. Oh, well! She's a sharp tongue and a wonderful soprano, likes to garden. She does things with her hands. Her favorite is to make potteries. That's it. Wow! Great job! Everything's correct but the pottery. She paints stones and fabrics and does potter about, but I've never seen my mother making pottery. Mother? Yes!

Annoyingly Tom said: Why Mother? I believed she's your girlfriend. She looked like 33.

Yes, at this age, she was exactly as you described her. Tom was still disappointed.

Einstein's findings time is nonlinear rushed into my mind. There's no past nor future. On the immaterial plane, everything plays in the here and now. About a year later my mother informed me that she learned the pottery handwork and started to create vases, flower pots, dishes, and bird's drinking troughs.

Since we still had time, Tom said, let's do another one. Okay, try Peter. I visualized my husband with his gray receding hair. Tom said: I see a handsome young man with full brown hair. He's got overalls on and a hand-knitted sweater with deer here. He stroked his upper chest. I mentally agreed since his mother had knitted him beautiful garments. His hands are besmeared with oil. Okay? Taryn said: It's time to come to an end. I said:

It's like before. You've seen my hubby during an apprenticeship at a car dealership.

On my way home, I asked myself about the just experienced phenomenon. Oma Lydia passed on when my mother was 32, Peter's father when his oldest son was 27. Boy, was he upset when he had to see Peter slaving away on cars instead of studying or having a position in his own company. Was he the sender of the telepathic information? To me, it made the most sense that Tom channeled Ernst-Peter Meyer and Lydia Augspurger from the ether to the material sphere. Our deceased loved ones still seek to speak with us through their telepathic efforts. But how are most of us reacting? With our ignorance.

The Para Research Inc. offered an astral research for anyone who knew the hour of birth. I had still hoped to find something about myself. So I ordered my astral portrait. I glanced over the first page:

... Sun in Sagittarius... Moon in Pisces. Your astrological combination confers upon you the gifts of gentleness and imagination. On page 6 of the 35-page pamphlet, I read: *... you are an intellectual worker with a keen and clever disposition to scientific research.*

I thought about my unfinished dissertation in Gerontology about the old age self-image of working and nonworking women. Since I didn't follow through with my scientific work, I can only hypothesize that women with a job have a more positive perspective of their old age than housewives.

Uranus symbolizes originality, freedom and the breakup of crystallized patterns and concepts. The manifestation of this planet's energy is unorthodox and unconventional, it's ultimate goal being the destruction of conventional attitudes to make way for the development of the new order. Your approach to life is unique, and you consider it totally your own. Freedom of self-expression and the need for change are very important. You dislike routine and anything that does not permit a free, spontaneity flow of expression. In this respect, you tend to reject society and the status quo because of the limitations they impose upon you.

WOW! Truly there's something to astrology!

Your relationships are often as erratic as your personality. You are attracted to the unusual and exciting in people and will seldom remain in one place or with any one person. As long as your environment provides a certain amount of change and does not become static, you are satisfied.

Aha! That's why I still stick with Peter. He allows for a lot of change, indeed.

You have a natural ability for understanding science. You have probably found it difficult to deal with people in authority as you have your own way of doing things. Work that requires original thinking and allows you to express your creative potential would give you the greatest success in life.

I'm still waiting for my water crystal photo research I described in *Water-Code Cracked?* to be recognized. My next work after the Cranberry book in English will be one solely about the water crystal photos since my findings are truly original.

Page 9 also didn't tell me anything new:

Memory is strong and of a pictorial nature; you remember many details of life, especially if they relate to emotions. That's true too.

I once asked my mother: Do you remember an occasion when you caught me in the middle of the night, sitting in my baby's bed? No.

I'd played with my things in the dark. All of a sudden the door opened. I saw your arm turning to the light switch. In the split second from dark to light, I thought, how will she react to my sitting in bed? What could I do? I knew you wanted me to sleep. But to lay down without your seeing it was impossible. When you caught my look, I suddenly burst out with loud laughter. You joined in laughing and misheard the falling stone from my heart.

You'd said with a low calming voice, but now lay down and sleep!

Well, I don't remember.

I even recognized the swinging of pride in your intonation. You thought what a positive little girl, not fearing the dark. Was this the dawn of my sunny disposition? I learned an essential lesson: laughing kills angst.

My mother said: I guess I did a lot wrong.

Why? Um! You haven't been in a "how-to-be-a-perfect-parent school" since there's none. So you don't remember it at all? No!

I see it crystal clear as if it would have been yesterday: the bed behind the door, your arm, then you opened the wardrobe ...

That can't be, yelled Ma. Impossible! Why?

The arrangements, that was still in the Zeppelin-house. We moved from there when you were 9 months old! How can you memorize anything from that early age?

Peter entered the apartment, pulling me out of my dwelling on thoughts of the past.

Guess who's visiting? You tell me.

Willie called from the Huntley's. He's flying this route often now. Marita and Bianca are with him. Oh, good! When will we see them?

Tomorrow, they want to visit the Paul-Getty museum. If you want to accompany them, they'll pick you up at around two.

Why, great! Yep! What a nice change. I will be driven around, this time. Oh! I almost forgot to greet you. He reminded me twice not to forget. Who?

Toshin. The pic of a bearded Dutch talking to Peter at the Pomona classic car exhibition flashed before my eyes. We'd been interested in a red MGB Convertible, but the owner wasn't there. I offered Peter to wait at the car. He said, no, come along, we'll look for it later. Toshin's wife Urga had the same idea and managed to buy it. We had a customer, so we got it from them for a few hundred bucks more.

The Rohdes picked me up in an all-American battleship. The jumbo jet flight engineer had bought the Oldsmobile Cutlass to be able to cruise around whenever he flew to L.A. Used to big machines, Willie would not drive any small cars. We shipped on, our eyes on the street that vibrated under the sizzling Californian sun. Did you buy any cars, lately? We got Yul Brynner's Gullwing. Really?

Yep! It's silver with green leather. Good condition. How much? 80 grand. Too expensive for me. Anything, I can afford? How about Grace Kelly's 190SL? You're kidding! I know it sounds fantastic, but it's true, we have that, too. By the way, how much is the entrance fee? What for? For the museum. Marita said with a broad smile: It costs nothing at all. Willie said, you just have to call up in front when you come with a car. There's limited space. (Now, in the new huge Paul Getty Museum on the hill behind the Holiday Inn on Freeway 405, no more parking problems.)

How's it financed? Paul Getty was an oil multimillionaire. In his legacy, he'd ordered the museum to acquire fine arts for several million dollars each year. The building is a replica of *The Villa of the Papyri* that was destroyed by lava. Really? I said. I've seen the remaining fragments on my trip with the Achille Lauro in the early 80th. Oh really? Uh-huh! Wow! Getty even copied the herb garden. Inside, Willie said, oh there's something new. Have you been here before?

Yes, we from Lufthansa often come here. I like to check on the new antiques.

Is that an oxymoron? Huh? New antiques. Yeah! You can learn a lot here, but you have to know, not everything is listed correctly.

Have you seen the adjacent park? Uh-huh! It's very relaxing. Gandhi's ashes are there.

Not only there. Look, just what I said. It says the chest's from the 18th century, that's not true. On the fixings, you can see it's built in the early 19th century.

Next day, we all went to the Santa Ana fleamarket. After picking up Bernd and Petra we had a boat's ride and went to a classic car show in Newport Beach. Peter said: This Jaguar could be a good deal. I said, my Renault Florid was also white with a red soft top. Peter bought the E-Type Roadster, most probably not out of sentiment. A few yards from it I detected a familiar looking mechanic plastic egg. The only door in front with the attached armature and the steering wheel hang wide open.

Excitedly, I said, my mother had driven such an orange colored Isetta. Peter said: Forget it!

Too dangerous, said Marita, turning away. I would never drive one like that. Me neither. Well! But until age 37, my mother only had a driver's license for motorcycles. This one and the Go-go were the only cars she was allowed to drive.

Next day, Marita and I rented bicycles and cruised the strand via Manhatten Beach to El Segundo. On our way back, we had the opportunity to watch a film crew working at a beach house. I said: Last time, I walked in the Venice Beach crowd a guy gave me a phone number from a film agency. Maybe that's the movie I could have been an extra. Didn't you call?

No. Didn't I tell you? I had a dream, in which I was a male actor. It felt real. I'm sure it was a past life. What's sense of making movies again? It would be another experience.

Yes, you may be right. I should have been an extra at least once. But I have too much to do, always looking for autos. Peter likes me to come along. In case he finds a car we can take it right with us. By the way, next month we'll have a rented house with a guest room.

I didn't know, you look for a house.

We didn't, our coworker Volker told us. He owned the house right opposite. Oh, could I send Bianca in her fall holidays? Sure. It'll be a break from business. She doesn't know what to do. She gets bored in Eichen. No, kidding, living in the middle of nowhere! That's because big houses in the cities are too expensive. And small houses are not for men managing jumbo jets. When he's cramped in the cockpit all day, he likes a place to spread out.

A few weeks later I picked up Bianca from LAX in a black 190 SL. I had to drive it since Peter needed the Toyota. Bianca said: Wow! Black with red leather! Is that Grace Kelly's?

No, we sold Gracia's right after you'd left.

A guy just was waving, do you know him?

I didn't look. He was cute. We get a lot of attention with the vintage cars, but I'd prefer my Toyota's easier handling. Now, we are almost there. Here Bel Air North Gate leading to the enclave of the very rich. Here starts Sherman Oaks. Now we have to drive half way down Scadlock Lane. We live as the cross flies less than a mile from Shirley MacLaine's estate in Encino. Oh! Living in L.A. you are surrounded by stars. We've more traffic than Shirley, but a spectacular view. Oops! I forgot to get the tires against the curb. You have to do that when you park on a hillside in an earthquake area. Inside, Bianca giggled:

How funny, a pool office.

Yes, we didn't get the desk through the door, so we left it right on the covered patio. Cute!

I think, we are in the wrong business.

Why? Our Landlord has a much healthier way of making money. Huh? Collecting houses. How? He jogs through the streets, and whenever he sees a for sale sign, he stops to negotiate prices. Does he also sell houses? I don't know. There was only a for rent sign. He may sell them when the real estate prices are skyrocketing. That way he can use the profit to buy more houses when the economy gets sour, and the house prices are falling.

Like Monopoly. Right!

Don't you mind Mama's sending me here?

Why should I? For me, it's like a vacation. Peter lets me stay at home quite often. We can do fun things, treating the little girl within. How about a tennis match tomorrow? Why? Yes! We can go to Hermosa Pier afterward and do some shopping. There's a $5-Store. I got two beautiful bikinis there. You'll like it. I still love to spend time in Hermosa Beach.

Next day after breakfast, we got tennis outfits on and left the house with shields and big sunglasses. We loaded the 190SL with the racquets and towels. After the match, we had an avocado vegetable pita at a beach restaurant.

We entered a boutique right next to the parking. Heading back to the car, I snatched the flyer fixed under the windshield wiper. My first and only parking ticket in the US! I had forgotten to re-feed the parking meter. Such a gorgeous day and such an annoying ending. Bianca asked:

Where can I buy a bottle of champagne?

You are 16. You won't get any alcohol.

Yeah, but you can buy it for me. Sure!

My mother told me twice not to forget it.

I've to go to Trader Joe's anyway.

Who's that? A deli with lots of health-food owned by one of the Albrecht brothers. Aldi, you mean? Yes. The emporium empire their mother had started. An employee once told me, Mr. Albrecht comes for inspection once a year. He always travels with 3 similar looking men all wearing trench coats and hats. Why? One brother was kidnapped in the early 70th. The Albrecht's paid 7 million for his release.

Oh wow!

That's the price for being extremely wealthy.

Roaming through the fruits and vegetables, I fetched lots of fresh food. At the time, I used to treat all my guests in the morning with a plate of fresh fruits, arranged in ever changing mandalas. I got some yogurt, sprouted grain bread, cheese, smoked salmon and a bottle of red wine. On the checkout counter, a woman at about age 25 glanced at the 2 bottles saying:

ID, please! You're kidding! Jane straightened in her gray t-shirt. Snappy, she demanded: Your ID, please!

I giggled. Why? I'm 38.

I took off my sunglasses. Don't you ... well, I guess you are serious. Cheering up, I searched my pocket. You made my day. I was just upset getting a parking ticket. This makes up for the trouble. Here, the ID. Luckily, I had it on! Did I say sure? One never can be sure.

Perfect psychic: Hilde running into John Hudson

On Christmas, Hans-Jürgen and Nicole had invited us to Brentwood. Peter had met the lawyer after an accident he had with Uli. The latter needed legal advice. A taxi had bumped into Uli's car, but he hadn't gotten a dime. The cab driver was uninjured! While still living in Germany, we were vacationing in HJ's house, twice. There were also other guests frequently. For Nicole and the three kids that must have been too close for comfort, sometimes. I realized this only after we had settled in L.A. When I had to handle the flow of guests myself I felt empathic with my friend. Is it a broader exegesis of an eye for an eye?

When we arrived at Bluegrass Lane, a petite elder lady was already sitting in front of the fireplace. HJ's introduction, this is lovely little Hilde from Bel Air, raised a pitiful smiling. While I shook her hand, he stated proudly, Hilde's husband was a rocket engineer. He came over with Wernher von Braun.

Taking turns looking at us, he added:

You look like sisters. I also sensed a familiarity with this woman and asked, what makes you think that? HJ shrugged, just a feeling.

Except for the curls, we don't look alike.

Changing the subject, I asked, why are you holding your cheek? It's swollen, I have a terrible toothache. Have you seen a dentist?

Why, yes. It's an abscess on a molar.

Why didn't he do anything? The swelling has to ease before he can remove the tooth.

If you want, we can try Reiki. What's that? It's the channeling or transfer of cosmic healing energy. Hilde looked oddly open. Well?

It's a hands-on healing system that harmonizes and balances. She said: Okay go ahead, it won't harm. You'll be my very first guinea pig. Well! Let's try it out. I held my hands about half an inch away from Hilde's cheek, avoiding to get into her silky blond locks.

All of a sudden, I felt a strong itching!

Hey! What's that? My heart at a gallop, I giggled, gosh, it's almost unbearable. A strong electromagnetic energy field between my hand and Hilde's cheek had built up. I sensed the importance to remain in this position until the vibration eased. So what happened to your husband? HJ told me before that your Heinz had Alzheimer, and you took care of him. Hilde smiled, her eyes searching nirvana:

He passed on three years ago after eight long years of slowly changing his personality.

I'm sorry! It must have been hard for you.

I got used to it. I couldn't go anywhere without him. No visiting friends, no shopping, had to take him with me like a kid.

But you couldn't take him in a shopping cart.

No, Hilde chuckled, I left him in the car. Luckily, he never found out how to get off the seat belt. Oh! Nix with *dem Ingeniör ist nichts zu schwör.* Tcha! But at home, it was difficult. Once, he came out to me in the garden, worn out looking but happily smiling he said: Well, that was heavy work, he said. Satisfied with his finished project, he'd led me to the bedroom. There I saw the piece of work he'd accomplished. The mirror and all my perfume bottles on the dressing table were broken and laid around shattered. Jeez! You may have spent too much time there. Well! Three years ago, he died. Though I'd gotten used to the situation, his passing was a relief. My blood pressure is still high at times.

A week later, Hilde called. I asked: How is your tooth? You won't believe it. In the morning after the party, the pain was gone. I still went to the dentist. He was astonished and said, there's nothing anymore. We can save the tooth. But that's not why I called. Yeah?

Do you know a good fortune teller? Why?

I'm thinking of going back to Germany.

Oh, no! Why? When you are older, it's better in Germany. What's better? The infrastructure for once. True. I don't need a car there. Here, it's always nerve-wracking to go to DMV to do the tests. All the time my blood pressure rises. What if my eyes get worse and I can't drive anymore? I'd be buried in Bel Air. So do you know any psychic?

I've never consulted one, but once I attended a group seance at Every Woman's Village. We were instructed to bring photos of deceased persons and something from them. I took my mother-in-law's picture and the diamond ring she gave to me. The psychic held it in her hand, looked at the photo and said: Oh wow! Well, you'll get a huge amount of money in October. Big money. Hopefully, it'll be invested wisely. Did you get the money? Yes, there was a property deal pending. It seemed to fell through, but it didn't.

So let's go to her. Okay, I'm going to call Marilyn right away. I still have her ad.

A few days later, we drove to North Hollywood. Hilde said I know a German bakery in the area. They have the best pretzels and a butcher who's known for his delicate meat in aspic. Um!

Arriving at the door of the psychic's tiny apartment, the blond woman greeted us:

Oh, hi, you are sisters, aren't you?

I swallowed the displease and the question, do I look that old? Our mother would have had a 30-year birthing pause. I asked:

How did you get that idea?

Marilyn winced. That was my first thought. We sat down on a little round table. The psychic sat opposite to us.

Do you want to know something specific?

Yes, I'd like to move back to Germany. I've friends in Düsseldorf and Frankfurt, and all my relatives live in Potsdam. I'd like to know, where I'd be better off. Marilyn handed the cards to Hilde. Please, shuffle.

Opening the cards, she said, I don't see you going to Germany. I don't see any moving in the next ten years. There's a heart knight. A lover is in the picture, some significant other. We giggled. Marilyn went on without losing her composure, you know the man from the past, you'd loved him before. I even hear wedding bells. Hilde released a smeared sound.

Calmly, Marilyn went on, yes, it's definite, within three months your destiny will change. I also see all your relatives in jail, but don't worry, they'll be free soon.

Hilde looked amused and a bit off. I said:

Since I'm here, why don't you read me, too?

Sure. Before Marilyn handed me the cards, she said absentminded, you've something to do with a king, I don't understand, oh let it be.

Shuffle the cards and part them in three piles. Okay. Are you Jewish? Not in this lifetime, but who knows for sure? Your mother is very pleased with what you're doing. Huh? My mother's still alive. Marilyn said firmly, no doubt, it's the mother figure. She had uterus cancer. Oh, you have contact with my grandmother Maria. She had a hysterectomy and was also my godmother.

What's your grandfather's name?

Ludwig. Um! No, that's not him. I forgot to give Marilyn my other grandfather's name, and she didn't ask.

You are related to Doris Day. Huh?

True. Ha ha! How?

From your mother's side. Oh listen, there's something with your brother, a kind of legal thing, quite odd, but don't worry, the affair will not have any legal consequences. Years later, my mother told me about the grotesque anecdote of my intoxicated relative.

Outside the psychic's apartment my friend said more amused than outraged, we'd better saved the 25 bucks. I don't know any man with whom I'd start a love affair. I also don't know any prisoners. This foretelling is a farce.

You're right, related to Doris Day, ha ha.

If I had checked on Doris Day, who'd already lived in Carmel as supposedly my father's relatives, I may have examined it more closely.

A few days later, Hilde called:

I want to invite you for a duck dinner. Can you come next Saturday? Hans-Jürgen and Nicole are coming, too.

Oh, great, of course, we'll come. We didn't know where Hilde lived so we drove to

Brentwood and arrived together with the Altenburgs at 418 Cascada Way. HJ rang the doorbell saying, you'll be delighted. Hilde makes the cris-piest duck west of the Mississippi. He rang a 2nd time. A beaming female with rosy cheeks opened. Hilde!?! Are you in love? The words just slipped out of my mouth. Hilde's elated laughter made HJ glance at her flush porcelain complexion. With the sharp eyes of a terrier, our lawyer friend tossed in: One could think so. Hilde ignored our frank statements. Smiling graciously she said: Come in. I've got to get back into the kitchen. The ducks are almost ready. Marianne would you please come with me? You could whip the cream for the dessert. What will we have? An orange sorbet, but not the liquid, watery kind. I make it with lots of heavy creams. Yum! Sounds delicious! Hilde gave me the hand mixer and a dish. Right off, I spilled a few drops on Hilde's midi woolen skirt and wiped them away as fast as they got there. Never mind! Though it was only the third time I'd met Hilde, I felt at home in her old-fashioned kitchen. I took the red cabbage, the potato mash, and the cranberry sauce to the table. Returning, I said, the dining room looks like from a castle. Hilde said it's just a replica. Our original furniture was bombed out in Berlin. All our belongings were gone. How awful.

That wasn't the worst. I'd hidden three days behind an oven in the cellar. Why? Because we knew the Russians were there and they raped every woman they got to hold off.

Were you ... where was Heinz?

He was kidnapped by the Americans. But at the time I didn't know anything about him.

So what happened? Hilde shrugged off with a lost facial grimace: After three days I was very hungry.

Two days after the duck dinner Hilde called. Guess what? Huh?

You were right. I'm really in love.

What? How so? It took place in the parking lot of the Bel Air Supermarket. My shopping cart was one of those intractable sorts. You know, the ones that you've problems on the straight already. But I'd to push this stubborn wire donkey up the hill. As I struggled a tall, attractive gentleman came by to help me. He looked at me and asked astounded: Hilde, is that you? I called: Wow, who was he? You won't believe it, the actor John Hudson whom I secretly admired, some thirty years ago.

So Marilyn was right! In what movies was he in? John was one of the soap opera doctors in *General Hospital*, but most successful in *The Racer* costarring Kirk Douglas. They were competitive car racers. John even got an Oscar nomination. Wow! But for the big success he's missing the synagogue key.

I guess I haven't seen him.

Why don't you come next Saturday with Peter? I'll make my famous hazelnut cake. Then you can get to know each other. You have much in common. Wow! Marilyn wasn't only right about the new old love. When the Berlin Wall went down, Hilde's relatives were free! Shame that we had not experienced that extremely emotional time in Germany.

5 foot 10, slim with full blond hair, Hilde's handsome lover greeted me with a compliment, you look like Jane Fonda. Really? Yes!

The blue eyes and cheeks. From my father.

Jane got her eyes also from her father.

You've something in common with Peter, Hilde said. He was a race driver. John said:

Oh, but I only in the movies. I got to know Phil Hill. A very nice guy. I contacted him to get acquainted with my role.

The 5 inches high tart with the whiskey and lemon soaked sugar crust did sit enthroned on the coffee table. Covered with the chocolate mesh it looks like a piece of art, I marveled. Proudly beaming Hilde replied: Do you want a big piece? Yes, please!

It's very delicious, John tossed in, even I eat it though I stopped boozing.

How come? I asked. I just cannot handle it. Too many strange experiences. One was with my buddy Jack Palance. How did you meet him? Did you make a movie together? No, we were both pilots during WW II in Italy. So, what did you do? We celebrated in my 71 Cadillac. We drank more than half a gallon of vodka. When we woke up next morn, we had not the slightest idea where we were. Peter laughed out loud.

Chewing my first bite, I said, yum, that's the way, I like whiskey! Hey, is that yummy! My mother made a similar cake when we had the restaurant using 10 eggs, the egg whites were beaten, 6 tablespoons sugar, 350g freshly ground hazelnuts, and 2 tbsp flour. She used only the lemon in the sugar covering. By the way, I thought the booze was causing Peter's hair loss, but you still have full hair.

I used to do headstands.

Yes, that may help. It also could be psychological caused. Too much stress. Meditating would be good. Eagerly Peter said, the booze helps me to relax.

Later, when we went to the living room, John turned to me and said absentminded as if reconsidering: You have to meet Marlon's sister. Why? You two seem to swing on the same wavelength. Jocelyn is a great therapist.

Where does she live?

In Santa Monica Canyon. She converted her garage into a seminar area. I'm going to call her right away. John disappeared in the guestroom. A minute later, he called me in. I listened to Jocelyn's centered voice: Can you come next Friday, the 26th? Why, yes.

Up to now, there are only 8 confirmations. With up to 10 persons the seminars working terms are fine. Okay, I'm looking forward. It takes place from Friday 5:00 p. m. to Sunday afternoon. Okay, I'll be happy to meet you.

Coming back, I asked:

How did you meet Jocelyn?

We played together. In a film?

No, on stage, in New York, on Broadway.

You still have contact?

Yes, I help her sometimes. She'd bad luck with her men. They'd beaten her quite often. I'd taken her to the doctors. Why would one stick with beating spouses? I ran away, even as a kid. Pa never raised a hand against us, but once it seemed close. When I did shake a thermometer to produce a false fever for Heini so he could skip school, I broke it. By running away, I spared Pa the undergo. Had Jocelyn beaten her spouse in a former life and needs to feel how it is the other way round?

On our ride back home, my thoughts drifted to the acts and obligations of the past:

Sermons and Neckar rides

This wet winter lasts forever, Grandma said into the thin air. A little later, come on, Dear! The divine service starts soon. Oh pleeease, Oma, let me sleep a little longer. I dreamed the Eberbach-Oma was in the hospital.

Well, you know the divine service. Why can't I stay home today? Why do I have to go every Sunday? I can pray in my bed, too.

I know, I always say, we don't have to go to church to be good Christians. As long as we can rest our heads onto the pillow without regrets about anything we've done during the day we can sleep as good Christians.

I thought, if I can't live or sleep according to Oma's opinions, how could I profit from 'em? Every Sunday, the same old story. Jannche, get up now, they're all sitting on the table yet. Oma brushed my hair. Patronizingly she said: Uncle Heiner's coming. Well, at least time would go by fast. Heinrich Roth's preaching wasn't any shorter, but interesting. We used to count his different word repetitions while suppressing our laughter. Every 2nd or 3rd sentence, Heini's godfather added: isn't it? Truly? Or: and the like more. We were hoping he'd reach 100. The highest counting ever was 79.

I plumped onto the chaise and stared at the set table. Pa asked:

Have you had good dreams, little onion?

Papaaa! This half sang warning not to overdue came with a curled nose and rolled up eyes. Very witty! If I ever could sleep longer, I could finish them too.

Papa ground the coffee in the squeaking mill and tossed the full drawer into the filter on top of the coffeepot. I pulled my icy feet under my butt and glanced at Oma's hand. On the kitchen cabinet's working plate she stirred Kaba into the milk and put the mug in front of me. Her stretched out arm yielded an expression of disgust on Mama's face.

Wanna you go to church with this sweater?

Why? The sleeves look like polished!

Insignificantly looking, the addressed shrugged her shoulder. That's why you never use oven cloth. Maria took her daughter-in-law's fussy quittance with another I-don't-care gesture. She paused and said:

I can tuck them up. She gathered a sarcastic:

Typical Holschuh's Marie.

With my awakened compassion, I wiped the drowsiness from my eyes and said: Oma, you still have that pretty wine red sweater. It's brand new and goes well with black.

That's dark blue sweetheart, corrected Papa. I thought Ma is the colorblind in our family.

Oma stroke lightly over her tidy woolen shoulder strap skirt that Mama had made her just recently. She'd bought the fine fabric from the fabric factory she worked in as a thread maker. On sales days for the workers, she'd frequently bargained some tasteful cloth and proved her tailoring skills.

I was proud of Mama's looks and felt sorry for Oma who could have made more of herself. In her big closet loosely hang two dresses, two apron dresses, two skirts, three blouses, a jacket, two jerseys and a winter coat. The shelf compartments consisted of a few sweaters, some undergarments and nightgowns, a few handkerchiefs with crocheted seams and two handbags. Mama who'd better hung half of her wedged wardrobe content there too, commented on this poor selection: My mother-in-law lives in higher regions. She doesn't care about the outward being. The kettle whistled and blue hissing flames licked forth. Mama got up in her energetic jerky manner. Her chair slid over the freshly waxed marmoreal lino. Its legs screeched against the ivory tiles. Eee! With both my forefingers I shut my ears. Heini said the girls in our class scream same way when the teacher scrapes with chalk on the blackboard. Switching off the gas, Mama lifted the kettle and carefully poured water onto the coffee scented heap. She opened the baker's oven. The noon before, I had warmed my icy feet in it. Now, a delightful roast smell filled the flat. Mama said: Almost done.

Seppel argued with his mirror image. The Sundays were no sunny days for the lovebird because he had to remain in the cage. Papa poured just a little water into the filter saying: If you fill it up right away, the aroma suffers.

I know, Papa, you told me before. I wormed my navel with the thumb. Itching again?

She was up all night, trying to expel her dinky droppings, Oma said. We've to purge.

In the living room, the couch table was already lifted up and extended to dining table position. On the white linen, the finest white porcelain shone with golden borders. With guests, we always ate in the living room. While the Sunday's roast roasted to the end, Oma cleaned Mama's homegrown Brussels sprouts and peeled the potatoes. The washed and dried salad waited with dressing on the side in the fridge. Papa snuffling at the milk before pouring it into his coffee said: Heiner comes in his leucoplast bomber. Lloyd LP 600, added Heini drily. After Papa had finished eating he lustily engrossed in his beloved *Spiegel*. Hey, you've to listen to this. Papa's feisty facial expression changed into a Faustus smile. Homecoming Schörner, the loud comrade, ah, the Soviets have pardoned the sucker. Who's that? I asked, not really interested. The boring mag was not at all my cup of tea. The Bloody Ferdinand, the Butcher of Riga, this crazy guy doesn't stop at anything. He'll probably now spy for the Bolshevist. This fanatic Hitler worshiper will be a great commie, ha ha! Now he can discipline the people's police. Mm... mm... mm... ta... ta... ta... there... he gave the cadets ice cold tactic lectures.

What are cadets? They are soldiers drilled to be officers candidates. How do you know?

Why! Listen! Though I didn't fight, I had the basic training, there you learn that. While reading further, Papa burst out in a hearty laugh. His face turned red and his body trembled. When the tears run down his cheeks, we were all infected by his utterance.

That crazy guy burned everything, by accident even the suitcase of the commanding general. He must have had fun, ha, ha. Mama said: They'd better taken a shrink along.

After a while of reading by himself, Papa said, stifling his laughter, one of three radar sites of a tank division had defected and should be brought to Libau in Kurland. On its way, the radio command tank had to stop on a cross way. „Schörner stopped the radar man, demanding the march orders. To Libau you want, is written here ... nonsense, take flight you want"... "Um! Colonel general Sir I have orders to drive to Libau."

Schörner: "Who had signed the march orders? The first general-staff officer". Then tell the first general staff officer that the traffic discipline of his division leaves much to be desired. Schörner turned around to his military policeman and ordered: Fuel!"

Haha! "The gendarme dragged in the fuel canister with 20 liters. Schörner himself poured petrol over the command tank and lightened it." Hahaha! "Till the end of the war, the tank division held hitherto only two mobile radio stations." Hahaha! We laughed more about Papa's droll behavior than about the weirdo Nazi. His jolting belly and trying to hold his wheezy laugh was hilarious. Oma said, while putting the butter back into the fridge, this is unbelievable. Mama said with a mocking look: With such bozos, they wanted to win the war. Wait, oh that's awful, Schörner was highly noise irritable. He shot barking dogs and punished coughing sentry posts ... ah, this is insane ... in the polar sea, he tore open a shot mule's mouth and looked at the tongue.

Since it was missing, he called in all the first sergeants from all the unities in the area and initiated a search action for the gone tongue.

I asked: Why had the mule no tongue?

Why! Haha! There were lots of hungry mouths. That tender piece of meat, Oma said amused, of course, it was already in a soldier's tummy. Naturally! Papa gasped as an asthmatic and tears were running over his cancer red face. His funny noises in the very back of his nose came out as a fine drizzle which dabbled onto the page of the magazine. I bent down a little and examined the strange uniformed man with the glasses on the front page. Heini said that fire-hazard military monster could make a funny movie. Mama replied:

Yes, but now it's enough, we've got to go. Smiling jeeringly, she added, that wasn't the right preparation lecture for the divine service.

My father started the sermon with happenings of the past week and consequently added:

We should stop all aggression and follow Jesus' advice to turn the other cheek. Mahatma Gandhi said, "an eye for an eye blindfolds the world." He showed us how to get out of the craziness. By his non-aggressive resistance and his famous fasting for freedom, Gandhi provoked the English Empire to change the laws. Through passion and fellow feeling, he'd led India into independence. And that is what we all can apply in our daily routine. Let us act according to the Great Soul's words: The way of love and truth always wins. Let us sing the hymn *The Power of Love*. Papa's favorite song was also Mama's pet part. With her bell light soprano, she'd led the small community to higher spheres. Oma Lydia was a driving force in the family's converting from evangelism. In the old days, the church had a choir.

She sang he played the harmonium. About a year before they met she'd seen him in a photo album as an adolescent. She had the strange feeling that this boy would play a role in her life.

At this age, Alwine and Ludwig met in the church.

Now, let's welcome our dear brother Heinrich Roth from the beautiful wine-growing Bergstraße. The addressed raised his dark haired silver interwoven head and walked to the desk. I liked his sonorous voice with a soft snug tone. So tranquil, I'd fallen asleep if there had not been the counting duty.

Dear brothers and sisters, we have come together here today in this beautiful antique school in the name of Christ ... my thoughts drifted to Heini's classmates. Instead of today's 26 members of the *Christen unserer Zeit*, on weekdays there gathered double the number of students.

... the Kingdom of God, His sphere of influence is inside of you, dear brothers and sisters.

What's in me? I whispered. Oma whispered back, God's within you. Huh? Just now?

Yes, most of the time. Only when you're naughty, Satan overtakes ...

... and who had discovered this inner psychic power? The oldest son of a mortal lumberman Jesus from Nazareth, ain't it? Truly? But how, dear comparatives does this creative power reveal? In its highest unfolding, it shows as love. But instead of love, the in-truth-holding many falsely call belief became the most important thing. The frame matters more than the picture, ain't it? Truly? The funny noise in the very back of my nose was contagious. Near me, the sound as if someone holds water in a hose back with the thumb increased.

... and thus we better bring our influence to bear my dear comparatives. Let the believers become lovers. This way we make people happy and raise their spiritual level. These thoughts my dear brothers and sisters we want to take home from today's divine service.

With 59, the output of the repetitions was well below average. A similar letdown was the blue Lloyd mobile. The tiny tin box with its ivory roof looked rather like a cough drop than a car. One had to wedge in oneself. I proudly remained leaning on the bent bonnet of our gray Beetle and looking with compassion to Oma who boarded the vehicle with her bent down head. On our way home, Mama said, did you know that your second name you got from uncle Heinrich's daughter Erika? No, but the first name I got from Heini because of the song „Mariandl, Jandel Jandel, du hast mein Herz am Bandl Bandl. Yes, he'd outvoted me, I wanted a Barbara.

Barbara? Why Barbara? Because you like rhubarb? No, I just liked that name. I felt sorry for Mama not to have gotten her will. I had named me Lea, Mara, Lara or Clara.

While Maria lured Heinrich into another slice of roast, he said: What a delicious meal again. Alwine, you could run a restaurant. She answered half ashamed, half proudly averting:

That's all I need! Apropos, what's missing? How about a schnapps for digestion?

Oma turned around to the buffet's built-in bar and said obediently, that durable Steinhäger is still from last Christmas. That doesn't matter, time makes it better. What a nice poem. Papa took a sip. His eyes widened as if he'd seen a ghost. His sharply shaved cheeks glowed like soup bones coating his face's education patina from all his reading. Speaking of poetry Maria, Heiner said, your poem Geist der Wahrheit has touched me deeply, especially the first strophe. Really?

Yes! Really! I even can recite it by memory:

Geist der Wahrheit, Licht und Klarheit
Trägst du in das weite Land,
dass verschwinde Nacht und Sünde.
Und der Vater wird erkannt.

Höchster Geist, erfülle nun die Herzen,
Tau des Himmels, heile alle Schmerzen.
Der große Tag des Herrn ist nicht mehr fern.

Maria blushed right up to the ears, and the little glass of wine increased the two red spots on her cheeks, reminding me of a circus clown. Papa said with his pointed forefinger in the direction of the buffet door: Darling, can you get the cigar case?

Ugh! I approached the credenza's dark wood door with its ivory embroidery. Though Papa did not smoke, on Sundays when external preachers gave us the honor the puffing was obligatory. I opened the box holding it under Papa's nose. He took two stinking sticks and cut out from each one end a V-shaped piece. Fetching the matches, I rattled out one of Oma's axioms: *Messer, Gabel, Schere, Licht sind für kleine Kinder nicht.* Tricky smiling, I stroke against the matchbox and gave the men fire. Sucking, spitting, and puffing they sat next to each other on the yellow couch with light gray naps. Dense smoke wandered around their heads. Papa's fine blond hair was in need of another anti-dandruff treatment. In these days only a few people knew that too much protein or animal fat respectively increases dandruff formation. But even if he'd known, Papa would not have given up eating his beloved fat sausages. So how's your Loyd? Papa asked. Heinrich answered:

I never thought I'd buy such a new car. I just took it, because it had run only 8000 km, quasi a demonstration car. Very reasonable, with radio 2.800 marks. In my frank Saggy manner I asked: Is it not a little small for a tall man like you? Smiling he said:

First I thought so, too, but I fit in comfortably. What would you say, Maria? That's true, said the addressed in her comfy chair, rotating a foot as usual. I sat well. Papa didn't want to hurt his fellow believer's feelings. After he'd left he said crafty, *wer den Tod nicht scheut, fährt Loyd.* I'd rather buy a two-year-old car and for the same amount I've something sturdy. Heini said chesty, Borgward builds good cars in general. Papa said:

Anyhow, this lawnmower isn't comfy for long distances and it has no crush zone.

Alwine asked the dish washing Maria:

Are you coming along to Eberbach? You haven't seen your sister for long. I don't know.

There's no flooding anymore. I'm sure Mina would be glad to see you again.

Oh no, just let me clean the kitchen since you did most of the cooking. You can start earlier, and I can accompany you next Sunday.

As you wish. Yes, it's better, I've to write to Hedi that I can't come to Glückstadt. Shall we tell Mina anything? Can we take anything along for the Schlickenrieders? Oh yes. You can bring Edeltraud the self-embroidered handkerchiefs and the diabetic cookies. Oma's chubby niece had suffered a shock from a war experience at age 13 and must shoot herself Insulin ever since. I never got a straight answer when I asked specifics, but I can imagine. I thought Oma wanted to read and write for the rest of the day. The idea, that she still suffered her husband's death hadn't crossed my mind. Seppl's chirping made us aware of the doorbell. I pushed the ball shaped button of the door opener and bent my torso over the stair-bar. Uschi's brown tuft of hair appeared.

I can't play with you today. We'll drive to Eberbach. Wait, I ask if you can come along. A minute later, Uschi glided down the rail and raced to the neighboring house. Like most of the time, her mother allowed her to come with us. In the Beetle, Alwine reacted to Ludi's

Monza like start with a rumpus guttural sound. Cunning, he said, Heiner wouldn't have the slightest chance to follow us and in a wailing voice, do you know why Mutti will not go to Glückstadt? Mama said:

She doesn't feel well. Such a thing one digests not so easily. You know yourself how it is. And they were longer together. I asked:

What is with Oma? Mama said: You know, that Opa had died. Now she's more than a year without him. But Oma still has us. You don't know yet how it is to lose someone close. Look down there! In this paper factory, your Papa had worked as an electrician. I said: I know, that was before you married. Yep!

Goes the paper, we give the ragman there too? Heini sang along this man's singsong: Taaa-tteeer, old iiireeen, paa-peeer!

Most certainly, answered Papa. A few yards further, the robust line keeper's house willfully looked down upon us. In front of the dark mixed forest, the light brownstone beamed in the bright sunshine. Finally, sun after this long storm period. It glittered on the frostily breathed on barren limbs of the flanked trees. The wavy meadows steamed out the rainfalls of the past weeks. When the pretty old building of the inn *Zur Marbach* appeared, Ludi's enthusiasm came through. This house could be made to something great. A lot of work was his spouse's reply. And it all would be loaded onto me. Ah, the Himbächel viaduct! Bonny! Who lives in that castle like building?

That was Hitler's vacation home. By the way, do you know that without Oma, the Himbächel viaduct wouldn't exist anymore? I looked back out of the split window at the grand bridge from the 19th century built from brownstones. A true eye catcher. Even in the cold time of the year, it gives its surrounding a splendor. Why Papa?

At the end of the war, a cohort of soldiers trampled over the line ties in the direction of post 19. Oma hurried towards them and asked: Well! What do you want here? The comman der said we're going to blow up the viaduct so that the Amis can't come further. Good God! Mutti shouted at him, are you crazy? You can't do this! Do you have any idea, how long it took the Italians to build it? They won't come again. He said: But we've orders to blow up bridges. Brave Marie said, why the war's almost over, there's enough destruction already. And besides, the Americans will certainly not come by train. If you want to blow up anything, there's a small bridge in Ebersberg. Heini said: Oma should get a medal of honor. That's true, I agreed proudly.

Uschi added one of Oma's proverbs:

Nothing is so hard as man's ingratitude.

In high spirits, we moved uphill Beerfelden. Papa intoned the song „*Wenn wir erklimmen schwindelnde Höhen* ..." and singing all together we ascended towards the top cross. The higher plains were covered with a spider web fine ice-crust. In Gammelsbach, the ceremonial of our red houses repeated the umpteenth time. Heini pointed outside, there's the red house, we're almost there. Nonsense, that's not red, it's red-brown. Uschi, what color is it? It looks brown. Sure, the real red one comes later. It took a long time to pass through the

Odenwald Malibu. Just before reaching the rail underpass towards the river of Neckar, it appeared. Ma said: There's your red house, Marianne! I shouted: Yeah, that's it! House was an understatement. The gelatin plant together with its new buildings along the river is today the biggest around the globe. Every 4th ton of animal protein used worldwide comes from this family firm. Had Ma acted upon her prophetic abilities by calling it my red house? Though, it has nothing to do with me personally the great-grandchild of the factory's founder Heinrich Koepff is Peter's beautiful daughter-in-law. Like my mother's folks, most of Michaela's relatives live in Eberbach, and by the way, she celebrates her birthday on the same day as Doris Day!

The brown opalescent river streamed slowly between the shore street and the wooded hills. From the fine emerging fog, the sun spun silky angels hair, like brittle silk shawls. It branched out over the black-green heights lingering up in layers between bushes and tree stumps. The horizon embraced in haze had some of an enraptured infinity and seemed to belong to another time. Loving the Neckar valley I asked the umpteenth time: Why don't we live in Eberbach? Aunt Hilde and aunt Anneliese live here, and Papa has no siblings in Michelstadt. Mama said with a slight regret in her voice:

Oma has her duties in Schönnen. Michelstadt is not as far away as Eberbach. Pity! The area was still a little flooded; the water reached the riverside road, but, except for a few small pieces of wood carried along, nothing disturbed our ride on the usual route.

We turned left since the Beetle needed fodder. We liked to get gas from this gas station since the friendly man used to give us little presents. This time along with chewing gum, we got a blue manikin from hard rubber. We delightedly twisted its overlong arms and legs in all directions. I was glad that Uschi came along. She was more entertaining than Heini and rejoiced so much at this diversion. For half a day, she was freed of family duties and from the clamor of her baby brother. In our family, we spoke our minds aloud but were over and done quickly, and the family stood firmly together. I sneezed noisily, Uschi said:

Wait I've got something for you. She proudly produced a novelty out of her jersey pocket and carefully opened a little bundle. I loved the way my best girlfriend jumped for joy for any tiny thing such as a re-closeable package of tissues. Though we had the first car, the first TV, and the first phone in the neighborhood, we still used rough linen hankies. Also, our fannies weren't as pleased as our neighbors' 'cause my father was a busy newspaper reader. So he'd cut old issues in handy pieces, pierced them with a puncher and hang them with a cord on a nail on the wall next to the toilet: until Marika from Kassel came to visit. Oma's cousin Louise's daughter introduced us to the fleecy cleaning matter. When the toilet got clogged up, she said, this wouldn't have happened with proper toilet paper. She then got two rolls of 8 m long live quality from the nearby grocery, one for each bathroom so all our butts could get used to this line of luxury.

Naturally, nobody in the family wanted to miss the bottom lavish anymore.

Speaking of Louise and her daughter Marika there's another coincidence for the album:

Peter's 3rd granddaughter Marika was born on my father's birthday. Her two older sisters Katja and Anika would have rather named her Louise! Are you guys having fun on the other side, checking if we pay attention?

On route to the Neckar St, we were curious if we could drive to the house this time. The Sunday before, the street was passable, but the house, our relatives lived in, stood on sloping land that had turned into a lake. Uncle Heinz had made the Gondolier with a plaster pan. One after another he'd picked us up from the sidewalk. Heini took a bath, if of misfortune or live hunger the 9-year old didn't tell. After dipping, he almost disappeared in a huge fluffy farmer's shirt aunt Hilde had fetched from her 6.2 tall Heinz. This time Papa was able to lead the VW to the entrance door. Our little cousin rushed by with his red cab. Such a car would have been my favorite Christmas present too. After cake and cocoa, Jürgen let us turn a few rounds. Karin could not reach the pedals and was more concerned about her cow. She milked her dolls wagon with an underneath positioned water filled spray bottle and brought her cow fresh grass, daily.

I proudly raced around the big yard like Huschke von Hanstein in his red Porsche Spyder. An enormous energy made my veins vibrate under the skin. With straight shoulders and exposed breast, I felt wonderfully free. Ever since a cabriolet was on my wish list for the future. Twice, I'd even dreamed of driving an open car through Michelstadt. Whenever I joyfully told my dreams at the breakfast table, Papa promised me a cab for my 18th birthday.

As the time had arrived this was no subject anymore since Pa was in the process of purchasing the brownstone house in Schönnen. But I had saved money and spent it on a used Renault Floride with what I found out later new paint over old rust. A real eye catcher: white with red leather and a red fold roof. Cruising through the old town, the unlimited freedom I felt in my childhood dreams turned to reality. If they were prophetic ones, will not be certifiable anymore.

Some 20 years later in L.A., I'd driven my 450SL down the beautiful San Vincente Blvd. An enormous energy made my veins vibrate under the skin.

Jocelyn Brando's writers-block workshop

Shortly after John introduced me to Jocelyn, I headed down the boulevard. The magnificent plantain trees formed a fresh protective cover over the heads of the joggers. When their beautiful red blooms bubbled over, I'd to be careful concentrating on the traffic. I turned right to Santa Monica Canyon, and just in time arrived at 338 E. Rustic Rd. After an introducing hug, Jocelyn escorted me to the others. Some gathered in front of the fireplace, some near the buffet. I helped myself with hot water from a beautiful brass samovar and focused on the tea bleeding out of its bag. I grabbed a few grapes and took a seat at the fireplace. Some of us introduced ourselves until it was time to start our mental exercises in the converted garage. The only younger African American male must have felt forlorn in our round of middle-aged female authors want-to-be and actresses with autobiographic literary interests.

Gracious Linda Ridgeway sitting on my left talked to Celeste Bonham, a former MGM manager. I overheard her saying something about her leaving the movie makers after eight years. The earnest woman with long black hair reminded me of my grandma Lydia. I asked:

What did you do at MGM?

Reading scripts. Oh, good. I wouldn't mind earning money by reading.

Linda said Rock had just written a book.

Celeste asked: What about? Yul's life.

Yul Brynner? I asked. Yes, Rock's father.

We owned Yul's silver Gullwing, I said.

What!?! Linda jumped up from her seat.

Wow, what a respond! Do you mean the car with the doors open like that? Linda raised her arms bowing over her head.

Yes, we are dealing vintage cars. We bought the Gullwing out of a garage. Really?

Yes! It still had French license plates.

Yeah, Yul had problems with the IRS.

Who has not? Suzanne, the actress CPI sitting next to Celeste intervened. Our host called for attention. With her long blond hair straight tied to a pendant ponytail and a pink sweater over comfy gray sweatpants, Jocelyn looked casual. But in her function as a seminar leader, she was right to the point: For the newcomers, this 3-day workshop intends to free writer's blocks by getting rid of inner hindrance and cramps. This work can also have a therapeutic effect. To loosen up, we start with a little exercise. Write down anything you want to get rid of. That's easy, I said.

Yes, but we only stress *our* change. It's not ours to say I want to get rid of my husband's smoking. You may say I want to get rid of people around me endangering my health.

Can I also say, I wish I had a nonsmoking spouse? Yes, but that you do when you work on the dialog dimensions or the imaginary extensions. So what do you think is the most important you want to dump?

My fear of not being loved anymore or not being able to love enough. And what do you think you can do about it?

Treat my inner child and getting a doggy?

So you know what you can do.

Before we go deeper in the twilight imaginary and the inner wisdom, we'll do a meditation, where we visualize our inward from the toes to the scalp. Sit straight with your feet on the floor. Take some deep breaths. Visualize the blood flowing through your toes. Feel the warmth. Relax your toes. Now visualize your forefeet and feel the warmth. When I reached the spleen relaxing the pancreas, a tear left my closed lid and rolled down my cheek.

I thought about my grandmother Maria, her unconditional love. I missed her. In the new house, I hadn't felt her anymore. No cross sum 11 and too much work fixing up the house room by room. The first thing to get rid of I wrote down our visitor's name reminding me of Henry Miller's friend Moricand in *The oranges of Hieronymus Bosch*. Gerd made me mad for staying months after months, asking Peter's help for his real estate deals. He most certainly had stolen his passport even twice. It had cost us thousands of dollars to get the treaty trader visa renewed.

I won't write down his name. Though, I know for sure I can't prove it. One time, when we still lived in the house, in Bergen-Enkheim, I was alone with my visiting mother when the door-bell rang. Two criminal investigators asked me if I know C.-P. Meyer. He's my husband. What is with him? Nothing, we only have to inquire. Is he there? No, he's looking for cars. When and where's he born? When I had given them Peter's birth date, they said yes that's him. Can you show me a picture of your husband? Looking at it, they shook their heads. Every time, Peter missed his passport this guy had visited us before. From another acquaintance, we have later heard that he used to travel with five different passports. When he was here with Petra, I had no time for myself. I had breathing trouble. My bowel refused to function. The inner child was hurt.

In the pause, I walked with Linda, Suzanne, and Celeste through the neighborhood.

You must have thought I'm crazy, Linda approached me laughing, but Yul Brynner was my father-in-law. That's why I was so excited. I've to call Rock. Maybe he wants to use the original car for the movie. I'm sorry we don't have it anymore. We sold it to a bodywork company in Frankfurt. It's red now. Turning to Celeste, I asked what are you writing about? My work as a managing director of acquisitions, how it ended, how I got back on track. That's the title. Back on track? Yeah.

Sounds great. Thanks! By the way, since you are German, do you know Udo Lindenberg? Yeah, everybody in Germany knows him. I once had to show him the Universal Studios. Oh, yeah? Yup! Accompanied by his physician and Fritz Rau. The guy was rather ill-humored. Really? Yes, I was astonished, too. He seemed so cool in his all black outfit. He was peeved by not being recognized.

Why? Does he think, he's known here too?

It was quite funny. After a young woman had approached him as a fan, his mood changed instantly. The barometer of public opinion soared. I wouldn't have expected that from somebody who's pretending to be so cool.

Back in my black cab, I resumed, why Udo's behavior had attracted Celeste's attention so much. Is it not the very thing we find fault with we have to work on ourselves? I just say sawdust and plank. Celeste is wearing black, and she can be genuinely grouchy.

The *Trail of Tears* and continued chronicle

I had three new girlfriends. One morning while hiking through the Santa Monica Mountains, I asked Linda, what did you do to find your potential relatives? Why don't you get in touch with your grandmother and ask her what to do? I did. I got, there's nothing to do. So let it be. I parodied the Beetles while looking down on Calabasas and the Woodland Hills skyscrapers. Wow! What? I wonder, how it had been here 50 years ago. Linda said, just farmland. You really should act. Why?

You are the type of actress who could make it. Blond, blue eyes with that sparkle and a great voice. Yeah, when I was with my parents in Vegas, I was asked twice for an autograph. Once in a dream, I was an English speaking male actor. I still may have this actor's aura.

Yeah, you should try auditions. I don't know.

You've got what it takes. You're such a natural. But what's the use of doing the same thing again? If I'd been a male actor before.

Now you're female.

I don't think I want to be in the limelight. Some change after a shepherd's isolated life.

In fact, until I dreamed of my girlfriend I didn't believe in a life after life. What kind of dream? Um, I had an eerie experience with my deceased friend. Since then I think anything's possible. Do you want to talk about it? Sure. I was sad about her early death. One night, I'd dreamed about her. She'd told me, don't be sad I'm not dead. Only my body is sunken into the grave, but I still exist. However, I doubted it to be true.

What changed your mind? I asked while sniffling on a scrub on my path side wishing to know all names of plants and their use.

In another dream, my girlfriend told me about a family secret and asked me to let her mother verify it. When she amazed confirmed the secret I was convinced our life does not end after death. Wow! Have you ever had contact with your great-grandmother? Actually, when I worked on the Trail of Tears I often had the feeling of automatic writing. I wrote without thinking. I know that feeling, I tossed in scraping a tiny mussel out of the slope. How does that come here? I also pictured her

with a chicken in her arm. You know they took their animals along for food. I visualized the kids, the sick, the weak and the frozen to death. They were just left on the roadside.

Um! Horrible! I read in Marlon's biography what they did to the natives. Do you think how many were forced on the death trail? Some 18,000, 1/3 didn't make it to Oklahoma.

Your relative must have been very young.

Gruesome! What do you think about an eye for an eye? Huh? I wonder if the ones who caused that brutal expulsion may have gotten frozen toes in the Nazi war's Russian campaign. Linda sighed: What's the point of suffering? A lack of love and sympathy or greed.

You are right. They found a vein of gold on the Cherokee territory. Where was that?

Georgia, in the southeastern parts of the US. Marlon wanted to make a movie about it. And? The money issue. Yeah, they negate this holocaust by making ever more Nazi films. Do you know why? Huh?

Because most producers are Jews.

Well, that's a fact. Yeah. Germans finance the movies as another kind of remorse. Are the liberators trying to liberate all Germans from confidence? What do you mean?

I used to feel an inherited burden of guilt. I think the allies are determined to let us feel that way. But we are all the same. Huh?

We are all capable of killing given the right incentive. We all should be rueful of the things we'd done wrong in past lifetimes. I think we not only reincarnate as individuals but also as groups. We had been murderers and saviors and part of genocide past lifetimes. Let's start with the assault of Semitic nomads on the Sumerians in Asia some 3 or 4 thousand years ago. We may have been there. Linda shrugged: You rarely find these things in books or lexicons. True. But Marlon wrote in his biography about the Sand Creek Massacre in 1864, where hundreds of women, children and old men were mutilated in the most horrifying way. Some cavalrymen bragged about their monstrous trophies. Can you imagine, they made tobacco bags from breasts of native women and saddles from their vagina.

Linda's ailing look made me say, sick, eh?

Could make you vomit.

After reading *The Investigation* by Peter Weiss, I'd actually thrown up. Why? It's about the trial of former Auschwitz guards. Those poor Jews surviving the Holocaust by stripping their people of everything usable, dental gold, hair ... and gassing them. It's hard to live with the guilt of following Nazi orders to industrialized murder. Horrible! Yeah. But we are all from the same source. So, why can millions of native Americans be slaughtered and no movie producer ever cares? Seems not fair.

Yes, but we can't escape the Universal Law. It is a reassurance we all have to repay.

Bending, I grabbed a stone. That looks like a heart. How pretty! I'm going to paint it for Peter's birthday. Why had Marlon excused himself for antisemitic statements? Any idea? Was it because he thinks the CIA men in the Vietnam operation Phoenix had not been any different from Heydrich or Himmler? Dunno.

On the other side, he acknowledged the accomplishments of the 18 million Jews compare to the 99 something % rest of men, their success in science, music, and politics; not to speak of movie business and economics. Einstein, Freud, Marx, three most influential Jews. By the way, Marx reported in his Capital that the New England society offered £40 for each Indian scalp. In Massachusetts-Bay, the reward was even £105. Yeah, about this genocide we don't hear much.

Yep. This eye for an eye thing will go on and on if we are not willing to turn the other cheek. Huh? We need to forgive ourselves and others; otherwise, it'll go on until the planet is ruined by destructive weapons and exploitation. If we want heaven on earth, we have to look back on our evil and evaluate our guilt.

What will your heaven on earth be like?

Looking in Linda's pretty face, I said every being should live in harmony, dignity and decency. Sounds decent. But how?

All men get basic necessities such as shelter, clothing, and food. We all respect each other's originality and learn from our differences. We stop looking at the speck of sawdust in our brother's eye by recognizing our own plank. Linda said: Your heaven on earth needs another society. Yes! Everybody making millions a year could keep only two or three and give the rest back to society. They couldn't make their dough without others working or cheering for them anyway. There'll be a pool of money to give each person a small sum for the most pressing needs, 800 or 1,000 bucks. The rest could be spent on education and innovation.

What do the rich get out of it?

If men can live with dignity, the rich will gain security, recognition, and love! Isn't that what we all want? But how? At a yearly held global event, the most honored philanthropists will be celebrated as pop stars. A tall guy neared. Oh, hi. How are you doing?

Pretty good. Are you working again? More or less. A few yards further I asked: Who's that? An actor I know. Looks familiar. Maybe I've seen him in a commercial.

Could be. Michael Greene often hikes here.

By the way, that Bronson movie you played in, what's its name? *The Mechanic*. I played Jan-Michael Vincent's girlfriend. I slit my wrist. An agonizing act. Killed my career, too.

Returning to Linda's caravan, she said: I like your idea of a basic income. With a gesture to her shabby 53 truck, she said I'd restore this and trade the caravan for a cute little house.

Acting-class appearance

Linda took me to her acting class in Hollywood and Suzanne introduced me to Sharon Chatten who's instructing actors in Brentwood and Santa Monica. I optioned for Sharon. The class temporarily took place in an old church since the original place was under renovation. Waiting outside until she arrived, I studied the faces of the colleagues. The tall blonde with broad high cheekbones looked familiar to me.

She didn't seem as confident as her sporty looks. When Sharon came with the key, we entered the dark wooden hall. Another woman who also reminded me of someone walked to the piano and started to play and sing. Had I not seen this childlike face with the curly mane in Pink Cadillac with Clint Eastwood? Sharon said: Your first improv will be a class reunion. She divided us into groups of two.

What's your name again? Marianne. Okay, you and Mariel, Chris and Berry ...

At the end of the day, I got Wes as a partner to prepare for a play called The Porch. I liked my role as a woman who made it as an editor in New York. But I misunderstood the instructions and learned the exact lines. My poor partner in the role of my former lover didn't know what to say. Sharon said: That's not what I want. You only have to know your role, not the lines. Driving home, I thought about myself in the role of a woman who just came to her hometown from New York. I pictured me sitting on the porch in front of my parent's house. My mother had already passed on. My father was in the hospital, the operation's outcome unsure.

On the next class meeting, Sharon put more emphasis on the grimacing of Strasberg's method acting. We sat in a half circle, our teacher in front of us. She said: At the end, I'm going to check your relaxation. After a minute,

Sharon caught my eyes and said, you could be a great actress, but you aren't coming out enough. Indeed, my facial gesture, the screaming, boxing, kicking or beating the air, was almost zero. I had followed the relaxation instructions I'd learned from Jocelyn by relaxing my body parts from toes to head. After about 5 minutes, Sharon came to the chairs next to me and lifted up my neighbor's arms. Trying to raise my limp limb, she didn't say anything. But her gesture and her puzzled looking made me think, my way to relax is working as well. Of course, when waiting for an actual stage performance I might be too worried and the physical workout might be best to calm me.

Starting our Improv I walked along the garden chairs that were arranged in an L-form. I nervously banged against each backrest and finally sat down on a chair alongside, feet up in a fetal position, arms around legs. I watched my partner walking towards the porch, answered his greeting but didn't move. We were beating around the bush for a while. I marveled his full head of hair and asked if he'd do headstands or eat lots of beans. But nobody would have taken us for former lovers. All at once my partner asked: What did they say at the hospital? I paused and lowered my voice by a few notches: could go either way.

Sharon jumped up from her seat.

Great, great, it didn't look like acting. Huh? I had never heard her critique the established actors this way. The only thing you could try next time to imagine the love in your life to create more intimacy. Just think of your lover in real life. Let it work for you. Of course, it's not as easy with certain partners. I mentally agreed. Wes was not my type, indeed. With Chris, it would have been easier.

By the way, Chris' father Peter Lawford had a recurring role as Doris's romance on The Doris Day Show 20 years earlier. At least my partner had no chance this time to show his effectuate impersonating with set up gestures as on his earlier Improv scene with a young man. After my last performance, he'd expected another disaster and wanted to have a second chance.

Anyway, I ended the class and left the group since I had developed stomach pains caused by stage fright. I also wanted to save the monthly $140. And what's the sense of doing the same work twice? Consciously or unconsciously I only wanted to prove my talent. I should have tried to make at least one film. This may be too late, or I'd be the oldest newcomer actress ever to make it in the Guinness book.

Party-George and property search

I love the way people in the US offer their houses. Every weekend, we roamed the areas and looked for open houses. Waving balloons on real estate company signs or mailboxes made us feel invited to enter. We also asked three firms to real estate agents to look for a proper property. But after the 3rd house, we had been offered we were already fed up wasting our time. The first one in Burbank resembles a library. The writer had also collected lots of other things. Unfortunately, no cars. She had even converted the garage into a library extension. There would have been too much work involved. The 2nd one, owned by an Indian family was too dark and had not enough space for cars either. The 3rd house in the Hollywood Hills we liked a lot, though, with $585,000 it was a little more than we'd wanted to spend. We offered 540 grant. But when we called again the house was sold.

Not wanting to waste any more time we told the real estate people, call us only if you can offer exactly what we want: A 2-3 bedroom home with 2 bathrooms, at least space for 5 cars and a view for up to a half million. Anyway, we were happy in the house on Scadlock Lane where we watched the deer passing the street at 6.30 a. m. on weekdays. On Sunday's later traffic they showed up at 8.30 a. m.

Peter sat on his pool desk. He flipped through Hemming's Motor News searching for parts he needed for an Adenauer Mercedes. I went to the bathroom and washed my hair. Making my towel turban I overheard Peter on the phone, to whom should the check ... Witchgram like the witch with the broom?

With a 'y' and without the 't'? WYCHGRAM, okay. What!?! I shouted and ran outside.

Ask him if his first name is Roger. He could be Uschi's ex, Renee's father! Is your first name Roger? Yes? I grabbed the receiver. Hi, Rog, this is Marianne, Uschi's girlfriend from Michelstadt.

Why! What you're doing there? I live here. I traded the lousy German weather for the Californian sunshine. I plan to come soon, too.

For good? No, there's a car show in Beverly Hills next week, I want to go with Wendy. I like you to meet her. Yeah, I heard about Wendy. Uschi said she's too good for you. Isn't she also a nurse? Yeah, I'm sure you'll like her.

You can stay in our guestroom.

When the two arrived, Roger asked: Have you got Tylenol? What? A Painkiller. No, we don't take pills, but I can get you some. I've to go shopping. I bought the smallest bottle. When I handed it to Roger he looked perplexed. What's that? Tylenol! In a way as if I'd insulted him or acted insanely, he said, they'll not last very long. Um! You only stay three days, don't you? So? I thought, you'd take 3 or 4 a day, and I can keep the rest for the next guest in pain. No wonder Uschi left Aberdeen with Renée after 2½ years. Huh?

It's not easy to watch hubby ruining his body. Roger made it longer than expected by people who knew him. He made his transition on May 24, 2012, meeting his Indian mother and his German father not inheriting his only child and grandchild a single dime. His 4th or 5th wife who got houses, cars, and cash did send them Rog's school reports, baby mug &, shoes as well as some dummy's. What's the message? Another karmic payback, I suppose.

Roger washed down six pills with water. Have you tried just water? That sometimes helps. Ignoring my praise, he said: What a great house for parties. Yeah, tossed Peter in, and the great view of the Budweiser factory. Only pity, we can't use the pool now. Let's party anyhow. We don't know many people who'd come at short notice. I can call Don Briton. You may know him.

Sure, the Texan, we'd some business together. They had a huge house. I'd been there twice. Don's wife Lynne is very nice. Then you know them better than we do. We could ask Mosy. Do you know George Moseman? Isn't he a musician from Michigan? Nice guy.

Small world.

I made the party food myself. Why spending money for stuff that mostly doesn't taste as good as homemade? For every taste, I cooked something: chicken, fish, hamburgers, potato salad, filled eggs, coleslaw, sliced veggies with dip and some other finger foods. I use to make lots of food. Some of it the guests take home, and some we eat the following days.

George came alone, but with flowers and a bottle of German white wine! I was impressed by his charm and wit and made a mental note not to party without George anymore. You could open a restaurant. Never! My parents ran a restaurant and cafe.

Where did you learn to cook? From age 14 on, my mother had made me cook every 2nd Sunday. Do you have any sisters?

No, only one brother, traditional upbringing: I cleaned the family shoes, dusted and dried the dishes, my brother handed in part of his salary. Petra and Bernd had long left, when I talked to Lynne about my metaphysical experiences. She said: The problem with the apparition world is, there are not only good spirits. There are also the ones that make fun of you. You think the two who appeared in my bedroom were not my father's ancestors?

No, I only mean, some channeled ideas may come from an evil source. But still, there's my consciousness. Right. How did they look like?

She'd white pants and a white blouse on, the man dark gray slacks and a light-blue shirt both long sleeved. His sleeves were hitched up a bit. She was about my age, round face with medium blond curly hair and looked like my friend Carole whom I met only after this experience. His face was elongated with still mostly dark hair and side whiskers. He was skinny, she a tiny bit on the chubby side just like Carole. I wonder if she can do that, how is it called when matter dematerializes and appears on another spot, teleportation? I know that using subspace conversion is possible. It's different from an out-of-body experience, isn't it? Yes, that's the soul moving. How would you define soul? As consciousness, electromagnetic radiation coupling with the body's magnetic force field.

Shirley MacLaine mentioned a silver cord that's connected, and when it ruptures, we'll die. The soul detaches from the body. Some people see the electromagnetic radiation emit from the body at the time of death.

Yeah, so I've heard. Had the spirits halos?

If I've seen their auras? Yes. No.

Have you ever seen an aura? Only my own around my hand, mostly when I take a bath.

Do you want to see mine? Why? Yes!

Do you have a room where I can sit against a white wall? Yes, let's go in our bedroom.

Turn on a dim lamp. I switched on the nightstand lamp and sat down on the floor, leaning on the bed. Lynne sat with her long dark hair against the opposite wall. Now take a deep breath and let everything sink, relax and look at me with half open eyelids as if you're about to sleep. I see it! Wow! It's golden like in holy pictures but not a hoop, it is from ear to ear. Why can you do it? I'd given seminars, but I'm not into that metaphysical stuff anymore.

In the early evening three weeks after the party the phone rang. Maurice, the realtor called with good news: I found your house on a ½ acre, 3 bedrooms, 2½ baths and a maids quarter you could use as a guest quarter. It's got a big garage, fits two cars and a motorcycle. Up the driveway, you have space for 5 or 6 cars, secluded from the street.

Sounds great! Where is it?

Encino, between White Oak and Lindley, on the border to Tarzana. Sounds good! How much? 465.000. Sounds reasonable.

But it's a fixer upper. Needs a little touch-up. It has a view over the Valley. You can see Woodland Hills, Northridge and the Sierra Nevada. But we've got to rush. There's another buyer, a Jewish businessman. Do you have time now? I could show it to you right away.

Yes, of course, sounds like our house.

I pick you up in 10 minutes. Like I said there's a buyer, he wants it for his son.

20 minutes later on this warm spring day, we turned left on Karen Dr. up to an asphalt driveway. Landing in the middle of wilderness, a beguiling odor of eucalyptus, citrus, and oleander welcomed us. A crowd of chirping cicadas tried to drown out the realtor's speech. You've got to have imagination. It's got lots of potentials. You could make a rock waterfall leading to the pool. What's that? I asked, pointing to an ugly shed. There's the pool equipment behind. Yuck! I'd replace it pronto. First, you better cover the slope in the front with deep rooting plants. It's full of gopher holes. Otherwise, you can just move in. Touch it up a little and sell it for 150.000 more. I rather do it for us then for somebody else. Walking to the garage, I said, what happened to the poor tree looking like a scarecrow. It's got more host organisms than leaves. Yes, this is a weed grown place! The owner's a single man with his son. His life companion ran away. Still, I hope we get it. The place is pretty shaped with the yucca grouping on the curve of the pool. It looks like an island. We walked towards the entrance path with flagstone bordering masonry passing blue blooming shrubs, a jasmine bush, tiny fan-shaped palms and a battered banana scrub. Standing

in front of the flagstone entrance with the wooden double door, Maurice said: You could cut the eucalyptus. It needs lots of water, the avocado may not get enough.

Okay, I said. There is more room for cars than at the Hollywood Hills house, and it's easier to find. If you want to sell anything, it's better to give easy directions.

So how do you like it so far? I know it needs touching up. It'd fit us perfectly. Let's have a look inside. I didn't like the beige linoleum on the entrance and kitchen floor. I'd tile that area. It's bright all over. Yes, most rooms have glass walls. Maurice pointed to the metal overhang out the kitchen window. But I had only eyes for the pepper tree, a neighbor's chaste tree and the snow covered mountains. You could walk dry around the house.

I thought it never rains in California!

Boy, was I wrong! Once, from heavenly pipe bursts, masses of water gushed over L.A. The house was flooded twice. My visiting parents helped us get the water out by the bucket. I had invented a measure to save the wall-to-wall carpet. I lifted it, set building blocks every 2 yards, bought 20 bags of cat litter with brightener, spread half of it under the carpet and half on top. I saved the white floor covering, and it was never as clean. We also had cat litter for a year.

But we'll never forget the televised dreadful drowning of a neighbor boy. The 15-year-old Adam Bischoff, from Woodland Hills, was swept to death in the rain-swollen Los Angeles river. We agonizingly watched the boy's fight in the swirling churning floodwater for hours. All trials to catch him failed. We were stung about the city's not being prepared for this danger with some retaining jigs. After that tragedy, they were. Too late for Adam.

Our steps echoed in the empty hallway. We sank into the white carpet of the family room, leading to a room with a fireplace. There you have the best view over the San Fernando Valley. Though, not as magnificent as in Sherman Oaks, since the house sits lower, in the Santa Monica Mountains. The living areas connected through two flag stonewalls, the one on the left side contained a built-in bookcase.

I mentally furnished the house, while we walked out the sliding glass door to the patio. I looked into the adjacent room with black shelves. Maurice said: It also has a glass door. Nice office. Let's look at the master bedroom and the bathrooms. The latter caused me a sigh: Rugs in bathrooms! Disgusting male's dropping around the toilet and seedy tiles inspired my demolition creation. The bedroom made up for the loathsome locality. It was large enough for aerobic dancing in front of the wall mirror, although it's not healthy to sleep near mirrors.

The owner couldn't make up his mind whom to give the house and wanted to talk to each party. The day after the meeting, Maurice called. You'll get the house, Peter. How come? Because Marianne told the owner about the missed house in Hollywood. He said this time you should be first. Well! Great!

Except for the garden furniture, we had few pieces to move. Thanks to Sam Shoen for only $29.95 we rented one of the thousands in the US running U-Haul trucks and worked ourselves. I got some spreading plants from Home Depot and started to cover the bald spots where the ivory had died. The ones with small leaves and tiny red flowers spread very fast.

Dr. Fett and our new friends

Suzanne called: Can I visit you this weekend? We could hike a bit in the mountains.

Why, yes, I'd like that.

Two days later, walking down Karen Drive, Suzanne said, the reason, I came is not just to eat your cake and drink your coffee. So?

I need a favor. Okay? I marveled our corner-neighbors manicured grounds. Isn't that a gorgeous garden? Yeah, all over blooming flowers. Yes. And did you see the tennis court on the upper level? I'd like to have one, too.

I'd like something else. Suzanne pointed to her eyes. Look at my backlash eyelids and the lachrymal sacks. Next Friday, I have a doctor's appointment to get them fixed.

Have you met the man of your dreams?

No. But those dark circles make me look tired and discouraged. I can only play certain roles looking so weary. So what can I do for you? I need you to drive me to the doctors office and back since I get an anesthesia. Okay, no problem. It'll take 3 hours at the most. I'll make my famed homemade lasagna. We can eat it afterward. An hour later, back at the corner of Boris and Karen Drive, I said:

I wish we'd be friends with those folks. I love to play tennis. I'll put it on my wish list.

The doctor greeted us warmly: So you brought my patient, Dr. Fett said heartily, shaking my hand. That is extremely kind of you. What a mellow voice! Such a gentleman! I had no health insurance several years living in the US and only once went to a dentist. But if I'd needed a physician, I'd had asked Dr. Fett for advice.

Just make yourself comfortable. He escorted me back to the waiting room himself. I had never met a friendlier and heartier doctor. In one of his *Architectural Digest* issues, I found an interesting piece: an outside sitting arrangement with built on side tables and a smaller shelf above the headrest. With a piece like this, it's not necessary to have tables. Since Hans-Jürgen wanted the couch back for one of his daughters the plan to make something functional formed in my mind:

I'd cut plywood according to my measurements and get light gray tiles for the outside of the cubes and the back shelf. Foam padding for the seats, velvet covers and pillows I'd sew by hands. Watching TV, I'm usually sewing, painting or creating something anyway. The time passed by fast. The assistant came: You can come now. I went into surgery. Suzanne still looked a little woozy. Dr. Fat said:

In a few days, you won't see the bruises anymore. Just this sentence made me feel at ease again. With a question mark I said:

Next, please? You don't need that yet. There's still no drooping. You have no vision problem. Maybe we'll do it in ten years if I'm still practicing.

In her Condo, Suzanne got cold-packs out of the fridge and put the lasagne to be warmed up in the oven. You don't use a microwave either?

Nuke it? No way! It's killing!

Isn't it a drag to taking care of people's tax matters? It's okay. What would you do, if money wouldn't be an issue?

I'd only work as an actress. That's your only wish? I'd also buy a sailing boat. And you?

I think, I'd only read, write, paint, get some pets from the pound and grow veggies. I'd be happy with a little farm with sheep and hens.

Returning home, Peter was installing an electrical sprinkler system using all different kind of water supply systems.

A few days later I had accidentally cut a drip mist hose. Peter came with his repair set and fixed it. Ever since I called him Dr. Sprinkler.

The ground cover patches had spread fast on our slope. A few weeks after the planting I replaced buckets full of the fleshy plant cuttings for the dried ivory patches. Almost finished, a tall Blonde with two same colored dogs on each side walked towards our house from downhill. Before she passed by, I said: Hi, could you by any chance use some cuttings? I still have plenty of plants left. The woman looked perplexed. Why, yes! She wound both leashes around her wrists to save the dogs. Well, it's Wednesday, my gardeners are just in the yard. I don't have the ones with the little red flowers. Aren't they pretty? The big pink ones, I've, too. But I still could use a few. Well, thank you. I live in the house on the corner. Really? The one on the tennis court?

Exactly. Oh, I love to play tennis. It's paddle tennis only. But if you wish, you could come in an hour. We could play a match.

Oh, great. I'll bring the cuttings along.

Leanne greeted me in her stylish home. I peeked at a big square plate with pastel paintings. Let's get into the kitchen.

The dogs rested on the parquet floor. May I introduce the dogs? You have seen them only from the distance. Rocky on the left is 6-year-old, probably a boxer mix, Honey's about 3.

She looks like a fox mix.

Yes, she's as shy as a fox.

Pretty kitchen! I always wanted a white one. I glanced at some painted pieces. I do porcelain painting. Well done, so delicately. My East Indian friend Maya also paints porcelain. You certainly have talent. It runs in the family. My maternal grandfather was sir Thomas Lawrence's descendant. You may know his famous painting pinkie. Um!

We walked along the kidney shaped pool covered with tiny dark blue tiles. The dogs ran ahead of us up the stairway to the paddle tennis court. The green mesh around it was high enough for mature mishits. Starting, I said, oh, it's different. Tennis is not as noisy. Two big neighbor dogs agreed with me regarding the annoying clapping sound.

After a while, their constant barking bothered me even more. I shouted OUT! Do you know, who's dogs you are talking to?

Nope. The Cassidy's. What Cassidy?

Oh, don't you know David Cassidy, the singer? Yeah!? I guess, he is the most famous of the actor/singer family. I think I love you. Huh? That's one of his songs.

By the way, do you walk the dogs every day? Why, yes. If you want to, I could walk Honey. Sure. I like to walk, but alone it isn't as much fun. Well! Great! Honey will love it. She's easy. You won't have any problems with her. Yes, I love that little girl with the pulled in tail. Yes, she had probably bad experiences. My daughter Laura brought her home. Rocky is a stray, too. He behaves, he, don't laugh, but he acts up like ... I think he is occupied by my father's soul. I said: I like to live here where people talk about these things openly. In Germany, you'd have aroused hysterical laughter.

Yes, but I have my own experiences. I've seen auras and a ghost when Laura was a baby. Really? Yes! How'd it look like? I saw it hovering over Laura's bed. A big white smoky moving thing as a thin cloud or a fine diaper-like fabric changing its form constantly. Your painter uncle? Well? Or your father! Possibly.

Reiki in Venice & metaphysics in Mexico

Peter awaited me. Where have you been?

At my new friends' house on the corner.

I've forgotten to tell you. Toshin invited us to his party. When? Now. I bet he'd invited us when you greeted me from him. Usually, I don't like short notice goes. But on this enjoyable day, I changed quickly as a flash.

When we arrived in Venice, Urga greeted us. Toshin was involved in a conversation with another bearded man. Peter found a colleague at once and started the usual car talks. I talked to Urga about my Reiki experience and more personal natural events. She said: My son has outstanding psychic powers. He was only 18 when he started channeling messages from the ether in front of big groups. Boy!

A curly grayish guy came in, slightly crooked and obviously in pain. He walked to the back room. I followed him.

Hi, I'm Marianne. Nice meeting you.

Likewise, Lars. What happened to you?

I injured my back by lifting a sink.

I know that kind of work. Lately, I lifted one of those toilets with an integrated water container. I was lucky nothing happened to me when I heaved it onto the glue sealing ring. Yo! The weight had taken my breath away.

Years later, for a year or two I had pain, several hours after lifting only 10-litre water bottles. Time, the world's best healer, took care of the problem. Or did the hopping ball help? I also took Schüßler salts # 1, 2, 3, 7 & 11 to help strengthen the connecting tissues. But as usual only a few days. If it is no food, like Spirulina, I forget it. I first thought it was a dropped bladder since Grandma Maria had this kind of problem. I write this down for this condition may run in the Victor family, too.

Lars said when you do this kind of work all the time you are not always paying as much attention as you should be. Don't you have men around? I only do these things when I'm alone. Peter hates my projects in and around the house. So I work when he travels. Boy!

By the way, I'm a Reiki novice. If you like, I can try it on you. Why, yes! I know Reiki. So? I've gotten it a few times. It relaxes a lot. Where exactly does it hurt? Lars pointed to the lumbar region. I put my hands over it. Ah!

Shortly after, Urga arrived: Ingrid will come later. She's also doing Reiki. It might be worth trying the concentrated energy. After a while, Lars said: It's much better already.

I went back to the dancing area. A few people were moving their bodies to Strawberry Fields. I was all eyes for a joyfully dancing woman in a partly transparent chiffon outfit with pointed ends. It gave her the appearance of a Greek deity. I rarely wear dresses, but in this, I'd feel free to move. When the Muse left the dance floor, I got bored and went back to Lars. Urga came and said, I've seen Ingrid. I'm going to tell her that you're here. The Greek deity in the white and brown chiffon appeared.

Hi, I'm Ingrid, are you the man in pain?

Yes, but it's much better already. So?

The concentrated energy won't hurt.

So, why don't you lay down?

Lars stretched his body on the floor. Ingrid sat down and took his feet in her hands. You can start on the head, and we'll meet in the middle. We worked quietly then lifted our hands from his abdomen. Aping Ingrid's thanking for the energy with the Dalai Lama-like sign we left Lars to relax. Ingrid said: I've never seen you here before. Are you a Sannyasin, too?

No, I smiled, never been in Poona, searching for enlightenment. No need for a master, though, I've been in Goa. Toshin sold us a car.

It's our first party with the Rolls-Royce-Bhagwan folks. Ingrid smiled devotedly with an elfin twinkle in her eyes. His name is Shree Rajneesh, but we call him Osho now. Before you told me, I didn't even know that Toshin and Urga are Sannyasins. I know everything about you guys from the *Stern*. Or was it the *Spiegel*? Both, Ingrid said, I once was in Augstein's mag. Really? Yes, they showed me in my orange outfit. I was the first art historian working with a data processor. I did the first science of art documentation with the help of a computer in the state government of Nordrhein-Westfalen.

So what are you doing here? I usually live on my land on Big Island. But Hawaii is not good for making money. Hence, I leave the island sometimes to work as a housekeeper in L. A. Right now I need $17,000 for my teeth.

That much? I just had to renew a ceramic bridge with four dentition. The price was only $1,050. A Romanian dentist had advertised a half price special. Why! You're bold My dentist is well known. Lots of celebrities go there. That's no proof for quality. Ingrid looked puzzled. You may be right. I've lots of problems.

Sounds familiar. My friend Marita also goes to a celeb dentist in the Rhine-Main area. She complains about her teeth whenever I meet her. Why don't you work in your profession?

I want to be free, work for a while and then I travel to India or Bali. Yeah, same here. I never could hold a job living with Peter. He needs me in the business, and we use to travel spontaneously. Where do you live? On Karen Drive in Encino. Really? My friend Anda lives on Karen Drive. She's also a Sannyasin. Okay?

I must leave now. But it's only 5:00 p. m.

My boss wants to have dinner tonight with a friend. I get $50 extra. I usually don't cook. I only clean, wash and do his grocery shopping.

May I ask, how much you make? 400.

A month? No, per week. Wow! I do cooking, cleaning, business and gave Peter my money so we can buy more cars ... I should try that, too. Sure! They look for white housekeepers. You just go to an agency and flip through the books. They have record albums with photos. You can choose your employer as per your interests. One of the Sannyasins is Robert Redford's housekeeper. Cool! Whom did you choose? He's a lawyer from Toluca Lake, the son of my former boss Mr. Green. Tomorrow is my day off. Why don't you come to see me? Well! Why not?

Wear something comfortable. We can go for Thai chi in the Hollywood Park. Just give me a call. Urga has my number. I've got to rush.

On sunny Saturday morning, I arrived at a big two story house, impressive from the outside. Inside *nomen est omen*: green, demode. I met Ingrid and her boss in the kitchen. She was nibbling on a carrot from a plate of raw veggies and said, oh, I like your ponytail. Her boss was preparing him a cereal.

Not a bad looking guy, tall slim. Was it an amorous glance just sliding over me? For a split sec, I visualized myself in this house.

Ingrid said: We better take both cars. I'll meet two friends afterward, and I don't know how long this will take. You surely can join us. Bo is a Swedish actor. Tobi writes lyrics. You'll like them. We left for the park. I followed Ingrid and almost hit her bumper since she all of a sudden stopped on the Freeway's drive up, though, there was no single car on our line. We joined some 30 sporty dressed people on the lush green lawn. I imitated the instructor's slow movements. It felt like slowly tossing an imaginary big ball and moving in space, lightly following with the legs.

Walking to a little coffee shop in Studio City, I said: Ingrid, why stop without reason? I'd almost hit you. I'm sorry. I know my driving could be better. I don't want to lecture you, nothing happened. But I don't want to lose my new friend. If a truck runs into you, you're dead meat.

The pecan pie was delicious. The conversation consisted of mostly private matters: Bo's wife, Tobi's work, Ingrid's teeth, my great-grandfather's family. After exchanging business cards, Ingrid said: Why don't we all go to the AIDS support group in West Hollywood on Wed in a week? You'll love it there. It's an extremely emotional event. It's every Wednesday, but Louise Hay comes only once a month.

She's very charismatic. I've heard from her. She writes a lot, doesn't she? Yes, Marianne, I'll introduce you to Louise, you'll love her.

On my way back to Encino, I felt light like a butterfly. The SL drove by itself behind a slow pickup truck. The speedometer indicated 35 mi/h! I didn't care at all. Usually, I lecture the slow mover. But on this sunny afternoon, I had all the time in the world and marked a bit in my cerebrum: more Thai chi movements.

Peter awaited me with a question. How about going with Ray's mother to Mexico? Just for fun? Looking for classic cars. She takes a translator along. Okay? I had a feeling we'd not find anything but the heck with it.

A few days later, we sat in the plane to Guadalajara. We had a day there. I liked to walk around the cobblestone city, likely the most European-like in the country. We rented a car and headed towards Mexico City. As I thought, we'd not found any cars, but I'd have liked to rescue some puppies from their sellers. In Mexico City, we hired a taxi driver for a day. Fernando drove us to the local car dealers. Carole and I stayed in the car.

I asked: Do you know the famous spiritual places in Mexico? Yes, there are many people coming to see them. Have you ever experienced anything metaphysical there?

Not there, but for 11 years, I meditate. For 6 years, I have out-of-body experiences. Wow! Yes. It's indescribably pleasing when the energy body moves up into the air. Yeah, I had a few forced experiences myself and in dreams. That's different. I can go everywhere. Mostly, I visit my mother and call her later on.

Cool! Yeah, every time, she's stunned when I describe her what she'd done or spoken.

Ah! I'd like to be a fly on the wall, too. If we all would be able to do that, we'd lead better lives since we'd count on unseen visitors.

We do have spirits hovering around all the time, said Carole. Yeah, but mostly the ones who left their bodies for good. As a fly on the wall, we'd get to know ourselves better. Peeping Tom would have to listen to his own infamy. I only left my body involuntary when I was ill or highly upset. Fernando said:

I do it because afterward I feel energized and no matter what I go about everything works better. But lately, I have not meditated much. Why not? I got panicked. How come? Twice I had problems coming back in my body. By the way, Fernando changed the subject, declaring with a proud facial expression, I've got a brother living in California.

Oh yeah? He's a lawyer. In our family, we'd all saved money to let him study.

Where does he live? In Hermosa Beach!

Hey! That's where we'd lived!

The men came back. You won't believe it: We just visited Alberto Lenz in his mansion. They live fenced like in a jail. That's the price for being rich. Mr. Lenz said you have a slight accent. Where are you from, Mr. Meyer? When I said, from Germany he said that would have been the least I'd expected. Then we can talk German. We all speak German in our family. It's tradition for the kids to study in Germany and marry Germans.

Later in the Hilton, we had a major fight, same subject as always: a job of my own. I gave you my money. You agreed to pay me interest. Let's say, this would be $200 a month. I have no gardener. I cook every day. I'm fixing up the house ... I have not told you to do that.

Do you think, I live in a house with pissed on carpets? The only thing I'd do is working as a housekeeper. Ingrid has more free time than I and gets highly paid. Then, I'm gone, and you can look for somebody else to cook and clean and search for cars.

You don't have a work permit. So?

Why don't you open up a pawn shop?

It's much too risky. You have to know a lot about what's worthy and what's not. Remember, your silver knife? A fierce eye shot at me. I thought about the 70th when I'd just moved into Haus Tania. I was about to hang a copy of Spitzweg's *Poor Poet* on the wall and didn't find a hammer. Searching in the silverware case for a knife, I got the dark old one. I thought if this get's stains, it doesn't matter. Likely with only one contact lens on, I had not seen the Claus-Peter imprint. We were too short together, and CP hadn't made any fuss about my mistake. But boy, once or twice a year he put that subject on the table! This time I had the chance to use it against him.

Wien in Beverly Hills, Hay in West Hollywood

On Wednesday afternoon, Hilde called, do you want to accompany us to the Wiener Ball? I've to get the cards as soon as possible. Well, if it's okay with Peter, I'd love to. What a week, we just came from Mexico. By the way, tonight I'll meet Louise Hay. Hilde who'd likely never heard a thing about Louise ignored my remark saying, the Mayor of Vienna will come. His wife Dagmar Koller will sing. Oh, well, I've never been at a Wiener-Ball. My mother would appreciate it even more. She loves to dance. When is it? In three weeks, on February 3. Oh, then we can celebrate Peter's birthday. But I don't have anything to wear for such an event. I don't want to spend a lot of money for just one occasion. I'm going to put it on my wish list. What wish list?

I learned about it in Shakti Gawain's book. You can ask for anything. You just visualize what you want in your life and as long as you don't have it just go on and use supportive affirmations. Positive thinking draws on everything you wish for like a magnet. What affirmations? You could say, with every day I feel better and better. If you say that every day a few times, it will eventually stop the ongoing poisoning we usually unwind in our heads. And what about the wish list? You write down 10 things you desire and describe them in all details. So, if you want a man in your life ...

I already have one. Or a friend. Characterize him or her, visualize the looks and habits. Whenever one wish fulfills you add another one to complete the 10. I wished Leanne as my friend and whoosh my wish fulfilled. Now I'm going to add a beautiful dress scratching out a less important wish, seems to work.

After I'd hung up I wrote down: A blue dress matching my blue eyes, long, size 5, accentuating my figure for not more than $20.

Opposite the *Blue Whale*, I saw Ingrid waiting next to the entrance of 647 North San Vincente Blvd. We walked into the huge dark hall of the theater looking for two free seats in the middle of the approximately 300 people, predominately young men. After the mass meditation, the chairs were put aside. On a long row of connecting tables in the middle of the hall, sales people offered big Spirulina bottles and other immune strengthening supplements.

It was the second time I got information on the blue-green spiral organism. A sign showed that Spirulina supposes to increase the white blood cells, especially the helper lymphocytes, also the lactic bazillions, beneficial gut bacteria. Some of the HIV-positive men claimed to take Spirulina to strengthen their immune system and to prevent AIDS.

Ingrid said something to Louise waving at me. I came close kind of drawn to this vibrant and charismatic woman.

In her elegant red dress with the floral print, she looked extremely feminine. So this is the woman who sells millions of books helping countless readers to get well! I especially thought about the writing of her being sexually abused as a toddler escaping the monsters of her childhood and showing us how the way.

Louise, may I introduce you to my friend Marianne; she's also doing Reiki. That's wonderful. After Louise left us I said, she's truly proof for her bestselling title *You Can Heal Your Life*. Louise sat in her chair on a table. Everyone could see her while speaking to us. Ingrid asked me to follow her onto the stage where some 20 Reiki practitioners and other energy worker acted on several massage tables. With a whispered greeting, she took care of the feet, and I held my hands over the crown chakra. We had kept this procedure whenever we channeled the universal life energy together. Our most dramatic time was on an India Festival in Yorba Linda with a young woman. Karuna's transformation was exhilarating. It was an eerie feeling treating in front of the crowd and then walking with the girl. Ingrid said, do you think about Jesus, too?

When he healed the lame man?

Yep, didn't it feel great? With a broad grin, I looked at her. What? I'd rather not tell. Come on let it out. What amuses you so?

Waving in Karuna's direction, I asked:

Is that what you have in mind when you use to say that your ego is still in your way?

Huh? Never mind. After some young men had talked about their experiences and the supporting program ended, we left the massage tables and went down to the others. We all sat down on the floor in circle rows. Ingrid and I sat in the outside circle. Someone passed me a yellow flyer: Louise L. Educational Institute creating the world where it's safe for us to love each other. We sang the three verses of Jai Josef's song I love myself the way I am: www.youtube.com/watch?v=TWATvSCXLeQ

After some kindergarten like floor games, it got more emotional when with dimming lights, we sang a canon together:

"Doors closing, doors opening, doors closing, doors are opening. I am safe it's only change, I am safe it's only change, doors closing..."

I enjoyed the harmonic atmosphere and the feeling of unconditional love many times. Later, Louise left the lead to Stuart, a young psychologist who's specialized in re-birthing. Since I always gave away baby mushrooms I'd grown for the immune booster Kombucha tea, I was known as Mushroom Marianne.

On Friday, we searched for occasion wear for the worldly Wiener-Ball, first at Designer Labels for Less. Peter found a trendy fitting tuxedo for a reasonable prize. He asked to put it aside. You'll come back, said the Hungarian salesman. At Ross, Peter tried several brands. I said, they all have the opening in the middle. It looks like your butt wants to take off.

No shit! Yeah! Two slits would be okay, but the one in the middle, no! I'd take the one from DLL. That has none at all. Not even the most expensive tux here fits as good. Did you find anything? Nope. Except for those jeans. If you don't want them, I get them for Andy. I couldn't resist this rich green. Oh, I forgot to tell you, Gerd is coming tomorrow.

Darn! Alone? No, with Petra. I hope, she'll not dry her socks on our office chairs again. Why? Why what? Grunt! I can't stand this honeyed hypocrite. He always whets his knife. I think his limp handshake says it all. Huh?

We better open a bed & breakfast, then at least I'd make some money. Chill out! You always tell me, I should look for a job, then you have me do all this extra work. How could I ever keep a job when you need me constantly? Come on! All morn, I've looked through the papers. You know prices better than I do. Yeah, I know lots better than you ...

Annie, get your gun. That doesn't mean, you can drop everything on me! I need time for myself, too. If you go on like that, I'm going to step in Ingrid's shoes. She's got two free days a week and doesn't even cook. When do I have got a full free day? On vacations. Free? How free? Free to listen to your litany?

A week later, I took some stuff to Goodwill on Ventura Blvd. in Tarzana. It was the first time I donated something. Usually, I went only there to hunt for books, antiques or paintings, especially after a seminar in Everywoman's Village. A large nice lady with a huge house full of antiques somewhere in Simi Valley, claiming to have been married to one of the Krupp sons appraised whatever we'd brought in. She taught us about antiques and told us about her divorce from the wealthy German.

Her mother-in-law had advised her to stay and kick him out. I said, with some hubby, you have to be as hard as Krupp steel. This time, I didn't look for antiques, only for clothes. On a round rack, I noticed a shiny blue dress in a dry cleaning bag. Wow! That's it! The long evening gown looked like never been worn. I searched for a label: no size, seemingly custom made. But the prize tag said it all: size 5. Original prize 19.95, reduced to 5.95!

On the eve of February 3rd, we drove with our black Cadillac Eldorado Cabriolet to Bel Air. In Hilde's living room I sat down on a wide white easy chair. That's the one on which Franz Josef Strauß had taken place years ago when Heinz still worked for Lockheed.

Ah, then you may know if our former secretary of defense got bribed or not? I don't think so. I have not picked up anything.

Of cause, nobody had dropped a bundle of bucks in front of you. Strauß was such a smart powerful man. Once, before election day, he said: I agree with any chancellor under me.

We left the Cadillac with the valet parking service and entered the Beverly Wilshire foyer. To get in the huge hall where the Wiener Ball took place, we had to step down a recess. The floor to ceiling glass wall and the people already in made the broadly carpeted landing not easily noticeable. Hilde and John walked hand in hand in front of us when all of a sudden they disappeared. They were so fast on their feet again that it looked like in a comedy picture. I couldn't help tittering. Hilde also laughed but with an agonized facial expression. I don't think, there is anything to laugh about, I think I sprained my ankle. I'm sorry!

I danced with Peter. A photographer shot a picture of the four of us. The event ended at

1:00 a. m. with a payback of my insensible behavior. Just past my favorite deli Trader Joe's, directly under the Freeway bridge on White Oak, we got a flat tire. So, in the 1st hour of Peter's 48th birthday, he had to change the tire in his tuxedo. He got the car jack from the trunk saying, Marianne, you have to step on the brakes till I'm done. It's just too dangerous. The tires are huge. I don't know if the jack stands firm. It's quite a shaky thing.

20 minutes later, my foot ached. Driving the remaining half mile home, I said: I'd better not laughed at Hilde's slip-up. I just couldn't help it. Such a cute clowning! Now my right foot hurts as much as Hilde's. Little sins get punished instantly. And why do I have to suffer too? Karma?

I hadn't had much contact with Hilde this summer not wanting to disturb the young love. I also had a lot to do fixing up the house. Peter was traveling abroad. Since he always argues when I start new projects I used the time to do all the improvements in his absence. To tile the kitchen and the hall, I ripped out the linoleum and began to level the floor with concrete. The kitchen had set two inches. I needed a lot of bags. After two days work, I figured I'd never be able to finish the project in the time Peter was gone. I had also underestimated the work on the deformed hall slope caused by earthquakes with a rented jackhammer. Near Home Depot I chose a Mexican from a group of day laborers. For three days the young man who called his mother each evening helped me straighten out the floor.

Peter came back from Germany holding a white cardboard with golden stripes on two grips. While kissing me, he kept it far from his body as if I should not see it. Want me to take your grip-sack? No, just take the briefcase.

What's in there? I asked jeeringly. I cannot believe you bring anything else than the usual dirty clothes. Peter chuckled. For sure, it also needs cleaning. I'll show you in the car. We walked to the park house. Let me drive. Peter put the box in the backseat. Miaou! Foxi!!!

Don't get him out! He's sitting in his shit.

Oh, poor thing! I gave him a kiss on his peachy forehead stripes. Pooh, now I smell it. Peter said, well, I felt quite sorry for the flight attendants. The stewardess asked me to leave him with them. Poor fellow. They may have given him milk. He's not used to it. Why didn't you take Carlo along, too? Foxi had fallen from a tree. He's still limping. I felt sorry for him and wanted to surprise you. Poor Carlo.

After a smooth bath, Foxi lounged about the bright rooms with the floor-to-ceiling windows. Overlooking everything he felt to be outside. Putting on an appreciating grinning, he forgot all about to dragging along his leg.

Back in Michelstadt left behind Carlo was pissed. He didn't quit on food but he dead stopped communicating with my mother for three weeks. She had taken Foxi to Peter's car.

A few months later Carlo made his entrance at LAX as the curio fat cat mimicking Caruso. The dog carrier with the tomcat had gotten lost. The search ended when the ashen-black-beige tiger had sent his tragic wailing of his Opera serial performance off to the last row.

All the stewardesses, employees, and passengers rushing to the container agreed never to have seen such a large common house cat. I was shocked when Carlo walked out of the big box Peter had dropped onto the kitchen floor. Opening all the reachable drawers and doors of the kitchen cabinet, Carlo asked:

Where's the food? What have you done?

Ma shrugging put the blame on Pa:

Ludi bought more and more sausages. He could not stand Carlo's heart moving beggary. Every other bite he shared with him.

How could you! He was 6 kilos you 80! Every tenth bit would have been too much.

I couldn't help it; he's such a good eater.

That he is, learned it as a kitten. Carlo was on his own and had food only on occasion. Whenever anyone filled a bowl for him he'd emptied it at once and searched for the next bowl filler. He had no security of regular meals. It's still influencing his life. My fellow student found him nearby the female jail.

I know, kids were pulling out his whiskers.

Yep! I'm sure he'd developed his sound intensity there. When the caring cons had thrown their titbits out of the barred windows, he'd for sure increased his caterwaul to get another goody. I don't know if you recognized that Carlo is also a genius in mind reading. Whenever I thought to keep a food rest for him, a few secs later he appeared saying don't bother to use a dish for this tiny bit.

Right, he did it with me, too.

I wonder that his box is still clean after all those hours. Yeah, 17 from door to door.

When Hilde saw Carlo first, she said:

By Jove is that just winter blubbery or frustration fat? Half a year later, on Thanksgiving, we invited Hilde and John. My friend was amazed by the change. Carlo was a speck-less cat again. His asthmatic gasping was gone as well as his audible snoring.

How did you do it? The trick was to lay him treats in front of the door. When he wanted another goody, he had to get all around the house and enter through the cat flap.

When the turkey and the veggies were on the table, Carlo came into the dining room and stared at the actor like hypnotized.

He seems to admire you. Well!

Carlo's tail whipped, the disruption turning out a bit awkward. Under the spell, the captivated performer cut a piece of turkey but taking over I laid a piece of meat in front of the door. Shortly after the tom came in dragging a heavy gopher between his teeth like a fetching dog. He stared at John. I asked: How did you do that in just a minute? John, he does admire you! You think so? Yeah! Maybe he wants to show that he doesn't need dead meat. Well! He'd never done this before! It must have to do something with you. He brought you a gift.

A few months later, my mother was astounded about cunning Carlo. Have you put him on a diet? After explaining the tactic I earned a big smile. That I should do with Ludi, too. The surplus movement melts fat.

Dan Barton commanding the bridal

Just after our yearly Gullwing group meeting in Dana Point where we'd went to with our 300 SL, Hilde called.

We are going to get married on Oct. 5, 1990.

Oh, congratulations! Wow, it's the day my darling grandmother was born 88 years earlier. Another coincidence!

Will you be there? Why, yes.

Can you be my Maid of Honor?

Of course! I feel honored.

John's Best Man is Dan Barton from Days of our Lives. The wedding will be at the Bel Air Hotel. We got father Ara for the ceremony.

Who? He'd just married Hugh Hefner, the Playboy editor. Dean Martin and Syd Charisse are coming, Finny Getty, the Ex-Mayor of Beverly Hills. 43 altogether.

Well! I better don't think about our special day. The least romantic event you can imagine. We went with our few guests from a fancy hotel to a students bar. In the evening, in a close by restaurant, drunken Pete threw his tough steak onto the wall. For the money spend, we'd have easily celebrated with all friends and family. After Hilde hung up, I thought heck another synchronicity! Was the 88th birthday of my emigrated great-grandfather's daughter a reminder?

But what could I've done besides asking all and sundry about finding my potential relatives? Jocelyn advised me to check on Ellis Island. All immigrants names are listed there. But how should I find someone if I don't have a name? He had certainly changed his name to Victor later. On the vessels' passengers list for sure was the name recorded matching his passport. I doubt he came with a fake one. Since I didn't know what to do, I tried several times to get in touch with Grandma Maria. But all the time I got the message not to have to do anything.

Marita had accompanied Willi on his flight to L. A. because it was one of his last ones. The computers made engineers aboard jumbo jets useless. The new technique forced them either to retire or to be trained to become pilots. Marita had extended her stay to visit us for a few days. Entering our grounds, she said:

Let's celebrate! I brought a bottle of champagne. Every time Marita came to visit, life was easier, more lively, more sparkly, and every time we parted I felt we had a good time. Peter opened the garage to use the short-cut to the guestroom. Glancing at the extra long 600 Mercedes' white leather interior, Marita made a valuing sound: What a black beauty!

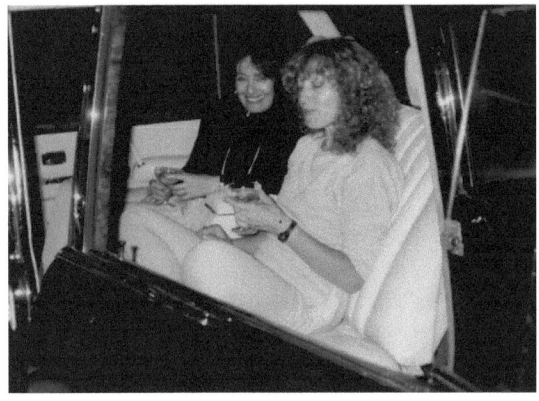

Peter grabbed the bottle and said, I better serve you the champagne in the car. But with a tux and a white serviette around the arm, please. Once again, with Marita's arrival, a mood of relaxed gaiety flew across the house. And with it the expectation of experiencing another cultural highlight. Most musical events we'd underwent with our lively friend. Especially enlightening was when we'd jointly attended The first Lady of Song in Frankfurt's old opera, in the early 80th. Being in our prime, we were impressed by 64-year-old Ella Fitzgerald's vocal range, phrasing and purity of tone. I surely mentioned my mother's similar singing voice. At the time, we didn't know of my relationship with Doris Day, who taught herself to sing by listening to Ella's records.

Listening to both singer's intonation of *Someone like you*, I liked Do-dos' lighter interpretation even better. Her idol had truly helped to develop her singing voice. And now I'm learning by listening to my relative's recordings.

What's new? Any musicals playing? On Friday we are invited to Hilde's wedding. Is that the little Lady, we'd been with at *Les Miserables?* Yep! Whom does she marry?

The actor John Hudson. Marita's eyes widened: Doris Day's ... isn't he ...?

No, John Hudson. He often played Westerns, and he was a doctor in the soap General Hospital. He was not as successful as Rock. I've just seen him with Larry Hagman and his bottle ghost Barbara Gordon. By the way, I still haven't found out anything about my great grandfather's family. Marita sighed:

Why you wanna find your bloody kinsfolk? I think you're wasting your energy. I feel it's important to know that life continues on another level of existence. Finding those Victor relatives would proof it. Do you think people will change if they know that ghosts exist?

Maybe when the catastrophes by our ruinous activities and the apocalyptic fears increase.

I doubt it. By the way, I want to surprise Hilde and John with our decorated Mercedes 300 Adenauer. Oh good, I'll help you. We may find something nice at Michel's.

I called Hilde for the exact time to pick them up. She said, four guests aren't coming. So you can bring your friend along. I have to pay the $39 per plate as it is. Oh, well, Marita will enjoy it. The big green Mercedes with the creme roof looked marvelous with the ivory flower arrangement. When we drove up Hilde's private driveway, a deer family of six made us stop. We never saw them at daytime. The deer coming to our grounds appeared also only after nightfall. It's as if they know what's going to happen. Did you ever see deer with such big ears? Nope. Now move! Peter pushed the horn. When he slowly started again, they leisurely moved their big brown bodies.

Father Ara kept the ceremony refreshingly relaxing. Hilde had told him to avoid religious talk since many Jews were invited, producers, actors, agents. When we all had taken seats in the dining hall, John's Best Man let a spoon clink on his glass. Dan Barton's lengthy smashing speech discouraged me. A mixture of intimidation, stage fright and serving the food made me kick my prepared mini delivery under the Persian rug. But after a stout woman got up and said something, I regretted my sheepishness. My words about how the excellent cook and private nurse had captured her old love would have been wittier. Also my wish only Hilde's palatal pleasing talents should be tested.

But 18 happy months later, her destiny conformed to the burden of another nursing job.

I sat next to a pleasant elder man. Mr. Gefsky showed interest in my diamond ring. I handed it to him. My mother-in-law gave it to me. What a beautiful setting with the baroque pearl. What are you doing for a living?

We're dealing vintage cars. How about you?

I'm a movie agent. Oh really? I had acting classes with Sharon Chatten. When she critiqued me better than the professionals, I took off. Don't you wanna work in the movie busi-

ness? Not really. So why did you do the class?

It wasn't a conscious thing. All came to me easily: John introduced me to Jocelyn Brando. Two actresses in her writer's block workshop talked me into showing me their classes.

Oh, I know Jocelyn. But I didn't know she's a therapist. She's a very talented actress. She has at least as much talent as Marlon. But she wasn't lucky at choosing her roles. Too bad.

Yes. It's a pity! I only remember her last role in Mummy, Dearest, a small, but not a bad one. Anyhow, acting isn't everything. The salmon is excellent, isn't it? Yes, so is the lamb. Do you know what kind of meat the steak is? Veal, I guess.

After the fruit shape Marita neared our table.

You've got to come with me. I met an interesting couple. Dr. Patrick J. Frawley is the co-founder of the Schick Shadel Hospital of Santa Barbara. His wife had given birth to 9 children. Goody! Yeah, but it doesn't show on her.

Mr. Frawley had shown me why people smoke and how to lose the habit.

Okay. I'm coming.

Turning to Mr. Gefsky, I said:

Excuse me. Sure, go ahead.

Reaching Marita's table, I said, I've heard promising things. My husband Peter had given up smoking for a year after his mother had passed on but now he smokes again. The doctor was wholly in his element. He came to our table and explained the way habits form. simultaneously: The brain has 2 independent mechanism. The Turning to Mr. Gefsky, I said:

Excuse me. Sure, go ahead.

Arriving at Marita's table I said, I've heard promising things on how to quit smoking. My husband Peter had given it up for one year after his mother had passed on, but now he smokes again. The doctor was wholly in his element. He came to our table and explained the way habits form simultaneously: The brain has two independent mechanisms. The subconscious memory works like a recorder the reasoning mind like a calculator. The touch is the strongest sense. Many positive impressions have been recorded with the way we touch the steering wheel and pedals. Now, you act automatically even in fast traffic. The same is with cigarettes. Dr. Frawley raised his arm as if he had a coffin nail between his index and middle finger, looked at it, smelled the imaginary smoke and said:

We have to consume an addictive substance repeatedly to imprint the subconscious mind. Talk won't bring on the habit, and similarly, talk can't break the habit that has been programmed by body reactions. I asked:

So what can break the habit? The doc said:

The subconscious memory must identify the substance alcohol or tobacco through odor, taste or appearance and experience a negative reaction to change the emotion associated with the habit. I asked: Should I slap Peter whenever he grabs a butt? All the guests on the table broke out in a hearty laughter. Yes, exactly. But the way we work is more subtle. And more expensive I thought. Let's compare the method with training a dog. If a dog wets the floor and you bring him back to the wet spot for a succession of slight slaps with a newspaper, it's brain will record the discomfort with the wet spot. If the slaps are not administered at the wet spot the dog cannot record them together and the correction will not be effective. Now, the Schick Smoking Control Center uses impulse therapy called the Morse Code tingle. The slight annoying impulse removes the pleasure associated with the habit. I said: I got the message. Dr. Frawley said, give me your address, I'll send you a brochure.

Walking to the table of the newlywed I asked: John, I miss your buddy Jack.

Oh, he's busy on the set making a movie.

Several months later, Jack Palance won the Oscar for Best Supporting Actor in the role as the tough cowboy Curley in City Slickers. At the Academy Awards, millions of people watched him doing a series of one-arm push-ups. Thus he showed the movie makers they must not offer him Grandpa roles.

In the following week, Jocelyn held another workshop. Suzanne called: Are you going?

I don't need to. My writing's going smooth. Okay? I'm still going. I need a break from Peter. So what's new? Nothing much. Peter has it with the celebrities, lately. So? He'd run into Steffi Graf on his way back from Germany. Really? Where? At Newark Airport. And? He asked her: Where are you heading? What did she say? Miami. What else? Yesterday, Peter dined at the Spago with Rod Stewart on the neighbor-table and I went to a group channeling. Jeau Michael channels several spirits. It's so funny when Maria comes through and he talks in a woman's voice. So what do you get out of this? Like the others, I asked about my lucky stone. It's supposed to be an aventurine. I also asked about my big book about all the different kinds of alternative healing. He said the same thing, Marilyn already told me. What? I don't see a big book, but 10 small ones. Wanna you go with me to church tomorrow? Huh? Marianne Williamson is doing her Course on Miracles. Well, why not? I like her books.

Entering the old church, Marianne greeted us in a baggy dark-blue maternity dress with tiny white flowers. She said: 10 years ago, I was pregnant once before. My partner left town, and I had an abortion. Oh! Yeah, but some time ago he came back. Now I'm pregnant again. Maybe, the same child soul had settled down with me again wanting this experience. I said to my namesake: I had something similar to undergo. I don't know how many times I tried, but finally, I came to stay with my mother as *Patentex-Marianne*.

A week later, I took the wedding photos along to Jocelyn since I thought she might be interested in seeing them. Suzanne was already there. I noticed that the dark shadow of resignation had vanished from her eyes.

Wow, you look terrific. I mentally moved back to Dr. Fett's office where I waited for my friend. This compassionate surgeon did a great job. I showed Jocelyn the pictures. A bittersweet laughter left her throat. What a flunky!

He didn't tell me he'd marry. These men just don't have the guts to speak up. Why? Should I've better not shown you the photos? No, not at all, it's just we were lovers, and he hadn't even mentioned that he was seeing somebody else. Yeah, men have a hard time to reveal themselves. What can you do?

It's too sad. Life is just a bowl of cherries, so live and let a-a-alone. Poor Jocelyn, she had no luck with her men. The bad ones had beaten the good ones left her.

Sizzling spring after warfare winter 1991

The most infamous affair of summer 1990 was watching a prewar preparation on TV.

Saddam Hussein invaded Kuwait. His government confined hundreds of citizens of Western countries to discourage nations from participating in military operations against Iraq. It was sickening when the hostages were held in hotels as human shields and extra vile when Hussein touched kids' head. On 6 December he dismissed 3,000 hostages. But since he did not want to leave Kuwait the coalition forces started the attack on Iraq on 17 January 1991 with a surface bombing. With more than 100,000 flights more than 88,000 tons of bombs fell.

Watching the coverage of the Gulf war was a telenovela replacement for many people: blaring air raid sirens and firing antiaircraft batteries attended by CNN reporter Peter Arnett's daily televisual report. In the initial hours of the US attacking the city, I remember a tense scene with Arnett and the CNN journalists John Holliman und Bernard Shaw, in the Al Rasheed Hotel, in Baghdad. Explosions knocked people back from the window. Holliman seemed to be torn between wanting to be where the action was and wishing to be with the majority of the CNN crew in the shelter. He went there, but came back to the room, challenging the Iraqi guards in the shelter. I'll never forget when Bernie while cruise missiles were flying past his window, found shelter under a desk. He'd described the situation as feeling like being in the center of hell.

A week after the first air raids, I looked out of the kitchen window and saw the little red mailbox flag pointing downwards. The evening before, I'd put several letters with checks in the mailbox and turned the flag up. Mentally praising the US mail delivery, I walked down the driveway. The US customer is king in many respects. I opened a letter from Germany. This time I recognized my father's handwriting. I delivered Peter's mail to the office and skimmed through the text at his desk. Oh, Pa's kidneys are pinching. He thinks this could be his last letter.

This won't kill Ludi, Peter said. He's got another art plate from the collection *Adventures on Pussyfoot*. He wants to send it if Heini and Andreas could not come. Why does Pa think I'm a collector? Of course, the painted kittens are cute, and the colors are matching the kitchen interior. Peter said, tell him not me! I like unbreakable things better, especially books. Euuugh! The share of the cost for the Ibiza apartment is 1000 marks more. Why that? Because of refacing.

He hopes to get enough bookings to cover the costs. We should sell it. He calls the Gulf War an epitome of human ignorance and thinks it will be a set back for years. So many natural resources uselessly blown. They should better think of the poor children in the world! At least Pa is thinking about his little goddaughters in Africa.

After the 3-week air campaign, Hussein's mother of all battles ended with the burning of billions of crude oil. For eight month his military forces forced wasting an estimated 5 to 6 million barrels of crude oil and 70 to 100 million m^3 of natural gas each day. Wads of smoke containing hazardous gaseous emissions stretched hundreds of miles. The smoke contained high levels of chemicals likely having caused the respiratory symptoms of Kuwaitis and Gulf War soldiers reported as the Gulf War syndrome. Were all the civilian casualties worthwhile? Why is history repeating itself? The same powers endeavored to finish off Hitler by "accidentally and unwanted" killing hundreds of thousands of civilians by explosive, fire and phosphor bombs. An answer of the Luftwaffe's aiming to destroying Britain's airfields and war industries. The London Blitz with 71 attacks on 16 cities had not caused as many casualties as Hamburg alone. http://militaryhistory.about.com/od/aerialcampaigns/p/gomorrah.htm

Almost a three-quarter century after the Nazi and Soviet invading of Poland and dividing the land between them, fortunately, there is no pressure against a neighboring EU country anymore resulting in the Nobel Peace Prize 2012 for the EU. Alas, globally, there are still people horrifically suffering for their brain sick leaders.

Beginning of March, I was watching another televised brutality. Peter come here. I think they're killing a black guy. Who? The bulls. Police? Yeah, looks bad. Why? I don't know why. I guess because he's black. About seven LAPD officers surround the guy, some of them striking him repeatedly. Though Peter hadn't left his desk, he still had the chance to see the beating of the motorist Rodney King following a high-speed chase since the video footage was displayed dozens of times.

There was no other subject for the next week's thanks to a resident who had witnessed and videotaped the brutal beating of the African American construction worker. The heat on Rodney King was turned up. A much-disputed point was whether or not he was resisting the police struggle to subdue him.

The footage was partly aired around the world, inflaming racial tensions. The video increased public sensitivity and anger about police brutality, racism and social inequalities throughout the USA.

Mid of April, Peter said: Why didn't I bet on a rising Dow Jones Index? Today it closed above 3,000 for the first time. Having had a quick flip through another letter from Germany, I ignored his remark saying, they want you to bring two blue kinds of toothpaste, the one with fennel, propolis, and myrrh. They don't like the German brands anymore and wish to have a Trader Joe's in Michelstadt. What's propolis?

A bee byproduct. Aha. I won't forget it.

But I don't know if I'll fly on Whitsunday.

Then they have to wait till summer.

Heini and Andreas can take them along.

Only if they come. They will. I had a dream. You and your dreams. Oh, my teacher will be 80 on April 30. I wonder why Pa has her on his calendar. She'll be pleased to get a greeting card from California. Didn't you hate school? Luise Walti was okay. I had no problems in German and biology. She'd taught us autogenic training. So? That was quite a show.

End of April, the race riots hell had broken loose after a jury trial, resulting in the acquittal of four LAPD officers accused in the beating of Rodney King. As expected after such an insensible fateful verdict, a lot of houses burnt in the so-called Black Forest of Watts and other deprived districts. On the 3rd day of the riots with all its widespread looting, assaults, and murder, we had a dinner engagement with Bill and Leanne for sizzling fajitas in our favorite restaurant on Ventura Blvd. in Studio City. Walking in the balmy evening air down Karen Drive, a prickly vibe made me feel alive. We arrived at our neighbor friend's house. Bill greeted us with a twinkle in his eyes and a gun in his hand.

Do you need that? With a big grin, the big kid opened his belt bag showing his metal toy.

Alright, Bill said approvingly. I said I doubt we'll have problems in the Valley.

But, Leanne tossed in, better sure than sorry.

Getting into Bill's white BMW, I asked, so who do you think will win the election? Bush, of course, replied Bill sassy.

No way! Think about all those empty stores on the Boulevards. That frightens people. They want a change. So Bill will win. And, mimicking Bush, read my lips, he'll even serve a 2nd term. You're out of your mind. I'd rather go for Ross Perot. Clinton won't do the job.

You will change your mind.

Placatory, Leanne said: Well, we'll see.

A few days later, I took the Olds to pick up Ingrid from LAX. Gliding along in the comfy sedan, I said, you missed the action.

No need. I could have done without too.

How was Bali? Absolut fantastic! Such a beautiful island. I've never seen more sensual people anyplace else. They're radiating aesthetic, kindness and peace. Here, it was less peaceful. Yesterday, the National Guard and the U.S. Marines were called to stop the rioting. There were around 2000 people injured. Any killed? More than 50. Omigod, where are we? Out of sheer joy and talking. I never got lost on the way back from the airport. Looks pretty wild here. Ah, there's a gas station, I'm going to ask. Rolling down the window, I noticed a leggy 40ish black male walking some 20 yards from us. I screamed: S i i i r ! The man stalled, looking puzzled. How do we get to the Freeway? The African American shook his head as if shifting his surprise. He pointed to the right. Thank you! A minute later, we were back on track.

Peter picked up my relatives from LAX. When they entered the house, I said: Hey, Andreas, I remember those parrot green pants. They don't look worn. Are you wearing them just to show me that you do? My nephew answered with an amusingly swerved nay, they are my darling pants. If you are lying, you are an expert. Laughing, the 18-year-old said, no really I wear them all the time. Perfect quality jeans then. So, now, you both can jump into the pool, or are you hungry? No, Heini said, we just ate on the plane. I show you your room. It was a maid's quarter. We use it for guests. I did all the tiling and the bathroom renewing myself. Runs in the family. Except for Pa, his fingers are all thumbs. Peter said, why, he'd cut the dead tree pretty well. Awful. I couldn't stay watching his kamikaze stunt. Oh, come on, he's used to it. He was an electrician and had to do this work every day.

Hey, looks great, like a marble room. I marbleized everything, so desk and nightstands look alike. Gorgeous piece!

I got it from a garage sale for 25 bucks.

Next morn, Andreas came into the kitchen. I pointed to the cat feeding bowls. Guess who was there? Huh? The coons! Why? They sometimes come through the kitty door to petty larceny of food. Really? Yeah, that's when the water is empty, and there are dusty rests of dry food in the water bowl. Why? They wash their paws after eating. Cool!

I reached Andy the plate with a gorgeous fruit mandala. He grabbed several pieces: Oh wow, I'd eat much more fruits if served like that. Peter said, what a charmer.

That's why Opa is taking you along on his bus tours all the time. I've heard you keep the fellow passenger's spirits up. Have you inherited this quality from me? Um, I'm just kind. But our unchecked laughter and the hay fever you've gotten from me for sure. No one else in our families has any allergies.

How about a tennis match? It's just two houses down at the corner. Okay?

When they'd started hitting the ball, the Cassidy dog's woof didn't bother me at all since my relatives pulled some great stunts. Heini was close on the net when Andy hit the ball in a high arch over his head. Heini ran as swift as an arrow but had no time to turn around. He hit it over his head without seeing where it went. It's inside the field! Andy showed off hitting it right back straight through his legs.

Incredible! You are artists with the ball.

When we came back, Peter said:

How about driving to San Francisco? Why?

I've bought a 300 SL from a German who lives in San José. From there it isn't far. So

you can show your folks the belle of the bay. That will take at least two days! I thought about Ma's intention, paying the flights so he can make a protective cover over the heating and cooling system on the flat roof. That way, the house would be cooler in the hot summers. I'd planned to pay for a 2-day trip to Las Vegas, the Grand Canyon and visits to Disney World, Sea World, and Universal Studios. But another 2-day trip was nonscheduled. Heini had read my mind: We stay 3½ weeks. But we'll need only 5 full days for the roof. You want to cover only the pipes, do you? Uh-huh! So, to fix the beams and the plywood will take two days three at the most. The rest is nailing on the Canadian asphalt shingles. That you can do, too. Peter said: Sightseeing will take a day and a half. The next day on our way back we'll get the car.

Two afternoons later, we drove in the Olds up a hill and reached a sturdy two storied house. That's not a pasteboard house as the once you see here, said Heini. It is made from real stones. Yes, but in an earthquake area, it's dangerous to live in such a house. Entering the living room Heini went right to the wall and pointed to a blue porcelain plate showing the famous Michelstadt city hall. In the next half hour, I was stunned by my brother's strange behavior as if we had changed personalities. I kept quiet, and Heini went on talking with those German strangers until Peter said: We have to hurry now. I want to be on the Freeway before it gets dark. We went outside. Heini, Andreas and I were already standing at the Olds when Peter went back to look for his key. Heini said with a strangely absent look: Now, this will take quite a bit longer.

What do you mean? I don't know ... something will happen. Peter came back. The key is nowhere. It must be in my briefcase. Where do you have it? In the trunk. Oh great! Peter jerked on the grasp several times, then turned around. I'll get a screwdriver. I've to get to the trunk from the backseat. Half an hour later, following Peter and Andy in the red convertible, we still got to the Freeway at dusk.

Back at home, we got a call from Karl-Dieter, asking if Kai and Ollie could come for two weeks. I moaned, how will I handle that, cooking three meals for six people, more shopping, keeping house, showing our guests California and Nevada and helping Heini with the roof.

On the other hand, for Andreas, it'll be good having two peers to roam around. I asked:

Is it okay for you to move into my office? I'd built a daybed that can be converted to a double plank bed.

Sure. Okay, then let them come.

A week later while Heini and I were nailing the shingles against the planks Peter and Andy picked up the youngsters from LAX. Heini said: I could have told you a long time before that we'll come for sure.

Why? I had a dream where Andreas and I were with you and Peter visiting a German who had the Michelstadt city hall on the wall.

I didn't know you've prophetic dreams, too.
Since I was 6. Why have you never told us? Mama knew it.

I guess if I hadn't had those operations and medications I had those things even earlier.

Are you getting instant visions at daytime?

Not that I know of, why? I had that recently. I was with Hubs and some other handball players in Paris. We were cruising around, having a beer here and a bit there and didn't pay attention where we were heading. All of a sudden, Hubs said: Good grief, where's our hotel? All of a sudden, I had a three dimensional town map in front of my inner eye. I could see parks, bridges, churches and even street signs vividly. I told him specifics about better taking a completely different route and gave directions. You should have seen their faces when we finally ended up right in front of the hotel. Wow! Was it telepathy? Dunno.

Next morn in the guest quarter, I rattled out Kai and Ollie our program for two weeks. If you also want to visit Saint Francis, you've to drive yourself. Huh? We've just been there. Where? In San Francisco.

Three days later, we were driving in the Olds on the 210 Freeway towards I-15, the Freeway leading to Las Vegas. After crossing the San Gabriel Mountains near San Bernardino, the Freeway led through the Mojave Desert with dunes, rock formations and crusted salt lakes. Close to Barstow, Andy said:

Hey, look at the mountain! It is written: Calico. Uh-huh! That's a Ghost town, a reconstructed silver mine town. It's interesting, we'll go there, it's only a few miles off the 15. I was there two times, once with Peter and once with Ma and Pa. Leaving the parking lot, we walked towards the 19th-century picturesque place. A weird looking full-bearded man in an antiquated black suit greeted us. When he raised his topper, Kai said: Marianne, why are you through with him? Oh well, I couldn't stand his beard any longer, it's like a grater.

The continuation of our journey turned out boring, mostly flat, few diversion. To kill the time, we estimated the length of the line till the next curve. In the early eve, we reached the ultimate playground for adults. Heini asked: Where are we staying? I think we'll get the best deal at the *Sands*. It was the 7th Hotel built on the Strip. It's not as splashy, but it's a historical place. In the 60th, it was owned by Howard Hughes. JFK was occasionally a guest of Frank Sinatra. And I was very lucky there with Ma and Pa. How so? I'd invited them for staying 2 nights with breakfast, a $5 chip on the roulette table, 4 quarters for the slot machine, a show and a dinner for just $189. On the roulette table, I'd pit on a number with my head demonstratively turned away from the table. The ball rolled and what came? The 19. And where lay my chip?

On the 19! Exactly. The croupiers greeted me whenever I passed their table. On the slot machine, I won another $25. So, I made a few bucks more than the special's value. Not a good business for the Sands.

When I came back from the check-in desk I said, you won't believe it. I got 2 suites with a jacuzzi for only 38 bucks each, also tickets for Splash in the Riviera. We had no time for splashing in the Jacuzzi since we were too tired and next morn we started early for our Gran Canyon tour. After 25 miles on I-515 and further on Highway 93 via Boulder City, we reached Lake Mead, one of the two lakes created by damming the Colorado River. The kids were impressed by a huge Hoover Dam. 75 miles further we reached Arizona's historical town Kingman. Andy who looked in the map said, there's Route 66. I glanced at it and said, oh Andy Divine Ave. A good omen! After a good deal of the Route 66 nostalgia, we got lost since our card didn't show the small roads. We took Antares Rd. Hwy 149. After miles and miles with no single soul in sight a flicker of hope: the Antares Rd. was now called Antares point, signalizing an overlook. After more miles and no sign of life, we got edgy. I don't know what had gotten into me. When I read Tanny Ranch Rd. indicating life, I said, let's see if we get water there. We've got only 2 bottles. But the ranch looked like a rotten, empty shed. Miles and miles of nothing.

Kai asked, what will happen if we lose a tire? It's so hot outside.

Don't worry. We'll be okay. I had a dream in which we got wet at the Sea World by a splashing whale and driving back on the San Diego overfly. That was funny last year there, your sister duck in fear of heights.

It was a mistake not to stay on Antares Rd, one we'd never forget and regret. After some more miles on a dirt road, all of a sudden we reached the canyon and had the impression as if no man had ever been here, absolutely still. No bird, no insect, nothing. Dead calm. Huh! Kai said: It looks like where Selma and Louise had their takeoff. What a view! An unsolicited place. Better than in church. I'd never felt that alive. After a while, Heini said in a solemn tone: I think we have to head back now. Kai said: It is the most peaceful place I'd ever seen! I could stay longer. Yeah, me too. But it's 2:00 p. m. already. You want to see the London Bridge at Lake Havasu too.

Arriving late afternoon, it was still broiling.

We listened to a big black soul singer at the bridge which was built 1831 over the river of Thames and in the 1960th was stone by stone dismantled and shipped, from London to here.

When we arrived at home late in the evening, we were greeted by Peter who had a little mishap with the wall and my self-made bookcase. Getting my sweat-suit out of it, I said: Oh, looks like you had a good time. Did you do some fashion designing? We will never forget these summer weeks with lots of work and fun, one of the best times ever.

I was in love with life. When Kai left, she said: You really have a fine family life. You were always there for us. I wish I had that at home, too.

Fire walking with Michael Big Bear

In February 1992 Ingrid invited me and my parents to an afternoon tea at Roy Orbison's beach house in Malibu. Her Toluca Lake lawyer had claimed marriage plans and Ingrid had to look for a new job. The economy wasn't as good anymore, so Ingrid had to take a lesser paid job with far more work. The late country singer's German widow Barbara and their two almost grown up sons had left for the weekend. Ingrid greeted us excitedly. You're lucky! It's my first time to watch whales. On the wooden terrace, my father prepared the video camera and filmed the grand gray whales. They appeared to put on a show, jumping out of the water and making funny sounds. They seemed to be at least as amused by our joyful laughter than we were by their wedding ceremony.

After about 15 minutes my filming father ended his efforts to tame the mammals on celluloid.

Ingrid said, Michael Big Bear's doing another fire walk. Oh, well! Expelling a cubic yard of air I said: Not eager anymore. I understand.

We'd experienced the onset of such a fiery event some months earlier. But the spiritual leader of the Inner Light Center had forgotten to inform the neighbors. Ten minutes after we had lit the two-yard diameter wood stack we heard the fire brigade's siren from the far distance. Three young men in yellow rubber coats terminated the approved holy ceremony at the Osho-Center. All lamenting didn't stop the black hoses' extinguishing the fire. The commandant, who had approved the fire walk was on vacation. He had not informed his colleagues. Ingrid said:

I don't know if I'm going to walk, but I'm cock surely going. I want to see it.

Okay, I'll go too. Looking at my parents' unhappy faces, I added: I'm pretty sure I won't walk. Later, we passed along the beach, valuing the houses of the rich and famous. If we'd have known about Ma's relationship with Doris Day earlier, we'd have taken a picture of her nearby beach house. It's almost as if Ingrid had followed her. First, she'd worked in a house in Toluca Lake that could have been the one Doris described in her biography. I shouldn't wonder with all the curious coincidences that Mr. Green's house once belonged to Doris's hubby Marty Melcher. That her agent and future husband had by chance lived right next to her house, was already strange.

Then Ingrid had a live-in job close to Doris's Malibu's beach house, and right after she'd left this world at the very day between my father's and my mother's birthday, I learned from my family relationship with Doris!

A few days later at about 1:00 p. m., I steered the Olds towards the 101 Freeway joining the flickering sheet metal line. The vibrating air and the wavy gliding in the comfy cruiser made me solemn and the ride appeared quite mystical. On Lincoln Blvd., the lobster sign woke me and some 60 seconds later I turned right into Victory Ave. Like Victor, another coincidence? All afternoon we pushed certain meridian points in search of our personal painful blockades. These possible imprints of pains or fails from early childhood or past lives released by crying out. I roared my lungs out. Had this to do with my dreadful experience as the beautiful woman in an earlier century? In my youth, I'd once woke up with the reminiscence of a dream in which I was pushed up on a rack wagon. It took me days to recover from sad feelings.

A quarter century later, watching the traditional Castro Marim procession in Portugal, I felt this bottomless sadness again. Several drumming groups were parading. While a group of some 30 drummers in brown and beige Middle Ages outfits had passed by a sudden sadness came over me. I wasn't able to stop the flow of tears. Had this kind of drumming preceded my execution in a past life?

After a light vegetable soup in a Venice restaurant the plaguing long procedure started again. The roughly ten yards long and two feet wide bed for the red hot coals was already dug out from the lawn, the logs of wood circularly piled up. After dry exercises and cleansing our bodies with burning sage we sat around the pile of wood. Three members with hoses tried to catch flying sparks with their water nets. 36 eyes stared in the glaze. Bits with questions were fluttering through our gray matter: walking or not walking? Our feet's safety was at stake. One time a colleague came out of the trance state. He'd not only burnt his flesh even the bones. I stopped listening. If he'd go on with his horror stories of accidents nobody will walk. Guttural sounds and shrill laughter could not belie the massive angst.

Now talk about your specific fears. Pointing to his girlfriend, he said go ahead. The woman half his age said I'm fearing unbearable pain. I said I fear to be a cripple. By the way, I don't have health insurance. Me neither uttered some other participants. About two hours later, the wood was burnt down. Big Bear's helper shuffled the red hot coals into the dig and waited behind the big plastic bowl of water at the end. Since we walked looking upwards, we had to choose a catcher for our safety. The water was for neutralizing possible sizzling coal chips between the toes. Michael Big Bear started to walk and stopped in the middle. We'd held our breath, when he even walked a bit backward some couldn't hold back the sigh or called out: Oh, God! Omigod!

After Michael's helper had walked he made photos from all other walking participants.

Ingrid in her white gown stepped forth to the starting point in an euphoric state. I felt in a Zugzwang. What if all except me would walk? My concern got concrete when three mere mortals including me had not walked. Hesitating I stepped to the starting point. Pure angst crept into my bones. I felt like a chicken whose throat is going to be twisted. After the fresh load of red hot coals had been dispersed, I cried, why am I so frighten? I followed the trained ceremonial procedure and said, I'll burn my fears and doubts and fill my future life with acceptance and love. As practiced I raised my arms and said three times I give my body whatever it takes to walk safely over the fire. I looked in the ¼ Cherokee's eyes, so he could appraise my trance state and said: I take the hands of God, I walk with God, I am God. Big Bear's grin showed me I was already initiated. From my toes, up to the hips, I sensed an electric vibration as changing to a higher frequency. Like numbed I doubted to be able to lift my legs. The repetition of the words I take the hands of God were nothing more than the inarticulate babbling of a drunk. When with the tip on my thigh Michael appointed a starting sign I forced forward without reluctance. To my greatest amazement, the sizzling coals felt not hot as if with my words I had neutralized the temperature. Open-mouthed I took fast audible breaths like a laboring woman.

The compeers on both sides called spurring, Gods Love, Gods Love. I fell in Ingrid's arms without feeling the change from fire to water. But my ecstatic scream of joy may have risen some neighbors from the horizontal. The releasing angst and apprehension made space for a forcible blissfulness. In the frenzied fever of my transformed fear, I'd fallen around many necks.

Like Pegasus, the light gray sedan we'd purchased from Willie flew winged over Freeway 405 passing the round building of the Hollywood Inn. When after the dark mountain the San Fernando Valley emerged brighter than ever I felt the tipsiness again and hoped not to get stopped. Who knows what kind of cosmic narcotic the body produces to make the fire walk wonder possible? Or was it a protective ectoplasm under the feet? Arriving at home in my erratic state Peter had a fit of the sulks. He stoutly stared at the monitor of his PC hunting moorhens. But he could not hide his relief. I asked: You were afraid, right? Nah! As if! Hearing noises from the guest quarter, I floated towards my parents. Both were glad to see me well and sound. Why did it take so long? Pa expected you to lie in a hospital with thickly bandaged feet. The spoken off said:

I was three times out checking on your car. I kissed my parents. At ease, they went to bed.

After planting a kiss on Peter's soft lips, the mimosa changed into a rose. On cloud 9 I floated to the bedroom. My 5 Tibetan Rites and the yoga dancing in front of the mirror took half the time while I was grinning like a goofy idiot.

Next day, I still floated in a world embracing mood from room to room, smiling from ear to ear. I wrote down my fire walk feels and send a copy to Michael Big Bear. On a small note I'd written, excuse me for not having translated it. But I feel there's somebody in your neighborhood who's interested in reading it and would be pleased to tell you its content.

A week later, Michael called from Sedona. Hi, is this the woman with the psychic powers? Huh? Let me demonstrate you the perfect performance of your trans-channel. I'm now leaving my apartment with the cordless phone. I'm ringing on my neighbor's door. Now you can talk to Erika. To whom? A fellow countrywoman from the Black Forest. The 73-year-old subscriber of the German psychic mag Esotera was indeed interested in my writing. We kept in touch even after she had moved back to Germany. Michael said: While writing you will have help from the other side. Hopefully, the good ghosts will help me publishing too. We all get help from the other side if we recognize our talents and use them. After experiencing the physically unexplainable phenomenon of the fire walk, I had an inkling of who we are, not just related to the double helix of atoms coiled along our DNA. Everything's possible if we trust.

A strange thing happened: Ten minutes after inserting Ingrid's fire walk photo it was marked: *The graphic cannot be shown.* It was a better one, showing the ditch in its full length, but instead add this photo. OK Ingrid?

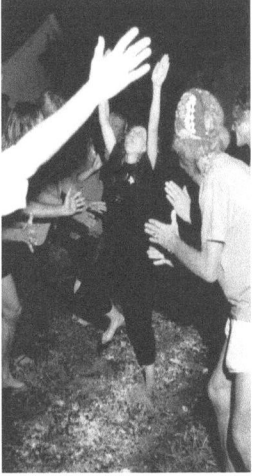

Later, looking at our photos I said, don't we look wholly gaga? Ingrid replied:

I guess that's what we'd been at this moment.

New carriers on the horizon

Ingrid called. What's up, another adventure?

No, I've to tell you something interesting.

Me too, I was at the Granita yesterday. Eh?

Then you must have seen Barbara. She had worn her green hat. Yeah, we've seen her and of course the hat. The boys had fun teasing.

You know I was looking for another job. Barbara's many parties are too exhausting.

Does she need steady domestic help anyway? When she came from the wedding in Texas and made us tea, she seemed so self-sufficient. Um! She'd be better off with occasional party helpers. Anyway, how was the interview? Are you working for Mrs. Disney now? No, she wants to give her former domestic another chance. Never mind. I just read a worker in the Dominican Republic who makes the Mickey Mouse t-shirts has to work all his life to make as much as the president of Disney in a ½ day. Okay? Now listen. I read two of Barbara's books. One's about Jung's concept of the shadow self and one about the power of prayer. The latter reminded me of the possibility to plead for an easier job. Okay?

So among others, I contacted the spirit of my first boss, Mr. Green, you know his son. Yeah, the lawyer from Toluca Lake. You won't believe this: He called me last week and asked if I could work for his future mother-in-law in Glendale. Betty's a single painter in her 80th, a very sweet woman. I'll get more money for less work, and I'll have a car again. Great! We just call for our needs and the cosmos passes along whatever we wish. Think about my blue dress for the Wiener Ball. By the way, yesterday, I found a promotional letter from the Holistic College of Nutrition in the mail. I applied right away. Good for you.

Yeah, now I can read books about proper nutrition and a healthy lifestyle without Peter's constant comments about wasting my time. Since I don't have a working permit, I might have my own business as nutrition adviser.

15 months and thirty interpreted books later, I called Ingrid who meanwhile resided on Big Island again. I just want to check if you're there and if you've got a little time for me. Yes, why? I'm coming! I don't believe it. Will you come alone? No, we are going to vouch for Bill's and Leanne's marriage vows. I knew you would not come alone. So you won't have much time. How long are you staying?

Almost a week. Where? At the Mauna Lani.

That's not on the Kona coast. Yes, but it's on Big Island. We'll rent a car. It'll be our shortest

and most expensive vacation ever, three times more than we spend for our yearly trips with the Gullwing group. A round of golf costs 280 bucks per person, the cart 85.

Have you been at Hasya's? Not yet. You really should go, you'll like it. Ask Anda to go with you. Okay. So, will you have time? Actually, yes! I work as a private nurse again. I found a great job. Why, great! It's the best job I ever had on the island. In a house of the rich and famous. I only work from Friday eve to Monday morn and make $600. Great! Yeah! The people are very gentle, but I'm on alert day and night. That's very exhausting.

Landing on a Polynesian islands again was not as emotional as years before in Papeete.

On the main island of Tahiti, I'd felt eerily at home. When Peter and our friends had waited in the hall for the onward flight to Bora Bora, I impulsively left the building and talked to a taxi driver about his family. I had a sincere feeling of belonging as if I had lived here before. I'd rather gone home with the man and to meet his family than flying to Bora Bora. Had this to do with my past life as the paunchy Polynesian or was I rather concerned with flying again? Due to a storm, it took an hour to start from LAX. Then the shaking was frightening still more the rattling of the gaps between the parts on the ceiling.

On Hawaii, I didn't feel as connected as on Tahiti. But I'd prefer living on Big Island. The language wouldn't be a problem. Plus, on the lush green Kona coast grows one of the best Spirulina algae. Our luxurious hotel resort in the middle of the desert with a seductive scent of Oceanic flowers, surrounded by a manicured carpet-like golf course seemed like an oasis. We were residing on the top floor with a private dining room. The free food and drinks we only used as appetizers. Later we tested the island's restaurants. In one we had sauerkraut, bratwurst, home brewed beer and black forest cake. I considered this romantic holiday an ersatz for our unromantic marriage. We were touched by our dear friend's ceremony right at the beach.

Next day, while Bill, Leanne, and Peter enjoyed a helicopter ride over the volcano and the Kona coast, I inspected Ingrid's beautiful land and my trees. On her birthdays, I'd usually send her money for woody plants. After the chopper ride, orchid lover Bill went with Leanne to an orchid nursery while we swam with Ingrid in the *Millionaires Pool*. The football field sized rocky pool once belonged to a millionaire. Now, everybody can swim for free in the lava stone heated water. A sheer treat. Peter's favorite place was the golf course, except for the tiny island where he had to strike precisely to land on the green. Most balls dropped in the Pacific. At lunchtime, we drove the golf carts in front of the hotel, and like step dancers clicking we entered the eatery.

A few weeks later, Ingrid called. Remember, I told you about Halima who cured herself of cancer with Spirulina, Aloe vera, green papaya and grass juice? Yes? She'll call you about her book. She wants to have it translated. I think that's good practice for you since you've to write your dissertation in English. What kind of book is it? Its title is *Stop Acidosis, Allergy, and Hair Loss.* Well! Sounds exciting.

When I picked up the health expert at LAX airport, I felt a strange familiarity with this weedy woman. Halima said: You look like the nurse who saved my life.

Really? Funny, her name is Marianne, too.

Where was that? Here, in L. A. after I lost my little boy. I came with $60,000. They used me as a guinea pig, tried chemo and cobalt. Um! Marianne and her doctor husband slowly reduced the morphine. These great people paid for my ticket to Hawaii and send me to the papaya doctor Dr. Kurt Koesel. Halima got a bottle out of her knapsack and placed some green pills on her palm. I looked curious.

Try one? A little lax, I said: Okay?

She handed me a tab putting the rest in her mouth. She pleasingly sucked them up like candies. I felt offended by the terrible algae flavor and swallowed the pill at once.

I didn't eat anything on the plane, just two apples. They served only junk. You could have ordered vegetarian. I did. They brought a white noodle mush; it looked like rubber.

Halima hadn't given up on getting me used to the algae. She covered its taste by mixing a delicious shake with a banana, a few dates, an apple, a tablespoon of Spirulina algae powder and a cup of water in the blender. In the following week, I had a big glass of this green slime every morning.

Wherever I showed up with Halima if at friends in the neighborhood of Little Tel Aviv, at the Body tree bookstore or Mrs. Goochie's, we were perceived as sisters. Halima knew about Ingrid's other girlfriend in the same street! We called Anda and walked up the hill.

Do you know how Anda survived the holocaust in the cellar of a Polish grain storage?

She must have been very young.

Yes, she was 10. At age 12 she was rescued. I always push her to write about it.

We walked up to Fidel Play's place. He's 27 years old. How old can horses get? In rare cases 50. Ponies have the better chances.

I didn't know that. His father was the famous race horse Foul Play. I can ride, Peter's too heavy. Here's my friend Yogi, the Great Dane with a lapdog soul. Hello, Anda, meet my new boss. I'm going to translate Halima's book. Can I buy a copy? Why yes. I've got a few with me. But they're not in English.

No job. I received my maturate in Munich. I still know some German. We agreed to come to the next sat sang with Robert Adams.

Sri Bhagavan Robert Maharshi came to Anda's house, twice a week. For a year and a half, I had a Guru in the neighborhood. After Halima's intro to Spirulina, I presented him with the powder every other month for his Parkinson. Anda made him the delicious fruit shakes he coined green slime. I wasn't a follower. But I walked a few times up the hill and got an impression of a master devotee relationship. I never desired a master. According to the Native Americans, persons born in Nov/Dec have a direct link to the Great Manitu. After Robert had moved I received a letter from Sedona. This message may be hard to grasp for persons in pain. But we can alter and change our lot by changing our habits leading to evil and disease. Our body possesses the ability to heal if we live naturally and simple and let our inner wisdom lead. It is also within our power to change our actions. Stemming from the same source, we better let love, compassion and peace run our relationships.

End of 1996 we left California. We didn't like to go, but the IRS was on our tail. Our ac-

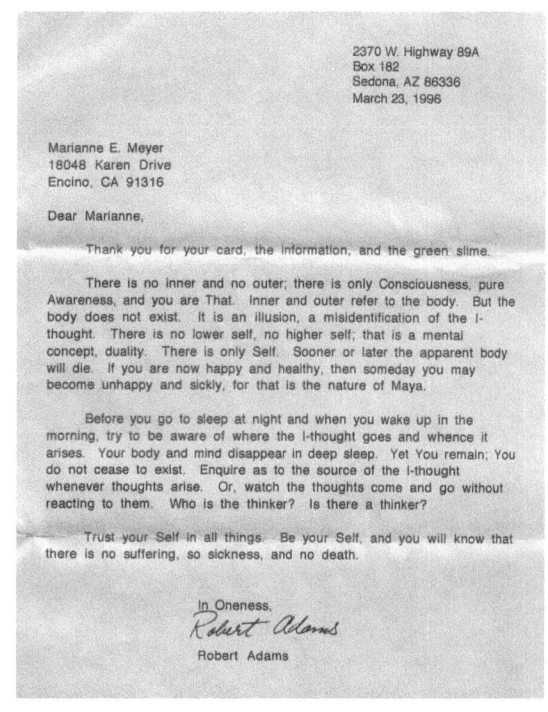

countant had passed on. Mr. Hoppe junior, who took over couldn't find the files. Two years were lost, and the IRS wanted about a third of all the money that was transferred from Europe in these two years. If a customer did send $100,000 for a 300SL Roadster, the IRS claimed about 30.000 though we made only 10.000. Based on these false premises, they asked an enormous amount of taxes. Thanks to Peter's above investments plus some $130.000 for Clemens Martin's movie business and $270.000 for João Gomes' Julio Iglesias concert turning sour, we ended up broke. We had not enough money to fight back. The lawyer Peter consulted said no problem just give me a retainer of 10 grand my hour is $580.

Therefore after protesting the summon, we left sunny paradise. Everything following seemed orchestrated. As soon as we had settled in an apartment near Frankfurt, I got a call from Barbara Simonsohn, Reiki master teacher and bestseller author of many books on

Reiki, Stevia, and other natural supplements. She had heard about my working for Halima and asked me to translate her papaya book. Incidentally, I mentioned my dissertation on Spirulina and the immune system. Shortly after, Monika Jünemann, head of Windpferd, asked for some test chapters. After reading them, she was wholly enthusiastic and said, of course, you don't need to translate anything. A few days later I signed a contract for three books, two on Spirulina and one on other measures to strengthen the immune system. I was appointed to a Frankfurt book fair appearance to introduce my books and to serve Spirulina drinks and treats.

Meantime, my father had made his transtion. The funeral was on the very day of my representation. Since the show must go on, Peter drove me to Frankfurt after the ceremony. And like a pin in a haystack my mother saw me in the Hesse Show on TV walking through the aisles and searching for the Windpferd stand.

All had happened as by itself. My hobby became my profession. Ingrid started the whole thing by introducing me to Halima. Later, not long after my own appearance on Prime TV as Spirulina expert, my mother called me. I've seen Halima on television. So? It was quite queer: as if I'd known her. Yes, I know this feeling. I also had it when I met her first.

The universe provides us with everything we ask for. I had a job to train my skills for writing a thesis. My allowance was a few hundred more than my college costs. Sometimes, the cosmos presents us without our asking. Or did I ask for Charley? Anda knew I was a dog lover and she had a perfect one for us. One evening Peter and I were sitting on Anda's kitchen table. Underneath, the 8-month-old cocker spaniel made himself comfortable on Peter's feet. Anda said he knows whom he has to convince. Charley was her married son's dog, and often on the loose since their house was not fenced. We agreed to a test time. Shiny black curled Charley was adoring. Peter took him on a leash bicycling. But whenever they came back there was sheer revulsion. Max and Mickey were acting unbearable. Wild whizzing, they jumped up the louvered windows. I used to lay with Max on my lab and Mickey next to my head on the self-made spartan sofabed working on Halima's book. Whenever Charley appeared, the terror began. My tummy or scalp got another scratch. The felines rattled up and hung hissing in each corner of the window. A week long I tried to get the toms used to Charley. When they went on hunger strike, we gave up.

Introducing Sandara bitch to the tomcats I was luckier. On Christmas 1998, walking along a ravine at Agadir beach a ball of wool barked at me. Coming closer I picked up the bundle of bliss and looked into the cave. All the other puppies and their mom were sound asleep. I said you seem to be a perfect watch dog. The circumstances were favorable to persuade Peter to take Sandy along. A few days earlier, while sleeping on a South France rest area, robbers had broken into our motor home.

In the Moroccan Himalaya, a woman said:

Your puppy looks like she's from Banana Village. Bingo, she is. Really? I'd seen her coming out on Nov 27. You're kidding! No, why? That's my birthday! I'm positive. My daughter's birthday is on 26. I watched the delivery next day. Coincidence? Jocelyn made her transition on my birthday. Marita had hit a truck fatally one hour before the WTC structures went down. It was no pleasure having a prophetic dream about the collapsing towers and Marita's crashing into a truck. And still another synchronicity for the album concerning Peter, Jocelyn, and John: In May 2001, while Peter raced through the Green Hell on the Ring, I watched the 24-hour race on TV. In the commercial break, I switched to the movie channel Kabel 1: A closeup of John Hudson as Cowboy kneeling with a pointed gun followed by a Western starring Jocelyn Brando and Montgomery Clift!

I called Jocelyn so she could check on her residuals. She said: For such an old movie it's pennies only. What are you doing?

Growing old gracefully.

No, I mean just right now. I'm clearing out.

What do you mean? I'm throwing out a lot of things. I don't want to leave as much stuff in the house as my sister. Please, stay put many more years! And better keep the letters. I suppose, Marlon was glad that Frannie had kept them. Without them, his biography would have been less vivid. Anyway, I just wanted to let you know that I'd never seen you or John on German TV, and tonight, Peter and two dear friends are on the telly! Well?

Who's orchestrating all these things?

You may find out. So, what else you want to do after clearing out? Well, one thing that's still on my agenda is another train ride to the East Coast. That I'd like to do ever since you'd told me about your trip on the double-decker Amtrak train. But then we'd to leave in a hurry because of the IRS problems. I was sad to leave you all. We could do it together.

Are you planning to come? I'd love to. You shouldn't miss out on this one.

Back to Sandy who made us happy with a course in dog love until she was run over in Bursin, near Geneva. 200 yards from the site of her accident Sir Peter Ustinov found his last resting place. Had she known about her passing? Leaving home, she acted distinctly. She rubbed her head against my mother's cheek and nestled between her thighs. 1½ years before I had dreamed, a French policeman gave me her neckband. Thus I advised Ma not to get too emotionally involved with Sandy since she may not get much older than 2 years. Sadly it was another prophecy, and at age 2 years and 24 days, our beloved bitch left her body.

Easy eye and **Malibu Inferno**

After leaving MGM Celeste invented a device against eyestrain. She'd worked in an open plan office without windows. The unit with changeable images does the same for the eye as looking alternating in a short and far distance. I invested my runaway money in her company though I was timid about doing it. I approved of the effect. She had gotten some ophthalmologist's support. But eyestrain was not my reality. I read for many hours without problems, thanks to Spirulina's carotene. But at the time some $1,200 wasn't much money for me. I wanted to help Celeste's device to get produced. Only, when she needed more dough probably for her new Cherokee Jeep, I didn't approve of Peter and Michael Lipke giving her $5,000. Mike got his share back. We could have also since, in her company category Germans weren't allowed to invest. I was pretty stupid to invest anyway. For my money, Celeste had certainly sold the blue aquarelle she got from Henry Miller. After the half year, she'd been his wheelchair moving buddy he'd asked her to choose one of his paintings for a present. Celeste wanted the clown. He said, anything except the clown.

Whenever I visited her in the rustic little Topanga house, my first glance aimed at the light blue watercolor abstract art.

Right after reading Big Sur and the oranges of Hieronymus Bosch I called Celeste and told her about my feeling of Henry Miller's likes with my brother. She knew Heini from his visiting me. For more than an hour, she told me a moving story from the time when Miller lived in Pacific Palisades. I scribbled two pages full. But at the end, my friend begged me not to write anything about that in my future books. Sorry!

I hadn't heard from Celeste since we drove to Mexico together. She had hoped to find a manufacturer for her device. I wanted to see Earthrise Farms' Spirulina algae growing. So at least I had a ride with the new car. We had cut through the dry flickering heat of the Californian desert until the algae odor made us stop. Watching the dark blue-green iridescent surface in the huge ponds felt like visiting a church. Instead of marveling the Madonna we watched the growth of ascendants of the very cyanobacteria that some 4½ billion years ago created the oxygen atmosphere. This first photosynthetic life form split water molecules with the help of sunlight thus producing its own food from surrounding gasses and minerals. From CO2 the cyanobacteria synthesized carbohydrates from nitrogen via the amino acids protein transforming the earth into a life-friendly system.

Had they also been the manna the Israelis had been fed on in the desert? Had the chosen ones been victims of an ET experiment? The 40-year duration and the intact clothes and sandals would account for this theory, so the stolen gold: the lifted offer for God.

In the southern California desert, a blazing heat of 43 degrees Celsius prevailed. After we had signed a confirmation not to make photos and to use our observance for business reasons, we had the opportunity to keep an eye on the culture. The trichomes, the chief chemist Dr. Belay had us look at under the microscope, were all tightly spirally coiled as screws tapering towards both ends. He also showed us the culture in the big glass bottles and the bottles with the liquid minerals and trace minerals.

In the future, we may have to rely on this compact food that produces oxygen and needs CO2. Globally, people could build ponds and produce Spirulina with their feces. NASA astronauts in space do it small scale to have always the fresh protein, vitamins, and minerals available. Some African countries take part in Spirulina projects growing the algae with almost no energy use.

Only 1 g of the algae powder mixed in the regular millet mush is sufficient to avoid nutrition deficiency. The *Green Gold* regenerates the cells and complements our depleted food perfectly since we might call this microorganism the mother substance of flora and fauna. It contains all we need. If a single matter in the body is missing, this could create symptoms no doctor may ever be able to diagnose. Therefore, whenever I don't feel well, I increase my daily dose or add some green slime.

We both looked through Dr. Belay's microscope and marveled at the tightly coiled micro-algae. They resembled green screws with small ends because it was real hot that day. In the cold, they look like worms, different to humans. We curl up when it is cold.

Later we shared a room in Mexico. Celeste got in a bad mood. I'd no idea why. When I first met her sitting on Jocelyn's couch she outright felt familiar but in a worried way. My dual feeling of closeness and respect, intimacy and distance reminded me of grandmother Lydia. During our friendship, I learned that their childhood experiences were similar, exceptionally bright, comparable characters and lifestyle. Our trip cooled off our relationship.

Weeks later, the heat got us together again. While still wondering what I'd have possibly done wrong the strong Santa Ana winds rattled the windows. I was about to call Celeste's friend Pia to ask her about a possible reason. The Dane model I'd met several times at Celeste's place also got me in contact with Uschi Obermeier, the jewelry-making mother of all supermodels. I sat on the floor with the ironing mat in front of me. My mother used to say I definitely accept your last lifetime as a shepherd not used to tables. Ironing isn't my favorite task anyway. Since I use to buy wash-and-wear things I manage to limit it. At 11.30 on Nov 3, I enjoyed a wonderful pinkish cloud when all of a sudden I realized it's forenoon!

There shouldn't be any pink clouds!

I switched to the local NBC channel 4:

A sea of flames had spread out from Calabasas in the direction of Topanga Canyon.

Pronto, I dialed Celeste's number asking are you packing? Why she replied rather angrily. I'm watching my favorite soap. You better switch to channel 4. There's a huge fire in your area. You can sleep here. Our friend Bebóo from Germany is visiting with his daughter, but you can sleep in my office.

Hilde called up: You know about the fire?

Yes, I just called my friend in Topanga.

It started near Motion Picture Hospital. John and the other patients had almost been resettled already standing outside in their wheelchairs. Luckily the wind turned. 3 hours later Celeste arrived. I asked did you take Henry Miller's painting? She looked at me as if I'd been nuts: I only got the wherewithal.

On New Year's Eve, we were invited to Hans-Jürgen and Nicole. I planned to get some appetizers from nearby Gelson's. But instead of turning left I impulsively made a right and headed to Trader Joe's. I detected a couple on a freezer cabinet. Following a hunch, I asked: Where are you guys from? Frankfurt.

Really? Me too. But four month ago I settled in California. My husband's from here. Oh! We may have acquaintances. Where did you work? At the Deutsche Bank. Me too!

What a coincidence! I don't believe in coincidences. I was working for Dr. Beine in the education department, but that was 20 years ago. Oh, yeah, I know a lot of people, I was a member of the works council. I like Mr. Gans.

Yes he's a darling, isn't he? I also played tennis with Mrs. Schultheis. No, kidding, me too! We were both singles at the time. Where are you living? In Woodland Hills. So we are neighbors. I live in Encino, on the border to Tarzana. Great. I just left the bank, premature pension. You certainly can retire here better than in Frankfurt. I've got to rush. Why don't you give me your phone number and we'll meet next week? Since Gertrude didn't drive, I visited her. Sitting near the pool midst of blooming bushes, I asked, how have you both met? In Venice. Oh, how romantic. After three years living with me in Frankfurt, we both had enough. It's much nicer here.

I agree. Have you been married before?

No, but my husband. His wife died of cancer. How sad. After gossiping about the former colleagues, I gave Gertrude a photo of me sitting next to our pool since she had planned a trip to Germany in Spring.

After their return, we cycled to their home. Gertrud said Mr. Gans was delighted. He still remembers Fräulein Holschuh.

Yeah, he'd seen me several times on the carmarts. Do you want a coffee? Sure!

Taking a sip, I said, gosh, I was known for my strong coffee but this one I can't drink. I'm now used to the American brew. Sorry.

Lowering her voice, Gertrude said, now I've to tell you something unpleasant. What's up?

Um, well. I've stomach cancer. No! Alas!

Why? Did you eat too many steaks? Why?

I just read Dirk Benedict's book *Confessions of a Kamikaze-Cowboy*. That's the guy who plays Face in The A-Team. He describes how he cured himself of prostate cancer with macrobiotic diet and no animal fat. He blamed his 3 meat-meal-diet for his cancer. In the morning he had eggs and bacon, a Hamburger for lunch and a steak or fish for dinner. Well?

Those are very acidifying fares.

In my case it's sausage, said Gertrude. I love all kinds of sausages. Do you drink lots of this coffee? 4-5 cups a day. If you avoid these goodies, the tumor disappears. I get you the book tomorrow. That will motivate you. Our body is a perfect instrument. You just have to play it right. Well? Yep! If we take care of a good tuning everything works smoothly. Bad mood or food gets us out of sorts. Um! Don't you think they erred? You look great!

No, there are already metastases. Gertrude touched her upper chest and throat area: Somewhere here. Are you in pain? Not at all.

Yeah, you look in the pink. Now, don't feel down, what comes into being will fade away eventually. You have to strengthen your inner healer, the immune system. I also bring you the cancer book by Michio Kushi. My friend Ingrid only recently got me these books as if she'd known.

But Gertrude had not taken the Kamikaze-Trip and tried the mainstream medicos. After the first chemo, she emaciated to the bones and lost her hair. I don't feel good about continuing, but they're all encouraging me. I don't. I know. I'm afraid of this. What's your inner voice telling? I still haven't lost hope. I vision the tumor getting smaller.

Good girl! Trust it! I should have listened to you. If I had envisaged this ... I'm constantly nauseous and the mucosa is sore all over my body. You have no idea how it hurts. I can't take showers anymore then it hurts even more.

Gertrude made her transition on June 20, 1994. I learned from her experience that we better listen to our inner voice and avoid letting outsiders shoulder our responsibility. We know best. Science is errors up to date or conflict of interest. Natch, the Merck Manual states diet plays no role in the genesis of stomach cancer. But the American Cancer Society lists cured meats to the cancer risk foods.

Dr. Bernd Winter from the *Gesellschaft für Biologische Krebsabwehr* (Institute for Biological Cancer Defense) told me years back in a phone conversation: "The success rate of cytotoxic therapy is only at 5 to 7%. It is a common error in medical practice to perform chemotherapy in cases of e. g. lung, stomach or bowel cancer. This therapy for tumors was developed for the reproductive organs, where the success rate is at 25-30%. Therefore there is no need to burden patients with other types of cancer with such toxins."

We better trust our feelings. If we suppress our intuitive knowledge and mistrust the inner wisdom, we expose our esteem and influence leading to feelings of helplessness, emptiness, or to bitterness if these feelings are suppressed to depression and death.

George's UFO, Anza's ET and another prophecy

Beginning of January 1996, the phone rang. Peter answered. Yes, we'll be here. Guess, who's coming. Huh? Mosy wants to play golf in our area. George arrived in the afternoon. We sat down outside around the pretty little white iron coffee-table I'd fetched home from a neighbor's garage sale for a fraction of the money paid for our other garden furniture set. It was the only time Peter had purchased something showing wealth except for the cars. He saw those sway chairs at Clemens Martin in the Hollywood Hills. There was only one hitch: Peter wanted 4 lounges and 4 chairs instead of 2 launches and six chairs. The latter would have been even less expensive. But Peter never listens to me.

After the general conversation with coffee and fruitcake, George seemed to brood on something. I've got to tell you some: It's a bit ... tensely, George grabbed his briefcase. Husky-voiced he said: Last month I'd been camping with my sons and a friend in the Anza-Borrego desert near the Salton Sea.

Oh, yeah, we know that area. I was there at the Spirulina Farm. George said, now composed: It was December 28 at about 7.20 p. m. We hiked with the dog to a nearby hill. With a sinking voice he spoke on: The night was clear with a ¾ full moon. He nestled on his briefcase and got out some drawings. Low-voiced he said, in the middle of the dark all of a sudden lights flashed up from the dessert and came moving towards us. Since there's a military area we thought about a helicopter squadron, but when the lights came close we realized it was a bigger flying object ... round ... huuuge ... flying from East to West about 5000 feet high. I said:

A flying saucer!

No, it was a mother ship! About 300 feet in diameter. You hardly can imagine how big! As a skyscraper horizontal ... as if the earth shakes ... or in the disco when the basses go all through. Nicolas, my youngest son was startled that such a big thing could fly so slow.

Max was agitated by the whole thing. Our German Shepard looked up like hypnotized with a downfallen lower jaw. Odd! The thing remained 5 minutes in our range of vision. To cope with the experience, I let the boys draw what they saw. George handed us the pages. We looked at the kid's UFO art.

What did you do? Next day, I called the ranger station and asked about possible military test flights. The ranger woman said, just go ahead and tell me what you saw. You won't believe it, her son-in-law is an astronomer. A year ago he'd seen this thing near Lancaster.

When I called the wife of the reverend from Borrego Springs, Marie Wright was in the next room. Two days later, the Methodist's wife called and told me about her experience with such a UFO that followed her some 20 miles when she drove home from Salton City. One time, she'd stopped. It also stopped hovering above her. As soon as she saw the lights of her town the UFO turned around and within seconds disappeared in the dark. Mrs. Wright also was most impressed by the size. Then she asked me, what do you think when this took place? Huh? In 1978. I yelled:

What? That's the time I saw something in Frankfurt at daytime hovering in front of the Taunus mountains. I was sitting at the kitchen table with the woman whose husband made bodywork on our cars. I said: Look, Erika what's that? Looks like a mini sun.

We observed that thing in the glare of the sunset for almost an hour. In the Hesse evening news, the UFO was mentioned in a single sentence. Next day, I searched German papers and the news. I couldn't find any citation, neither in radio, nor TV or newspaper. Isn't it about time to stop the mystery mongers?

The day after George's visit, I talked about this with Leanne on our morning walk. She reacted perplexed: This cannot be true. Why? What a coincidence! Yesterday, my masseuse told me about a crashed UFO in Roswell. In the first news report, military officials had confirmed the discovery of remains from a flying saucer. Next day, they demented their statement. My masseuse said there were survivors. 4 Native Americans had cleaned up the area and gave their information to their 8 sons. 6 of them died mysteriously. According to one of the still living sons, the survivors of the UFO had been reptile like. Allegedly they'd been rescued and brought back to the mother ship. Until today, officially the crash of the UFO is vehemently denied. No wonder!

George had talked about his experience to a sensitive who'd induced an out-of-body. He'd seen the inside of the mothership describing the image of the crew beyond of average people could bear. Looking at the green creatures, he expressed his feelings by saying: It scared the shit out of me. This angst he felt though he intuitively was convinced that the crew had no spite intentions! So what science fiction?

Shortly after I went shopping. On my way home from the supermarket, I noticed a black car with the personal license plate DICTOR.

All agog with curiosity, I followed what I thought Dieter Victor's descendant. With all the queer happenstances it was possible my migrated great granddad's offspring was our neighbor. The man stopped his car opposite Anda's house on Karen Drive. After explaining him my curiosity, the nice man said my name is Dictor, but we still share something. I can as well come up with an abandoned pregnant grandmother. At Anda's house, a fascinating communication waited. A visitor with dark curly hair said I belong to a UFO unity. From there I know John Lear had detected a huge ten-thousand-year-old metal mass many 100 yards underground.

The Learjet inventor? No, his son. He'd spent millions. The metal thing seems to stem from a foreign civilization. It was used to drill underground tunnels. Aliens? Well!

My friend's husband, Heinz Richter had worked for Bill Lear. Hilde told me he'd quit his job because he often had to fly the Learjet inventor around in his free time while Bill made passes at Hilde. Yo! Anda said: I have something strange to share, too. A few years ago, on hot summer nights I used to sleep outside. Once, I woke up when a man in black, 7 feet tall, bowed over me and lifted me up. After the anxiety had diminished, I felt a soothing warmth and a positive energy. I lost consciousness. Lying on a table bathed in bright light I woke up and lost consciousness again. Later on, I felt a lot better. I think this was a healing contact.

Could you have been hallucinating?

As a physicist, I wasn't willing to look at this other than a dream activity at least at first. But I talked about my experience with a UCLA professor in parapsychology. Since he had not ruled out the possibility of an encounter of the 4th kind he somewhat convinced me that I'd contacted an ET.

Three weeks later, the phone sprang to life. Peter handed me the receiver.

George wants to talk to you. What's up?

You won't believe this. We'd been in the Salton Sea area again. So?

On Highway 371, I stopped at a small store in Anza. There was this young blond employee who looked like a North European. I said:

You have chosen a pretty area to live in.

He spontaneously replied: Weird area would be more to the point. Um! So?

After we'd stocked up with enough provisions the young man said, I don't know what you think of UFO's, but here you can see enough of them. I bet all here living people have at least one photo of a UFO in their albums. Anda was enthusiastic about the news.

Anza is my real name! Then, let's go there!

Yeah, let's trip up. We can take my car. I've got a tent, too. I'd looove to camp again.

Me too!

Next morn, Leanne called as usually.

I'm on my way. Okay, I'll come down.

At the end of our driveway, my friend waited with Honey and Misty, her new Rocky replacing golden retriever.

Have you heard about the plane crash?

Yes, the TWA flight 800, Long Island

Awful, Leanne said excited, it just exploded.

Perhaps Arabs. You think it's an act of terror? Looks like, why should a plane just explode? Well? More than 200 people were killed, many students. I feel so sorry for the parents. Patty's lucky. Her son almost had been on the plane. His father had a premonition. What Patty? Eskander?

No, Patricia Klous, the head stewardess Judy Mc Coy from the Love Boat.

I don't know her. Of course, you do. Huh?

You told me her dog's often coming to you.

Oh, yeah, that cute gray cuddly one who often escapes by digging the soil under the fence. I brought him back several times. Didn't know she's an actress. I never recognize celebs. I hadn't even known Mariel Hemingway when I did an improv with her on my first class meeting. Only recently, I stood at least 5 minutes face-to-face with Maria Schell and her brother Max not having recognized them.

Maximilian! Really? Where?

At the Vienna Marriott Hotel.

My thoughts drifted back to another strange synchronicity experience, one making the orchestration of the spirit world clear.

Attaché without a clue for taking the train

Visiting our cold homeland, Willie picked us up from FRA airport. We stopped at the railway station in Hanau to buy tickets for Vienna. There we wanted to meet Jerry and his family three days later.

The former youngest LH board engineer then got us to his magnificent mansion in the Wetterau where the whole family was waiting. Jacky, the family dog approached me with a ball in his mouth. As a former handball player, I threw the ball way out in the leave-showered park. The drama followed when cumbersome bending in the poor fellow slowly carried himself. I felt so sorry for the beautiful Munsterlander mix, whom Marita got from the pound. Calming my conscience I rummaged through my travel bag for the Spirulina tablets. Jacky licked them lustfully from my hand as if he knew about their anti-inflammatory effect. I said: It looks like he has a full blown arthritis. He apparently had too many cream tarts.

Marita sight with a what-can-I-do eye rolling. Yeah, the Grannies often drop a piece of cake under the table.

In the evening, I gave Jacky 3 more 1 g tablets and the next day 9 g over the day.

In the morning of our leaving day, we were pleased with the positive effect. Jacky walked a lot better. Marita was also stunned about his shining fur. Two weeks later, we got the good news: The dog had gotten rid of the joint inflame! Ever since the family is using the blue-green algae daily to stay healthy.

Sitting at a window, I enjoyed the lush green of the rushing scenery. Peter had escaped to the smoking compartment. After a few minutes, I rummaged about in my suitcase in search for the three books I'd bought for the long train trip. I ever more nervously groped for them, but there was absolutely nothing book like. Darn! I had shown Marita the books. I must have left them in the house. I got up and walked towards the dining car. There was no free table. I asked a young woman, would you mind if I sit down here? Sure, go ahead. Looking questioning to the opposite sitting man I said I forgot all my books at a friend's house. The man introduced himself smiling: Ahmed Ashy. What kind of books? As a nutritionist, I bought the newest health books. Mr. Ashy opened his briefcase and got several books out. Yo! These are the books, I forgot! How so?

Here I'm the Saudi culture attaché in Bonn, but in my homeland, I was a professor in biochemistry, so I'm interested in these works.

Why do you live in Austria?

I married an Austrian. All of a sudden, I detected Peter a few tables apart. Oh, there's my hubby. Looking in Peter's direction Mr. Ashy said puzzled: The man with the ponytail? Yes.

I've seen him at least twice before. How so?

Does he sometimes fly to Austria? I usually fly to Graz. Yes, last year Peter visited his wealthy friend twice. They had a business together. He owes him 30 grant. Since he's not paying, Peter goes there for holidays. He gets picked up by his friend's chauffeur with a stretch limo and uses his yacht. But, why do you use the train now? Actually, I don't know. I don't believe in coincidences. We may have to learn some from each other. I live in the States. Shoot! My son wants to study there.

Well, I could give you an address of a family who may be interested in exchange students.

Would that be close to the ocean?

Yes, about two miles away.

That would be great because my son has trouble with his respiratory tract.

Hey! That's odd. I just read in Carl Pfeiffer's book. With high histamine levels in the blood or allergy and asthma one should take calcium gluconate 500 mg, zinc 10-30 mg, manganese 5-50 mg and methionine 500 mg to excrete histamine. Huh? I write it down.

Spirulina helps, too. It contains all those salts and a lot more. Also essential: lots of pure water! When the body doesn't get enough, it releases the water regulating mediator substance histamine. How come you know the amounts?

I'm good with numbers, and I have stress-related respiratory problems too.

A few days later, in the Marriott lobby in Vienna, we were waiting for the elevator quite some time. While I was talking with the Spellman family, I studied a handsome tall man with a long pepper and salt thatch. He was accompanied by a petite lovely lady. The beau had some pages in his hand and ever once in a while, he glanced at the text and then up in the air as to memorize the words or to call upon heavenly hosts. The setup mimic and gesture made me curious while studying the opera plan. It was Friday and our last opportunity to visit the state opera, but I had not the faintest notion of the Fri's performance. Finally, the elevator arrived. On the spur of the moment, I had the feeling the mellow woman now standing face to face with me knew about operas.

Excuse me, what do you think about the 'Andrea Chenier' by Giordano? Oh, this is a very lovely opera, but of course, I don't know your preference. Oops! The melodic voice matching the most heavenly blue eyes ... of a sudden, I knew whom I'd asked. The elevator stopped one level under ours. The lady and her gallant left. The posters on every 2nd street lantern popped into my mind. Maximilian Schell made a guest performance in *My fair Lady*. I had talked to a real art expert. And, in my opinion Max had better not cut his hair. It had improved his look a lot.

Hilde's karma uncovering

I always enjoyed my family as guests. This time, Aunt Hilde had accompanied my mother on her usual winter vacation.

Preparing an avocado dressing, I looked out the kitchen window for Hilde's new Oldsmobile she'd bought after John's stroke. As the spouse, she would have had to pay for his costs. But she was allowed to keep $68,000. At the time she owned about $86,000, so she got a few things. Four years, John exuded his charm in the Motion Picture Hospital.

Hilde visited him three times a week. I also came once in a while to this homey health facility and was not only awaited by him. Joe, one of the 3 Stooges and Judy Garland's agent Al Rosen liked the little conversations with me too. The latter Methuselah asked me twice if I'd seen him in his office. Not that I recall, I said, but who knows? Again I talked to a person who was important to a friend of Doris.

Because Encino is located between Bel Air and Woodland Hills, Hilde stopped by once or twice a week. In summer, she used to come more often for a half hour swim to cool off. This time she wanted to meet aunt Hilde since both had some in common, not only the same name and a hubby with the same name. Both had to take care of their Heinz. Hilde Richter had Alzheimer. Heinz Walz lost his foot from diabetes as his sister years before and spent his last years in a wheelchair.

Another mutual, both Hildes wearing wigs.

Of course, my aunt has no choice since she's bald except for a little hairy island in the back of her head. I had planned to take the girls to the hospital and before to buy veggies from the Calabasas market. I also wanted to guide them through the famous old farmhouse opposite the clinic.

While munching a veggie pita and salad, Ma asked, what could we bring John? Smirking, I said, he'd like a bottle of vodka. But he'd quit boozing. Yep, this may have been the problem since he still smoked some cigarettes. Nicotine constricts the vessels while alcohol widens them. It's better to quit on both. He'd also quit on headstands. Hilde looked at my aunt's missing fingers. Does it hinder you in any way? Not really! All my life was work, work.

How did it happen? Well, I'd just finished school and began my compulsory domestic service at the Helm farmers. They had a mill. Every day, I had to clean the chaff cutter. It ran with water. When I shut it off, I had to bend over. One braid got into it and twisted around the iron shaft sticking out. I tried to get it off. Ugh!

Ma said that's because you had your braids always in front. Anneliese and I had them in the back. Hilde shrugged in a what-ya-can-do manner. It twisted around my fingers. They were wrung off and my scalp ripped off. Ugh! What's it like to endure such? I sank to the floor. When I woke up again and saw my fingers, I screamed, a woman came out. I pushed her away and ran to a big mirror. When I saw me ... yuck. I turned around and screamed. I wanted to run home. They caught me. Willie, the oldest son of the farmer ran to a general room and called the Gütschow office. They informed Mamme. Ma tossed in: That was the darkest day in our family's life. I and Anneliese collected the fingers in a matchbox and buried them.

Mamme only saw me when I already had the bandage. But the farmer woman sat there in shock. The professors in Heidelberg didn't know what to do. I was their first such case. They didn't believe I'd survive it. Chuckling, my mother threw in, you know what she said the very next morning when all the doctors came in for their visit? Huh? When they asked how are you, she said: fine. Ha ha.

Mamme remained with me in the hospital. At night, I'd thrown up from the ether. If she wouldn't have helped me, I'd died of suffocation. Ma said she got blood directly from a woman. Hilde has AB, a rare blood group. That was the end of October 40, said Hilde. I was in the clinic until Eastern 41, a half year. Then I was in a convalescence home, in Heidelberg-Schlierbach. That's a recuperation institution. And then?

I served my tailor apprenticeship. Three years later, I got my finals with the best grade.

So, you really worked off some bad karma! Maybe you'd scalped an Indian in a former life. Haha! Bel Air Hilde asked, what the heck is karma? All my friends talk about it and I'm getting somehow what they mean, but I'm too sheepish to ask. Karma's cosmic justice, the concept of cause and effect. We are responsible for our actions, for our reality. What we cause, good or bad, will have an effect on us. Huh? If in a past life you were constantly bedridden and other people had taken care of you, you know people having near death experiences use to see their life unwind like a film. After that life, you'd see yourself sickly lying in bed and being taken care off. So you'd decide to play the opposite role in your next life. The soul reincarnates to learn all facets of life. Thus you'd married twice men who allowed you to do private nursing jobs to paying off debts. Aha! Hilde hailed with bright eyes and rosy cheeks. Heinz and John had not been my only patients. So? When I'd lived with Heinz in an apartment, I had taken care of my friend in the neighboring house for seven years. And Linda needs care, too. I shop and clean for her. Hilde joyfully let the cat out of the bag.

I admired her friend who's real name was Elisabeth Fabiani. I cherish the things I inherited from her. She had chosen the name Linda = Beauty. Linda started as a ballerina. She was married to a known violinist. Then she was an interior decorator and at the end of her career a registered nurse.

Hilde sighed, so that's karma? Yes, you now learn to be a caretaker meaning, you are working off your karma. If I'd taken care of you all my life, I'd not need a nursing job this time around. Ma said: Let's hope me neither. You were quite a job: pneumonia, pleurisy, mumps, ear infections, cataract. Ah! I didn't think of that. So, whenever anything weighty seems to drag us down we can say, what lies ahead will serve my spiritual maturing. Anyhow, everything's only temporary, nothing remains like it is, except for the essential ethereal part. You talk like a priest. I'm a preacher's daughter. Pa still does funeral sermons for not religiously organized people.

Arriving at the hospital, I said, the Western town I'll show you later. Here we are, look on the wall, all the movie stars! In the back, we passed the dementia division. Some seniors sat quietly in a row of chairs as in a doctor's office, waiting to be next and watching us passing. Two ladies had bows in their hair. I said: How pretty. Turning to my folks, I said you'll like John's room. He overlooks a park-like area with ducks around a tiny creek.

John was still in bed.

Hi John, how are you doing?

I'm okay. How are you?

Fine. May I introduce: this is my mother Alwine and here's my aunt Hilde. His eyes wandered from one to the other. After another glance at my mother, his facial expression showed astonishment as if he recognized her from somewhere. I looked out of the glass wall saying hey, where are they? Huh?

John, where are the ducks? Oh, they're at the bar, they needed a drink. Haha! Still the same funny guy!

You look like Doris. Doris Day.

I laughed: Isn't she blond with blue eyes?

Yeah, but the solid hair, the features, the nose, the complexion. I'd long forgotten the fortune telling. While writing, it came back to me. Plus, the psychic had allowed to tape the reading. Leaving the building, we walked across the street and entered the oldest house of Hollywood. It was removed from there and built up again in this Western Town. The visitors can walk around and see the old rooms and work tools. I like to buy fruits and veggies from this working farm. They are tasty and inexpensive. At the time they had only quinces. Aunt Hilde made great jelly from them.

Buddhism & Reiki - Connecting past and present

Carole called: Hi, how's everything going?

Great! Peter left for Germany. I'm enjoying myself. Good for you. What's he doing abroad? He invested most our money in Portugal and now he's trying to get some of the dough back. Well! Good luck. The reason I'm calling, I plan to come to L.A. on Wednesday?

Why? Great! On Thursday, I have a date with Hilde. She needs to see a lawyer in Beverly Hills, but other than that I'm free.

Well, that's gross. I need to go there, too. I'll bring some stuff from my mother I'd like to auction at Sotheby's. Oh, yeah! We were there lately, with what I'd hoped to be a Modigliani. Unfortunately, it was an imitation. Too bad.

But the good thing is, I still own the red-headed woman. If it would have been an original painting, I couldn't enjoy it anymore. Either I had sold it or I'd be anxious all the time somebody could steal it. Carole laughed.

I like your optimistic way looking at things.

On Thursday afternoon, we headed Southwest. We'll take Scadlock Lane, so you can see the house we had rented. That's it: 3710.

Great view! The heat made the air vibrating and everything blurred. The beer factory in the distance, the skyscrapers, and everything around looked like a surrealistic painting. On our way up, Carole asked, what's that huge building? The University of Judaism. Just had a seminar there with my neighbor Sandi Steinberg. She's a script surgeon and helps screenwriters with their work. Why'd you go there?

It's the thing with my great-grandfather. I thought if I'll write a good script ... through a movie, I could find my relatives in Carmel.

So how's it going? Well, when I read that very part aloud, a female director in the seminar said, it's great material for an Ingmar Bergman movie. What did you do with the script? I wasn't ambitious, only advertised it in a booklet, Clemens Martin had co-published. I doubt any director ever got hold of it.

Who's that Martin? He's the OPM guy Peter gave our good money for movie deals. Still, owes us a bundle. He lives quite well with other peoples' money. Playing polo isn't cheap. Here we are, that's Hilde's driveway. Well?

We may see some deer nibbling away Hilde's roses' and lilies' buds.

No ruminant in the woods, but a wooden surprise waiting on the chimney. Hilde let us in her space home. Do you want coffee or tea? Carole said: I quit on coffee. I said, so we both take tea. While Hilde walked to the kitchen, we passed by the chimney. Resolutely, Carole walked to the right side of the mantlepiece, picked up the little Madonna and dropped it in my arms. Tell me, what you feel! I stalled. My eyes filled with tears. I gave the wooden statue right back and walked to the family room.

While Carole put it back onto the board, Hilde said: The Northridge shaker threw the Madonna from the chimney but it didn't get a scratch.

Sad and disturbed, I sank onto the comfy couch and nibbled on my chocolate eclair.

Carole didn't bother me any further. But on our way out passing the chimney, she laid the ten inches carved piece in my lab again. Rivulets ran down my cheeks.

Just tell me, what you feel. Grief, distress ... deep sadness. Carole said softly:

This was the only thing the owner was able to leave her dear relative. The circumstances were inconsolable.

Back in Encino, Carole got her massage table from the car and set it up in our family room. I'll give you a master attune. She got some stones and stuff out of her pouch and placed them on certain energy points. In her function as Reiki Master and hypnoses therapist, she gave me one of three grade 3 initiations. In the night, I'd a dream where I was again in the body of the very beautiful blonde I had dreamed about many years ago. In the former nightly vision, I was pushed on a rack wagon. Though I had no other recollection, it took me a week to recover from the burden of the saddening impression. This time, I felt good.

I fixed a plate of fruits as my daily mandala.

When I'd completed the outer ring of apple cuttings, Carole came from the guest quarter.

You spoil me! Well? What a piece of art.

My shy smile made her ask: What's up? I had a dream. I took care of my sister who was bound to bed all her life. She laid in layers of bright white feather pillows and bedclothes in a huge 4 pole bed with a canape. I devoted myself as if I atoned for something and avoided all the looks of my many admirers. I'd stolen the statue from the church. Why?

I thought, if my sister can't go to the house of God to pray to the Madonna, I've to bring her home. I wanted so bad to help her get well. The dream ended when I was taken away by officials. But it had nothing to do with the theft. I was an eyesore to less attractive women. Yeah, said Carole, great beauty can be a handicap. Envy, jealousy, and false accusations were the beautiful woman's curse.

I wonder why I not have gone through the actual dying as in my past life dream as the young shepherd. There I had an uplifting feeling after being shot in the back. Or as Polynesian, the relief feeling from the unbearable pain the tar caused on my skin.

What do you think had happened to you?

I think I was burnt. My fear of walking on red hot coals was intense. As a kid, I loved to layer and burn twigs in an ashtray.

Well? Yeah, but I may have been impaled before. What makes you think that?

The seminar before the fire walk was about pressure points, imprinted pains. I guess I was staked and re-experienced that pain. Otherwise, why would I have screamed so much? By the way, tomorrow is a Buddhist meeting not far from here.

Okay? Wanna you go?

Well, have you been there before?

Once. Did it work out for you?

Um! I don't know. Their chanting NAM MYOHO RENGE KYO supposes to bring luck. Well? You came here. You gave me 3rd grade Reiki and private lessons. Am I not lucky? So you said.

I also asked people to try it out. Yeah?

Just recently, Armida, our neighbors' maid came to me with her success report. As an Avon adviser, she had to visit her customers all the time. Never before they called her. But a week after the daily chanting, the first customer called and ordered something. Since then, she had four other calls. In Miller's love letters to Hoki Tokuda, I've read that he also had more luck with saying the magic spell 50 times per day though the translation "there's nothing more exclusive than the law of the

Lotus sutra" doesn't seem to evoke such a decisive effect.

The phone started on ringing when we were about to leave for a visit at Leanne's. It was my ersatz daughter. Because I knew Carole was coming I suggested Ines trying our concentrated Reiki energy for her neurodermatitis. Spirulina had made it less itchy and distinct, but it had not disappeared entirely. Okay, we'll see you tomorrow eve around 6 p. m. Tonight we'll attend a Buddhist meeting just two blocks from us in Tarzana. Is it the temple near Topanga? That's a Hindu temple. I was there with our Indians and with my parents. This meeting's in a private home. Are you interested? Not really. I don't have time.

That's your problem. You need to take more time for yourself. I was there once. That mantra NAM MYOHO RENGE KYO may help you.

Why I could check it out, how's it spelled?

I'll write it down for you. If you change your mind, we'll meet tonight at 7:00 p. m. at the hairdresser on Ventura between Lindley and Havenhurst not far from our favorite breakfast place, same side. Why there?

I need that non-chemical perm liquid again.

Why'd you perm your hair? Peter's gotten to know me with curls. He doesn't like changes. And it's easier to handle that way.

There was no chemistry between Carole and the Guatemalan hairdresser. We were warmly welcomed by some 20 people. The owner of the house just talked about her experience with 26 tumors in her breast: When my surgeon set an appointment for an operation, I said okay, you can cut the tumors out, but give me four more weeks. I didn't explain to him why. I just wanted to give the NAM MYOHO RENGE KYO the chance to heal me. Every morning and every evening, I chanted for 5 minutes. When I had the check up, my surgeon couldn't find any growth. But you won't believe it. He responded nohow pleased.

A tall woman in her 50th said: Yeah, the doctor gains by cutting not by praying. I'd chanted for my 80-year-old mother. My father passed on five years ago. Since then, she'd been alone. I visualized a desirable partner for her, and hard to beat, she just married a handsome 84-year-old millionaire.

When Wolfgang and Ines arrived next eve, the massage table was already set up. Carole said, do you have any book where I can show the kids the chakras? How about Hands of Light? Yeah, great one, I know Barbara. Flipping through Brennan's big blue book, I found a double page picture showing the auric energy flowing around the seven chakras. That's good. Turning to the young couple, Carole said: It's just to show you what you may feel when we work on the table. So Ines, hop on it.

Wolfgang, you hold Ines' feet. I walked towards her head and held my hands around it. While Carole worked on the body, I looked in Wolfgang's pale face. I sensed the strong whirl in my palms as if the air of a big balloon deflated at once. The young man's eyeballs popped out. I smiled at him. Well? Wow! You feel it, too? Uh-huh! Now you know that this energy thing isn't just baloney. Carole said:

You'll be okay. The skin rash will diminish. I can see you'll be having a little girl and later, another one. You'll be well off in all respects.

I asked: Are you pregnant? No. Carole said: You'll be soon.

When the kids were gone, I said: Wow, Carole, that's the second time this year I felt the universal energy so strong.

When was the other time? You know Lanoo?

Isn't he the guru who's on TV all the time?

Yes, he's a known German singer. Okay? Every day from 7 to 9 p. m., he's meditating in his Book of Light Academy on San Vincente Blvd. You know I helped Hilde to clean out her friend's apartment. In the eve I always drove by. Last Good Friday I saw Christian Anders in his white thin cotton garb walking to his suite 101. I stopped the car and joined the small group. We were only four people in the small apartment, equipped with cushions. The atmosphere was intimate. Lanoo got our crown chakras spinning by pressing his circular arranged fingers on our head, mine swirled. After the singing and meditating, I was talking with Lanoo and virtually took over the question time. By the way, you can listen to the meditation. He gave me the tape and a booklet. When the others left, we talked generalities in German. He gave me an energy boost by moving his hand over my face. I've never experienced my eyelashes to flutter like that. I wonder what this might trigger.

Hasya and Hollywood's Osho Community

Ingrid called from Hawaii. I bought an avocado tree from your money. Oh, good! I love avocados. To the umpteenth time, Ingrid asked: Did you go Hasya's? Not yet. You really should go with Anda. OK! You'll like it there, especially the huge charcoal pool in the middle of her living room. Though I wasn't eager to marvel at people's pools, I said okay, I'll ask Anda. Do it! Believing that everything happens for a reason, I considered there could be something important waiting for me in the house of the famous movie producer. Withal, as a friend of the *Godfather's* sister I could befriend the movie producer's wife as well. Maybe Francoise Ruddy could help me find my folks via getting interested in my script.

On September 11, 1996, Anda called.

Wow, I was about to call you, too. Ingrid asked me again to go with you to Hasya. Um!

What's doing? Do you know anybody who might be interested in a white lion? A real one? No. Stuffed? Just the head is left. It can be used as a rug. I don't know. It's a very rare thing. You may be lucky. Why?

Hilde has a lunch date with Finny Getty. She's Paul Getty's widow. The museum needs to buy new stuff all the time. I'll call Hilde in a sec. She can ask her friend about it. Why don't you write about your experience? That could bring you more money. And it'll be great therapy. My sons think so, too. Yep! Considering how many times Anne Frank's book went over the counter. And she had a better life in the attic. But she died? Anda, as usual, turned the end of her sentence towards a question mark. True. I understand why my sons urge me to write. But why do you want it? It'll be good for you. And, maybe I'll find me. Why? When we first met I felt oddly close to you. We may have been related in a former life. Um! Reincarnation, isn't it wishful thinking?

Not for me. I'd like to believe, thinking of Germans reincarnating in Jewish families and vice verse, to learn to love each other. I'd like that. I think, it happens. I once had a dream where I walked to a provisional store. I held a younger girl on my hand who had blond braids like mine, not Jewish looking. I have blond and blue eyed boys! I know. Sometimes I also fall into the cliché trap. Anyway, I knew the salesman, but he didn't respond when I smiled at him. I said, don't you recognize me? I'm Miriam from the ghetto. You also lived in a Polish ghetto before your father hid you in the grain storage cellar. It would explain my affinity with the Judea children. I can't believe there are only 18 million. I know many myself. Most my profs were Jews. I worked voluntarily with seniors and as a family counselor in the Jewish Community, in Frankfurt. Our landlady Mrs. Weber was half Jewish. The brother of Peter's friend Uli killed by Nazis. We now live in *Little Tel Aviv of the Valley*. In the morning, I hike the mountains with Sandi, Bette, and Estelle all ...

Omigod, I must rush ... the photo shooting. I'll come right back. Need a passport? No, I had that Garcinia interview with reporters from the biggest Japanese woman's magazine. What's that? You may know the plant's name better, tamarind. It's supposed to reduce weight. Ah, yeah I remember. Sour. Yep!

I'd use it if it works. I said if I want to lose weight I go on a one day fruit and veggie fasting every week ... works for me.

An hour later, I showed up at Anda's. She handed me a handwritten page. That's a poem I just made about my endure. You'll write the book!?! Yesss! Anda raised her arms. You all got me to do it. Ay! Great! I hugged my friend.

Can you read it to me? While Anda read aloud, my eyes filled with tears. You should show it to Hasya. Maybe Ingrid's pushing me to go with you is for you. So let's go. Yeah, let's do it, said Anda with a conspiring twinkle in her beautiful eyes. Got her number? Nope. Then I call the Osho-Center in Venice. Eric gave me Hasya's number. After a brief explanation, she invited us to come this very Wednesday evening.

A few hours later, we entered the grand building. In the dressing room right passing the entrance, I got rid of my tight pants and choose a comfortable white gown. The renowned charcoal stone pool in the living hall attached to a large fireplace surely impressed me. But I'd rather have the floor to ceiling ART DECO bookshelves on the backside of the sitting area. I made a mental note to look for bamboo-like strips to make my shelves look like those.

Two women recognized me from somewhere, perhaps from a let-go or a healing session. Forgiving myself, I swallowed the memory failure. My lively nature may have attracted their attention. We were seven women and four men. The bit 'a double eleven again' fluttered through my cerebrum: it was 9.11! The 9 is my number because I was born on Nov 27 (2+7=9). 1+9+ 9+6 adds up to 7 like the cross total digits of my birth date! Seemingly, a perfectly chosen date for me. But nothing unusual happened. Except for Hasya's peculiar behavior. During the afternoon hours, Francoise Ruddy tried to X-ray me with her beautiful dark eyes. When hugging her goodbye, she'd not let me off for at least a minute. The longest hug ever made me dizzy.

Because of increasing distress with the hopeless IRS problem, I had no chance to come for a follow-up event. Years later, Peter Biskind's book Easy Rider Raging Bull gave me a possible reason for Hasya's queer performs. The author mentions that Melissa Mathison at age 12 started as Coppola's babysitter. Supposedly, she'd been one time Francis' lover. The woman, who had later earned an Oscar nomination for the E. T. script and married Harrison Ford was described in the book as if she had been me. Even the intimate part and the horse like gum showing when laughing. The similarity and same initials may have made Hasya think I also could be dating her Godfather producing husband and wanted to check out my rival.

Next morn, I picked up Leanne for a hike. It's going to be a nice one. You bet. Are the other girls coming, too? Bette for sure. She still has my juicer. Ay! She said you can take it after the walk (including an interesting biotope as I found out later).

How was your press conference?

Pretty good, fortunately.

See, I told you not to worry. Yes, there were only eight reporters, a number I can handle. I only hate big crowds. I loved my neighbor friend for reassuring me all the time. Leanne had earned a bachelor in nutrition and proofread my dissertation. When we rang the bell, Bette wasn't ready yet. She let us in. Al and Bette only lived in the bedroom because of their never ending refurbishing project.

We walked over torn tiles. I asked:

Why don't you live in your big motor home? The redhead in shorts shook her shoulder. Somehow, she looked younger this morning. Had her art director hubby done nonfiction wonders in the heat of the night? Bette said:

Sandi and Estelle will join us.

We entered Sandi's beautifully restored home likely mirroring her success in the script surgeon business. Estelle, her roommate, and real estate agent came down the stairs.

Walking up on Boris Drive, we talked about the coming election. I said, after reelection, I'd like to present Bill my oil painting of the famous city hall with the church in Michelstadt.

What makes you think he'll win again?

I knew it the first time too. How so? Remember Leanne, when we drove to *Carlos & Pepe* in your BMW? I said: Clinton will win and mimicking Bush, read my lips, he'll even serve a 2nd term. Don't you remember your Bill's aiming at me? Leanne looked questioning. But why would you want to give Clinton your painting? Looking down on the brain surgeon's huge house, who's Carthusian-mix tomcat Sebastian had marked our freshly painted home, I said: Bill had sent us a check for $8,000 for the earthquake damage. I thought of it as a good idea 'cause the church behind the city hall was built in 1492 the same year when Columbus discovered America. Sandi said: If you want to meet Bill Clinton I could arrange that for you. Why? Henry Waxman is my in-law. Really?

Yes, it'd be no problem.

Isn't he's health and environment? He may have even read the letter I wrote to Hillary. Anyway, thanks for your offer. I'd love to meet Bill. When I see him on TV, I feel like he's family. But I'd like to do it on my own. I want to deserve it. Sandi said: He could not keep the painting anyway. Whatever the chiefs of states get during their presidency, they've to give back. Then I'll wait.

In chatting groups by twos, we reached the top. Down under us the sparkling San Fernando Valley in the morning sun. I asked Bette:

Have you heard of speaking in tongues?

Yes. Why? We were new apostolic. So?

My mother said, there were women all of a sudden speaking in foreign languages.

That's known in the Seventh-day Adventist Church, too. So we have a similar upbringing. Passing a ruby blooming hibiscus bush, I said:

Those are edible, good for the immune system. Bette stopped abruptly. Huh? What? Um!

Gazing at me, she said: You'll have a message for us in 10 or 12 years. Wide-eyed with goosebumps all over, I asked:

What kind of message? Had Bette a vision? Was she now speaking in tongues? Um ... something with crystal ... wait ...

What do you mean, Christ?

Maybe. I don't know ... Cranberries? No, wait, it's got to do with water. Huh? Dunno.

Arriving back on Boris Drive, both big Cassidy dogs were out on the street. Let's hope they don't remember our paddle tennis sounds.

I shouted: *Was habt ihr hier zu suchen?* Go back where you belong! Lifting my left arm, I showed the dogs their way. One moved a few feet, the other not an inch. He neither barked nor acted aggressively. Both looked at me with a facial expression no fear, honey!

Water-Code cracked?

11 years later, back in Germany, I'd written some self-help books on Spirulina and the immune system. One of my studies with the blue-green algae was with Jürgen Görke. The health practitioner diagnoses by using the Kirlian photography (KP). As electrical beings, we emit measurable or photograph-able energy. The higher our intake of silicon, germanium, selenium and copper, the stronger is the emanation and the more extensive is the aura.

Spirulina contains all these semiconductor substances. Görke made a Kirlian photography of the energy fields of my fingertips and toes. I then took 7 Spirulina tablets with a glass of water. 7 minutes later, he did another KP. He stared at it, then grabbed the first one again. Dr. Meyer, how's that possible, so fast? The inflammation points ... most of them are gone! That's why Jacky's arthritis had healed so fast.

Jürgen Görke belonged to my support team on the Tour der Hoffnung, an event to collect money for kids with cancer. Every year, professional cyclists and celebrities are wheeling their bodies from town to town, collecting checks. After a 15 mile hilly tour, the last station was in front of the castle in Erbach.

I talked with Costa Cordalis about Spirulina which he also used. The famous singer spun round me and scrawled his name on the back of my self-made T-shirt, directly above my fabric color writing SPIRULINA HEALS NATURALLY. Costa then stepped up the stage in order to ask jointly with other celebrities for donations. When the compere said, this is today's last opportunity to contribute I felt a strange urge to move forward. As in trance, I walked towards the platform. I took a promotion card and a pen out of my pants pocket vouching for ten big bottles of Spirulina. Costa thanked by hugging me. I walked towards the master of ceremonies, took his microphone and without a spur of stage fright, I said, yo, I'm out of breath, but happy to be part of this tour. In many studies, the nutritional supplement I'm donating is proven to prevent and heal cancer. My mother and a female reporter in her company among the audience wondered about my performance. So did I. Had my father, the big spender and speaker overtaken? Or had the exhaustion released a lot of endorphins that made me act in such a cool manner?

I did send my book to the nearest oncologists asking for an interview. I had in mind that children with cancer would get the Spirulina and that the producer later would supply unlimited amounts for the oncology childcare's wards of all clinics. One of the profs put me off. The other one invited me. But what I have heard made even the heaven cry. It rained all the way back home.

In a 45 minute conversation that's imprinted in my brain, the prof first accused me of financial interests, then he ridiculed my idealism. I showed him photos of a 4½-year-old boy from my book *Spirulina, Survival Code*. The boy's mother had a job related led and cadmium contamination. His hair had grown for the first time in his life after taking the blue-green organism for two months. Since the prof didn't comment on it, I said:

Spirulina can also be used on intercontinental flights since it eliminates radiation and helps with jet lag problems. Otherwise, the life expectancy of the crew is some 65.

That's why I'm not a pilot, he replied pertly.

I replied: Doctors' lifespan isn't vast either.

To make a long story short. I was not even allowed to give my gift to the kid's parents. The oncologist said: If you first prove the effect. Well, you haven't read the book I'd send you. Seven pages of references from scientists around the world proved Spirulina's cancer-healing and cancer-preventing effect. He snarled: I don't approve of cancer preventive measures. We need cancer because of the overpopulation! Huh? After all his careless comments this one left me speechless. I was sure he meant the elderly, not his patients. But I gave up on getting in touch with the other profs participating from the tour money. On my way home I felt slapped. While the rain slapped the windshield and the wipers clicked furiously back and forth I came up with the title of the above-mentioned book's remake: *So halt ich mir den Arzt vom Leib*. If certain doctors don't care about their oath, we better take our well-being into our hands and keep them at bay.

Masaru Emoto's water crystal photos pulled me out of the dive giving me an instant lift making me think of writing about my experience with water. In my book Wunderwesen Wasser, I also describe Johann Tikale's wonderful work which via certain frequencies leads to detoxification by cleansing the lymph.

Emoto's findings of water transforming vibrations such as sound, color, writing and action in visible form add to this. I also inform about how to activate H2O to spring water quality and give an account why this cluster water stops allergy, Alzheimer, cancer and other diseases. The book also contains data on ways to avert our forced medication from the faucet. In 2007 my book *Cranberry Powerfrucht* was edited, some ten years after Bette Rohm's assumed speaking in tongues. I found the oldest centenarians live in cranberries consuming countries. The sour fruit appears to stretch the arteries. It seems their phytochemicals turn the clock back. A few month later I received an e-mail from Peter Groß, the inventor of the award-winning water activator which is now called Aqua-Lyros. He added two water crystal photos (WCP) acquired according to Masaru Emoto's method.

The one taken from regular tap water looked muddy. The other one taken from the same water passing through the activator was crystal clear. I called Peter Groß and asked for the artist photographer's phone number. After an hour's conversation, Ernst F. Braun offered me some soul stars saying: You only have to write your name on a small piece of paper and send it to me in an envelope without anything else. I'll place it next to a tiny bottle of distilled water for a day. Then I'll take a pipette and put 22 drops of the informed water into 22 glass dishes and quick freeze them at -35°F. I'll then take them out one after the other. With a microscope camera, I'll take the pics at -5°F. I've about 45 secs per WCP.

A few days after sending my signature, I received an e-mail with 15 WCP! E. Braun cited this amount as highly unusual. He normally gets 4 or 8. At first, I considered them just gorgeous. At the 2nd sight, I discovered very private matters reflecting my characteristics, likes, experiences, and stepping stones!

What's this wondrous work telling us? Who did the job? Due to highly personal messages and because of my former extrasensory perceptions of deceased relatives and friends, it dawned on me, who informs the water. Our Dead! Spirits! Souls! H2O seems to be a medium for souls. Since they exist on a higher oscillation level most people don't see them, though, they exist around us. Apparently, my grandma had not given me a song and a dance after all when she said: Your grandpa in heaven can see what you're doing. I probably wouldn't have understood this so fast if I hadn't read Friedrich Jürgenson's book *Voice Transmissions with the Deceased*. In the book, the painter and opera singer clearly established the connection with the beyond. While monitoring taped bird's voices, the voice of his late mother appealed to him with his nickname: Friedel, can you hear me? It's Mammy. www.vtf.de/schweden.shtml

Inexplicable phenomenon on the PC may also be spirit activity. At times, I'm quite sure about it. Especially if apparently unwanted text disappears, and I later write it much better and think: good that it had vanished. One time even the copy disappeared when I tried to get it from the USB stick.

My personal WCP reflecting pleasant experiences were forming beautiful crystals. Crises in my life like two useless operations appear dark and barely shaped. E. Braun had printed the WCP showing a praying woman on her knees on a card and named it High-priestess (p. 187). Our almost separation shows a divided crystal with a broken heart and Peter's profile. Our neighbor friend Scöpi commented on a lovely one: Looks like your wedding photo. I said, if this WCP is designed by souls, shouldn't they know we aren't similar tall?

Oh, wait a minute ... I pointed to the Saturn-like thing. That's the moon hopper! Huh?

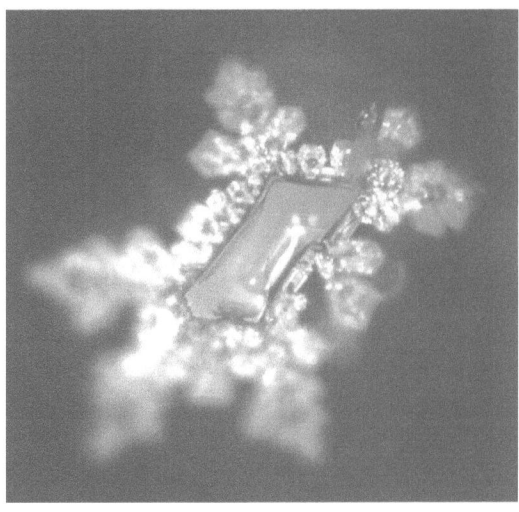

That's where Peter had helped me get on the hopping ball! On it, I'm almost as tall as Peter. This sports tool made my back muscles strong again. Our gospel choir conductor had let us stand up all the time. I had back pain. But after a few weeks of hopping, I was able to stand for hours without suffering.

See, this one. Our sun sign!

Yes, an archer. Oh here, isn't it a divine picture? A dog, the ears like Sandy's and trees! Yep! You love dogs! That's for sure!

And trees, I paint trees all the time.

Later, when my sister-in-law called I told her everything about the WCP and said:

I'm going to write a book on it. Renate said:

Are you sure you want to do that? Don't you think to embarrass yourself with it?

The thing is too important. There's too much at stake, no regard for personal feelings.

Renate chuckling: Just, high priestess.

Oh, well! Had not been all naturalists who had discovered something new revealed to the absurdity?

Several weeks later, Maddie MacCann was kidnapped. Because I interpreted some of Ernst Braun's personal WCP correct, I thought I could help to find the little girl by trying another experiment. Ernst was on one of his 1,000-1,500 miles walks he does every summer. So I did the test with his daughter Sarah Steinmann who also knows the high art of microscopic photographing frozen water drops. She informed the neutral water with the most shown picture of the little girl and the written words: Where is Maddie McCann?

A few days later, Sarah did send me 8 photos per email. The very first WCP looked like a motive: An ice skate with a phallus symbol and a horned animal with a boomerang. Skating on thin ice? The dupes are usually called cornet. Could that mean, Gerry committed adultery? Had the deceived taken Maddie as compensation? I hope, the girl didn't end up in an elitist circle of pedophiles. Anyway the WCP suggest the kidnapper is very wealthy.

One WCP shows an estate with a kidney-shaped pool and a runway. I recognize three females. The one on top seems to protect the property with its illumined runway by a heavy weapon.

Another WCP looks like the inner part of an airplane. On a kind of hybrid WCP, there are house numbers and probably a golf course.

A round of people shows a little girl standing on the left, a blond or bald headed man in a black shirt and tan shorts sitting sidewards talking to a heavyset younger man in black pants, white shirt, and full black hair.

I see house numbers 2, 3 and 5. There is also a WCP that looks like a map taken from a 5-mile high flying plane. Most WCP I painted in acrylic without mentioning the experiment. Since I wanted to be of help, I talked to Mr. Thielke, a criminal investigator from Frankfurt. He advised me to send an email to k45@pp-ffm03.de

I did it, but I've heard no more from the police. They may have called it baloney. I'd also send info to the UK police, Oprah Winfrey, and Prince Charles. Until recently, I couldn't find any address of the McCanns. The Clarence House responded but I'd never heard anything about anybody working on it either.

It lasted two years after my book *Water - Code cracked?* was on the market, that it dawned on me why I had more soul stars (WCP) than usual. Two men were playing an important role in my life: my ex-lover Edmond Dembinski and my fatherly friend Jochen Gestering. Both happened to have been artist painters! Mr. Braun's other clients may not have as many artists on the other side; not to forget Peter's uncle Adolf and Edi's mother Wanda von Dembinski.

The seven tests with Ernst F. Braun reassured me about the souls' interacting with us. The one with my father made me happy. I had written down my name and two questions for him. I'd hoped, this way to find his writings.

I'd walked with my husband to the post office to send the handwritten questions to E. Braun. My mind was in the other world. I mentally asked my father to give me a sign.

On our way back my eyes were pinned on a promotion poster with all kinds of sausages. Though I avoid most animal products, I was attracted by the Russian shop where I used to buy only Siberian cranberries. Giving way to a strange urge I pointed to a chicken salami and two other sausages. With a full plastic bag, we left the shop. My husband with a surprised and delighted glance at the Russian. We'd made it up the steep Kisselberg and sat down on the fountain edge. Suddenly, I felt a craving for meat: Let's try the salami. Throwing all hygienic objections overboard, CP hacked with his key at the salami. Chuckling, I said:

Hopefully, none of my readers come by thinking of the one whom I often met walking this route on Shank's pony. Just seconds later the very one passed by. I spluttered: What's happening today? Then, in a quiet moment the scales fell from my eyes: Didn't I ask my dad for a sign? I meant an indication regarding the water crystal photos. Had he arranged this so amusingly? Transferring me his immense lust of sausage and sending me the health conscious reader just at the moment I thought of him? If so, thanks, Pa, for your cooperation!

After the usual procedure, I received a PDF file. One WCP of great radiance seemed as the illumination of the purest soul. I felt a similar sense of pleasure when my late father used me as a medium. Still, in the flesh, he always had doubts on a life after life. I used to say sooner or later you will get to know it. Hopefully later, but then please, give me a sign. What a wonderful sign of his existence it was! He planned his whole mourning ceremony with chorales and biblical passages, which he made sounding in my inner ear: 'I worship the power of love' and 'See I am with you every day …'

All mornings, I woke up with another verse. I was most receptive on the first day. On the

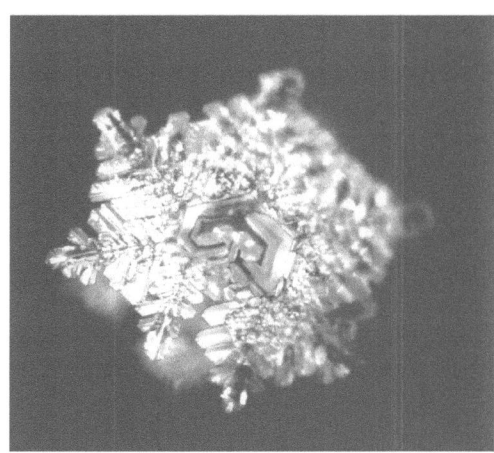

eve of my father's transition, I puzzled about the cause of his passing. In the morn, I woke up with a clear hearing of The Internationale.

My mother had an explanation right on: At the end of election nights the party pals of the social democrats usually sing: So comrades, come rally. My father's weak heart was overwhelmed with joy for the SPD winning the election after so many CDU governed years. He probably sang aloud and accidentally swallowed his partial denture, for we never found it and I detected an eversion on his throat.

The inside of this bonny crystal resembles the attic of a house. An eye on the left roof side looks to a rectangular object next to the nook. My mother went with me to the attic. I walked, bent down, far out in the direction of a shelf. Yes, my mother yelled excitedly, there he has his written stuff. In a file, I found manuscripts from 1951. My father had sent them to an agency. He was offered: For 12 marks, we'll send 50 copies to different publishers. His novel about the 40th, I'd read later. Instantly, I was interested in the mini story: How I became a writer.

In Germany, the authors' affairs haven't improved much in the last 60 years. Thus, my dad's writing I'll attach with the wish, the much-discussed citizen money may soon stop the concerns of creative people:

He was not skillful working with the drill. Dire hardship may have made him apply for the job. Day by day he laid the thin metal sheet in the stencil. And day by day, he came to me to get the broken drill sharpened again or replaced. So we got to know each other. For he had never reached the demanded quota, I realized that he was accustomed to another kind of work. One day I spoke to him:

"Tell me, colleague, this way of earning money is not particularly appealing to you too, isn't it? What is your real profession?"

Self-consciously with a swelling breast, he declared: "I'm a writer!"

I had an idea of this occupation and therefore, my inner man instantly got two heads smaller. Full of empathy I asked: "But why do you have to earn your living as a laborer?"

"Well, in Germany the poet and thinker were never valued much. Here, the genius may starve to death!"

When we played skat my father used to say: He who writes remains. Now Pa, you will too. In the two weeks after he made his transition, I was full of love. When Marianne and Helmut came for a game of rummy, I'd never before had these heartstrings towards them. I felt my father's presence. No wonder, he loved to play.

The idea of interacting souls may appear bizarre to some men. Watching child prodigies as Jay Greenberg help to understand the subject. As a toddler, he asked for a cello by drawing one. In a music store, Jay got a little cello and began to play. By the age of 12, he'd finished composing five symphonies. Jay wrote The Storm in a few hours. He speaks of multiple channels, and the music comes involuntarily. It just fills his head.

http://www.wimp.com/musicprodigy

The psychic painter shown on the video is another example of channeling from the other side:

www.youtube.com/watch?v=URM8KGpjztE

When Shirley MacLaine had watched Luiz Antonio Gasparetto in his home in Orange, California, Henri de Toulouse-Lautrec came through and spoke about her former life as a courtesan in Paris. No wonder, Shirley earned an Oscar nomination for Irma la Douce.

Ingrid, my most-travelled friend, was once Antonio's translator in Brazil. Nobody has to believe in the soul, or an on-going life to be amazed by this film. Luiz paints in trance old masters by using crayons and paint tubes. The spirit artists are using him as a channel to tell us: Look, we still exist!

Also, the souls of Dr. Barnard, Dr. Sauerbruch, and other famous surgeons may be working through spirit operators like the ones Oprah Winfrey had shown:

www.youtube.com/watch?v=PNIbvItdjws

Who knows on how many distinct projects the spirit world works with us? Gasparetto is painting at breathtaking speed without looking at his doing. After 2 or 3 minutes a Modigliani, a Renoir or a van Gogh is finished. He is in contact with the painters and lends them his hands and feet so to speak. We can visit him and see how he works. Water crystal photos are similar surprising. We just send our own or a loved one's signature or photo to Ernst Braun www.wasserkristall.ch or ernst_braun@bluewin.ch) and can examine the soul stars shortly after. It would be best for science to stop being blind against the fact that the other world exists! As long as they still are, we may search for ourselves and find out how the human spirit is corresponding via water.

Learning from experience is genuine science. By recognizing the power of love within we do not have to fear dread or death. Knowing where we come from and go to makes us free. It makes life sincere.

Coming home to Berlin at last

After 55 years abroad, Hilde sold her Bel Air house and moved back to Berlin. Living in

California was not her choice anyway. After WW II, her husband was forced to work for the liberators in the Californian dessert. She later followed him. It's remarkably common that people at old age want to return home. When we'd visited Linda in the hospital, I'd soothing speaking stroked her head. She'd said: I'm back in Berlin, am I not? Lately, even I was moved to tears while listening to the song Heimweh (homesickness) https://www.youtube.com/watch?v=ootzkW_-hqY. So someday I may end up moving to Michelstadt or to the brownstone house my mother had planned to inherit me. She'd thought a house is a sure thing. But these days no one knows what happens to the property. If you have to go in a nursing home or the broke state installs a dictate mortgage or you trust a relative, you may end up losing it. The latter happened to Hilde. Her niece had rented an apartment. Later, she'd supposedly found a large house where Hilde was suppose to have an apartment. She'd given her niece a few 100 thousand up in front as a down payment for a house she'd never bought. Since the niece kept the money, Hilde had less to live on and to move in a less expensive home. Meanwhile, she'd fallen in love with a younger man, a divorced architect whom she'd met in a coffeehouse. A third love at almost 80! He moved her into another apartment, a much better deal.

At long last, destiny made it possible to visit my sister friend, check out her 3rd man and see how Hilde was doing in Berlin. I had called her often, but this time, I surprised her: If you want me, I can come and visit you next week. Why, great! Will you come alone? Yes, I'll do two interviews in the Hanover area and would then take the train to Berlin.

What do you mean by alternative?

One of them had erected with body alignment a crippled woman whose spine was totally bent. How did she do that?

It's a mixture of the Alexander, Rolfing, Feldenkrais, and Hakomi technique. Never

heard of it. But you know that stress, hassle or shock can cause reflex cramping. Uh-huh!

The muscles fail to be obedient. The brain loses control over the neuron muscular system. After several months the woman was 90% aligned again. Okay, you can tell me then. Can you stay over the weekend? Yes, I'd like to head back on Monday. Oh good. Because weekends Thomas always takes me places. We can see the Wannsee and Potsdam.

A week later, I'd taken a taxi from the station to Grunewald's Wachenheimer St 14. Walking towards the freshly painted yellow residence, I recognized a plate with a famous name.

Giggling, I hugged Hilde: You didn't tell me you live in Dietrich Bonhoeffer's house.

Whose house?

Don't you know about the theologian, who was in the resistance against the Nazis and was arrested by the Gestapo and hanged? No.

That's funny, I'm sleeping in famous people's houses, lately. Last month, I slept in Nicki Lauda's bed at the Fuschl Lake. Now I'm going to stay in Bonhoeffer's ex-house.

Do you know that racer?

No, Bob Hartmann bought his home. Nicki's self-made bed is just under the roof. Funny, its wood frame is nibbled on by a dormouse. Nicki's ex-wife Marlene loved the rodents.

Next morn, while Hilde did her extensive makeup, I asked, how was it when you lived here with Heinz? There was war. Um! Well? We didn't see each other much. Heinz was working on this wonder weapon. Okay? A highly dangerous task this rocket plane. Why? There was something wrong. They'd lost one. Many pilots had perished. So Heinz had to fly the plane himself to find fault. A split second before it exploded he identified what was wrong. At the dead last moment, he managed to blow off the ejector seat.

Jeez! He was injured and taken to the hospital. Hilde giggled, all the Nazi leaders came for a visit and congratulated him. That's gross!

What? Your husband worked for the Nazis and you live in the house of a man famous for his resistance against the Nazi dictatorship. I didn't know we also work off karma unconsciously or on the other side.

After lunch, Hilde said: I've to make Thomas's sandwich. He comes every day at 2 sharp. At 2:00 p. m. the doorbell rang. A set of keys rattled. Thomas's way of greeting Hilde made it easy for me to believe that he loves her. His voice had a whole different nuance when he talked to me. While he ate his bread with air-dried ham, we talked about the book I'd given Hilde and our plans for the weekend. Later, when Thomas drove back to work, he dropped us in front of the KDW department store. Hilde bought five mocha chocolate bars. I got white herring, potato pancakes and a salad that reminded me of coleslaw. I also bought some other fresh food from a nearby grocery because looking in Hilde's fridge would have caused a mouse to weep.

Next noon, we climbed into Thomas' big new model Mercedes. My last doubt about his earnestness melted. Also, his family's fate made his searching for a mother substitute understandable. Passing two large mansions, Thomas said, the white one belongs to Joop, the terracotta one to Jauch.

Really? This white romantic palace doesn't seem to belong to the fashion designer. The other one looks like a building, Ayn Rand's Roark in Fountainhead could have designed: Straight and simple. Ayn Rand? I've heard of her. Yes, she's a US novelist. Your age group. Republicans like her modern conservatism. Some say she must be Reagan's mother. Though I consider me a red green liberal, I can relate to the principle of her philosophy.

Which is? The reason is the mental faculty that identifies and integrates the substance supplied by man's senses. It rejects any acceptance of faith as a means of knowledge. Well!

After a walk and fruitcake in a coffee-house, our excursion ended in a content state of mind. I had the feeling that Hilde is in good hands. About a year later, after a slight stroke, Thomas moved her a third time: in a prestigious nursing home. Hilde made her transition on the winter day like my beloved grandma some thirty years earlier, and I still had not found her father's relatives in California.

What's on my wish list?

Since I didn't get hold of Doris, I felt obliged to try again on our way back from Palo Alto. I assumed, all the relatives from Neckarhäuserhof were expecting me to meet Doris. They'd probably envisioned me presenting her the photos personally.

On Sunday, after another abundant breakfast we left the Matta family. Past noon, we sat at

Rudy's bar. I had another Caesar's salad, highly surprised by the chicken topping freebee. Had Rudy tried to check if my appetite is as ravenous as Doris's? I sure passed the test. I once won a potato pancake eating contest.

Driving around the precious Carmel Valley area, we were lost. I saw a Gandhi lookalike working in the garden.

Yo, wait! Let me ask the old chap.

Ines stopped at the curb. I got out and walked towards the kneeling man. I bespoke the shield of a whitish baseball cap.

Sir, excuse me, do you know where I can find Doris Day's estate? Certainly. The smiling greybeard pointed straight ahead. It's about a mile from here. You just take the next right, then turn left and follow all the way down on Carmel Valley Road. Thank you very much, isn't it a lovely Sunday? I would have liked to talk to this nice man about his gardening. But we had not much time since Ines had to be back on Monday. Reaching the fort like gatehouse, we stopped about 20 yards away at the parking on the side. I opened the trunk and rummaged through my suitcase. But all grabbing and feeling for didn't bring forth any pictures or the summer cap I made for Doris. Ines said: Hurry up! Why?

The gatekeeper is coming out. Continuing my searching agitation, I asked: Is he coming here? Not yet. He's carrying the garbage can. Alas! I must have forgotten everything in the Matta's house. A minute later, the gatekeeper came half the way towards the car and called, what are you doing here? Thinking, Doris seems to be well protected we walked in his direction. I said, I'm a distant relative of Doris. I'd like to give her pictures from her Neckar folks. One set I'd left at the Cypress Inn desk, we'd stayed a couple of days ago. Um! Ines asked: Is Doris there? His nodding move was almost as deceptive as the East Indians'. Is it possible to ... why don't you write a note, the man said in a way that didn't allow to drum up … I'll get it to Doris. Leave a number and your address. Not thinking straight, I rushed back to the car, got one of my book's promotion cards, scribbled something and reached it to him. He looked at it. And your address? I took the card back and wrote down the post box in Castro Marim though I usually use the Tavira one. Suddenly, the man tensed up and got agitated. With wide open eyes, he pointed to my writing and hollered, what's that?

Curiously, I answered, that's my address!?

A bit relaxed, he said: That's my name, too. Probably, the Latin was afraid we had a bomb in the Beamer. Back in the car, Ines asked:

Are you disappointed now? I really would have liked to meet Doris. It was high on my list to see her in real life: if she reminds me of my mother like in her films. But I'm not leaving California empty handed. Only for my Neckar relatives, it will be disappointing. The trip was still great. You and Situ made me happy. Well? Really, you were very supporting. Maybe I can see Doris some other time.

There's not much time, Ines replied drily. How old is she? 87. See. People with pets live longer. Clara can easily be 100 plus.

Clara? She likes that name better than hers.

So what else is on your vacation wish list?

Meet Carole, Brian, and Imara, maybe Herta and Wayne. I also want a photo from Doris's footsteps. That's easy. We can take the girls along. Only on June 17, I'm not free. It's Giulia's graduation ceremony. You'll like it.

Yeah, that's something new. Um! What?

In the ten years, in California, this will be my first graduation ceremony, Ines replied:

At the Waldorf School, it's a little different.

My thoughts drifted back to Doris's estate. If Mr. Castro wouldn't have made his intimidating Cuban name cousin all honors or if I'd been on my own, I'd have tried harder. On our way back South, I got another glimpse of my great granddad's decision to settle in this area. In the sunset, the mountains were dipped in an infinite light as if emitting sparks. The trees and bushes in the canyons appeared razor sharply outlined, vague the depth of the space between the stems, leaves, and needles. The rocks chiseled by creation draped in the ocean's haze as huge creatures. There was such a solemnness in this. Tears rolled down my cheeks. No wonder, my relatives had fallen in love with this lovely spot. Later, lying in the king size Seacliff bed some hundred miles South, I regretted not having thought about trying to get hold of Doris in her second office. According to her friend Clint Eastwood, you can find her at Safeway, shopping for her babies. If we would've had one more day!

In the early morn, I took a picture out of the window. Absorbing the beautiful panorama in the fairy-like fog, I realized, it might be my very last time in California. On our way back, looking at the motor homes on PCH, I said: That's our lilies of the field way of living, using solar energy. But I guess they pay. Oh, look! There's a kind of money drop box.

I'd like to travel to Northern California in a motor home with Peter and find my family. In spring 2014 we could celebrate Doris's 90th birthday. Afterward, I'd like to repeat the kind of trip we'd done with Jerry's Mercedes Cabriolet end of 1986 when Peter had the idea to combine business with pleasure. What trip?

Jerry had a brown SL. He had wanted us to drop it at a garage in Miami. It all started with a warning by Jerry's roommate Wanda. She's a pretty good psychic. So? Yep! When we were about to leave, she said: When driving on your own always keep the window open a gap. In Dallas, we bought a red E-Type Roadster from a couple living in a house with an indoor pool and a square footage of more than 12,000! We made a down payment and arranged to pick it up on our way back to L. A. Okay?

Our next vacation stop was New Orleans. Have you been roaming the quarter? Uh-huh!

The infectious beat of the swing style music and the Creole/Cajun cuisine kept us 4 days. And once again, another ship I was on, ended in trouble. How so?

Not as with the Achille Lauro. The Mississippi steamship had an engine problem, just lost its steam. Have you seen those hot fudge boys putting on a real show making their famous sweets? Nope! They were as artistic as your Italian pizza bakers, throwing the cloying dough in the air. We were quite touched by the Louisianan soul. In Memphis Tennessee, we savored a colorful symphony in the sun lightened glorious Graceland: late fall leaves in red, yellow and brown shades. Like it there? Well! It's a magnificent mansion, gracious exterior, huge park-like garden. I took a pic of Peter next to Elvis's pink Cadillac and a fleet of other cars. But the interior didn't leave me speechless. I only remember a giant brown leather couch. I liked the openness and the large high rooms, but I missed the caramel voice sounding through the hall. They should offer Elvis songs and movies the way they do Doris's in the Cypress Inn. What else?

Oh, well, something strange. Huh? In downtown Memphis, we suddenly learned how it feels to be different. What do you mean?

There wasn't another Caucasian soul in sight.

All faces we looked in were pitch dark. So?

We were frightened but of some aggressive squirrels. They approached us with their sharp teeth and troubled us like the beggars in India. Nobody else was bothered by them.

Those Hitchcock birds turned radical rodents made us head for a safe haven of the Peabody's. Headfirst, we dipped onto the planet of the chosen ones. Huh? The Grand Lobby was full of light faces. No single mulatto in sight as if there were still racial segregation.

Ines' cellular rang. While she talked with an employee, the images of the rest of our vacation rolled by my inner eye:

We'd ordered apple pie with our tea and joined the admirer's horde by gazing at the exquisitely decorated Christmas-tree, the chandeliers and the grand piano. We had just digested the squirrel shock when it was the birds' turn once again. At 5:00 p. m. all eyes followed Duck master Pembroke, pacing to the fountain. The former circus animal trainer started the traditional parade of the mallard ducks. I said: Do you think, those birds are enjoying their lives in this marble basin in the middle of a hotel vestibule? Instead of waddling on a red carpet behind a gentleman in tails, they'd rather dip into natural waters and flying into the wild blue space. Peter said:

They might be used to that lazy life.

Reminds me of Herr Gans. Who? Head of Deutsche Bank's education department. Why? Nomen est omen. He's swaddling like a goose. He may have been a domesticated fowl in his past life. I wonder what would've happened if I'd remained Dr. Beine's secretary. We may have never met. Well, you never know. Would I have missed the freedom, I enjoy now? It was certainly not my worst workplace.

I forgot, what did you do? I'd listed the books and helped to prepare trainee and manager seminars. The colleagues were great. Opposite to my room was the office of two women. I forgot the psychologist's name 'cause she didn't open up much. But Mrs. Linke, the pedagogue, I still picture as if it had been yesterday. She'd married just after I had joined the team. I wonder if she's still with that man.

Why? She talked about how upset she was at first seeing his hair in the sink and how she got used to fixing these little things ... wish and away with a tissue, just another routine. But isn't that a form of slavery, too? Wouldn't it be great if you hubbies could make it your routine? As long as you are in love, we'd have the best chances to train you to clean up your mess. I blue it too. Indeed? Yes! Well!

Anyway, those preparations would prolong relationships because the many little things use up a woman's lifetime. And later on, when the love life becomes more routine, the wife may want to do more of the things she loves to do. The lesser time there's left, the harder it is to tolerate hubby's shortcomings. Especially, when other little things like kids add to the 8 hours work in the office and the housework. The reason why lately stress related diseases such as heart attacks and strokes are increasing among women. So what?

If men are not making enough money to hire help, they better cooperate. Otherwise, women feel used and may end the engagement.

You didn't. Right. Must be a karmic thing.

They're gone, said Peter. Let's go too.

Out in real life again, we got a local paper and a *Recycler*. Searching the press, we found another red Jag in Lafayette, called and made an appointment for next morn. After leaving the motel, we bought the Jag from an elder widow and left it to be picked up later.

Thursday eve, we reached a small town called Marianna. Peter moaned, here we'll rest.

Oh, how funny, on my birthday, we'll stay in Marianna. Peter stirred the SL in the courtyard of the Marianna Inn.

Come on! Have you turned into a romantic?

I didn't arrange that. So who did? His smiling was not conclusive. Next day, on the road again CP pointed to a signpost: Panama City. Here lives Alois Pfeffer. Huh? The guy from Aschaffenburg who sold us the Rolls-Royce with the golden Emily. Kenny Rogers PR car. Have you heard from him, lately? From Sef? No. I guess, he's still involved in that King of Atlantic thing. Had Sunny not been on TV? Yeah, as King Roland from Helgoland. The way Sef behaves, he could have been a king in his past life. Leave me alone with your past life chatter. Behave, it's my birthday!

In Miami, after dropping Jerry's SL, we rented a car. Peter asked for the smallest one. The woman asked: Are you sure you're going to fit in there? Yesss! Peter whispered in my ear. Most small cars are rented out anyway. Grinning like a Cheshire cat he approached the silver 4 door sedan. Near St. Petersburg, we called Bob Bilovesick who lived there with his German wife. He also bought a car from us in Frankfurt. Peter said:

Hi, Bob, we are in town. How about having dinner together somewhere? And can you recommend a nice motel where we can freshen up? No way, you have to stay with us. Hotels are impersonal. We told him where we were.

You are pretty close to the shopping mall where our card shop is. I'll pick you up there in 15 minutes. Many neighbor houses were surrounded by black mosquito net looking like huge bird's cages. In the hall, a 5-month-old German Sheppard greeted us friendly. My dog love made Annegret ask us to stay longer. After four days of their howling hospitality and tasty turkey and fish dinners, Peter got edgy. The pleasure part shouldn't overtake the business part. Trying to gain one more day, I reasoned: We could wash some clothes and tomorrow morning, we can invite our hosts to their favorite breakfast restaurant. So we'll be early on our way to Key West. I got my way.

The ballpoint pen stains in Peter's yellow sweatshirt were not removed. I blamed the detergent, but after the 2nd circle with stain remover and a stronger detergent, the blue lines were still visible. I said, with our German washing machine I'd never any problems with such stains. Peter repeated one of his favorite mantras: You are in America now, forget about Germany. Later, when I'd gotten reconciled to the less perfect things by appreciating the many better ones, my mother commented her first laundry experience in California: What a wacky washer! How can dirt be removed when the water flows in hot? In our washers, the water slowly heats up; therefore stains can dissolve. I'd told her, we have to do a cold circle before a hot one. She'd said: A waste of time and energy.

In Miami, we had to navigate our way out by our sun source. As long as the sun was sinking on our right we were heading south. Eventually, we were bound to hit the Highway That Goes to Sea. About 150 miles further we'd passed more than 40 wide spanned bridges enjoying an ever changing scenery of water and islands. Behind the wheels, Peter did the chicken dance and said with a cheerful heart: We're cruising through the Golf of Mexico in a car. Oh, look there's a dolphin. In Key Largo, I pointed to two beautiful parrots. Peter said: We should catch 'em. And then? Sell 'em. What a nasty business! Don't you think the birds would rather stay here than sit in a filthy apartment? Don't do unto others what you would not have done unto you. Amen. But we could stop at Key Largo on our trip back. It's a great place for diving. Oh, come on! Why not? We could at least snorkel a few hours. There's the only living coral barrier reef in the US.

The mirror in our next hotel made me smile.

All my crow's feet are gone! Like a rough-dried apple soaked in water. That's the vantage of humidity.

The Earnest Hemingway house felt familiar. Absorbed by my thoughts about living here and taking care of the cats, I hadn't listened. Why had his wife placed the cent in the cement? She'd built the pool when Hemingway was as a journalist in the Spanish Civil War. He was upset by the cost and said, you may as well have my last cent. Papa Hemingway was as tight as you in matters of home improvement. Men like to spend money in bars or on cars, not on houses.

Jeez, no single cat is interested in small talk. On the Southfork Ranch, I saw only one, and she even liked to be carried around. You better look for vintage cars. We need no more cats.

And I need no people telling me what to do.

A young man came near us, waving with a flyer. How about a free lobster candlelight dinner and a glass bottom boat ride? A value of 38 Dollars each. Dunno. No strings attached! Scanning the writing, Peter said, but I don't buy anything. You don't have to, just come and see. Why not? Well! How about tomorrow at 2:00 p. m. Sounds good to me. Okay! After the guy gave us directions where the boat starts, I said, that's not for us. I don't mind the lobster dinner.

I'm not even fired up for it. Lobsters use to lie heavy on my stomach. Maybe you can have your beloved salmon.

The boat ride took half an hour. I don't recall seeing fish through the glass floor, but the shark in the building left a lasting impression. We stopped in front of a gray blue wooden apartment complex. It consisted of two large structures. With other potential buyers, we entered a bright apartment. The shining creme-colored furniture matched the native American patterned bedspreads. The ocean view from the 6th floor was splendid. We were asked to fill out a questionnaire inquiring our income, hobbies, how long we usually vacation, where to, where we want to spend our next holiday and how much we spend on vacations. While we were shown a big luxury apartment, another sales rep had time to read our questionnaire and awaited us a few minutes later asking: Could you picture yourself for a week or two in one of the apartments? Yes, of course. Who could not?

How much would you wanna spend for it?

Right now nothing. We've seen the area. On our next vacation, we want to see other places.

Where d'you wanna go? Peter said:

South Africa, South America, Australia.

We're in Cancun. How does that sound?

Good. In the conversation, we learned about how time sharing works. You buy an apartment for 1 or 2 weeks a year and you share it with some 30 other owners. If you don't like to be there every year, you can exchange it with other apartment owners in other areas. I said: We aren't planning long in advance. We decide on the spur of the moment. What d'you mean? For instance, one winter morning in 1976, Peter said, let's hit the road. We loaded our Opel Diplomat and drove to Algeciras in Spain. On a ferry boat, we made it to the Canaries, but after seven weeks we had enough.

The sales rep tried some more, but 10 minutes later, he gave up on us and called for help. A man in sea robber design appeared: long hair of silver streaky color, bushy eyebrows, heavy treasure diver's decoration. I'm knocked up, said the worn looking salesman. Where's the problem? I stared at the weighty gold chain that would make me walk like an old woman with osteoporosis. The serious weight-lifter, who wanted folks to know raised his broad wristband hand and straightened his mustache. His biceps flexed and bulged. The white shirt unbuttoned down to the navel stuck to his hairy chest. The shark tooth smile under his the face fungus didn't promise to let us go easily.

Peter said, your salesman did a great job, but we are just different to the typical Americans.

A great job, you say? He gave him a smirk look. I took him out of the gutters. If he's not selling you an apartment I'll kick him right back. Oh, come on, I said, looking through the sales gimmick. I'd learned about subliminal methods of commerce at one of my college's socioeconomic seminars. Because his pitying method didn't have any effect, he said:

Wanna you fly with the eagles or scratch with the chickens?

Nice try! With a sneaky smirk, he asked:

Where are you staying? Was he trying to implant fear? Since we openly spoke of our hotel, the sea bear finally flashes a toothy grin giving up on us. Because all his subtle maneuvering didn't work, he seemed more impressed than maddened and even complimented us.

Later, in the restaurant, Peter said:

Three hours work for just a dinner. If we'd searched through the papers and looked for cars, we could have made more. But it was worth the undergo. Something new.

We flew from Miami to Dallas and visited our other customer friends, Jim and Saskia Hadsell. In the early 80th, we'd been invited to their wedding. They'd taken us to the world's largest Honky-tonk where several bands were playing at Billy Bobs in Forth Worth. There had even been a cattle ride arena.

From the Dallas suburb, we got our Jag and drove back to our second red roadster. I chose this one for my driver because it was an automatic car. After half an hour, Peter lost a tire. Two hours later, I lost one. Peter said: The road is bumpy, we better try to avoid the holes. After another two hours drive in the dark, a Highway Patrol siren blasted from behind. Lights flashed. I stopped on the roadside. A deep male voice boomed through the loudspeaker. I couldn't see a thing.

Get out of the car, hollered one of the two lawmen. You drove in wavy lines. Yes, I bellowed back. The road is so bad that we already lost a few tires. They came close since they were not frightened anymore that I'd fire at them. Where d'ya bound for? California.

Then good luck.

After a 10 hours ride behind Peter, I had enough and gave him flashlight signals. He stopped and walked back to me. I said, I'm dead tired. I can't drive anymore. Peter said in cheering up manner:

Let's do just one more hour. Otherwise, we'll need a day more. About ten minutes after we'd passed San Antonio and looked down with its sparkling lights, I suddenly lost control of the car. Spinning around the Jag slipped somewhere through the meadow and landed at a road guard. When I got out of the car, I was quite surprised. It was icy! When I'd hopped in the car in Lafayette, it was 76°F. Whoever is familiar with a British classic car knows how hot it becomes in the legroom. How could I've anticipated gliding on an icy bridge? I said: It's because you never listen to me. I'd better taken the stick shift car. If I'd slipped a few yards earlier, I'd landed a lot lower. Later, in our motel room Peter said, luckily, it's the hood only. We'll still make money on that one.

At some remote period, it dawned on me: I had dreamed about this long before. Wanda had warned me to roll down the window a bit. Then I'd have felt the cold. Could I've avoided the accident if she'd told me everything specifically or would I've forgotten it anyway? Can we change future events?

Still thinking of this adventurous time in our life, Ines said, here we are in your old area. Yikes! I was in the past again. I'd like to come back with Peter in a motor home, visiting our friends. We'd be independent and mobile.

Where should I turn?

Can I call Leanne? Go ahead. It would be great to say hello. You know her, too, don't you? Yep. She's on Odessa. Let's get off White Oak. I want to see a little more of our old home. Hi, Leanne! I'm near you. Can I say hello? Minutes later, I hugged Leanne, Laura, Lea and the rest of the big family, thanks to Laura and her husband. They were helping Leanne to move to her new big house and guest house where they all will live together. Bill was missing, at least his cancer hag-ridden body. I'm sure, his very being was there with us, too. I made a mental note to park our motor home in her large new lot in a few years. At the moment, we were both not really free to do what we'd liked so much: spend a lot more time together!

Two days later, Ines took Giulia, Chiara and me in the AMG to the crowded Hollywood Blvd. I said: Drives nice, the black beauty. Peter had test-driven these rare items before anybody else. By the way, why didn't you buy Arnd's baby? Huh?

The Gullwing, Peter's son had developed. They call Arnd the Chassis-Guru. I don't know. You have to ask Wolfgang. What's his other son doing? He's at Lufthansa, could have been chief of freight in L.A., but he's happy in Frankfurt, attached to his native soil.

Here, we are. It changed a lot, didn't it?

Not as much as Vegas. When I watch new movies, I don't recognize it anymore. Swallowed by an underground park house and up three escalators, we assimilated in the mass. Head down, we kept moving on the Walk of Fame, noticing some of the celebrities' names on the brass stars. I wasn't curious about the

VIP symbols. But I photographed Muhamed Ali's star on the wall outside the Chinese Theater. I have a soft spot for people fighting injustice. Searching for Doris's imprints, the girls found them amid the 200 concrete surfaces. I laid my left hand in Doris's imprinted hand. Ines took a photo. Yo! Fits perfectly.

The stars should have stepped barefooted in the wet cement. Most women wore high heels for the feet to look smaller. The picture of the poor Chinese women with bound feet passed my inner eye. Why do we allow men to cripple and to mutilate us in so many ways? They'd better know, next time around it's their experience! Sure? *You* have your girls in the Waldorf School. I'm pretty sure it was Steiner who said we reincarnate alternately as male and female, I think that accounts for the many gays and dikes.

I'm mostly involved money wise. You can talk about these things with the other parents you'll meet after the Rose Ceremony. Huh?

There's a party on the eve on the grounds of a classmates' parent.

With the picture in the box, I was happy.

Now, the only thing left on my agenda was to find some memorabilia with Doris's picture on. Entering a smaller souvenir store, I asked:

Do you have anything of Doris Day? Huh?

Doris Day! Who the heck is Doris Day?

A tall Latino with a black pomaded thatch came closer. A bit left handed, he drew a book and asked, what's her name again? Ines said:

Day! The juicy blonde and the Latino asked as if with one mouth: How'd you spell that?

The thought crossed my mind they might get subventions for hiring handicaps. Gently smiling I said softly, Day like in Sunday but without the sun. The giant's forefinger rushed down the rows of stars and shrugged. He said:

No! She's not there. Smirking at them and barely hiding my doubt I said: I can't believe this. Doris Day is the most successful actress of all times. And she is not known in Hollywood! That's holy smokes weird!

Shrugging his shoulders, the young man closed the book. With a labored grin, he turned around and walked to a rearmost area. I said to the woman, if you check the internet you'll find her millions of times.

Ines shook her head in a what-ya-can-do manner and turned towards the exit.

Oh, look up there, James Dean on a one dollar bill. I tried to reach the framed fan item. Looks good, better than the first president. But hard to get. Ines said:

Oh, wait, come Chiara. Ines lifted her little girl who pulled down the souvenir. The blonde cashed the 15 bucks with an ironed smile.

Not a bad profit. Not keen on selling their stuff. The icon on the top shelf! At least, he's there. Doris made 36 more movies than James Dean and sang some 600 songs!

Outside, a human cluster had formed around a Michael Jackson lookalike. Waiting fans for to be photographed with the pseudo-pop star. We entered a larger store. Lots of postcards, posters and t-shirts with funky colored star photos, but no Doris. I searched up and down a high rack of CD's: no Doris. We looked through pens, cups, and cans: no Doris. Not a single item with my relative's picture. After searching through some more memento stores, we gave up. I'd better asked at the Cypress Inn front desk.

On our way back to Pasadena, I said, maybe I'll find something at Goodwill. Good luck!

It's not crucial to come back without that. But I'm terribly sorry I can't support Michael Lipschitz with anything for his article. He'd put so much effort in it. Who's that?

He's doing all the research on the history of the Neckar area where my mother's and Doris's grandmother were born. He also looked into our relationship to Doris and had informed all of us, in the *Grüne Baum*, in Neckarhäuserhof. Family repetition again: Doris' mother worked in her brother's tavern. My mother worked four years in her restaurant and later in the bed & breakfast. Doris bought a bed & breakfast hotel. What happens now? Mr. Lipschitz wants to bring a 2-page report in the Heidelberg newspaper after my return. Now, there's not much coming from my part.

So what you want to do now?

What I'd like to do would be costly.

Why? If I had the money, I'd hire a director who admires Doris and who'd produce a movie on the base of the biography she wrote with Hotchner and my book. Well!

Doris's life story is so gripping ... we'd need an athletic actress. Why? As a teenager, she won a contest for the longest handstand.

Really? Yeah, she was even able to walk up and down stairways on her hands. Wow!

At age 14, her likely career as a dancer was shattered by a locomotive crashing into the car Doris was in. She suffered complicated leg fractures. I still feel sorry for Jerry Doherty. I even remember his name. Who's that? That was her dancing partner. Okay! The boy lost his promising career, became a milkman. In the year and a half of Doris's recovery, Alma paid for her singing lessons. She then sang in big bands and married a jealous psycho who almost shot her in her 8-month pregnant belly.

Oh, no! Yes, her life story offers material for more than a movie. It could make a gross series. Reading her biography, I figured why the book was never translated into German.

Why? Most people in the movie business are Jewish. And German editors wouldn't risk being pegged as Nazi publishers. Why?

Her story is the same trouble we had.

What do you mean? Well, what Doris and her hubby and Peter and I had to go through might too well serve the cliche of the evil Jew. Huh? We'd both lost our dough, she, thanks to Mr. Rosenthal, we, thanks to the Rosen brothers, but with two zeros less. How? The Rosen brother's cubic software thing didn't work out. However, Anda said they'd bought land! Peter should have invested in land himself instead. Oh, let it be. In the movie, I wouldn't dwell on that, rather on the eye for an eye thing. Huh? I believe we deserve all we get since we've done wrong in a past life. What will you accomplish with the movie?

That the people better stop their wrongdoing since it comes back. Turning the other cheek. Getting off the karmic payback wheel. Um!

And I want to find my folks. Well!

I'd compare living here and abroad. My mother was the Hausfrau and Mom Doris wanted to be, preferable to a movie star. Her family of origin wasn't a great one. My mother had sung on stage too, but she was never supported as Doris. Both are only two months apart and look-alike. When I'd flipped through Doris's book and shown my mom the photo with Doris and Frank Sinatra sitting on a couch, she pointed to her and said flabbergasted: Oops! That's me!

Really? Who's going to play?

I'd like to have Jessica Schwarz from Michelstadt playing their parts. By the way, my father was likely her first employer. Okay?

When she was 12, he gave her promotional handbills from local companies to deliver on households. What did she play? She was great in Mann's Buddenbrooks, and she got a Bambi for playing Romy Schneider. That was on my 60th birthday, my only uplift on that day. Have you seen The Perfume? Uh-huh!

She played the prostitute. With my intense shame from childhood on, I'd passed on that one. But times have changed, and some of the best actresses show everything. I know.

Whenever I watch Jessica in interviews or movies, I feel a certain familiarity. My mother was also a beautiful woman in the 50th. She was somebody too, but only in Michelstadt. She was known as singer and town councilor. But talking in public was more my dad's thing. He was party chair of the self-employed Hesse South. I think she only did it because he wanted it. Once, we sat with the ex-mayor at a gathering. He'd said: Alwine never talked much, but when she did it always mattered.

The familiarity feeling with Jessica could also be our same birth number 7 and name number 3. What's that number thing? Numerology, known in many cultures. Persons with same numbers have similar talents, characteristics and things to learn. How you get the name number? You write a row from 1 to 9 and below the letters from A to Z. Adding the numbers of the letters and you get the cross sum:

```
1 2 3 4 5 6 7 8 9
A B C D E F G H I
J K L M N O P Q R
S T U V W X Y Z
```

We reached peaceful Pasadena with its pleasant wide tree lined streets. Gnarly old sycamores nestle around traditional houses. Bougainvillea bushes climb up chimneys or spill as pink avalanches from wrought iron baskets.

Here, we are. Let's cook something zesty. I'm hungry. Chiara and Giulia rushed to their rooms. Ines got salmon and veggies out of the huge fridge in her modern kitchen. The Teenager came back with a few pieces of frizzled outfits. Ines said: I cannot believe it. What?

This morn was the fifth time in two days you used the washing machine. I need this for tomorrow. You poor thing! Do you have only three outfits? Nothing I like is clean. Oh, come on. You're wasting way too much water. Leave it here. I later look if I have something, too. Grumbling Giulia left.

I forgot to call Eva. Who's Eva? Ingrid's friend, a nurse from Santa Monica. Go ahead.

Hi, Eva, I'm Marianne. You know about Ingrid? Yes, too bad. Sigrid said she handled her illness sovereign, regulated her matters and made her passing easily for her friends. Well! Are you here? Yes, I wanted to see Doris Day. Why? I'm related to her through my mother.

What a coincidence! D'you know Eveline Popp? No. She's my friend. She made Doris's cloths. What? Why? Edith Head had hired her because she'd worked eight years for the Ice Follies. Can I meet her? Sure! Let's have a party. Um! I'll call her outright. Eveline Popp makes puppets now. She made the Shrek and a Michael-Jackson puppet. I call you again. What a small world! I call Imara & Brian. They live nearby and could come to Hill Street, too. Ines said: Dave lives in Hermosa Beach. He can drop you in Santa Monica. Well? Thanks! Sure. I'll pick you up later. What's with my number? You're born on a 13th like Situ. Okay?

Wait a sec, I'll ask the google boys: http://numerologystars.com/numerology-number-13-thirteen/

"Number 13 in numerology is a complex figure. It is seen as unfortunate, but it's wrong, and this recognition is up in the bias. Number 1 and number 3 are very strong and mean a successful career. On that date, births are practical, good planners, vigorously and systematically implement their plans." Check! What's Doris? A 3: creative, popular, confident, articulate and musical. Sounds like you. Thanks! Names add up to numbers too. Marianne adds up to 3. I forgot, how are you related to Doris? I think her great-grandmother and my great-grandmother were sisters. Lipschitz thinks about another relationship. Since not all names of kids are listed at the registry office, it's hard to tell. Huh? For instance, my mother had two sisters, but Hilde, the middle wasn't listed. And my mother was listed as Alberine instead of Alwine. So you can't trust those listings. How do you know all that number stuff?

I wanted to write a book on numerology and memorized the most significant traits from Strayhorn's book. When I meet someone, I ask about his or her birthday and try to find out if they fit the given attributes. It's fascinating checking the celebs with same numbers. Reading their biographies, you can compare their traits with yours or someone you know well. I tried to find a big woman to work with me on my psyllium reduction book, so I checked on

Marianne Sägebrecht. Reading her autobiographies, I found out we have a lot in common, name, birthday 27, hers on 8-27-1945 = 36 = 3+6 =9. She's a double 9; mine 11-27-49=34=3+4=7; I'm a 9 and a 7. I'm a Saggy. Her ascendant is Saggy. We both worked as doctor's assistants and with AIDS patients and received a letter from AIDS dissident Dr. Stefan Lanka. Huh? He's a molecular biologist like Prof. Peter Duesberg from Berkeley who was ever so kind to send me his newest works when new editions of my books on Spirulina or the immune system are in the planning.

What works? About uncovering the AIDS myth. I'll get you an interesting link: virusmyth.com/aids/hiv/tbcure.htm

Marianne Sägebrecht also experienced a big Californian earthquake when she worked on *The War of the Roses*, playing Kathleen Turner's and Michael Douglas' housekeeper. And the outcome with the Roses was as bitter as ours with the Rosens. We both lost our lieu's. Did you get her for the book? No! Why not?

I should have anticipated it. Why?

Neither for *Sugar Baby* nor for *Bagdad Café* or *Rosalie Goes Shopping* Marianne lost a single pound. I remember another synchronicity. Huh? While working on the set, John Hudson's friend, Jack Palance, fell in love with her. I also had the feeling that John had a crush on me. So, two elder US actors and veteran buddies were in love with us. Who else did you ask? Heide Keller, the chief stewardess on the German *Love Boat*. She called me back, but losing weight was not on her agenda either. I had even tried to get Wolfgang Rademacher to make a sequence with me as a nutritionist and send him a script. He called me to ask specifics. He's got a cute Berlin slang. But he seemed to be not interested. Ah!

Heide said, all of you out there think acting is easy. I didn't tell her about my acting class experiences. Doris is different. She says if I can do it you can do it. She knows we're all ONE. Okay? You know Hella von Sinnen?

Yes, the comedian. She wrote me a real nice X-max card back and suggested to ask Cleo Kretschmer. But we were already in the process of moving. Before, I had asked Angela Merkel and Oprah Winfrey. Really? Yep. Because with a Celeb on board, my editor would have given me full power promotion for the book. But it's been reviewed in several health magazines. Yeah? Yep. Can I cut the onions? With my lenses, I don't need to cry. If you want to. Ines is an 11. What? Numerology. Wow, you're right. Well? You're a quick learner. By the way, Doris has an 11 name number too and her birth number is 5: 4-3-1924. What kind of movie you've in mind?

Biopic with music. I'd love to sing Do-do's soft rock song *This is the way I dreamed it* and *Someone like you*. But Jessica has a great voice too. I know it's illusory. It would be an enormous film genre turnaround.

You think Doris would work again? Not really. So? You never know if it's for goodness' sake. She'd do marvelously. But I doubt she'd do the handstand at the Academy Awards as she did on her 70th birthday.

Really? Yep! I saw it on the net. She'd worn a blue top and gray pants. I can't find it anymore. Um! I'd donate half the profit to her animal foundation, and to pounds in Michelstadt, Tavira, and North Hollywood. Aha!

Remember when we got Tommy from there?

Yeah, I picked him. He was your only real tomcat. The others were just pussies. Whenever we'd come home from walking he'd given Sandy a smack on her butt. But he wasn't our only juicy one. You have not known Carlo. He opened boxes, removed pot covers and even a tile from the bathtub covering to have his own little house behind the tub. Really?

Yes. He also asked us to open the door and roamed House Tania visiting neighbors.

On one of my last days, I went with Ines, Wolfgang and the kids for a prime rib dinner, the first after 16 years. I rarely eat red meat, but sometimes, in the company I ruefully enjoy it a lot. Try the bread, it's delicious! I quit on bread, Wolfgang said. Why? I had high cholesterol. How so? I was often tired and in pain right after a meal. What did you do? I was checked through for about $3,000. They only found the high cholesterol. When I'd read about all the negative side effects of the prescription drug, I thought, no way! Good boy!

Most my family members died at 55 or 60.

On Lipobay? Dunno. But I'd like to enjoy my live longer than that. So what did you do?

I saw a homeopath. With kinesiology, she found out I've got a gluten allergy. I see.

I'd quit on gluten, ever since I feel great. I lost weight and have almost normal cholesterol. Great! That's omething to blog on my website. What website?

Marianne-e-meyer,com

A little farm after all

Returning from my first trip to California after 15 years, Peter picked me up with news: Anna has to give up the house. We can move in. Really? Why? Their tenants moved out of their apartment. Now, they move in themselves.

I'd always liked the cozy little house on about a ¼ acre with an adjacent arable ground. Inside it's like the houses in Westerns where the fireplace dominates the room. The flagstones around the inbuilt kitchen area and the clay floor tiles give it a rustic ambiance. One room has high French windows with a door to a terrace. My first project was building a bar opposite the counter top for more work space.

The little farm is an ideal artist's place: high beam ceilings, the smallest of the 3½ rooms has a light desk area in front of the window, perfect for writing. There, I build a loft bed for more storage. Peter tells me, he'd only need the motorhome, but from day to day he's taking more root. One day he says, things are going well, next day he's complaining. He's sawing and hacking the wood that he cuts off from dry trees or I collect while roaming with the dogs through the wilderness. Taking care for 5-year-old Mia and triple as old Leo was part of the deal: a dream came true. We both experiment with planting. Peter cares for brunch. I make dinner. Until he's ready cutting the veggies, I work on my laptop in the bedroom, the coolest place in the house. Outside there are three sitting areas. One's floor I covered with the rest of the clay tiles. Since there were not enough, I combined them with square parts of river stones.

The summers are hot, but the thick walls of the house keep the inside cool. The rent is low. I could afford it even if I'd remain alone. We activate our water, so we have a well-water quality to use for coffee, tea, and cooking. I'm allowed to grow vegetables on our landladies' adjoining field. In the first fall, I'd sown 5 rows peas and broad beans. Since we had almost no rain that winter, the output was poor. On March 25, Lisbella lamented about the missing rain. The NAM-MYOHO-RENGE-KYO came into my mind. My Portuguese isn't terrific, so I painted a scene with a person praying the Lotus Sutra mantra and clouds with rain falling on the ground. I told her to chant five minutes in the morns and in the eves. Had it helped? Three days after the chanting it rained for six days after three months of drought.

Lisbella at age 75 still cultivates many acres of fruit trees, olives, onions, potatoes, cabbages and other veggies to sell. She is rich considering owning several houses and lots of land, but she works from dawn to dusk and mostly dresses like a bag lady. What I don't grow myself, I buy from her, from the market or the discounter, 3 miles away, sometimes by bicycle. In the summer, we cool off a ¾ mile from us in a little lake with a waterfall called *Pego Inferno*. We may keep the place if we'll move to our house on the golf course *Quinta do Vale*. We'd need less furniture to move. In the summer we could rent the house and stay in the Quinta. The fortune teller had said: It'll take a vast amount of time for your investment to blossom. I'd never guessed that long. At least we'd the chance to play free golf and look at the unfinished house from where we'll have a view of the fairways and the river with the bridge. That would be another family similarity: Doris can see the Quail Lodge Golf fairways.

The wish for making a movie is still high on my list. Today, people learn rather by watching than by reading. Why is Ghost with Demi Moore, Patrick Swayze, and Whoopi Goldberg one of the most successful movies of all times? Because we deep inside know who we truly are. Love is the answer. It's most important in our lives that we love ourselves and all living beings and what we are doing.

I'm thinking about the uplifting event of the Waldorf School graduation ceremony. In the US people know how to celebrate. When I left school, I felt like a freed slave and had nightmares of being in test situations for years.

The school subjects I liked were arts, crafts, music, typewriting, and sports. My most hated one was algebra. Doris's biography starts with the *Que Sera* text. In the 2nd strophe, the girl at school asked the teacher what should I try? Should I paint pictures, should I sing songs? I had best grades in art related subjects. But we weren't used to getting jobs according to our likes. Developing talent needs assistance and approval like the one, I got a little too late:

Walking with my mother through the forest a minute from our flat in Michelstadt next of the famous Bal Schem's grave, I had let out an own version of a gospel song we had learned in the Igelsbach choir: *Soon I will be done with the trouble in the world.* Perplexed, Ma said: I didn't know you've such a good voice.

During the ceremony at the Waldorf School, I thought about my not being used to celebrating accomplishments, not even after having earned two masters and a Ph.D. That's not relevant to me. Done ticked off. Next project. Holding the Waldorf School's graduation ceremony program in my hands, the image of the children in front of the Scripps Hall flashes before me: We listened to their singing Over the Rainbow. I asked Ines: You know this is a Doris song, too? She answered with a counter-question: You know what it means? Huh?

Passed, completion, reaching maturity.

Do we ever? With the poem from *The Little Prince* (Antoine de Saint-Exupéry) on the back of the Pasadena Waldorf School's program, I'd like to end my book, too:

> "Goodbye," said the fox
> "And now here is my secret,
> a very simple secret.
> It is only with the heart
> that one can see rightly.
> What is essential is invisible to the eye."

It's quite hard to come to an end of a book when coincidences are coming rushing in:

I walked with Peter and the dogs. After an 8 minute walk, we saw a car with German license plates parking at the hunting club premises. A lady with a dog got out of the car and walked with us uphill. Are you living here? I asked. We own a house in Germany and one here. My husband is an osteopath in Munich. I'm a teacher. But I work voluntarily. My husband makes enough money.

Yes, I know what you mean. I used to work voluntarily too when we made lots of money. I visited kids in hospitals and seniors in nursing homes, and I gave Reiki to AIDS patients. I wanted to give back something for being so lucky with our business. Well!

That's why I plead for a basic income. With it, we had much more volunteer work. That's true. We can't give anything to society if it's difficult to make ends meet.

When we reached the hilltop, kids were running out of the yard to greet Mrs. Robert.

Incredible but true: The midget school is a Waldorf School! The other teacher appeared. When I told her about my recent experience in Pasadena and what Ines and Wolfgang pay for two kids, she said, that's exactly the amount we get from the parents for all the 14 children we have. And we don't know if the school can survive much longer. It's hard these days. Um! It'd be awful if we'd have to close. There are only three Waldorf schools in Portugal, one in Lagos, one in Lisbon and this little one here.

Still another coincidence for the album:

We had an American guest for eight days. Ken lives close by. The container he used to live in when he rents out his house had burned down. Since he had guests in his house, we'd let him sleep in our motor home. I thought that's my chance for having a proof-reader at home! When writing in a foreign language one always need to have it proofread by a native. But Ken is a chatterbox like Peter, so most probably he's no reading type either. On the 3rd day of his staying, he hadn't gotten past the first three pages. I told Ken about the *Escola do Malhao*. My wife, Irene was directing this school 20 years ago. She died on thrombosis at the end of her 2nd pregnancy.

When I told Ken about my relationship with Doris, we may have detected some other coincidence or a secret love? Ken asked: What's the actress's real name? Doris Mary Ann Kappelhoff. Mary Ann? That's the name of James Cagney's boat! What boat?

A 43 foot Chesapeake Bay buckeye ketch.

Um! She'd made three movies with him, *The West Point Story, Starlift*, and the best one *Love Me or Leave Me*. According to Cagney, "the perfect script". Okay? Doris thought of Cagney as "the most professional actor she'd ever known." Was there something else going on between those two? I don't know. In 1976, when her biography was published, all the Cagneys were still alive. Doris once mentioned a secret affair with an actor from the East Coast. Did he say why the yacht was named Mary Ann?

He wanted a plain old-fashioned name.

How do you know? Jimmy Jr. was my best friend at the time. He was an adopted child, but I think he was Cagney's real son. He looked like him. Even the manners. Those can be acquired. Right, but still, his mother was from Nevada. Aha! Maybe a showgirl who'd no time for the baby? Probably. Anyway, we sailed a lot together. I was often on Martha's Vinyard. Is that where he lived?

Yes, Cagney had a farm on that island just south of Cape Cod in Massachusetts. Have you seen him? Quite often. Once when he was already old, I was rowing him from the boat to the shore. He was in the backseat, tried to get up, got back, tried again and said:

Don't ever get old, boy, it's a bitch. How'd you met Cagney's son? I had a car business. I sold him import cars. Where was that?

Newport, Rhode Island. He'd also owned a competition racing team, Cagney RT. It was a fart in the wind, never did anything. The Cagney family's end had all the makings of a blockbuster movie.

Doris's story, too, that could make a Hollywood movie plus miniseries. So how'd it end?

That you can all read on the internet. But Jimmy Jr. was with me shortly before he died. He wasn't feeling well, so he went to Georgetown University Hospital for five days. They didn't find anything wrong. Happens often!

In the night before his aneurysm death, he was at my house in Newport. He went on a trip, getting divorced. That girl in Virginia, his Polish wife Annie was a horrible bitch gold digger. When they were making love she'd stare up at the ceiling and say, Jimmy, you've got to fix those cracks. Really? Really! He met her at my house. Does it make you feel bad? I introduced her to him. So, he was at your house before he died? He'd called from Virginia telling he's coming up. He called Casey, his sister after he'd called me. On the phone talking to her he died. Oh!

The end of the Cagney family was an absolute American tragedy. Isn't this the case with many fame families? Maybe. I know, why I didn't want to become famous.

Later, when Ken checked on his house, he showed me a 1984 article about Cagney Jr's death at age 44 by John South. I skimmed it "... Cagney is brokenhearted over the sudden death of his only son – because he hadn't ended the long sand bitter feud between them."

Oh, who's that friend? Huh? It says: A friend of the star said: I saw Cagney shortly after his son's death – he looked like he'd just shriveled up overnight and his eyes were red from crying. He told me: 'I didn't realize that something like this could happen - so quick, so final. Jim was a good man. We had our disagreements, but basically, he was a fine person. I just wish to God I hadn't been so bullheaded, that I'd set things right between us before he died. I hope my son can forgive me now. I know I can't forgive myself.'

I didn't write this down because that friend may be Doris. I write it down for the readers who may want to avoid the mistake not to come to terms with friends or relatives. I always wanted to be a life enhancer. However, looking at

www.youtube.com/watch?v=cCPZ-BkpU0w

and seeing Doris saluting James Cagney at the AFI Life Achievement Award makes me think about the fact that my relative hates to talk to a mass audience as much as I do. Love could make one go out on a limb. Cagney made three movies with "Doris Day, an actress he admired" (Wikipedia). There I also found that between 1961 and 1986 Cagney "made few public appearances, preferring to spend winters in Los Angeles...", "… his close friend Ronald Reagan gave the eulogy at his funeral." Doris was also a friend of the President. They both loved to venture onto the dance floor.

When Ken moved back in his stone house surrounded by its grim smoky landscape and all the wrecked containers and cars, the fire had chased a few other hungry mouths on velvet paws away. As the refugees turned up in our area, I said: How will I feed all those hungry mouths? The answer came after I'd emptied the first bag of cat food: Renate, my sister-in-law teacher, told me about an offered job as a pedagogue. Though it's a real small job, it pays for the pet food and is an opportunity to gaining experience and advancing towards understanding, harmony, and balance. Thus works the world. It provides us with everything we want. But we have to be clear in asking. On the day, when Ingrid had talked me into buying the top model's outfit, she'd complained of back pains. I said: What's that? I can't remember when I had any. Sure enough, this very eve for a few hours, I got the opportunity to experience severe back pains.

Though I messed up by not choosing a profession in the field where I could have developed my artistic talents, at my former workplace monte-canelas.net, Tanja Grandy gave me the chance to use all of them in one job.

Kids better study in a domain of their desire. Do what you love to do, and the money will follow. You will be one of the happiest people under the sun. Working according to our talents, we avoid inferiority feelings. This sense of being not good enough on occasion scraped my soul like sandpaper. Earning much money is less fulfilling as earning credit. Isn't sharing our gifts and making others happy the meaning of life?

While writing this, I received an email from my cousin Heide Bayer, who now works in the field of her likes too: Animal communication. I'd emailed her a photo of our dog Leo who was all of a sudden limping. "With the reading of thoughts, the mediator asks the animal a question and instantly knows the answer. On Heide's question, what happened, she immediately saw Leo walking backward and another dog she described me as a light brown smaller one with some white on the neck, apparently his girlfriend Mia. Then, Heide suddenly saw something red swoosh passed. That was probably the always speeding Englishwoman, the only red car in the area." (*How Water Connects our Worlds,* page

43). Via blood test, the vet ruled out an inflammation, made an X-ray appointment and gave me pain pills. Heide "asked Leo about pain. Leo: Sometimes. Heide: But Marianne gives you medications. Huh? Leo showed a wholly surprised face. I had never told him that in the sausage or a piece of cheese was a tablet. Afterward, I always showed Leo the yellow particles I pressed into the goodies and said, here your medicine". (ibid)

With her working for animals Heide confirms what Stierlin calls the family's cross-generational value system. Doris does it since 35 years:

http://www.dorisdayanimalfoundation.org

This book's profit goes to DDAF. My mother at age 84 developed angst and canceled her subscriptions to red cross and others, except the one for animal welfare, the family's value system!

Before I collect more chance events, I better end the book with Doris's account of the above poem from *The Little Prince* on her newest recording (see cover back):

My Heart holds touching songs. I was impressed how well Doris sings. Hearing the end of *Life is just a Bowl of Cherries*, so live and let a-a-alone, I recalled that Jocelyn once had given me this exact line, and I mused about this swerve since I did not know she'd recited a song. I liked Do-Do's voice best on the soft rock piece, she sang at about my age:

This is the Way I Dreamed It.
I'm still dreaming and praying for
Heaven on Earth
and singing with my friends in the sun.

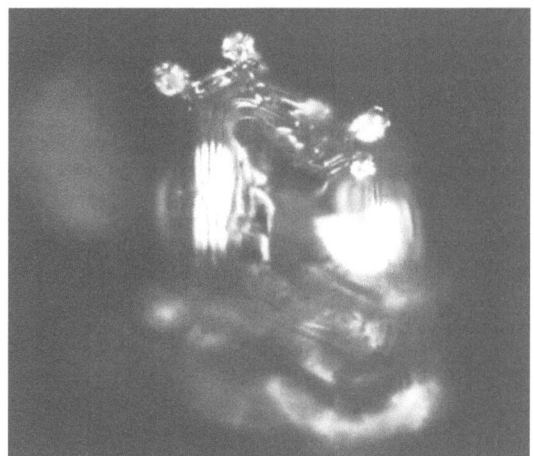

Acknowledgments

It takes a village to raise an author. It also takes houses to make literature public. I thank Books on Demand for fair conditions and exceptional handling. I'm also thankful for Grammarly. This partly free grammar checker helped me to improve my grammar and vocabulary.

Heartfelt thanks to my community, friends, and family. Quite a lot of them are already on the other side, helping me in different ways. I'm still counting on you! Forever grateful, I'll be sending this work on a Journey leading to love and light. I wish that this book will generate a resonance in my readers giving a deeper meaning to their lives and work.

Special thanks go to my dear friends Leanne Dodge for proof-reading the first half of the first book and Carole Madrid for helping me correct the cover text. I also thank Taryn Krivé for some corrections of the chapter *Developing psychic powers*.

I am also going to thank my readers in advance for giving me notice of any Victor family whose ancestor emigrated in 1902 from the Rhine-Main area in Germany.

For my mother's relative
Doris Day,
my father's
not yet known
Californian cousins
and my comparatives
on this side and beyond.

This captivating book wins by a clear statement on the mystery of changeability and storage ability of the water. Inge Schneider, head of the Swiss Jupiter-Verlag, found in her book review in the NET-Journal the author's findings that the water is the "interface between the physical and metaphysical reality" particularly appealing.

The reader will find disturbing facts about the quality of commercial waters. Anyone who believes that a tap water is clean, is encouraged to think and act. M. Meyer advises to activating water adequately. After all, who tastes for the first time naturally vitalized, oxygenated and alkaline water from the tap, want to drink no more soda water from plastic bottles. Pure water is the ideal solution for all health problems, especially if they affect the brain.

Ultimately, the author introduces free energy researchers and their technologies. She also shows what to do, so space energy can soon flow in all households.

ISBN 978-3734736919 104 p. 17x22cm €7,99

If your attention span suffers from this reading or you find health books difficult, I have an exciting book for you. Instead of getting the bullet directly through the eye, so to speak, I shoot from the back through the chest in the eye. Because in this novel, health tips come at best from medical miracles on two legs, which we have met in Morocco. In addition to Spirulina, there are other ways to get rid of blood and lung cancer or other modern epidemics.

Also, wintering in a country where there are neither fat sausages nor cheap beer and wine is like a 3-month fast. You hardly notice how you shrink healthy. My hubby used to lose more weight in Morocco than me because my lifestyle in Europe is not much different.

Delicious recipes you'll find in the back, less with Spirulina rather exotic sharp. If you click on this book on my website www.marianne-e-meyer.com, you can read it at Amazon. But you get cosmic benefits only when you order it from your bookseller. Can you imagine why?

ISBN 978-3738609571 94 p. 17x22 cm €7,90

We all need Spirulina. Why? Because of infertile soils, we can hardly get energy from our food. The blue-green alga is concentrated solar power since it contains all the colors of the spectrum and thus all frequencies of light, just like the water of Lourdes.

Marianne Erika Meyer introduced Spirulina, the blue-green miracle via her same-named German bestseller and an appearance on Prime TV in German-speaking Europe and Russia. Ever more people supplement their diets with the beneficial protein food. And dentists use it progressively for discharging amalgam and other poisons.

Stunning studies & reports around the globe prove: With Spirulina we strengthen our immune system as well as stand up to pain, depression, diabetes, MS, cataracts, allergies, anemia, arthritis, liver fibrosis, Parkinson's disease, and even AIDS and cancer.

In the illustrated book with delicious recipes, the doctor of nutrition covered each chapter in note form and highlighted important parts.

ISBN 978-3734728525 104 p. 17x22 cm €7,99

Since I do not find any handbook on the Cranberry in English, my next book project will be a revised translation of my above work from Windpferd.

So for the Cranberry season 2017, my readers will be well informed about the health-promoting power berry. Since 1914 Cranberries are researched and already used for bladder infections, acute cystitis, and conventional urinary tract infections. In this book, you'll find the latest study results pointing to the potential of preventing and curing some 80% of all health problems including cardiovascular diseases (especially atherosclerosis), rheumatoid arthritis and cancer.

The reader can also find out how to turn the clock back and to get as old as Methuselah.

Refined recipes from Marianne's health kitchen and trendy cocktails complete the book with the red round fruit.

The book will be available latest in July 2017 for €7,99